The White Rose Weeps

Grace Farrant

Grace Farrant

MENTOR
BOOKS

This Edition first published 2002 by

Mentor Books
43 Furze Road,
Sandyford Industrial Estate,
Dublin 18.
Republic of Ireland

Tel. +353 1 295 2112/3   Fax. +353 1 295 2114
e-mail: admin@mentorbooks.ie
www.mentorbooks.ie

ISBN: 1-84210-086-6
A catalogue record for this book is available
from the British Library

Copyright © Grace Farrant

The right of Grace Farrant to be identified as the author of
this work has been asserted by her in accordance with the
Copyright, Design and Patents Act 1988.

All rights reserved. No part of this publication may be
reproduced, stored in a retrieval system, or transmitted in
any form or by any means electronic, mechanical,
photocopying, recording, or otherwise, without prior
written permission of the publisher.

Cover Illustration by John Berkeley
www.holytrousers.com
Design and layout by Mentor Books
Printed in Ireland by ColourBooks

For my sister Helen

Chapter 1

Lizzie Mulvey stared out of the window of the single-decker bus from Barnsley taking her home to her family. Or was it still home? She shuddered. Bitter memories of the poverty in the Yorkshire mining village where she had grown up, the hopeless struggle to survive that went on behind the net curtains of the huddled rows of miners' cottages, stirred once again a feeling of anger. Moving to London to escape being dragged down in that struggle had freed her physically but not emotionally. Her pay as a nurse in 1930 was pitiful enough, but there was talk of raising it to thirty pounds a year. That was hers to spend as she wanted. It would not find its way from her father's pocket to the bar in the Miners' Club.

Huge piles of coal dust came into view, the ugly slag heaps scarring the landscape and reminding her with a jolt that the bus was coming into Colethorpe. She gripped her case firmly and made her way to the exit.

A young girl standing at the door of one of the cottages was scanning the arrival of the bus.

'For goodness sake, child, come away from the door. You're making a right draught. Our Lizzie'll be here soon enough. The bus is due any minute now, so—'

'Mam! Mam! She's getting off the bus!' Ignoring her mother's calls to come back in, thirteen-year-old Sarah wrenched the front door open wide and hurtled down the front garden path, out of the gate and straight across the road to where the bus had stopped.

The smartly dressed young woman deposited her small suitcase on the pavement in order to fling her arms open wide to embrace her sister.

'Oh, Lizzie, I thought you were never coming. I've got our room ready and Mam's making tea and—'

'Hang on a moment, Sarah, let me get my breath,' she laughed, amusement lighting up her brown eyes. Although not exactly pretty, there was something about her that attracted attention. Lizzie had a ready smile that brought glints of gold into her wide-set eyes, and a thick mane of glossy dark chestnut hair that swung heavily with each movement of her head. Her proud, upright carriage announced a woman who was prepared to take on whatever life had to offer.

'Sarah, love, you've grown!' she exclaimed. 'And just look at your hair.' She stroked her sister's wild red curls, which she had envied always. One day little Sarah would be a raving beauty with that hair and her slanting green eyes. Her pale creamy skin would need only the slightest touch of make-up. Surveying her sister, Lizzie frowned noting the shabbiness of the girl's dress. Nearly fourteen with just the slightest swell of a bosom, it was time that Sarah was dressed more in keeping with her age.

Both were unaware of the whispered conversations taking place on the bus. 'That'll be Jim Mulvey's eldest, went off to London to take up nursing,' one thin-lipped matron informed her neighbour unnecessarily. 'Left the little 'un at home to help out.'

'Come on, Sarah, let's see how our mam is. She is all right, isn't she?' Her welcoming smile disappeared to be replaced by an anxious narrowing of the eyes.

Sarah looked away before replying. 'She does get a bit tired lately.'

Her mother had complained a lot about being tired, said it was her age, but still Sarah worried, not understanding why it was that her father never blamed his tiredness on his age. He worked long hours down the pit, which was a good enough reason for him to be weary at the end of a shift.

The road that the girls now crossed was quiet, the bus having left for Brierly Common. There were few, if any, private cars in Colethorpe; the modes of transport available were either the bus or a second-hand bicycle, the latter generally owned and used by the men who worked down the pit.

Lizzie pushed open the black iron gate which led into the tiny front garden of their home. Nothing had changed there except for a clump of stunted daffodils struggling to exist among the blades of straggly grass that passed muster as a lawn.

Her Mother was standing at the door, a smile on her lips.

'Lizzie, love.' Joanna held her eldest daughter closely. 'Oh, you look so well,' she announced, pride filling her eyes with tears.

'No need to cry, Mam.'

'I'm not really, just so pleased you managed to get time off to get home for Easter.'

'I was lucky. One of the girls wanted to take time off later when her parents get back from the Far East. Daddy's a diplomat, you know.'

Lizzie affected an aristocratic drawl, wiping out totally her broad Yorkshire vowels.

Joanna smiled. Lizzie was always a good mimic.

'Right, I'll make us all a nice cup of tea. Just you go up with Sarah and put your things away. The way our Sarah's been cleaning up, you'd think royalty were coming.'

The two girls clattered up the narrow staircase, chattering about all the things they would do over Easter. Sarah waved her arm, pointing to the improvements she had made to the bedroom in Lizzie's absence.

'I've made a runner for the dressing table and see, I've embroidered it with daisies. Dad says I'm a right good little homemaker.' She beamed with satisfaction at her efforts. Aware that her sister was making no comment, Sarah repeated her remark.

Lizzie blinked, suddenly ashamed of her lack of attention. 'Sorry, love, you've made a really good job of our old room.' She sat down on the edge of the bed, sinking into the soft feather mattress. 'Wow, this is a sight softer than the beds in the nurses' home. They're like planks of wood. Good for the back so Matron says, but then she's so hard herself, she wouldn't notice.'

Sarah was all compassion. 'How awful for you. Are you sure you like it in London?'

Lizzie leapt to her feet. 'Oh, Sarah, you've no idea. It's a different life in London, what with the shops and . . . oh, just everything. I wish you could see it. I'm never coming back to Colethorpe, not ever!' Lizzie pronounced, her pale cheeks suddenly pink and her dark brown eyes flashing amber glints.

'But what about our mam and dad and all of us? Don't you want to see us ever again?' Sarah felt that if her beloved sister stayed away forever, she would have nobody in whom to confide her hopes and fears. She scrubbed the back of her hand across her cheeks to wipe away the tears, partly reassured by Lizzie's no-nonsense reply.

'Don't be daft, of course I'll come and visit, once I've got my nursing exams out of the way. They keep talking about raising a probationer's pay to thirty pounds a year but I have my doubts. I might even go as a wealthy old lady's companion when I'm qualified, you know the sort of thing, look after her when she wants to go on holiday, on a cruise or spending the winter in the south of France.'

Sarah gazed at her older sister in wonderment at her driving ambition.

'You are clever, Lizzie. Fancy thinking of all that. I wish I could be clever, but all Dad says is that I was born to be a worker and you were born to be a lady.'

Lizzie let out a snort of a laugh. 'A lady! He ought to see me emptying smelly bedpans and washing old men's private parts.'

'Shh, you mustn't say words like that. What if Mam hears!' Sarah protested in scandalised tones.

An affectionate smile lighting up her face, Lizzie hugged her sister.

'Still the little girl, aren't you? Never mind, perhaps it's best to stay like you are. Here give me a hand to clear my things off the bed, or we'll be sleeping on the floor tonight,' she said, anxious to bring a smile to Sarah's lips. The two sisters spent the next few minutes discussing where to hang Lizzie's clothes.

'Ooh, proper silk stockings!' Sarah held up the gossamer hose to the light. 'I can't wait to get out to work and have some money like you.'

A momentary frown creased Lizzie's forehead. 'Has

Dad said anything more about you going into service? He did say you'd have to when you're fourteen and that's only a week or two off now.'

'No, he's said I can stay at school a bit longer.'

'Well, you might as well make the most of it – it took long enough to build it with all our tanners going to buy a brick every week.' Suddenly overcome with a fit of the giggles she collapsed on the bed, holding onto the brass knob. 'Oh, do you remember the Monday our Patrick said, "Bugger Father Kelly, let's spend the tanner on sweets," and we had a bag of gobstoppers each to go to school with?'

'Yes, and I remember the leathering Dad gave us when Father Kelly asked him why we hadn't taken our money for the brick on Monday. We couldn't sit down for a week.'

Lizzie closed her eyes, savouring again the taste of the illicit sweets in her mind. 'Old Mrs Painter sold bloody good gobstoppers though.'

The giggles subsided. Lizzie walked over to the window and opened it. The view hadn't changed since she was a child. Beyond the back gate, a narrow cobbled alley ran between the row of miners' cottages opposite. At the end of the alley, a well-trodden path tramped on by generations of colliers led to the mine, the only source of earning a living for the menfolk of Colethorpe. From the day they left school until the dreaded pneumoconiosis turned their lungs to stone, the men struggled on underground to bring home a wage for the week.

Each cottage was identical, with tiny concrete areas to the rear – rough yards blackened by layers of coal dust and enclosed by a brick wall and the only recreational area the children knew.

Lizzie saw the midden still there at the bottom of the yard by the back gate. She shivered, recalling the icy morning trips to sit freezing on the wooden seat in the foul atmosphere. The smell was even worse in summer, catching the back of the throat when the midden man came to empty its contents. Shutting all the windows did little to prevent the stench permeating the whole house, lingering in every corner and clinging to one's clothes. She laughed turning to Sarah.

'Do you remember the time our Patrick locked Joe Daible in when he'd come to shovel out the muck?'

Recalling Joe Daible's language, Sarah's eyes twinkled. 'I know, our Patrick took Mam's key off the back door.'

'Does she still lock it every night?'

Sarah nodded. 'No wonder Mam made Dad get a lock and key after she found that dead cat in there one morning. You could hear her scream for miles.'

Lizzie laughed. 'It was a good job Dad never found out who'd thrown it in there, else he'd have killed them. Mind you, it must have been terrible for Joe Daible stuck in that filthy hole! Do you remember he yelled for hours before anyone heard him and let him out and the rest of the street wondered why his cart was stuck outside our midden?' Without waiting for a reply, she took a cigarette from her bag, lighting it with a silver-plated lighter.

'Lizzie! What if Dad catches you?' Sarah's eyes rounded in horror.

'Dad's still not back from the pit and Mam's busy getting his dinner. Anyway, everyone smokes nowadays – clears the phlegm off your chest, so the doctors say, and they ought to know.'

'Can I try? Would it cure my chestiness?'

'It might, but I wouldn't recommend it until you go out to work.'

The White Rose Weeps

Lizzie had made up her mind while still at school that she was not going to work behind the counter in the Co-op, nor was she going to end up slaving away in service for a pittance. She knew she had missed her big chance at a formal education when she was only eleven.

'The scholarship's tomorrow in Barnsley. Now you know where to go, Lizzie. We're all counting on you to pass and go to the Grammar School,' Miss Pendent had said, beaming at her star pupil. Her expression had turned to one of astonishment when Lizzie turned up at school two days later announcing that she had stayed at home instead of going to Barnsley to sit the scholarship.

'But why? All you had to do was get on the bus by the Catholic church and it would have dropped you off right near.' Miss Pendent's shock had angered Lizzie, arousing in her a burning resentment and frustration that this old spinster had no real inside knowledge of the poverty endured by most of her pupils. Just because the front doorsteps were all scrubbed white every morning did not mean that the proud women carrying out this ritual had eaten any breakfast. What would she know about pride and empty bellies? Food was for the man in the house followed by the children, and there was often precious little left for them.

Passing the exam would have been easy, you stupid woman, she wanted to shout at her, instead biting her lip and gazing at the pool of drying ink surrounding her inkwell. How could she explain that her Mam didn't have the money for the bus fare and even if she had, how could her parents ever have afforded the school uniform, the daily bus fare and all the other requirements of a posh education? So she had made up a story of being ill to cover her embarrassment. It wasn't until her ambition to be a nurse had very nearly been thwarted by her lack of higher education that she had resented the poverty which had deprived her of her rightful place at the Grammar School. Her present success had been due to her determination and a hospital that had decided to give her a chance. And her ambition did not end there. She was not going to marry a penniless labourer, live in a slum cottage and bring up a brood of rickety children. Her sights were set much higher. Young Doctor Holdsworth had paused to give her a bright 'Good morning' more than once.

'Listen to me, Sarah.' Lizzie's grim expression frightened her younger sister. 'Don't you go taking the first job that comes along. Not unless you want to end up living in a miserable hole like this watching every penny, never knowing when your man's coming home or, worse still, if he's going to be brought home in a hearse? Get out of here, promise me!'

'You mean I ought to go away into service?' Sarah's green eyes opened wide in bewilderment. 'I thought you didn't want me to go away either.'

Lizzie sighed, the corners of her mouth turned down. 'I dunno, sometimes I do wonder what is the best. At least, you'd get away from Colethorpe, see somewhere different before being tied down like our poor mam. You mustn't waste your life tied to a man who gives you a baby every year and leaves you slaving away while he sups his wages down at the club.'

'But I don't want to go and live in someone else's house,' Sarah protested.

'Well, I'm living in a hostel with twenty other nurses and believe me I sometimes think it's a prison, but when I get my day off I can go all over London, have a cup of tea in Lyons Corner House, sit in the park watching the people go by and, oh, see so much.'

Sarah smiled at Lizzie's enthusiasm. 'You really think I'd like living in Blackpool?'

'Why not? Seven shillings and sixpence a week all found isn't too bad. You'd soon make friends with other girls in service, go out to the flicks, enjoy being free for at least one day a week. You're never free here, are you?'

Sarah was about to confide in Lizzie about her secret ambition, then stifled the words forming on her tongue. Perhaps one day. She finished hanging up her sister's last new blouse, then sighed. 'I'd better go downstairs and give Mam a hand.'

'OK, tell her I'll just finish unpacking and I'll come down and help.'

Their mother's eyes crinkled with amusement at the message, grunting slightly as she lifted the heavy black iron pot on to the stove. 'Aye, she'll be down when the dinner's on the table will our lady daughter.'

Her husband was right calling her the lady of the family. Right from being a toddler, she had avoided hard graft and soiling her hands, and yet she had chosen to take up nursing. Strange that, unless it was the attraction of the uniform and mixing with doctors, even though at a respectful distance. There was no denying that Lizzie was an attractive young woman; her silky brown hair and liquid amber eyes would not of themselves be considered worthy of a second glance, but her whole being was possessed of an animal vitality which drew men to her. Joanna's only fear was that it would be the wrong kind of man who would capture her Lizzie.

'Right luv, get the plates out to warm and Dad'll want his coffee nice and hot.' Unlike most of his workmates,

Jim did not drink tea to replace the gallons of fluid forced out of his pores as he sweated underground, preferring instead hot, black coffee made straight into the mug. Joanna always cringed as he drained the last drop, somehow avoiding the grounds in the bottom of his mug.

She rattled out the ashes in the fire, stoking up with more shiny black coal. 'This blasted fire's been playing up all day, I've hardly had enough water for the washing and the potatoes still aren't boiling. If your dad's dinner isn't on the table the minute he gets in there'll be the devil to pay.' She wiped her hands on her wraparound pinafore before clutching her forehead.

'What's up, Mam?' Sarah asked, concerned at her mother's white face as she knelt down.

'Nothing much, just a bit tired I suppose.' She stood up, rubbing her back as she tried to straighten up. 'I miss Patrick. He was always so good with the heavy jobs around the house and somehow I find them all a bit too much lately.'

At forty-one her red hair was scarcely touched with grey and her green eyes still burned with a youthful vitality, but yet she had to admit that recently the household chores had been more wearying than hitherto. Perhaps it was her age, or . . .? No, please God, not another child on the way. These miners' cottages with only two bedrooms and an attic were scarcely big enough for a family of four let alone the five children she had already borne. Jim would be pleased; he had long blamed her for an empty cot, forgetting that she was fast approaching the change of life and not up to the sleepless nights a new baby would bring. She had been luckier than many, losing only her little Nellie out of the five, taken off with pneumonia.

'I could help more, Mam. I don't need to stay on at school any more. I could stay home and do all the jobs our Patrick used to do.'

Her mother did not reply. It was going to be hard telling her that her father had got other ideas. His wages barely kept them in food and his pint at Colethorpe Miners' Club. How could she break it to Sarah that he intended to send her away into service? Someone he'd met at the club had a sister who ran a boarding house in Blackpool and needed a girl to help with the cleaning. Sarah would have her own room and board plus a wage so that with everything found she would be able to send a few shillings a week home, just keeping a shilling or two for herself.

'Why can't Bernard do a bit to help round the house? Why, Mam, why?'

Joanna peered into the saucepan to check the potatoes before answering. 'He's had enough by the end of his shift down the pit. I'm lucky to have reared him so far.' She turned to face her young daughter. 'Do you know, when he were born, the midwife put him on one side and told me he'd never survive and best let him slip away. I told her straight that I was his mother and she'd better hand him over fast before I gave her a right good clout round the ears.'

She sat down at the old deal table covered with an oilcloth now worn with frequent scrubbings. 'It's his heart, I can tell. She was right, that woman was, about him being a weakling I mean, but wrong about me rearing him. I sometimes wish he could get some other work, but what else is there but the pit?' Joanna sighed, dragging herself to her feet. It was true, there was little else to do except go down the pit and slave while the coal owners got rich and collected their knighthoods. Jim said it would all be different one day; the workers would own the means of production and benefit from the profits, but that day was a long time coming.

Grand Mr Hetherington had spent more on having his name on a large shiny wrought iron arch over the pit entrance than he had on safety precautions for his men. His chauffeur-driven Buick costing over four hundred pounds would have kept a miner's family in comfort for four years.

At least Patrick had made a move to escape from the filth and drudgery of working on his hands and knees miles below ground, with the ever-present threat of a roof collapse. The mine owners always pleaded lack of funds when it came to better safety measures or providing simple amenities such as pithead baths and showers. Too bad if a few miners paid the price from time to time – accidents were soon forgotten. As for baths, didn't they get some free coal to heat the water to fill a tin bath at home in front of the fire?

After one week down the pit, Patrick had made up his mind. At a gangling six-foot-two and lying about his age, he had volunteered for the army and was immediately drafted into the Coldstream Guards. Pronounced underweight, he had been put on double rations until he filled out sufficiently to be a useful member of His Majesty's armed forces. Not that he was likely to be needed in combat. The League of Nations had been formed to prevent aggressive nations from preying on weaker neighbours, so that the massive slaughter of the Great War would not happen again.

The letters from Egypt, written in a beautiful

copperplate hand – the result of his education in the army and no thanks to Father Kelly, were read and re-read. Patrick's gift of painting a picture with words had Joanna transported to the sights and sounds of Alexandria and the desert, making her forget for a few minutes her daily struggle of trying to care for her family on a miner's wages.

She stood up to check if Jim's dinner was likely to be ready as Lizzie entered the kitchen. 'Right, Mam, what do you want me to do?'

Sarah exchanged a grin with her mother. As if Lizzie would do much to help! In spite of herself, Joanna burst out laughing. 'Sorry luv, I don't mean to mock, but how on earth can you do anything in that lovely frock? It'd be ruined in no time. No, just you sit down and tell me all about your hospital and your new friends.'

Lizzie made a half-hearted attempt to assure her mother that she really did want to help, but did not press the point.

'These potatoes are just about done,' Joanna said, 'and not before time either if I'm not mistaken. Here, Sarah, you get on and give them a good mashing, and no lumps this time.'

Sarah set to with the big fork her mother always used. She wanted to prove that she really could be of use if her father would allow her to stay at home and help. As Lizzie chatted on about some of the more difficult patients, Sarah struggled on. Her tiny hands began to ache with the effort, beads of sweat forming on her forehead.

'Come on luv, give them here, no need to make such hard work of it.' Joanna examined the result carefully. 'Wonderful, I'll tell Dad you've got the makings of a grand little cook.'

'Oh, Mam, do you really mean that?'

Sarah had always cherished a secret notion to become a cook in some posh establishment. Once on a trip to Barnsley to the hospital, she had seen well-dressed couples entering the County Hotel for lunch and had read the menu outside.

'Mam, what does "pommes frites" mean?' she had asked.

'Chips! That's what posh folk call chips.' She had laughed at her daughter's reply.

'Well, one day, I'm going to own a big hotel and cook.' She peered at the sign again. 'Posh chips,' she announced proudly. With her family scarcely able to afford to buy a cup of tea there, Sarah had not even begun to calculate how much money would be needed to own such an establishment. One day, she told herself fiercely. Didn't Sister Immaculata always say, 'God is good, he will take care of tomorrow.'

'Never mind that daft talk, we've got to get off to the hospital and see what they've got to say about this chestiness of yours.'

'Oh, Mam, it's nothing. You should hear Lily Batty's dad. Sometimes, he wheezes so bad, you'd think he'd stop breathing. Is he going to die, Mam?'

Joanna had bitten her lower lip. Fred Batty was in a poor way after twenty years down the pit. There was no cure for what he'd got – miners' lung – and even worse there was no more chance of earning a wage. What Gladys Batty would do with four little ones and not one of them old enough to work was a mystery. Joanna had clutched the rosary in her shabby black coat pocket. Please, Mary Mother of God, don't let my Jim get that.

The sound of the back gate being slammed shut alerted Sarah to the arrival of her father. Her mother busied herself.

'Quick, the pair of you, hand me dad's plate and I'll make a start. Sarah, get me the coffee out of the cupboard. The water's just on the boil, thank God.'

Sarah caught sight of her father striding up the path, his step still firm even after a long shift underground hewing the shiny coal from the unyielding seam. Her eyes threatened to fill with tears at the sight of this big handsome man reduced to spending half of his life bent double, buried away from God's daylight and in constant danger. And for what? Just to provide a meagre living for his wife and all of them. No wonder Lizzie had gone off to London to see if she could break the pattern of poverty and drudgery.

Her musings were cut short by his entrance. She could not fail to see the pride in his eyes when he registered Lizzie's presence.

'So, our clever daughter has decided to spend Easter with us?'

'Oh, Dad, I'm not clever,' Lizzie protested, rushing over to kiss him.

'Steady on lass, I've not washed yet, you'll get black all over.' He grinned with delight, talking over his shoulder to her, the cold tap water running down his arms, sending swirling black bubbles into the sink. 'Just let me get my dinner down me and then you can tell me all about this nursing.'

Black hair, still abundant and curly, said by many to be a legacy of the beached seamen of the Spanish Armada, betrayed his beginnings on the west coast of Ireland. Built like an ox, his strength was a byword in Colethorpe and he would often boast that his grandfather had been the strongest man in Galway, although how this had ever been put to the test had never been mentioned. Certainly, no man with any sense of self-preservation would dare question the truth of the story.

'And our Sarah, what have you been doing, helping your mam, have you?'

'Yes she has,' his wife put in quickly. 'She's got the makings of a right good little cook. Tell her your potatoes are nicely mashed.'

Sarah waited for words of praise from her father. She knew that he favoured Lizzie and tried not to feel jealous.

He patted her hand. 'Good lass, you're a grand little worker, soon be bringing a few bob home to help me and your mam.'

'I'll be fourteen soon, won't I, so can I start looking for a job, Dad?'

Her father did not answer at once, giving all his attention to the plate of mutton stew and mashed potatoes placed in front of him.

'Clean your plate and then we'll have a talk about it.'

In spite of feeling sick at the thought that he was about to announce his intentions to send her away, Sarah forced the food down, barely aware of Lizzie's lively chatter conveying a colourful description of her daily hospital routine.

'And there was this old man who kept insisting that the nurses were stealing his false teeth and all the time he had got them stuffed underneath the mattress.' Lizzie's warm brown eyes sparkled at the recollection of the incident, bringing a smile to her father's face.

'I'm glad you're making a real go of it, lass, I really am.' If Jim Mulvey cherished a notion that one day Lizzie would marry a doctor, he kept such thoughts to himself. Surely his children would escape from the grinding routine of unremitting hard labour. At least Patrick was seeing a bit of the world, fine so long as there were no more wars. For the time being, his younger daughter's future was forgotten.

Sarah waited for the moment when her father would push his plate to one side with the usual comment to his wife, 'Thanks, lass, that were grand.'

'Dad?' she began, half-afraid that she would be told to hold her tongue while the grown-ups talked. A hitherto repressed feeling of resentment towards her older sister welled up. 'What about me?' she blurted out, regretting the outburst as soon as it was uttered.

'All in good time. I want to talk to your mam first. Clear the table and get the pots washed, Sarah.'

Lizzie made an excuse to go out into the yard while the ritual of clearing away the pots was carried out.

Sarah fetched the black pan which had been left to steam on the range while they all ate. It was a struggle for the tiny girl to heave it over to the deep white sink and pour some of its contents over the dishes. No one moved to help her, it being assumed as always that Sarah, small as she was, was built for hard work and that would be her portion in life. Not until all the pots had been washed, wiped and put away in the big cupboard on the right of the range did her father speak to her.

'Right, lass, sit down and listen. I've been speaking to Frank Bass at the club.' There was no need to ask who he was; everyone in the community knew Frank Bass, the manager of the local Co-op and a councillor.

Sarah hardly dared breathe. Was he the man whose sister ran the boarding house in Blackpool? She clenched her fists under the table dreading what was to come.

'He tells me there's a job going for a lass who's prepared to work.'

'In Blackpool, Dad?' Sarah's voice was barely a whisper.

'Don't talk bloody daft. What put that idea into your head? He's nowt to do with Blackpool. No, he's got a job going behind the counter since Effie Farnton left.'

'Oh, yes, wasn't she the girl who had to leave—'

'Never mind why she left, she was no better than a trollop. Still what can you expect from people with no proper faith?' That was Jim Mulvey's way of saying that the girl came from a Nonconformist family and therefore was cut off from God's saving grace. 'Anyhow, I've fixed up for you to go and see him Monday morning at eight o' clock. If he likes the look of you, you can start the day after your fourteenth birthday.'

Waves of colour spread from her throat washing over her usually creamy pale cheeks until her whole face glowed with happiness.

'And don't go getting any daft ideas about your wages, do you hear? You'll tip up, bring your wage packet home to me unopened and I'll give you something back for yourself.'

Sarah nodded in acceptance. That was what she had expected in any case. There would be no squandering her money on silk stockings like the ones that Lizzie had, nor would her mother get much more to spend in the house. If Sarah felt any resentment at the thought that some of the money she earned would be spent on extra beer at the club, she repressed it. At least she would not have to go away to a distant town, living with strangers miles away from her family and all that was familiar.

'What about her schooling?' asked her mother.

Sarah could not help remembering the passion her father had shown in his dealings with local councillors regarding the provision of a Catholic school. Hadn't Councillor Blakey visited their house to try to talk reason to her father?

'Look here, Jim,' he had explained, 'if we let the Catholics have their schools, the Jews will be wanting them next.'

'And a bloody good thing too. Why shouldn't they have their schools too?' he had thundered. No wonder Councillor Blakey had shaken his head at such an obvious lack of understanding of the issues involved and had left.

'Use your sense woman. What's a few more months at school worth when there's the chance of making a few bob for us? Besides, I can't afford to go on feeding a growing lass like her forever. Lizzie's off our hands, Bernard's doing all right down the pit, and Patrick's making his way in the army. Now it's Sarah's turn.'

The fact that neither Lizzie nor Patrick sent any money home was not mentioned. It was also considered reasonable for Bernard not to have to tip up, instead giving his mother a fixed contribution each pay day. He was a man and courting, so he needed cash in his pocket. More often than not he spent his evenings at Iris's house where her mother welcomed him already as one of the family. A few dinners would soon pay dividends with Iris, the last of her brood to be got off her hands. She had dropped several broad hints to encourage her daughter in getting Bernard to the altar. Even if they weren't Catholics like the stuck-up Mulveys who thought they were God's chosen, Iris had stated quite plainly that she was willing to 'turn' for him and would soon be demanding that he bought a ring and got on with helping her plan a wedding. He had become a bit cheeky lately, half-suggesting that they might go further than a fumbling and intimate exploration with the hands. Iris was strong-minded enough to make sure that she did not end up like Effie Farnton at the Co-op, an object of scorn, whose mother hardly dared to show her face outside the door. If he wanted to go all the way with her, it would only be when she had a wedding ring on her finger.

Lizzie was well aware that any money sent home would go on household necessities. Her help consisted of sending items of clothing for her mother in the knowledge that at least her mam would not always be in the same threadbare skirt and blouse.

'She's not going out to work just so that she can spend her money on the fancy stuff her sister's got out there on the line.'

'They're mine, not Lizzie's,' Joanna told him, a glint of defiance in her narrowed eyes. 'Lizzie gave me some things she didn't need any more.'

'What? Does the lass think that I can't provide for my wife? Does she think I'm letting my wife go around in rags? Tell her there's no need for charity,' he thundered, ignoring Lizzie's muttered protest.

Joanna's Irish spirit fired her with an instant desire to rebel against his overbearing assumption that she should have no say in it.

'If my daughter wants to send me clothes it's only because she's ashamed of what she's seen on the line. She knows as well as I do that most of the ragged old clothes I wear are enough to give the neighbours a good laugh.'

For one moment, silence hung between them, both half-afraid of what was to come. Joanna waited for an explosion which would have sent her husband slamming out of the house and down to the club. Any climb-down on his part would have been seen as relinquishing his role as ruler of the house. He threw some coins on to the table.

'You've only got to bloody ask if you need owt. How's a man supposed to know what a woman wants? And as for our Lizzie, she can send what she likes. Let the bloody neighbours know we've got a clever daughter who's doing better in the world than their half-wits.'

He grabbed his coat off the hook behind the scullery door with a muttered, 'I'm off.'

Joanna had been holding her breath throughout this tirade, finally exhaling in a loud rush of air coinciding with the slamming of the door. Lizzie and Sarah grinned at this triumph of commonsense over male authority.

'Now then, you two,' she warned, frowning sternly. 'Your dad's a good man. He works damned hard to keep this family going and he's got his pride, so mind what you say or I'll tell you, Lizzie, not to send me any more clothes.'

'Oh, Mam!' Lizzie protested.

'Never mind that, just you pay your father some respect.'

Sarah and Lizzie exchanged glances. When their parents stood foursquare, it would be a foolish person who would defy them.

Chapter 2

Jim had met Joanna when she was still a wide-eyed innocent seventeen-year-old who had never been allowed to walk out with a young man back home in the village in County Mayo. Jim's father had crossed the Irish Sea to seek his fortune in England, finally settling in Liverpool with his young wife and baby son. Whatever he had forsaken it was not the faith of his forefathers and young Jim was brought up to obey the teachings of Holy Mother Church. Work being almost as difficult to obtain in England as it had been for his father before him in Ireland, Jim had joined the army.

He soon found on his first posting to Ireland that he was reviled by the Irish natives, who looked upon him as a traitor. Out on night patrol, he had come across Joanna and her brother. An ancient bicycle was lying in the road, its twisted handlebars being wrenched at by a young woman. The sound of a man's voice that seemed to come from nowhere caused Jim Mulvey to cast around himself anxiously. He did not want to end up in a hedge with his throat cut, the fate of unwary English soldiers.

It was all the fault of that English Prime Minister, 'Bloody Balfour' the Irish called him. He had declared in the English House of Commons only a few years previously, just before the turn of the century, that he would be as relentless as Cromwell in enforcing obedience from the Irish. There was not a child in Ireland who did not understand the significance of that remark. The massacre of three and a half thousand at Drogheda and Wexford in 1649 by Cromwell's army was a historical fact never to be allowed to be forgotten.

'What's going on?' he called out.

'What's it got to do with you?' the young woman replied. 'You can come and have a laugh at my daft brother if you like.'

Jim felt suddenly pleased that it was her brother and not a sweetheart that this lively redheaded Irish girl was out with.

'Look at him.'

Finbar had been giving Joanna a lift on his crossbar, but having consumed several pints too many of the potent ale sold in McNeil's bar, he had steered the bicycle into a ditch. Joanna was standing by the ditch, leaning over at the sodden creature floundering in the mud.

'You drunken idiot! Look what you've done to my only decent dress! It's ruined! You'll give me every penny for a new one before I ever let you set foot in McNeil's bar. It'll be a long time before you taste his beer again my lad!'

Jim thought she was the most beautiful girl he had ever seen with her riot of red curls reaching almost to her waist and her green eyes flashing revenge at her brother.

'Can I help, Miss?'

A look of relief crossed Finbar's face as his sister's scorn was diverted to the English soldier.

'You, a filthy Englishman? What do you take me for? I'd have to be on my deathbed before I'd accept help from one of your lot!' She was standing face to face with

Jim, or would have been if she had been a foot taller.

'Perhaps your brother feels differently, Miss. In any case, I don't expect you'd be wanting to see him die of pneumonia with no priest here to give him the sacraments.'

Joanna had stared hard at the tall soldier, whose features resembled more those of her dark, curly-haired cousins than those of the fair Englishmen who paraded their power and weapons throughout Ireland.

'Are you English or what?' she asked, peering at him in the pale moonlight.

'Well, my father came from Galway and that's where I was born. I was brought up in England, but I'm as good a Catholic as any of you, so you needn't stand there looking so sure of yourself, Miss.'

'For Christ's sake! Will the pair of you stop arguing,' a plaintive voice begged from the bottom of the ditch. 'You can be a bloody heathen Chinaman for all I care, just give me a hand to get out of this bloody stinking ditch.'

Jim's courting the young Irish girl had not met with the approval of Joanna's family who viewed the English soldier with suspicion and barely concealed dislike. His being a Catholic made them despise him even more, treating him as a turncoat. It was not until he had been posted back to England and had left the army that he had been able to send for his beloved Joanna. First there had been a stint in India before he could get back into civilian life and although giving up the army had been a wrench, he would have walked on coals to have Joanna as his wife. What man in his right mind would want to give up the chance to travel the world in order to slave underground? Joanna knew the sacrifice that he had made to win her love, and returned his love with a devotion that ignored his wild outbursts of temper and frequent bouts of drinking at the club.

'Come on, you two, never mind your dad. The kettle's boiling away there and I could do with a cup of tea.'

'I'll get the cups out, Mam,' Lizzie offered. 'You sit down and we'll wait on you for a change.' She studied her mother's sudden pallor with a professional eye. 'Are you sure everything's fine? You don't look too grand to me.'

Joanna gave a little laugh, shrugging her shoulders. 'Oh and since when have they made you a doctor, my girl?'

'I may not be a doctor, but I can recognise when someone's not one hundred percent well.'

Sarah carried on making the tea, now forgotten by her sister who had sat down again opposite her mother. Most of the conversation was a puzzle to her, but Lizzie's tone frightened her.

'So, what is it?'

'I've told you — nothing. It's just my age, that's all.'

'You mean you've missed?'

'Don't you be so cheeky asking your mam questions like that.' A bright pink flush spread from her neck upwards, suffusing her cheeks with an unnatural colour.

Lizzie was not to be put off by this show of indignation. 'Are you expecting, Mam, tell us.'

'I don't know, I mean, I don't think so, it's too early to say.' A tiny bead of sweat hung on her upper lip. 'It's my age, I keep telling you. Now, can we have that cup of tea?'

Sarah leapt up to tip the contents of the black kettle into the huge brown teapot. Concentrating on measuring the spoonfuls of tea and putting milk and sugar into the cups proved to be almost impossible.

'For goodness sake, Sarah, one sugar's enough for me,' Lizzie protested. 'I swear you've gone and put two in all the cups.'

'Well, you did say you were going to make it.' There was just the hint of rebuke in Sarah's tone.

'Oh, the thought of going out into the world to earn a living has loosened your tongue, has it?' Lizzie laughed, standing up and going over to her sister to give her a hug. 'You'll need to stick up for yourself, lass, it's a hard, cruel world out there. Just you remember that.'

'But if Mam . . .' Sarah stopped. If another baby was on the way, then that would be another good reason for her father not to change his mind about the job at the Co-op. He would surely make sure that she stayed in Colethorpe to give her mother a hand.

Washing the cups up after the tea filled her with an unexpected pleasure. She wouldn't care how many times she had to stand at the sink so long as she could stay at home with her parents.

The clock in the front parlour began to chime. It was an old Viennese Regulator, produced by the thousand in Vienna towards the end of the nineteenth century. About four feet in length, ornately carved with a curved glass front revealing the gleaming brass pendulum, it had been a wedding present from Jim's parents. Too good to be in the kitchen where the smoke from the range and the steam from the washing would have taken the sheen off its silky walnut finish, it hung on the wall in the best room. Every half-hour it reminded everyone of the passage of time.

'The sheets!' Joanna clapped a hand to her mouth. 'Sitting here talking to you girls, I've forgotten Aggy Hudson.'

Aggy lived in the next street identical to the one where the Mulveys lived. Her husband came in from his shift, had his bath in a tin tub in front of the fire, and ate his dinner, then left with barely a muttered word of farewell to spend his earnings at the nearest public house. If Aggy and her sons were to fill their bellies, she needed to scrape enough pennies to buy scrag end to make a nourishing stew eeked out with mashed potatoes and turnips. With plenty of coal to heat water and a hot fire to dry the clothes, Aggy took in washing. Not that many miners' wives availed themselves of her services, unless there was another baby either on the way, or just born. The presence, too, of an elderly incontinent parent in the house would bring women to her door bearing foul-smelling bed linen. All of this Aggy took in her stride, welcoming customers whatever their requirements. The windows of her tiny kitchen constantly streamed with condensation from the ever-boiling copper. At thirty-five, Aggy looked fifty.

'I'll go, Mam,' Sarah volunteered.

'Do you want me to come with you?' Lizzie asked, her expression clearly indicating that she expected her offer to be refused, although Lizzie would have been shocked if anyone had suggested that she was growing away from her roots in the mining village. Her mother registered the look and was saddened.

'No!' Sarah's refusal came out as a shout.

'Hallo, what's this? Not meeting someone special, are you?' Lizzie teased.

'That's enough of that sort of talk,' Joanna admonished. 'You know our Sarah's only a child.'

'Don't be daft, Lizzie.' Sarah went out into the hallway at the foot of the stairs where her old brown coat hung on a nail. She hoped that Lizzie and her mother hadn't noticed the colour surging into her cheeks at the mention of meeting someone special.

With a nonchalant, 'Won't be long,' she picked up the few pennies to give to Aggy Hudson and strode off down the back yard and out into the narrow alleyway.

It was dark now with no street lighting to help guide her, but Sarah knew every cobblestone and could work out the exact position of each back gate along the alley. She loved to linger, dawdling outside any gates left open so that she could observe the scenes being played out in the back kitchens.

Number twelve had a special appeal. Harry Wilby lived there with his parents and younger sisters. Harry was nearly twenty and had worked down the pit since leaving school. In Sarah's eyes he was the most handsome man she had ever seen with his thick thatch of corn-coloured hair and the bluest of eyes this side of heaven. Sarah fantasised about him, picturing herself at eighteen standing with Harry at the altar of Saint Patrick's Catholic Church. Every so often her heart would miss a beat at the prospect of some other girl capturing him. Many men were already married by the time they were twenty. What if Harry fell in love and got married before she had had the chance to grow up?

With no Harry to be seen in the kitchen of number twelve, Sarah hastened her step, pausing again outside number sixteen. Strange gasping noises coming from behind the wall adjoining the gate aroused her curiosity. The coal shed and midden were housed in a brick outhouse two feet away from the back wall, leaving a gap where bikes could be parked. With this narrow passageway not visible from the road or the house, it was an ideal place for the activity engaged in by the two people.

It was too dark for Sarah to see what was happening

and her knowledge of what went on between men and women was vague to the point of ignorance.

A woman with her skirt up over her waist was leaning up against the outhouse wall. Moans and grunts were coming from the man who was moving rhythmically back and forth against her.

On hearing the woman gasp what sounded like Harry's name, Sarah leapt back, her heart thumping rapidly. Whatever it was Harry was doing, the woman seemed to be enjoying it. Sarah suppressed the guilty thought that she wished she could be that close to Harry in case it could be construed as being impure and have to be confessed to Father Kelly.

The sound of a gate being slammed was followed by a man's footsteps. Whether he was coming in her direction or not, Sarah did not wait to find out, running as fast as she could to the haven of Aggy Hudson's steamy kitchen.

'You are in a state, love,' Aggy greeted her. 'Here, sit down while I fetch your mam's sheets. They're all nice and dry. I've just got to fold them, then you can carry them better.'

Lines rigged up from one corner of the kitchen to the other sagged under the weight of newly washed sheets. A fragrant warm vapour hung in the air wafting across the room from the sheets airing by the fire. There was no one to give Aggy a hand, with her husband out at his usual pub and her sons hiding in the front room.

'Can I give you a hand?' Sarah felt guilty listening to Aggy's wheezing chest, the legacy of hours spent in a hot, moisture-laden atmosphere.

'No, don't you worry yourself about me, luv, I'm used to this.'

Sarah watched as the red-faced woman deftly swung

the snowy white sheets folding the corners so neatly that they would have passed as brand new.

'There you are, tell your mam I'm not taking any time off over Easter, so if she needs any extra doing, what with your Lizzie coming home and all that, well, I'll be able to manage.'

No need to ask how she knew about Lizzie when everyone knew everyone else's business in Colethorpe. Sarah handed over the money, clutching the still warm sheets to her chest.

'Goodnight, Mrs Hudson, I won't forget to tell Mam what you said.'

Going past number sixteen was going to be an ordeal, especially if the man and woman had recognised her and were still there. Ignorant as she was in sexual matters, an inexplicable instinct had told her that whatever they had been doing was not really right. She told herself that as long as she kept looking straight ahead she couldn't be accused of poking her nose in where she wasn't wanted.

'Sarah, isn't it?' A man's hand on her shoulder startled her making her cry out in fear. 'It's only me, it's Harry, no need to be afraid, Sarah.'

Sarah's heart was thumping not only with fear but also with a strange excitement she had never experienced before. Harry Wilby here with her in the darkness and touching her.

'Harry? You made me jump,' she stammered, trying to explain her sudden reaction to his physical presence.

'Here, let me give you a hand with the laundry. Been to Aggy Hudson's have you?'

Sarah relaxed at the ease with which he dropped into casual conversation and handed over the heavy bundle.

'Poor Aggy, who'd want to do what she does for a

living, but I expect there's plenty glad to have her about.' He walked a few more steps in silence. 'And when are you starting work, Sarah?'

'I'm nearly fourteen, so Dad says I can start looking.' She didn't think it advisable to say too much about the possibility of a job at the Co-op. Harry had two sisters who were older than Sarah and who would not have been best pleased to hear that little Sarah Mulvey's dad had been able to pull strings on her behalf.

'Oh, quite grown up now then, are you?'

Sarah looked up at his face trying hard to decipher his expression, wondering if he were mocking her, but the darkness hid his features from her.

When they reached her gate, Harry handed over the sheets.

'I can see your mam in the kitchen and is that your Lizzie?'

'She's home for Easter, then she has to go back to London to her nursing job.'

Harry ruffled her tight red curls. 'Don't let them send you away now, will you? We want you here.'

Before she could fathom the meaning of his words, he was gone leaving her standing by the open gate. Harry Wilby had touched her, had said that he didn't want her to go away. It was not until the echo of his footsteps on the cobblestones had finally died away that Sarah reluctantly went indoors.

'You took your time,' Lizzie said, taking hold of the sheets. 'Come on, give me a hand, Mam says these are for our bed. Honestly, Sarah, wake up, you look positively starstruck.'

Sarah wondered if she ought to confess her meeting with Harry Wilby to her sister, but for once hugged the secret to herself. This was too special to be talked about and Lizzie would only tell her that she was too young to be having silly romantic notions.

Chapter 3

'Right, let's be 'aving you, then. Hmm, not very big for your age, are you?'

Frank Bass, the manager of the Co-op leant back in his chair, his watery grey eyes travelling up and down Sarah's figure and seeming to dwell over-long on her burgeoning bosom. A skinny man in his mid-forties, whose pasty face matched the dirty white of his grocer's apron, he had spent all of his working life at the Co-op and was now the manager. Not that his position meant that he could spend all day at his office desk. In order to make sufficient profit to pay out a healthy divvy, he had to take his turn serving at the counter and fussing over the customers however small their orders. Whatever the situation, it was well known that he would not give credit. The old trick of sending a child with the message that money would be forthcoming in the morning did not hold water with Mr Bass. The area manager praised him regularly to his superiors thus ensuring that Frank Bass had a job for life.

'I know that, Mr Bass, but I can lift and carry ever so well.' Sarah wanted this job so much, she would have agreed to fetch and carry until she dropped. Anything rather than be sent away to Blackpool.

'Aye, that's to be seen.' He gazed at a spot above her

head, then glared at her. 'And do you know your tables? Can you do your sums?' He did not wait for an answer before continuing with, 'It'd be your job, that is if I do agree to take you on, to weigh out the sugar, the currants and sultanas. No mistakes allowed, you understand. We can't 'ave the customers complaining about short weights, and nor can we see all the profits that makes up the divvy lost through giving 'em too much.'

Pointedly ignoring Sarah, he shuffled some papers on his desk, pretending to scan one or two closely. Sarah waited, hardly daring to breathe in case he turned her down without giving her a chance. After a long three minutes he looked up and took a deep breath as if to announce that he had arrived at a momentous decision.

'I'll tell you what I'll do. You come here first thing tomorrow. See Dolly and she'll give you some things to weigh out and if you get them right, I might consider taking you on – as a favour to your father, you understand. Right, off you go, and tell Dolly I need her in here.'

'Oh, thank you very much Mr Bass, I'll work really hard, honest I will.'

The manager waved his hand, dismissing her. 'Get Dolly and be off with you.'

Sarah closed the office door behind her, hardly knowing whether to be pleased at the chance to try for the job or worried in case she did not match up to Mr Bass's standards.

A short plump girl whom Sarah recognised as Dolly Redmile from number sixteen was counting out change to a woman with a small child.

'Another tuppence please, Dolly, if you don't mind. I can't afford to keep Mr Bass in pints.'

Dolly grinned, showing a row of even white teeth. 'Sorry, Mrs Wainwright, good job you noticed. It won't happen again.'

Pacified, the customer left, dragging her little boy away from the Co-op window where he had been desperately trying to climb into the sack of currants in order to grab a handful.

'Hello, Sarah.' Dolly's smile was genuinely welcoming. 'I hear from Fr . . . er, Mr Bass that you might be coming to work here in place of Effie Farnton. She thinks she might get her job back after the baby's born, but believe me, she doesn't stand a chance. Customers wouldn't like it and anyway Mr Bass is a strict Methodist and sticks to his principles.'

Sarah was comforted by this assurance even if she felt embarrassed at the reason for her good fortune. Dolly's friendly smile gave her spirits a much-needed lift.

'Oh, I nearly forgot, Mr Bass wants you in his office right now.'

Dolly brushed her straight black hair back behind her ears underneath her white cap. 'Suppose I'd better see what he wants then, after all he's the boss.'

Her easy-going attitude astounded Sarah. Mr Bass was the boss; surely it couldn't be right to talk about him in such a casual manner.

'Charlie, watch the counter a minute, there's a good lad.'

The tall, thin lad looked up from the window display where he was trying to clean up round the sacks of sugar and dried fruit. He could not be described as handsome with his spiky, mousy hair sticking out at angles on his head behind batwing ears, but what he lacked in looks, he made up for with his general air of affability.

Without waiting for his acquiescence, Dolly pulled off her cap, shook her long hair out over her shoulders and strode off to the manager's office.

Charlie sighed, laying down his broom and cloths. He wiped his hands down his grey overalls before taking up a position behind the counter.

'Hello, Sarah, I'm Charlie, general assistant, delivery boy and dogsbody. We don't do deliveries on Mondays, so I'm free to help clean up the yard, count in the goods and serve behind the counter when Mr Bass and Dolly need to discuss important matters.' He gave a knowing wink, adding, 'If you get my meaning.'

Sarah nodded, totally baffled by his remarks, but nervous of showing her ignorance of the daily routine of a large grocery store.

'You'll soon get the hang of things here. Dolly and Mr Bass see to the money. All you'll be allowed to do is run around fetching and carrying. See that ladder – well, that's to reach the tins on the top shelves. Believe me, you'll be up and down them steps a hundred times a day.' He leaned over the counter, dropping his voice to a whisper. 'Mind you wear a long skirt. You don't want him looking up your legs every time he sends you up the ladder.'

Sarah blushed, horrified that any grown man should deliberately try to get a glimpse of her knickers. Perhaps she should tell Mr Bass that she did not want to work here after all.

'Don't worry, Sarah, I'll look out for you. You'll be fine.' Charlie assumed a paternal air which sat odd on his pimply young face, making Sarah beam in happy anticipation of her initiation into the rites of the grown-up working world.

'How long have you been here?'

'Oh, let me see . . . since I left school, so that'd be exactly three years.'

'So that makes you seventeen,' Sarah informed him without pausing.

Charlie whistled in admiration. 'Quick at your sums aren't you? You'll do all right here, Sarah, probably end up as manageress.'

The two young people giggled at the joke, as if either of them could aspire to such positions of importance!

'I'd better go,' Sarah said. 'See you tomorrow.'

The Co-op enjoyed the most prominent position in the row of shops in Colethorpe High Street. With its double frontage and wide doorway, it was the largest store in the town. To its left there was a sweet shop and tobacconist, further along a hardware shop, a chemist and a barbershop. On its right there was a greengrocer, fish and chip shop, and finally a draper's.

The gents' outfitters occupied tiny premises opposite, the miners having little need of new outfits. A Sunday suit was exactly that and lasted a lifetime. One black suit priced at an incredibly expensive one pound thirty-seven shillings and sixpence was discreetly displayed at the rear of the window. Although priced as if for sale, it was generally known that Mr Peddar, the proprietor would hire it out for funerals and weddings.

The women made do with the discreet ladies' dress shop, which also sold dress materials as a sideline. Corsets in a bright pink satin with a long row of hooks down one side were advertised in the window at nine shillings and elevenpence; identical to the ones sold in the large London stores, Miss Enderby claimed. Sarah stared in wonder at the contraptions; she had seen them on her mother's washline and could not understand why they were necessary unless of course that was the only way to hold up your stockings.

The owner of the shoe shop displayed only the most practical of footwear, knowing the requirements of his customers. Boots for the men, hardwearing flat-heeled shoes for the womenfolk and comfortable slippers for the elderly. Plimsolls at one shilling and sixpence for children to wear in the summer were also good sellers. Being generally cheaper in Barnsley, any larger items such as furniture involved a trip on the bus to the larger town.

Just off the main street, Queen Street, narrower and less well-lit, boasted a number of second-hand shops selling household goods and clothes, all of which did a brisk business. A shoemender's premises did a desultory trade, most men being able to fashion soles and heels on lasts at home, thus saving on unnecessary professional repairs. Metal pegs that had been hammered on the soles and heels of shoes rang out on the pavements and cobblestones of Colethorpe.

One establishment was well patronised. A steady stream of customers bearing bundles to the pawnshop, also in Queen Street, bore witness to the poverty of some of the Colethorpe inhabitants.

Sarah crossed the road to press her nose against the window of the ladies' dress shop. A pretty blue cardigan caught her eye. At four shillings and sixpence, it was far beyond what she could ever afford, but if her father let her have enough of her wages back, she might be able to knit one in the same colour. The shoe shop held no interest for her having nothing to compare with the shiny high-heeled courts worn by Lizzie. One day, Sarah vowed, she'd go and stay with Lizzie and they'd go out to all the big shops and buy absolutely everything.

Leaving the shops behind, Sarah reached the row of houses ending in number one. Time to stop daydreaming and go and tell her mam what had happened at the Co-op.

'Well, it sounds promising,' Joanna said, amused at the excitement in her younger daughter's voice. 'So, if you do everything right, he'll give you the job.' She pursed her lips, wondering what Sarah ought to wear on her first day at work.

'I'll need a long skirt, 'cos I have to go up and down ladders all day.'

'But you'll trip up over the hem if it's too long.' She sensed embarrassment in Sarah's worried frown. 'I expect you'll need something fairly long though luv, for decency's sake.'

Sarah's relieved smile told her that she had guessed correctly.

'Now, let's see what we can do. You seem to be growing out of everything. I know, how about that dark blue skirt our Lizzie sent me? I haven't worn it yet – can't seem to make it meet round the middle. I could take it in at the side seams and perhaps an inch or two off the hem as well.' She looked at Sarah as if seeing her for the first time. 'You know, I do believe you've shot up these last few months. I won't have to take too much off the hem. What do you think? Would you like it?'

'But Mam!' Sarah protested. 'It looks practically new! Our Lizzie wanted you to have it.'

'Never mind. It's too small for me by a mile and you need it more.'

Sarah was thrilled at the prospect of starting work in a posh London skirt. 'I'll do the washing, Mam, if you want to get on with the sewing,' she offered, her eyes bright with expectancy.

'And your dad's dinner, and fetching the coal in, and collecting your dad's boots from the mender's and ironing Bernard's shirt.'

Sarah set about the tasks, her face shining with enthusiasm and spurred on by the thought of going out to work dressed in proper grown-up clothes.

'I'll do the veg first, then I'll get the coal in. The copper can be boiling while I fetch dad's boots. I'll hang the washing out when I get back. Bernard's shirt will have to wait, but I won't forget it. Can't have him looking scruffy when he goes round to see Iris.' Sarah gave a little smirk. 'Iris won't be so keen on him when they get married and she finds out how fussy he is over his shirts.'

Not for the first time that day, Joanna realised that her little girl was not only on the verge of womanhood, but that she was also determined to work hard to achieve any objective she might set for herself.

'Quite the little organiser,' Joanna told her reaching for her sewing box.

Flying round getting everything done before her father arrived home, Sarah felt proud to be given such responsibility and slightly surprised that she had actually managed to fit everything in.

'I've got to show Mr Bass that I can do what he wants, Dad, and that I can pick things up, then he said he'd give me the job.'

'He'd better. He's not likely to get such a good lass as our Sarah. Just look what she's done round here today.'

Jim's eyes took in the line of washing, the neatly ironed shirts and shining range given a good blackleading by Sarah. Joanna had also told him that she was almost certainly expecting.

'Good lass. But remember, if you do get the job, you'll still have to help your mam with the jobs that want doing. There'll be no coming in and sitting around expecting to be waited on.'

It was on the tip of Sarah's tongue to say that Bernard did exactly that, but then so did her father. It was only the women who were expected to slave all day and half the night however bad they might be feeling. This was no time to be starting an argument.

In spite of her great excitement, Sarah slept the next morning until she felt her mother shaking her gently.

'Come on, luv, I've brought you some hot water up so you can give yourself a proper wash all over before you get dressed.'

'Oh Mam! I could have got that myself.'

'Well, it's your first day so I thought I'd spoil you. Hurry up, now, the porridge is on and there's a nice cup of tea for you.'

Sarah couldn't wait to put on the new skirt and preen herself in the tiny dressing table mirror. Lizzie had left behind an old white blouse with long sleeves and revers. To Sarah it was the epitome of fashion. So long as Dolly Redmile did not think that Sarah was trying to outdo her. The thought struck her, that in spite of Dolly's seemingly friendly manner, there had been a hard line round her mouth and a questioning in her eye when she had seen Sarah emerge from Frank Bass's office.

Sarah presented herself at the Co-op promptly at eight o'clock. The door was still locked, leaving Sarah shivering outside in the freshness of the May morning. Even worse, several of her mother's acquaintances stopped to speak to her, enquiring the reason for her waiting so early outside the Co-op. These enquiries presented Sarah with a problem. Jobs being like gold dust, questions would be asked as to why she should get the chance of a job when their lads and lasses were looking desperately for work. If Sarah explained that she was only being tried out, then news of a possible subsequent failure to secure the post would soon get around.

'I've got to see Mr Bass,' was her answer. If she gave the impression that she was waiting to do some desperately needed shopping for her mother, then so be it. Sarah pressed her lips together firmly and volunteered nothing further.

The doors were opened soon after eight by Frank Bass who ushered Sarah in before locking them again.

Half-past eight was the official opening time and customers were not allowed in until the manager, Dolly and Charlie were all at their posts ready to start serving.

'We're a bit low on quarters of butter, so you can make a start on them. Dolly'll find you an overall and show you where to wash your hands.'

'Come with me, Sarah.' Dolly led the way through a large storeroom where tea chests, sacks of dried fruit and sides of bacon gave off mouthwatering odours. She turned to see Sarah's expression of astonishment at so much food in one small area. 'Touch so much as a broken biscuit and you're out on your ear, lass,' Dolly warned.

The door out of the stores led to a back yard with a brick outbuilding. Dolly took a bunch of keys out of her overall pocket, selected a large door key and signalled to Sarah to go in.

'Here's where we hang our coats and leave our sandwiches. That gas ring on the cupboard is for heating a kettle of water for making tea or washing your hands, but Mr Bass doesn't expect us to be forever wasting gas.

You'll have to let me decide when it's to be used. We wash up in the sink.'

'Where's the lav?' Sarah asked, nervous tension making her aware that if she soon didn't get to a lavatory, she'd wet her knickers. Besides, it had been a cold wait outside the Co-op that morning.

Dolly pointed to the narrow passage leading off the cloakroom area. 'Down there. Perhaps you'd better go now while you've got the chance. You won't get another break until eleven and that's if you're lucky.'

'Come along you two,' the manager yelled from the storeroom doorway. 'No time for a mothers' meeting, there's work to do.'

Sarah set to work weighing out quarters of butter just as Dolly showed her. To start with, the butter slipped all over the place and once she dropped a slab on the floor when no one was looking. A quick wipe with a cloth and no one would be the wiser. After a while, she got the knack and quarters of butter were soon neatly wrapped and stacked.

'Good, good,' Mr Bass nodded his approval. 'Now do the same with that sack of currants in the window. You'll find blue bags in the drawer behind the counter.'

Customers began to enter, waiting at the counter to be served.

'Well, hello Sarah, fancy seeing you here.' Sarah was to hear that remark from practically every customer who came into the Co-op. The tone varied from genuine pleasure that the little lass had got a job and would be able to help her parents out with a few bob, to downright jealousy that she had received preference above their offspring.

Sarah did not have time to interpret nuances of tone

with so many tasks being heaped upon her. She was grateful to be told that she and Charlie could take five minutes off for a cup of tea in the back.

'And I mean five minutes,' the manager said, tapping his watch meaningfully.

'You watch me,' Charlie said, tipping exactly two cups of water into the kettle. 'Quick, grab these matches and light the gas. Put two spoons of tea in the pot and when the kettle boils, tip it in the pot. I'm going outside for a smoke.'

'What?' Sarah was horrified. 'Are you allowed to?'

'Course I am, daft. I'm not a kid you know.' He sauntered out, pleased that he was impressing Sarah with his man of the world act.

There was just enough time to gulp down the scalding tea before Dolly came to remind them that they were due back in the shop.

'And you've got the deliveries to do, Charlie, so get a heave on. And don't let Mr Bass catch you smoking, or you'll be for it.'

He reddened, rushing off to do Dolly's bidding without a backward glance at Sarah who was sharing a conspiratorial smirk with the older girl.

'Mr Bass will be having a break now, so you'll be in the shop on your own, Sarah.'

'But what about you?'

'I've got to make the tea for Mr Bass, but if anything happens that you can't manage, come and knock on his door. Don't forget – knock and wait until he tells you to come in. Do you understand? Don't just go barging in.'

Mildly affronted that she should need reminding of the ordinary courtesies expected of a junior member of staff, Sarah gave a stiff nod. 'Of course.'

The smile creasing Dolly's plump round features was replaced by an unfriendly narrowing of the lips. 'Just thought I'd better tell you – no chance of any misunderstandings then.'

As it happened, the only customer to enter the shop was Aggy Hudson, in for her usual massive weekly order for soap and soda.

'Eh, fancy seeing you here! You didn't say you'd got a job.' Aggy's red-rimmed eyes took in Sarah's smart skirt and blouse. 'You look a picture I must say. When did you start?'

There was no point on trying to escape telling the truth. 'Well, Mr Bass is giving me a bit of a chance – nothing definite as yet. We've just got to see how things go,' Sarah told her, giving out just as much information as was necessary to prevent further questions. 'If it doesn't suit me, I can always tell Mr Bass that I'd rather not stay.'

The disbelieving, 'Gerraway!' from Aggy warned Sarah that she was beginning to say too much. Plenty of girls in Colethorpe would have gone on bended knee for the chance of such a job and to pretend that she was not really desperate to be accepted by the manager was stretching incredulity too far.

'Well, I hope it all works out for you, luv.' Aggy picked up her bag of soap and washing soda, placing a half-crown coin on the counter. Sarah searched around frantically for Dolly or Mr Bass, but neither showed any sign of emerging from the office.

'Don't forget your divvy slip, Mrs Hudson,' Sarah said, filling it in as she had seen Dolly do countless times. 'And your change.'

Aggy checked it carefully. 'Good lass. Give my best to your Mam.'

With the till still open, Sarah waited for Dolly's return.

'I didn't like to disturb you and Mr Bass and you did say I was to carry on,' she babbled.

Frank Bass who was close behind Dolly cast a look at the till and divvy duplicates.

'I don't think we're going to need to look any further for Effie's replacement,' he beamed. 'Come into the office and we'll sort out your pay and hours right now.'

'You're sure, Mr Bass?' Sarah asked, totally overwhelmed at this change in his attitude. She wondered what it was that Dolly had given him with his tea to put him in such a generous frame of mind. Perhaps it was the chocolate digestives she had taken in with her. Whatever it was, it meant that her future at home was safe. Filled with impatience at the long wait before she could tell her mother the good news, Sarah worked frantically all day to prove to Mr Bass that he had made the right decision.

'Steady on,' Dolly warned her. 'You're making us all dizzy, you've been up and down that ladder so many times.'

At half-past five, Mr Bass told Dolly to take the divvy duplicates into his office so that he could check the day's takings against the amount of cash in the till.

'Off you go then, Sarah, we'll see you tomorrow at eight on the dot.'

The huge doors were locked behind her and Sarah stood for a moment watching the comings and goings in the High Street.

A weary woman in her late thirties clutching a shabby brown shopping bag was just getting off the bus from Barnsley. Daisy Murray had a slate loose everyone said, but was good enough to slave all day in the posh houses doing the laundry and scrubbing for a pittance.

Miss Enderby was running a discreet duster over her shop front door. She patted her wispy grey bun, glancing up and down the street in the unlikely event that there might be a late customer needing underwear or stockings.

Just like all these people working in shops and down the pit, the bus drivers, the delivery men, she was now part of the real grown-up world, earning a living. The first thing she would do this weekend would be to write to Lizzie to tell her of her good fortune. It was all very well Lizzie advising her to leave home and go into service, but what would Mam do without her? Sarah had overheard the conversation between them, which although only partly comprehended made her suspect that a baby was on the way. Deep down, a consciousness of her awakening sexuality told her that she did not want to be too far away from Harry Wilby. One day he would see that she was no longer a child.

'Hello, little dreamer, what are you doing here standing outside the Co-op, can't you see it's shut?'

Harry's deep blue eyes, filled with amusement, were taking in her rapt expression. Sarah, suddenly aware that the object of her dreams was standing close to her, put a hand up to her mouth, half-afraid that she had been voicing her desires out loud.

'You look very smart and grown up, I'd hardly have recognised you, Sarah Mulvey. A little bird tells me that you've got a job here. Is that right?' His strong hand crept round her shoulder resting there, its heat searing right through her thin blouse.

'Well, I've only started today to see if I would do and Mr Bass has just said that I could have the job.'

The White Rose Weeps

'You didn't tell me you were starting at the Co-op when I saw you the other night,' he reproached her. The only answer Sarah could think of was that it was not really anything to do with him. She bit her lip before venturing, 'I didn't know you'd be interested.'

His arm tightened round her shoulder. 'Everything you do interests me.'

Panicking at the unexpected intimacy of his reply, Sarah jerked herself free and ran across the road. What would her father say if someone told him that she had been seen in the High Street with Harry Wilby's arm round her? A quick glance behind her told her that he was still waiting outside the Co-op. With a pang of bitter disappointment, she realised that he was there to meet Dolly Redmile.

Her mother's delight at the good news of Sarah's job wiped Harry Wilby's words from her mind.

'Your dad will be pleased for you, luv. Now come on and sit down while I make you a cup of tea.'

'Oh, Mam,' Sarah protested, 'let me do it.'

'Get your best things off first, otherwise you'll have nothing to wear to work tomorrow.'

Sarah savoured the words as she went up to her room to change. Somehow her old clothes seemed to belong to another time and to a different person.

'Mam,' she said, on her return to the kitchen, 'these old things hardly fit me. What am I going to do?'

'Hmm, it looks like you're going to need your money for the next week or two to get you rigged out for work. Your dad won't want to be shown up with you not rightly dressed in the Co-op for everyone to see.'

Sarah was half-expecting a tirade from her father on vanity and waste of money, but for once he had been reasonable.

'I mean, Jim, she's going to be on show to all of Colethorpe, isn't she?'

Jim forked a few more mouthfuls of his dinner into his mouth allowing them to digest along with her words. Clothes were a waste of money, but he wasn't going to have his lass looking untidy. In any case, Frank Bass would expect her to be smart now that he'd given her the job.

'Aye, well mind she doesn't buy rubbish. A smart dark skirt that'll last and some hardwearing shoes – I'll leave it to you Joanna, but nothing like our Lizzie has for London, mind you.'

The next few weeks were a blur of hard work, saving each Friday to go and buy suitable clothes to wear. Dolly wore a tight black skirt that was shorter than the current fashion and showed the backs of her fat knees. Her blouses were equally tight and even the white shapeless overall could not conceal her full rounded breasts. Sarah, envious of Dolly's attractions, had taken to surveying herself in the mirror and measuring her chest. Her firm breasts were just big enough to give her hope that she was approaching womanhood.

With money she had earned to spend on clothes, the trip to Barnsley on her Wednesday afternoon off was a real treat. She and Joanna spent hours searching the shops for suitable bargains, with Sarah indulging herself by trying on one fashionable skirt after the other.

'You can't wear your skirts that short,' her mother had chided, as Sarah twirled in front of the shop mirror. 'Remember what you said about going up and down ladders. There'll be time yet for you to show off your legs, but work isn't the right place. Besides, it's not as if any decent girl'd want to copy Dolly Redmile.'

Sarah wondered what her Mam meant by decent and

The White Rose Weeps

why she had thought fit to mention Dolly but deemed it prudent not to ask too much.

'Seems daft though, doesn't it, Mam? I mean, it seems as if I'm going out to work just so as I can afford the clothes to go to work in.'

Joanna laughed at her daughter's logic. 'Don't be so downhearted, luv. It won't be too long before there's some left over for yourself.' Privately she doubted whether there would ever be enough for Sarah to spend on fripperies and her heart ached.

The contribution that her daughter made towards household expenses was already improving their daily diet. Instead of New Zealand neck of mutton at ninepence a pound if she bought the whole neck, she had been able to treat them on Sundays with the occasional joint of beef and Yorkshire pudding. Silverside at one shilling and tuppence a pound was a welcome luxury after a week dining on mutton stew.

A sensible navy blue skirt and two dark blue blouses having been decided on, Joanna paused by the department selling baby clothes. Sarah observed her silently. Although she had guessed that a baby was on the way, her mother had not told her definitely. It seemed that now an announcement was to be made.

'You don't need telling, I suppose,' Joanna sighed, 'that there'll soon be a pair of lungs waking us up at all hours of the day and night.'

Sarah was not sure whether to say that she already had an inkling. She squeezed her mother's hand firmly.

'Well, you'll be needing some things for it. Don't worry, Mam, you can have all my pay now that I've got my clothes for work.'

Sensing that in some way their roles had been

reversed, she assured her mother that the new arrival would present no problems.

'I'll help look after you and the baby at the weekends and when I get in from work, you'll see. I'm glad that Dad let me stay at home with you.'

'So am I, luv, so am I,' her mother told her. 'Now come on, let's see what they're giving away today.'

Chapter 4

Jim averted his eyes. He remained silent mulling over what he ought to say. How could he tell Harry that there was always the possibility that if they tried to dig themselves out, there could be worse falls and even the risk of underground waterways being diverted into the tunnel? What was it the old miners used to sing?

> We're up to our knees, up to our knees,
> Up to our knees in water,
> Silly buggers just like us,
> Don't know what's the matter.

They knew all right what the matter was but just had to pray that the streams did not become torrents hurtling through the seams and swallowing up men before either drowning them or dashing them to death against the jagged rock walls. Jim and Harry remained for three hours wondering what help was being organised. Most of the time was spent in complete darkness with Jim carefully sparing the use of the candle.

'Do you reckon the others got out, Jim?'

'Well, if the fall is worse than just this section, then we're going to need a miracle to get us out of here before we run out of air.'

'Perhaps we ought to start praying.'

'I already have,' Jim said. 'I'm praying for all the bastard mine owners to roast in bloody hell.'

Joanna had heard the siren as she was hanging out the washing and chatting to her neighbour. Both women dropped their bags of pegs, rushed indoors to grab a coat and joined the other stricken women hastening to discover if their men had been buried alive.

In spite of her advancing pregnancy, Joanna struggled to keep up with the straggling group advancing on the pit, until a sharp pain in her side forced her to slow down.

'Don't know who's missing yet,' she heard one man say.

'Sounds as if it's near where Joe Smallburn's men are working.'

Joanna clutched her side, leaning against the wall for support. Wasn't that the name she had heard Jim mention once or twice on the rare occasions he'd said anything at all about his working day? Please God, not my Jim, she prayed.

Sarah was at the top of the ladder in the Co-op handing down tins of peaches to Dolly who was serving a customer clearly better off than most. Whoever heard of anyone wanting three tins of peaches all at once?

'It's our Rita's wedding,' the woman announced, as if some explanation was owed to account for such unlikely affluence. 'His people are helping with the wedding breakfast – not short of a bob or two, they're not, so I'm making the trifles.'

'Very nice too. She's a lucky girl your Rita.'

One thing about Dolly, Sarah thought, she always seemed to know exactly the right thing to say to people.

The sound of the hooter stopped conversation.

'The pit!' Rita's mother hastily paid for her purchases and fled.

The colour draining from her cheeks, Sarah scrambled down the ladder.

'I'll have to go,' she whimpered. 'It might be Dad.'

'No one's going anywhere, young lady, so just get on with your work,' ordered Mr Bass. 'If there's any news, good or bad, I'm sure we'll get to hear of it the minute word reaches the pit top.' A lifetime spent in the mining areas had taught him that men trapped underground did not get out before many patient man-hours had been spent trying to find a safe solution to the problem of rescuing them. Working in the grocery trade might not be too well paid, but at least he wasn't risking his life every day in order to keep the nation's fires burning.

He set Sarah to work tidying up the front window. Charlie, upon whom this task usually fell, was out on deliveries and not expected back for at least two hours.

'That lad's got just about as much idea of cleaning as I have of knitting,' the manager muttered. 'Mind you shift the currants and get into the corners. The customers'll wonder we're not run over with rats if they see the mess he's left.'

Dolly was quieter than usual, going about removing the streaky bacon from the slicer in a slow automaton-like manner. Sarah guessed that Dolly, too, must be concerned about her own father. A thought struck her; would she wondering about Harry too?

Time passed slowly as they waited for news. No one entered the shop, all having gathered at the pithead either to find out the fate of relatives or give support to those whose husbands or sons had been reported as missing.

'It's your dad, Sarah!' Charlie came bursting in the rear door from the storeroom. 'I've just heard – there's been a fall. It's him and another, I think they said it were Harry Wilby.'

'Now then, lad, stop your shouting and tell us what you've heard,' the manager commanded. 'And you, Sarah, just sit yourself down a minute until we hear what this idiot's got to say.'

'They're trapped, that's all I've heard.' Charlie's thin chest rose and fell rapidly as he gasped for breath.

'Oh, Mr Bass, I've got to go to me mam,' Sarah pleaded, a sick churned-up feeling in her stomach stripping the colour from her cheeks. Great sobs issuing from the very bottom of her tiny chest bore witness to the unspoken thought that her dad might even be dead at this very moment, lying crushed in the blackness of the pit.

'Right lass, off you go, but you're to come back the minute you find out what's happening. We've a business to run here and you're paid to work.' He stared coldly at Dolly. She needn't think she was going to run off to see how that great fair-haired giant, Harry Wilby, was faring. 'You can go and make us a cup of tea, Dolly, while Charlie here minds the shop.'

'Right, Mr Bass.' Her voice trembled, but Dolly made no attempt to plead her case, jobs not being easy to come by. Her safest bet was to fall in with his wishes rather than risk the sack.

Sarah ran past the shops where anxious traders, all aware of the desolation a pit accident could wreak on the community, stood in their doorways, ready to pick up the first available snippet of news. The row of cottages appeared to be deserted as was her own. There was no reply to her anguished cry of 'Mam!' when she reached the back door, and rightly guessing that her mother would by now be at the pit, Sarah took a deep breath and flew to join her.

Insinuating her slight form through the crowd, who gave way when they saw it was Jim Mulvey's lass, she reached her mother.

'It's Dad, isn't it?'

Joanna's face was grey, black smudges framing her sad, green eyes.

'Bernard's down there helping,' she whispered. 'All we can do is pray.' Joanna's faith was unquestioning. She did not expect to be especially singled out for God's favours, accepting that 'Thy will be done,' could so often be a cruel will as far as God's creatures were concerned. She fingered the rosary in her pocket, reciting soundlessly the Pater Noster and the Ave Maria.

A man appeared at the doorway of the pit deputy's office. Joanna recognised him as being one of the few for whom Jim had any respect

'Mrs Mulvey, would you come and sit inside? It's going to be a while before we hear anything.'

The day was now raw and grey with the wind blowing in chilling gusts. Joanna was about to refuse when Sarah answered for her.

'Thank you Mr O'Flaherty, Mam'd be glad of a sit down.'

'Only if Harry's mam comes as well,' Joanna insisted.

John O'Flaherty nodded. He pulled his grey cap down over his lined forehead. 'Of course, I'm just going to call her over.' He strode over to where Ethel Wilby was flanked by two of her neighbours.

It was clear to see from which of his parents Harry

inherited his Nordic good looks. Ethel was a handsome woman, long-limbed and broad-shouldered. Childbearing and drudgery had wrought some havoc on her once beautifully proportioned figure, but now in her late forties there was still an echo of what she must have been in her prime. Her blond hair, untidily scraped back with hairgrips, no longer had the lustre it once had and her blue eyes were sore and reddened from weeping for her son.

The two women embraced in acknowledgement of their shared anguish, then followed the pit deputy into his office. They sat stiff-backed on hard wooden chairs, both not daring to relax in case news should come and they would have to rush out. Neither insulted the other by offering useless consolation for their plight; there would be time enough for that if the word came that Jim and Harry had perished. The strong mugs of tea remained only half-drunk on the deal table, which served as a desk.

'Listen!' Harry leapt to his feet. 'Can you hear it?'

Metal striking stone had set up slight waves of vibration echoing loudly enough to penetrate the thick wall separating Jim and Harry from their rescuers.

'Quick, your shovel, Harry. Start tapping whenever there's a gap in the digging on the other side.'

For the next hour the two men communicated in this way with the team endeavouring to reach them until finally, a familiar voice was heard close by. Jim lit the candle and was cheered to see the face of an old mate.

'By the . . . Albert Cornwhistle, you took bloody long enough.'

'They're alive! Come on lads, give us a hand.'

'What for?' Jim protested. 'We don't need any help.' He

caught sight of Bernard. 'You daft bugger! What the bloody hell are you doing here?' An unspoken fear that his wife might have been left with neither husband nor son to support her, sharpened his tone.

'Be honest, I'd have got it in the neck from you later if I hadn't come, wouldn't I, Dad?'

The others laughed, slapping Bernard on the shoulder, recognising his relief at finding his father safe.

'Right, let's get the bloody hell out of here,' Jim said, picking his way over the piles of rubble and broken pit props. Although the danger was over for the moment, there would still have to be investigations to find out what caused the slide and whether it would be safe to resume work in that seam.

Harry was feeling slightly dizzy, but faced with Jim's stoic bravery, he too had to act nonchalantly in the tradition of all miners who had been snatched from imminent death.

'You know, Jim, if the candle had been a bit better, we could have finished our game of cards. Just as I was winning too. I'll see you tonight in t' club. You're not getting away with it.'

Laughter born of relief that no one had died was passed along the tunnels from one man to another until the men waiting at the bottom of the shaft were able to relay the good news to those waiting above. In spite of their protestations the two men were gently assisted to the cage and supported as it began its ascent.

Suddenly sobs and laughter intermingled as a roar ran through the waiting crowd. Ethel grabbed Joanna's hand, helping her to her feet and out of the door.

'They're safe!' Sarah flung her arms round her mother, who was staring at the pit shaft as if mesmerised.

'Thanks be to God,' she whispered. Her unborn child would see its father.

Sarah was still dancing around not sure whether the noises she was making were laughter or weeping. As she stood with her mother waiting for rescuers and rescued to appear, she realised with a pang of guilt that much of her grief had been for Harry Wilby and not solely for her father.

At last the two men stumbled into the daylight, both blinking after the hours spent peering blindly in the blackness of what had very nearly been their tomb.

Harry was limping, suffering slightly from the effects of a bruised calf muscle. He was fortunate that the boulder that had struck his leg as he tried to escape, had merely glanced off his calf and had not landed more squarely. He could never have come to terms with joining the ranks of the crippled miners – all objects of pity, and all poverty stricken. With the doctors in the pay of the pit owners, compensation was hard to come by.

'I'm all right, Mam, honest I am,' he grinned, his white teeth contrasting with his coal and dust smeared face. He winked at Sarah over his mother's shoulder, as he submitted to her powerful, maternal embrace.

Sarah blushed, lowering her eyes in case her confusion should be noted and interpreted by the watching village women.

Grim-faced, her dad was talking to a couple of officials, who were anxious to hear the details of how the accident had started. From their expressions, it was clear that he was telling them what he thought of the maintenance of the pit roof in his section. They were joined by two union representatives equally keen to make submissions.

'We've been warning management long enough about

that section,' they were heard to say.

Jim shrugged his shoulders. All he wanted to do was get home with Joanna and let her help him bath in front of the fire to ease his battered body.

'I'm off, if anybody wants me, they know where to find me. You an' all, Bernard, you've done well, lad.'

Joanna, now relieved that her Jim was safe and ready to return home, took his arm for support, the long vigil having drained what little physical strength she had. Bernard went to link his arm in hers, but she pulled herself away gently. Her weakest child had proved that he was as tough a man as the next, shrugging off danger in order to save his father. She kissed his cheek.

'I'm fine, luv,' she told him. 'You go off and see Iris, she's been worried sick about you. She'll be as proud of you as I am.'

Iris had been hanging back from the Mulveys wondering whether to interrupt, and had just decided that it would be a good move to go up to Bernard's father and say how pleased she was, when Bernard turned away from his mother and held his arms out to her. Her heart beat faster with relief and recognition of the fact that he was now hers, and had publicly acknowledged her claim on him. Time to move on the wedding plans.

Amidst all the well-meaning neighbourly remarks and the effort needed to get herself and Jim home, Joanna did not notice Sarah's worried expression.

'Mam.' Sarah had to repeat herself to attract her mother's attention. 'Mam, I've got to go back to work. Mr Bass said as soon as I knew how Dad was I had to go back and make up the lost time.'

A flash of fury crossed Jim's weary face. He had spent the day not knowing whether he would live or die, all due to the poor safety regulations in the pit, and now Sarah was at the beck and call of some snivelling shopkeeper.

'Go back and tell him you'll make up the time another day. Your mam and dad need you at home. If you're not home in ten minutes, I'll be in that Co-op and—'

'Right Dad, don't worry, I'll tell him.'

Terrified now at what Mr Bass would say and what her father would do if she were made to stay at work, Sarah ran all the way back. Letting herself into the back entrance of the Co-op by climbing over the back wall into the rear yard where the washrooms were, she smoothed her skirt and went into the shop itself through the storerooms.

'Oh, so there you are, lass.' The manager's face was flushed and his eyes shone with an unnatural brightness. 'Good news we've heard, good news.' He rubbed his hands together.

'I'm sorry I'm late, but me mam's not too well and I had to stay with her.'

'Aye, that's as maybe, but I gave you the time off to see how your dad was, not to look after the rest of the family.'

Sullenly checking the divvy slips and cash in the till, Dolly stopped what she was doing and glared at him. She opened her mouth to speak, then thought better of it.

Her glare, intercepted by Frank Bass, appeared to change his mind.

'Well, all's well that ends well, as they say. You might just as well get off home now, I'll be shutting up in five minutes.'

Sarah had been anxiously watching the door in case her father carried out his threat to come and fetch her. Always at the back of her mind was the fear of losing this job and having to go into service in Blackpool.

'Thank you, Mr Bass.' She smiled at Dolly and before she could stop herself added, 'I'm glad that Harry Wilby was all right as well.'

'That's nothing to do with anyone here, Sarah, so just you be off right now.'

Why Dolly had frowned at his words, Sarah could not fathom. Surely Mr Bass had seen Harry outside the Co-op lots of times, so why should he be nasty? Anyway it was nothing to do with her the way some grown-ups behaved; best get home while she had the chance. Mam'd be needing help with Dad's dinner.

All the same, she regretted not having been able to speak to Harry after he had winked at her. She cherished the memory of his handsome face, desperately wishing that she were not still too young to have a young man courting her.

The back door was open when she arrived home with the kitchen full of people and loud, excited conversation. She stood outside listening, half-afraid to join the group.

'A wedding and not before time,' she heard her father saying.

'You'll make a lovely bride, Iris, and our Bernard's a lucky young man.'

Sarah doubted both statements. She might be only fourteen, but she had seen how Iris had flattered him, waiting on him hand and foot whenever she got the chance which lately had been more often than not with invitations to have his dinner at her house. Mrs Webster had encouraged the match, telling Bernard that Iris had cooked specially for him. Bernard, always the spoilt one because of his poor start in life, had begun to resent the fact that his mother's pregnancy had made her somewhat less attentive, and with Sarah out at work, his best shirts were not always as well-ironed as he would have liked. More than once Iris had taken the shirt off his back to go over it with the iron before they went to the pictures in Barnsley. Iris was not the most beautiful girl in the world with her thickset figure and dull complexion, but she had given him the promise of what she would do for him in bed once they were wed, which was enough for any man.

'And what about the bridesmaid? You couldn't have chosen a prettier girl to follow you down the aisle, Iris? Have you asked her yet?'

Sarah froze; Harry Wilby was in there too. How on earth could she go into the house now with her feelings written all over her face for everyone to see?

'Where is the lass?'

'Here, Dad. It's all right, Mr Bass said I could leave early.' Sarah stood in the doorway, hanging back, half-afraid to push her way past Harry who was standing between her and the table. Physical contact would have been too wonderfully unbearable. Bernard was grinning shyly whilst Iris was trying none too successfully to smile without appearing to be triumphant.

'Come on in, lass, you do live here,' Joanna told her. 'Iris has got something she wants to ask you, haven't you, Iris?'

Iris's attempt at coyness did not do her looks any favours. Unattractive red blotches spread from her neck upwards contrasting with her usual unhealthy pastiness.

'I, that is, we want you to be my bridesmaid. Bernard and I are getting married in August.'

Aware that all eyes were upon her, Sarah stammered her acceptance.

'I . . . I . . . yes.' Then noticing Iris's disappointment at her lack of enthusiasm, she took a deep breath and added, 'I think it's wonderful news. It's just that I've never been a bridesmaid before and I don't want to spoil things.'

The roar of relieved laughter at Sarah's self-deprecating remark restored some levity to the gathering. Harry repeated his earlier overheard comment that she'd be a beautiful bridesmaid. He had the good sense to intercept Joanna's warning frown not to compare Sarah's beauty with Iris's distinct lack of good looks. She would not want to be told that her bridesmaid would be attracting all the admiring glances.

'Well, who's to be your best man, Bernard?'

'You know, Dad, that I'd have asked our Patrick, but Egypt's a long way off and it'd be doubtful if he'd get leave to come back here just for my wedding.' He looked hopefully across at Harry. 'I don't know if you'd be best man, Harry. It seems that after what's gone on today, you're almost family.' This was a long speech for Bernard, which somehow seemed to sum up everyone's feelings.

Harry leaned across the table, grabbed Bernard's hand and shook it vigorously. 'I'd be proud to be your best man. Your father and I won't forget that you were there to help us today.' Suddenly changing his tone, his blue eyes shone, reminding Sarah of cornflowers on a summer's day. 'On one condition – that I get to kiss the bridesmaid.'

Amidst general laughter, he brushed his lips lightly over Sarah's cheeks. Sarah half-closed her eyes, in agony in case her mother interpreted correctly her telltale burning cheeks.

Chapter 5

From the day of Bernard's announcement that he and Iris were to get married, plans for the wedding were the sole subject of conversation in both households. Sarah worried constantly about her role, how she would look, and whether she would manage to hold Iris's bouquet without dropping it.

'I'll feel really silly with everyone looking at me. Why couldn't Iris have chosen some more bridesmaids instead of just one? When Jean Batsford got married she had six, all in pale pink.'

'Yes, and it took her mam months of going out cleaning at that hotel in Barnsley to pay for it. Not much to boast about there. Iris may not have the looks of a film star, but she's got her head screwed on the right way. She won't go wasting Bernard's money.'

'Why have I got to wear blue?'

An impatient sigh from her mother told Sarah that perhaps her constant harping on what she would look like, was causing annoyance.

'Really, Sarah, you're beginning to get me down with all this fussing about how you're going to look.'

What was underlying all the complaints was Sarah's trepidation at being in Harry Wilby's company all day with everyone staring at her and sure to guess how daft she was about him. They'd only make fun of a lovesick fourteen-year-old. In any case, Harry would only be nice to her because it was expected of him.

'I suppose we'll be told the real reason for all this carping before long. Just drop it for now, will you? Come here and give me a hand to put these shirts through the mangle and for goodness sake talk about something else.'

It was not simply the exasperated tone which told Sarah to be wary, but also the searching look in her mother's eyes warning her that before long she would demand a fuller explanation for all the complaining.

'Sorry, Mam, I didn't mean to make you cross.'

With the wedding in August and the baby due in October, Joanna had enough on her own mind not to delve too deeply into her daughter's reasons for dreading the wedding. As the bridegroom's mother, she would be on show and well aware of the sly glances at her swelling stomach and comments on her late pregnancy.

'What are you going to wear, Mam?'

'A tent I should think,' she sighed with faint reproach.

'Oh Mam! Why don't you get Miss Enderby at the shop to make you a special dress?'

'I might just do that. Right, you finish the mangling while I do your father's dinner. After he's gone out we'll get on with your dress. It's cut out and tacked ready for a fitting. Best not to put things off much longer. Iris is sure to be asking how things are going. You know how particular she is.'

Weddings always caused a bit of a stir in Colethorpe. For one, the steely-eyed matrons took it upon themselves to see if any slight bulge below the waist of the wedding dress was hiding a shameful secret, which would not be long in making itself apparent. Unmarried girls used the occasion to prompt reluctant swains to come to the point and pop the question. All it needed was a sly reference to the intimacies the groom would be experiencing that night.

Capturing Bernard had needed careful planning, with flattery, promises of sexual delight after marriage and liberal helpings of home-cooked meals. Iris's mother had come up trumps more than once in assisting her daughter to lure Bernard to the altar, inviting him to sit in the front room undisturbed with Iris while she prepared the dinner.

'Mind you, the stew was easy, Bernard, it were Iris that made the apple pie. Lovely light hand she has with the pastry.'

Fired with Iris's careful sexual teasing on the couch in the front room and filled with her apple pie, he had made up his mind to pop the question. She may not be a raving beauty, he told himself, but she'd do him fine. Any qualms he might have had about getting married and taking on the responsibilities of a married man had been swiftly dispelled by Iris, who promised him that she would carry on working for a while and put money by for when they had a family. With Iris's father knowing Sid Cornthwaite, the housing manager, a well-kept miner's cottage had been allocated to the young couple to rent.

The day of the wedding dawned bright with a promise of clear skies. Iris sat resplendent in front of the mirror in her bedroom. Today was her big day, and with just young Sarah Mulvey for a bridesmaid, all eyes would be on the bride. Iris had no illusions about the looks nature had handed out to her, recognising that she had inherited her father's heavy jowl and her mother's poor skin.

Apricot powder liberally applied had given Iris's grey

complexion an unusual healthy glow as well as covering up the odd spot or two. Whether her father approved or not, she had bought a deep crimson lipstick to add fullness to her small thin mouth.

'You look really lovely, Iris,' Sarah told her. 'Our Bernard's going to be thrilled when he sees you coming down the aisle.'

'That's real nice of you, Sarah.' Iris was genuinely pleased and surprised. A more searching appraisal of her bridesmaid had made her realise just how pretty young Sarah was, with her emerald eyes and flawless skin needing no enhancement. She could hardly guess that her pretty bridesmaid was suffering at the thought of being close to the best man and having to cover up her feelings in case acute observers detected the truth.

The sound of a car engine backfiring made them both jump up.

'That'll be Uncle Len from Barnsley with his car. He said he'd take you and your folks to the church. You'd better go down, luv. Best not to keep him waiting.'

Sarah had stood for what seemed like hours in Iris's bedroom, first helping her and talking to her and now she was in the front room waiting for the car that was to transport her to St Patrick's. When the front door was opened, it was to reveal a crowd of well-wishers gathered outside the gate.

'Ooh, isn't she a picture?'

'She'll put Iris in the shade and that's a fact.'

Her blue dress, although made of cheap taffeta, complemented her red hair which Iris's mother had tied back with a matching ribbon. Whilst Iris had endeavoured to cover her pasty cheeks with the orange-coloured powder augmented by two bright red spots of rouge, Sarah had sensibly refused the offer to share the make-up. Nervousness usually stripped her complexion of colour, but today excitement had had the opposite effect, heightening the delicate pink of her cheeks.

Totally unaware of her breathtaking beauty and the effect it was having on all who saw her, Sarah made a dash for the car.

There were so many people outside the church that Sarah was thankful for the presence of her parents and Lizzie, who had managed a weekend off for her brother's wedding.

'You look a picture, lass, and no mistake,' her father told her in a strangely gruff voice. 'Nearly as pretty as your mam when I first saw her.'

Joanna's coy smile lit up her green eyes. Today there was no evidence of the weariness this last pregnancy had been causing her of late; instead there was a youthful glow making her look younger than her forty-one years. Jim had been furious when she had suggested getting Miss Enderby at the shop to run her up a little dress to hide her bulge.

'Just you get yourself off to Barnsley and get a proper rigout for our Bernard's wedding. I'm not having people think we're paupers.'

The arrival of the bridal car caused another flurry of excitement.

'Right, we've got to go now, luv, so just wait and do as Iris tells you.'

'Save me a seat, Mam. I'll stay here with our Sarah until Iris and her dad are ready.' Lizzie put a comforting arm round her young sister's shoulder. 'You'll have everyone looking at you, really you will.'

Dismay threatened to fill Sarah's eyes with tears. 'But I

don't want everyone looking at me. I feel a right idiot all on show.'

Lizzie bit her lip. 'Sorry, Sis. Well, just remember that it's Iris's big day as well as your brother's, so try and look happy for their sakes. Go and help the bride and try to put a big smile on your face.'

Sarah took a deep breath and went forward to greet Iris, fussing over her veil as instructed and smoothing the creases out of her white satin dress.

'Come on then, luv,' Iris's father whispered to his daughter, giving the signal to Sarah to move forward clutching the train.

Following Iris down the aisle was just about bearable until she saw her brother accompanied by Harry waiting at the altar. Both men turned at the sound of the 'Wedding March', Bernard's round brown eyes gazing adoringly at his bride, whilst Harry Wilby's eyes were firmly fixed on the lovely young bridesmaid.

Sarah hung her head, afraid to meet his searching scrutiny and wishing more and more that it could be Harry and herself standing at the altar exchanging vows. One way of trying to forget where she was consisted of fixing her gaze firmly on the Latin inscription over the altar.

'*Tu es Petrus, et super hanc petram,*' she got as far as reading when a hiss from Iris brought her back to earth again.

'Sarah, my bouquet.'

She gave a guilty start at almost having forgotten the duties she had rehearsed a dozen times with Iris. The flowers chosen would have filled several vases if removed from the bouquet and Sarah had to struggle to hold them safely until the ceremony was over. The vows and responses seemed to go on forever with Sarah feeling that all eyes were boring into her back.

If the service in church was an ordeal, the reception held in the Co-op hall was an even more arduous test of Sarah's endurance.

'Best man and bridesmaid sit next to one another,' Iris's mother announced bossily. 'There you are dear, no need to look as if Harry's going to bite you.'

A devilish grin as he said, 'Don't be too sure, she looks good enough to eat,' brought the colour flooding into her cheeks once more.

Chinking of glasses, speeches, excited laughter at the innuendoes concerning the patter of tiny feet, all went by in a misty haze, as Sarah tried to concentrate on not letting Harry's thigh press too closely against hers at the crowded table. She was thankful when the ritual of cutting the cake was over and Bernard led Iris out to dance to the three-piece band hired for the event.

'Right, Sarah, the bride and groom are out on the floor, now it's our turn,' Harry told Sarah, taking a firm grip of her arm.

Horrified, Sarah shrank back. 'But I don't know how to. I can't!'

'Trust me, sweetheart, I'll just lead you round once. Follow what I do.'

It was everything she had ever dreamed of, having Harry hold her in his arms, almost lifting her off her feet, and carrying her slight form around the dance floor. Even so, she was relieved when he left her to dance first with Lizzie and then with several other girls.

In accordance with local custom, Iris had invited most of the girls who lived in the street to celebrate her day of triumph. Whatever the cost, no one could be left off the guest list. Dolly Redmile had arrived at the reception late, unable to get the afternoon off work to attend the church service. Her bright floral dress with the lowest of necklines soon had the men nudging one another and winking. To Sarah's dismay, Harry made a beeline for her, grabbing her closely to his chest and whirling her round the floor.

'I bet our Bernard won't be the only man here getting his way tonight,' Lizzie remarked to one of her old school friends who was sitting beside Sarah.

'What do you mean?' asked her sister.

Lizzie looked shamefaced and patted Sarah's knee. 'Oh nothing – it's just that Harry Wilby is certainly taken with Dolly Redmile.'

'Shouldn't wonder if they might be next down the aisle,' her friend agreed. 'I pity Harry in some ways. Everyone knows she'd cock her leg up for anyone.'

Hugging her misery to herself, Sarah crept out of the hall to stand outside in the fresh air for a while. It was true what Lizzie had said about Harry; he was always hanging about outside the Co-op waiting for Dolly. Vague recollections of the night she had heard a couple behind the wall flooded back into her mind. The secrets of what went on between a man and a woman were beginning to take shape, but as yet were so mixed up that she decided she would ask Lizzie to tell her the truth.

Later that night all alone in her bedroom with Lizzie having taken over Bernard's old room, Sarah closed her eyes and went over the magic moments when Harry had held her so close to his heart. Please don't let him marry Dolly Redmile, she begged an unheeding deity.

With Bernard married to Iris and settled in a miner's cottage in King Street, there was space to spare in the Mulvey household.

'Just me nòw, Mam.'

'Until the baby arrives and then we'll see how much room there'll be, what with the cot and pram and extra washing.'

'Are you pleased, Mam?'

'About what? If you mean about having another baby at my age, well . . . it'll take my mind off Lizzie and Patrick being miles away and Bernard married.'

'You've still got me.' Sarah eyes were brimming with tears.

'Come here, luv, of course I have.' Joanna held her daughter close to her, kissing her gently on the forehead. 'And what would I do without you? Now tell me, are you happy about working at the Co-op?'

'Of course I am! I'm getting really good at things. Mr Bass says I might get a rise at Christmas.'

It was true; things were getting better all round for the family. Sarah's contribution to the family budget had made some difference, but not as much as it should have done with her father now spending more time at the club since the accident. Although he would never have admitted it, Joanna guessed that his unspoken desire would be to work above ground. There were jobs, but for the favoured few, and Jim's pride would never allow him to risk the humiliation of having his application for a change of job refused.

Sarah threw herself heart and soul into proving to her parents how invaluable she was to the household. Even if this new baby had been a surprise, Sarah was determined that it would have everything. With the little money left over from her pocket money, she bought some pretty yellow gingham to line a Moses basket she found going second-hand in the pawnbroker's shop in Queen Street.

'But that's lovely!' Joanna's face lit up, smoothing away the tired lines etched by the demands of her advancing pregnancy. 'This one'll be the first to be so pampered.' She kissed her delighted daughter. 'If only I could have done this for all of you.'

'Mam, don't say that, you know how much I like sewing and cooking and everything.'

'Aye, like your dad says, you're a good little worker.'

'And I'm making a start on a new shawl.' She showed her mother the white wool she had chosen. 'I'm having it put by for me, so I only have to pay a bit each week when I get my money.' Sarah bit her lip, eyeing her mother through her long fringed lashes. 'What I'd really like is to save some money at the post office for when I'm older. Do you think Dad'd let me have a bit more for meself? I don't want to leave you short, Mam, but well, you know, I've always wanted to be able to have a bit put by.' Anxiety creasing her forehead, she waited for her mother's reply.

'Well, I never!'

Joanna sometimes wondered where Sarah had got her brilliant organisational skills from. She couldn't recollect Patrick, Bernard or even Lizzie being so far-sighted and determined. As for her dear Jim, any hopes he had entertained of a career in the army had been cut short when they married and had a family. With money always so short, life had become a dreary living from one day to the next. Would Sarah be the one to break the mould and really forge a good life for herself?

'I'll have a word with your father,' was all that Sarah could elicit from her mother.

Chapter 6

It was late in October, as the first hints of the cold Yorkshire winter to come were being felt, that Joanna had an inkling that she was starting in labour.

She had been feeling tired all day with a niggling ache low down in her back and every chore weighing her down. Thankfully, she had got the stew on the go and the vegetables ready. Sarah had put all the washing through the mangle on Sunday.

'I don't care what the neighbours say about Sunday, Mam. I'm at home today, so that's when the washing gets done. I've been to Mass so I've done my duty, which is more than them what criticises my line of washing can say.'

Joanna had laughed at her daughter's outspoken comments. Since going out to work Sarah had acquired more confidence. My lass is growing up, Joanna had thought to herself.

When she heard the back door open, she gave a sigh of relief.

'Mam!' Sarah cried out, throwing her bag and coat down on to the floor. 'What on earth are you doing? You look terrible! Come on, up to bed with you, while I make a cup of tea.'

'In a minute, there's your dad's dinner to finish and

coal to get in.' A sharp pain in her side forced a gasp from her lips, stripping the colour from her cheeks and leaving her breathless.

'Bed, Mam,' Sarah ordered, 'and you'd better tell me when I've to get the nurse and what I've got to get ready for her. And you can stop worrying about Dad's dinner, I'll have that ready in no time. In any case, if he has to wait five minutes for once, he won't die of starvation. Come on, lean on me and let me take your weight.'

In spite of her assumed air of being in charge, Sarah was secretly terrified and excited at the same time. Childbirth might be considered to be the most natural thing in the world, but there were still women who died, leaving a squalling infant behind to be cared for as best as the family could manage.

'Put clean sheets on the bed first,' Joanna gasped. 'You can take these to Aggy's later on. My clean nightie's in the drawer over there. Put some water on to heat, then get on with your dad's dinner, there's a good girl.'

Any further argument would have only caused her mother to fritter away her strength, Sarah rightly guessed, agreeing to everything once she had gently assisted her into bed.

Working at a frenzied pace, fetching in coal, putting pans of water on to boil, heating the stew and mashing the potatoes, Sarah managed all the tasks by the time that her father came home. He did not need telling twice where Joanna was, racing up the stairs to see how she was faring, cradling her head in his arms as she winced in pain.

'Mind the pillowcase, Jim,' she whispered, as his coal-stained fingers stroked her cheeks, 'I've got all clean things on for the nurse. And stop worrying about me. I'll be fine, this isn't the first one after all. You just go and get your dinner and have your bath, then we'll see if it's time for Sarah to go round and get the nurse.'

The next three hours passed in a blur with Sarah up and down the stairs fetching and carrying. Her mother's cries of agony tore through her heart and had her begging the nurse to do something to stop the pain.

'It's perfectly natural, as you'll find out one day. When an apple is ripe it falls, and not before,' Nurse Wiggins informed her.

'Oh, Mam,' Sarah wept.

'Go downstairs now,' the nurse said, detecting a change in the expectant mother's breathing. 'It won't be long before you hear a baby crying, I promise you.'

His face grey and lined, Jim was sitting upright in a chair by the door, listening to the muffled groans coming from upstairs. This one would be the last, by God! He'd been a good Catholic all his life, with his wife having given birth to five babies and only one taken from them. No more, he swore to himself.

'Mam will be all right, won't she, Dad?'

Jim stretched out a hand over the table to comfort his daughter, but whatever he was about to say was stopped by the faint cries of the newborn baby.

'There what did I tell you?'

Standing up ready to follow him upstairs, Sarah did not tell him that he had said nothing.

'Just give us a minute,' Nurse Wiggins called out, 'then you can come and see your new daughter.'

The yells of the young sister, who would now be centre stage in the Mulvey household, brought a relieved smile to her father's face.

'She's got a sound pair of lungs on her, that's for sure.'

The White Rose Weeps

'What are we going to call her, Dad?' Sarah asked, but her question remained unanswered.

'I'll just go up to your mam, then I'll give you a shout when she's ready to see you.'

At that moment, Sarah felt alone and excluded, trying to suppress the feeling, that she was the one member of the family who was needed only for the contribution she could make to the welfare of the others. Bernard had been mollycoddled on account of the poor start he had had in life. Lizzie was treated as someone special, looked upon as the lady of the family because she was nursing in London. Patrick, so far away in Egypt, had always been her ally, even if he teased her mercilessly, often getting her into trouble before sticking up for her.

Unpalatable as the truth often was, Sarah realised at the age of fourteen that her tenure in the family household was safe just as long as she could be seen to be of use. In order to remain at home, she would have to go on working with little return for herself, making her contribution to the household expenses as well as doing more in the house than any one of her brothers or sisters. Well, with one exception and Patrick was miles away. Much as she loved Harry and wanted him to be the centre of her future life, she could not envisage herself like her mother, painfully struggling through each dreary day with barely enough money to survive on. There had to be something better. If other people could work and make a lot of money, so could she. Perhaps her own hotel might seem to be a silly fantasy, but then how did you get started? Taking in lodgers? Getting a little boarding house? Sarah sighed at the impossibility of her present situation.

Her self-pity faded the moment she held the new baby in her arms.

'She looks like me, Mam,' Sarah murmured, astonished at the tiny red curls sparsely covering the tiny head.

'Well, she is your sister,' both parents laughed together.

'What are we going to call her?'

'How about Maureen after your mam's sister in Ireland?'

Sarah frowned. 'But I've never met her and Mam's not seen her for years,' she protested.

'Aye, but it's a family name and who's to say your mam won't get the chance to go over to see her sister soon?'

Sarah was about to suggest her own favourite name, but before she could utter the name 'Rose' she was interrupted.

'Now, then,' Nurse Wiggins commanded, 'that's enough excitement for now. You two be off while I settle mother and baby down for a rest.'

As soon as they were back in the kitchen, Sarah got on with stoking the fire and making cups of tea for her mother and the nurse.

'And bring her up a little soup, will you, luv?' Nurse Wiggins ordered. 'She needs to keep her strength up if she's to have enough milk for this little one.'

Joanna's red hair, tangled and matted, was spread out over the white pillowcase. Sarah's heart ached seeing her mother so washed out and weary. She longed to stay and gently tease out the knots in the lovely hair, combing and brushing until she looked young and beautiful again, but more practical matters called.

'I'm just off to wet the baby's head, won't be long,' Jim called out from the bedroom doorway.

Sarah knew what that meant. By the time his mates in time-honoured custom had all bought him a drink in celebration, it would be late before he returned home.

In between running up and down the stairs, Sarah managed to do the washing-up, ironing and preparing food for the next day. It had been arranged that a neighbour would care for her mother during the day while Sarah and her father were out at work, although the money she received for this attendance during the lying-in period did not cover any actual housework. This would all be waiting for Sarah on her return from the Co-op each evening.

'Very nice, I'm sure,' her boss greeted her when she imparted the news of the arrival of her baby sister. 'So long as you don't expect any time off to help at home.' The thin smile accompanying the remark, far from reassuring Sarah, served only to emphasise the threat contained in his words.

'Oh no, Mr Bass, we've got Mrs Letten to help out when I'm here.'

'That's just as well then. Right, Dolly, the morning's plans.'

'Miserable old sod,' Charlie muttered once his boss was safely out of earshot.

'Charlie!' Sarah was shocked.

'Well he is,' Charlie repeated unrepentant. 'He makes himself out to be so holy, preaching every week in the chapel, when all the time he's up to something with Dolly.'

By this time, Sarah's shock had given way to curiosity regarding Dolly and her employer. She raised an encouraging eyebrow.

'Yeah, haven't you noticed how much time she spends in his office?' With the blood rising in his cheeks, as he prepared to expand on his tale of Dolly's misbehaviour, his spots positively glowed bright red.

'What are you still doing here?' Frank Bass had flung open his office door and stood glaring at the errand boy. 'On your way at once!' he yelled, his boiled onion eyes glazed and watery.

'Right away, Mr Bass,' Charlie answered in the most obsequious manner he could manage, nodding and half-bowing as he retreated.

'Tell you more later,' he whispered to Sarah, before flying out of the door with his bicycle loaded so high that his progress down the High Street, weaving from side to side, warned other road users to keep well clear of him.

Puzzling over Charlie's remarks, Sarah observed Dolly throughout the morning, but was unable to fathom his meaning. It was true that Dolly went into Mr Bass's office whenever he told her to, presumably to go over stock requirements or make him his morning cup of tea, which did not seem to Sarah to be anything worthy of sly comments.

It was not until later that afternoon, on her return from dinner, Sarah thought she detected a guilty look on Dolly's flushed faced, as she emerged from the manager's office.

'What do you mean about Dolly and Mr Bass?' she asked Charlie when they were collecting their coats that evening.

'It's obvious, isn't it?' Charlie said, grinning. 'He's up to no good with Dolly when we're not around.' His scanty ginger eyebrows came together in an uncomprehending frown at the extent of Sarah's ignorance. 'Have you any idea of what I'm talking about?'

Not wishing to appear stupid, Sarah shrugged her shoulders, replying, 'Course I have. I expect you mean he

The White Rose Weeps

kisses her and that.' Her blushes at making such accusations confirmed Charlie's suspicions that Sarah was ignorant of what went on between a man and a woman. He burst out laughing.

'Well, put it like this. There's already been one girl leave here because she was having a baby and wouldn't say who done it.'

The sound of the door into the storeroom being slammed silenced him and no more was said.

Dawdling on the way home, Sarah regretted not having asked Lizzie the all-important question when she was home for Bernard's wedding. Until her mother volunteered the information, Sarah had to be content with only half-formed ideas, which were beginning to approach reality, but did not go far enough.

What did strike Sarah, was that Harry Wilby did not appear quite so regularly to meet Dolly out of work.

Chapter 7

'You're taking a lot of trouble over yourself just to go round to Bernard's aren't you.'

'Don't be daft, Mam.' Harry Wilby caught a glimpse of the speculative narrowing of his mother's fine blue eyes as he stooped, peering into the mirror set too low for his powerful frame.

'A tie an' all, our lad, eh?' she glared again, suddenly protective of her handsome son. 'So long as it's not that Dolly Redmile.'

'Give over, Mam, will you? No, it's not Dolly. Like I said, Bernard and Iris have asked me to go round and have a cup of tea with them.'

'Hmph! That Iris Webster's getting a bit above herself, asking folk round for Sunday tea, isn't she? Are you trying to tell me that Bernard isn't flat out sleeping off his dinner-time boozing?'

Harry finished buttoning his jacket before turning his attention once again to his mother. He recognised her carping for what it was, no more than a combination of protectiveness and inquisitiveness.

'Believe me, Mam, Bernard's Sunday drinking is a thing of the past. Iris has properly got him where she wants him.' He laughed, showing gleaming white teeth. Unlike many of his mates, whose teeth had rotted at an early age through poor diet and neglect, Harry had inherited his mother's strong Scandinavian genes, programmed for generations to withstand lack of visits to the dentist.

'So what's this all for then?'

Harry sighed. 'I've no idea, Mam, but I'll let you know everything as soon as I get home. Now is there anything special you need to know, such as how good Iris's cakes are, what pattern she's got on the lino, or whether they've got a three-piece suite?'

'You cheeky bugger,' she laughed, watching proudly as he marched, shoulders firmly back, down the back yard.

If he had omitted to tell his mother that Bernard's parents and young Sarah were to be there too, he had his reasons. For one, Sarah had just passed her fifteenth birthday, growing lovelier with each passing day. Meeting Dolly after work outside the Co-op was simply an excuse to see Sarah for a few excruciatingly frustrating moments. Christ! She was a vision with her wild red hair now tied back demurely and her figure blossoming with the promise of a more womanly shape yet to come.

Fifteen! He could not even hint to her how he felt about her. Perhaps one more year and he could ask to take her to the pictures in Barnsley, that's if Jim Mulvey would allow it. But unlike the other girls he had dated, there would be no taking of liberties with Sarah. Accepting Bernard's invitation, aware that Sarah would be at the house, meant that he would have to be on his guard with her, but the promise of being close to her was something he could not deny himself.

Bernard had managed to find a terraced cottage to rent similar to those in the High Street where he had grown up. Used to a home where floors and doorsteps gleamed with the frequent application of Mansion polish and step whitener, he had been dismayed to find that the previous tenants of number nine King Street had found no use for such frivolities. He had been pleasantly surprised at Iris's reaction of stoic acceptance at finding her new home in need of being scrubbed from top to bottom to make it habitable, and congratulated himself on having chosen a sensible wife.

The price of Iris's stoicism had been new lino in every room and a three-piece suite for the parlour to be duly admired by a stream of visitors, family and friends, nearly every Sunday since the wedding.

Harry took in the shining white doorstep and crisp floral curtains at the front window. Bernard had certainly found himself a houseproud wife if outward appearances were anything to go by. He allowed himself a minute or two to fantasise on what life would be like married to Sarah, having her to himself every day and night. The physical pain of knowing that it would be years before he could hold her sweet body close to his almost made him groan out loud. Forget it you fool, he told himself sharply.

Iris opened the door. The contentment marriage had brought, clearly suited her and had even improved her skin, making her appear almost bonny.

'Come on in, Harry. Bernard, take his coat,' she ordered, leading Harry into the front parlour where the Mulveys were already seated.

Jim and Joanna had been given pride of place in the armchairs either side of the fireplace, with baby Maureen contentedly cooing in her mother's arms. The one bright rug in front of the fireplace was an imitation Axminster – none of your homemade peg rugs made with odd pieces of cloth from old clothes for Iris. Its brown and rust pattern toned in nicely with the mock parquet pattern of the lino giving the room an air of working class gentility.

With the armchairs occupied, the only spare seat was on the sofa next to Sarah. Harry hesitated, then made for one of the high-backed chairs by the table already laden with Iris's fruitcake, buns and sandwiches.

'No, on the sofa,' Bernard insisted. 'There's plenty of room next to our Sarah, she's only little.'

Harry drew a deep breath in an effort to keep control of his desire. He smiled at Sarah. 'Aye, but growing prettier every day.'

Sarah bit her lip anxiously wishing that she could make a fitting reply, as his weight depressed the springs on his side of the sofa, tipping her almost into his lap.

'Now then, our Sarah, don't go throwing yourself at Harry like that,' Bernard warned, enjoying the joke with his best man.

Sarah hung her head, desperately trying to conceal the bright red patches on her burning cheeks. If only she had known that Harry had been invited, she could have made excuses to stay at home. On second thoughts, that would have upset Iris, who had clearly worked hard to show off her home and her abilities as a housewife. Sarah knew that it was important to Iris that her in-laws should think highly of her. A means of escape suddenly struck her.

'I'll help Iris with the tea, Bernard. You can stay and talk and look at your new baby sister. I'm lucky – I can see her every day.'

'Aye, and hear her every night,' Joanna laughed. 'Go on, Bernard, hold her. You'd better get some practice in before yours come along.'

The sofa, although cheap, was well sprung, and this combined with Harry's weight made it difficult for Sarah to release herself from its engulfing depths.

'Come along, Sarah, let me help.'

Harry turned towards her, his face just a few inches from hers so that she could feel his warm breath on her cheeks, and with his arm round her waist, gently lifted her up.

Grateful that all eyes were on Bernard as he nursed his baby sister, albeit somewhat awkwardly, Sarah fled to the kitchen where Iris was waiting for the kettle to boil.

'Never mind me,' Bernard was saying, 'it's high time I were your best man, Harry. Who've you got in mind to be Mrs Wilby?'

Just before the kitchen door was shut, Sarah caught some of Harry's reply but had no time to reflect on it with Irish eager to show off her kitchen.

She looked shyly round the spotless kitchen with its gleaming black range and scoured sink.

'You've got everything really beautiful, Iris,' she said, her eyes shining with admiration.

Iris smiled in gratitude. Her young bridesmaid was proving to be a true ally in her attempt to win over the in-laws. Perhaps later on when Sarah was married, they would be able to share all kinds of confidences. Iris was longing to tell someone that she thought she was expecting, but it was too early to make a general announcement.

She beckoned to Sarah to join her as she stood with one hand on the handle of the kettle.

'Can you keep a secret?' she whispered.

Sarah nodded, intrigued at the air of suppressed excitement in Iris's voice.

'I think I'm going to have a baby next January. I've missed twice and I've been sick in the mornings, so I'm almost sure, but don't tell anyone, promise?' Iris's face was pink with the thrill of finally entrusting her secret to someone.

'That's wonderful!' Sarah flung her arms round Iris's neck. 'I'm going to be an auntie.'

Sarah's knowledge of pregnancy and childbirth had been slightly advanced with the birth of Maureen. So far her mother had not told her all the facts of life, merely telling her when her monthly cycle had begun last winter, that she was now a woman and could have a baby.

'Don't you let any lads go taking any liberties with you until you're married, understand?'

Sarah had nodded agreement still only half aware of what constituted a liberty. With Iris taking her into her confidence over her pregnancy, perhaps she might explain the rest of the mystery to her.

'Hello, what's all this about?' Bernard had appeared in the doorway to enquire what had happened to the cup of tea. 'We're all gasping in there.'

'Well, gasp for another two minutes,' Iris told him, deftly pouring the boiling water into the large brown teapot, which she then transferred to a red tin tray, another of her wedding presents to be shown off that afternoon.

Much as Sarah would have preferred to remain on her feet passing round the sandwiches and cakes, she was firmly put back in her place next to Harry by Bernard.

This was Iris's show when all had to admire the crockery, cutlery and tablecloth, commenting on how lucky she and Bernard had been with their wedding presents. It was then up to the men to tell her what a wonderful cook she was and, even though they were really full up, they could manage another slice of the fruitcake. Throughout the ritual, Iris assumed an air of pleased satisfaction that this first rite of passage had passed so successfully.

It wasn't until the ceremony had ended and Sarah was back home in the haven of her bedroom that she had time to ponder on Harry's reply to her brother when asked who he had in mind for a wife. Amidst the gently banter, Harry had replied that he had someone in mind but that he had not yet popped the question.

'Well, you'd better get a shift on,' Jim had said, 'in case someone else beats you to it.'

Harry's enigmatic, 'I don't think that's likely,' had filled Sarah with desperation. Who could it be? Please don't let him ask Dolly Redmile.

'If I can't have him, I know he's worth someone better than her, even if she is nice and friendly with everyone,' she whispered to herself.

Harry kicked several inoffensive stones hard, making them ricochet off the solid brick walls backing the yards of his neighbours' houses. He could not go home yet, not with his mother eyeing him keenly and wanting to know every detail of Bernard's house and furniture. Just the mention of Sarah's presence would have her ice-blue eyes penetrating the secret he struggled to hide in his heart. He didn't need anyone to tell him he was a fool harbouring a passion for a girl who was only hovering on the brink of womanhood. The recollection of her sweet young body against his on the sofa stirred him into a frenzy of longing. He turned away from the back gate, heading for the one place where he would find some temporary release from his frustration.

That Sunday was to be the pattern for many others. With Iris's pregnancy now general knowledge, Sarah was pleased that Iris frequently asked her round to keep her company whilst Bernard was on the late shift, beginning to look upon her as a friend and confidante. Iris's one topic of conversation was her pregnant state and such was her preoccupation with her swelling womb that she did not seem to notice that Sarah was often puzzled by some of her comments.

However, in her typically methodical manner, Iris had borrowed some books from the library in Barnsley in order to make sure that she had all the necessary facts at her fingertips, determined to be *au fait* with whatever the midwife had to say when the time came. These books contained graphic descriptions of the development of the human embryo from conception to birth.

'Just you take a look, Sarah, while I put the kettle on. It's really amazing how babies grow inside you.'

It was not the diagrams of the human embryo which had captured Sarah's attention, but the description of the male and female genitalia with detailed explanations of how conception took place.

'What's the matter?' Iris had asked, noting Sarah's pallor. 'Don't you feel well?'

'I . . . I'm fine, just a bit hot actually,' Sarah had lied, carefully pushing the book away so that Iris would not connect her anguish with what she had been reading.

On the way home, the feeling of nausea at what she had read overpowered her, leaving her clinging for support to the railings which ran alongside the park. The pictures of the man pushing his penis into the woman's most secret part of her body swam in front of her eyes until she vomited violently into the scraggy bushes by the park gate. How any woman could want that to be done to her was beyond Sarah's comprehension. Once the feeling of nausea had passed, she began to reason more logically that with so many people keen to marry and have babies, perhaps it was not so horrible. Even so, she could not envisage herself wanting to do it, not even with Harry. An inexplicable emotion seized her, sending sensations washing over her, sensations that were not altogether unpleasurable. Then again, perhaps with Harry it would be right.

Clapping her hands over her ears to shut out the thoughts which she knew to be wrong, she ran, her feet pounding the cobbles until the pain wiped out the longing in her body.

In the Co-op, this new awareness threatened to affect her normally easy-going relationship with Charlie.

'Why can't you come over to Barnsley with me this afternoon? We might as well make the most of having Wednesday afternoon off and there's a really good film on.' He sighed. 'What are you shaking your head for, Sarah? Surely your dad wouldn't say no to us going out in broad daylight.'

It wasn't so much that her father would have put his foot down at the suggestion that she should spend an afternoon with a young man at the cinema, but more her fear at being alone with Charlie in the dark. What if he tried to kiss her? She'd heard from Dolly that all kinds of things went on in the back row and now that Iris's book had educated her, she was even warier of being alone with a man.

'I've said no and that's that Charlie, so don't mention it again, please.'

Dolly smiled widely as she counted out the takings in the till. Young Sarah was a right prissy miss and no mistake.

'Do you say no to all the boys, Sarah?'

The White Rose Weeps

Sarah's scarlet cheeks gave her the answer. Perhaps it was just as well that the girl kept herself to herself. With that flaming red hair and eyes the green of a pure tropical ocean that a man could drown in, she'd need a pair of bodyguards to keep her safe. It had not escaped Dolly's attention that whenever Harry Wilby came by to meet her from work, he wore a dark brooding look as his eyes sought Sarah.

'I've a lot to do at home, helping Mam and our Maureen. Besides, I like going round to see Iris. I'm making some things for her new baby.'

The conversation was cut short by Frank Bass coming to close the door.

'Come along now, it's one o'clock, time to go home you two. I've still got some work to do in my office. You young 'uns don't know you're born, you really don't.' His yellow teeth bared in what he intended as a rueful smile, reminded Sarah of the big bad wolf in *Red Riding Hood*, chilling her to the heart.

Flinging off her apron, she fled, glad to escape to the world outside the Co-op. Passing the wool shop, she suddenly remembered that she needed another ball of the baby wool to complete the matinée coat she was knitting for Iris's baby. Seeing the 'Open' sign about to be turned over to 'Closed', she pushed the door gently.

'Oh, please, can you just stay open a minute while I get my last ball of wool?' she begged Miss Potter.

Anything for a sale, the sharp-eyed spinster thought, reaching for the wool put by for Sarah some weeks previously.

'On no!' she gasped, embarrassment flooding her cheeks crimson. 'I've forgotten my purse.'

Miss Potter's wry expression clearly expressed her

view that she did not believe a word. 'No credit, my dear,' she said, replacing the wool in its pigeonhole with the other white balls.

'I . . . but I don't want credit. I've left my purse at work.' Sarah's eyes began to fill with tears at the implication that she was trying to obtain the wool without paying for it. 'Can't you give me a minute to go and get it? Please,' she implored, 'it's only in the Co-op.'

A minute, what was that? Miss Potter mused. There was no one in the flat upstairs eager to have her company, not in the next few minutes, not that afternoon, not ever.

'Right, just one minute and that's all. I've got things to do and people to see, you know,' she lied, almost willing herself to believe that there was life outside her little shop.

Delighted at her victory, Sarah raced back to the Co-op only to recollect that Frank Bass had locked the front doors and would not hear or heed if she knocked. The back wall was the only way that she was going to gain access to the cloakroom behind the storerooms where she had left her purse.

Hoping that no one would think she was a thief trying to break into the Co-op, she scrambled over the wall, dashed to the door of the cloakroom only to find it locked. Mr Bass's bicycle was still propped against the shop wall, which meant that with a bit of luck he would still be in his office and would open the cloakroom door for her to retrieve her purse. She smoothed her hair, tucked her blouse into her skirt and took a deep breath ready to go in and beg Mr Bass to re-open the cloakroom.

The well-oiled door to the back storeroom gave way to her gentle push without so much as the hint of a creak.

The White Rose Weeps

The only strange noises to be heard seemed to be coming from behind a pile of boxes stacked on the right almost reaching to the ceiling. Fearing that animals, perhaps a couple of dogs, had got into the storeroom and were snuffling about seeking food, Sarah approached on tiptoe scarcely daring to breathe. She did not want to risk being seized by sharp-fanged dogs.

She peered round the corner, leaping back instantly. The sight of Mr Bass lying on top of Dolly, his trousers down at his ankles, his spotty backside pumping up and down, brought bitter waves of nausea to her throat, the acrid bile threatening to choke her. In spite of the horror of what she was seeing, Sarah's curiosity overcame her initial disgust and she stared silently at the couple. Dolly's knickers and stockings were lying discarded on the sacking used to cushion the pair of lovers against the cold concrete slabs that made up the storeroom floor. Dolly, naked from the waist down, her legs in the air, gasped in rhythm with her lover's thrusts. Sarah could not understand why Dolly kept her eyes closed nor why her features were contorted as if in pain when all the time she kept urging the man on with cries of, 'Don't stop! Frank! Frank!'

Mesmerised, Sarah waited until the frenetic coupling had ceased. She wanted to run away, but her legs were firmly glued to the ground and with her throat constricted so tightly that she could hardly breathe, she did not even have sufficient strength to force out a sound to make the two aware of her presence. It was Dolly's scream as she opened her eyes that brought Sarah to normality.

'You nosy little bugger!' she yelled, thrusting Frank Bass to one side as she struggled to sit up and pull her skirt down.

'What the bloody hell!' Frank Bass tottered on one leg, staggering drunkenly, desperately trying to grab the waist of his trousers in order to pull them up to hide his now flaccid penis, which Sarah was gazing at in wonderment.

'I came back for my purse ...' was all she could manage to croak through her dry lips.

'Oh, yes?' By this time, Dolly, with her face blotched purple and her black hair straggly and witch-like, had stood up and was grasping the collar of Sarah's blouse, pulling on it so hard that the stitching gave way. 'You say one word about this to anyone and I'll bloody kill you.'

Frank Bass grabbed her arm, twisting it cruelly.

'Dolly's right. No one's going to believe a word. Don't forget I'm a respected churchman, my girl.'

He smelt of stale sweat and something unidentifiable but noxious as he leant over her. Sarah cringed against the high boxes of sugar and tea behind her, frantically seeking a way of escape.

'You're sacked,' he told her, grinning in triumph. 'I'll tell the area manager that I caught you stealing from the till. Dolly will back me up. Believe me miss, you'll not get work for miles.'

Sarah's meekness suddenly evaporated in a surge of anger at the sheer unfairness of this unexpected attack.

'Wait till I tell Dad,' she threatened, her voice high and tremulous. One final shot as she slammed the door shut nearly proved her undoing with Dolly leaping to follow her as she added, 'What will Harry say?'

Her momentary fit of bravado faded the minute she had scrambled over the wall, soon to be replaced by deep sobs. She had done nothing wrong and now had to explain to her parents the details of what Mr Bass and Dolly got up to when there was no one about in the

Co-op. Charlie's hints about Dolly and Mr Bass, incomprehensible at the time, now became crystal clear. Clutching her torn blouse tightly round her neck, she ran, oblivious to the inquisitive stares and solicitous comments.

Miss Potter glanced at her watch. That Mulvey girl had not come back for her wool after all. The story of the forgotten purse had simply been a ruse to obtain tick. Well, she didn't fool me, Miss Potter smirked, satisfied at her business acumen, yet annoyed at having been made to stay open after one o'clock and be forced to have a late lunch. Dear, dear! The sound of pounding footsteps made her look up. Whatever was happening now?

The sight of Sarah running past, heaving great wrenching sobs audible even with the shop door closed, aroused her curiosity for a second, but Miss Potter did not want to get involved in the goings on in Colethorpe. Had it not been for the fact that an elderly aunt had left her the shop, she would never have settled here with these rough, hard-drinking colliers and their huge families. She pulled down the blind and turned to go upstairs to her quiet little flat and undemanding Tibbles.

'Mam! Mam!'

Joanna turned from the stove where she was stirring the aromatic contents of a huge stewpot. Sarah's wild-eyed terror made her drop the spoon and come running to gather her child up in her arms.

'Mam! Mam!' was repeated in a gasping croak.

'Come here, luv. Sit down and tell me all about it.' The soothing words familiar to Sarah ever since she had been a toddler had the effect of calming the rasping sobs.

'Oh, Mam, it's Mr Bass and Dolly and now he's given

me the sack.' She began to wail again. 'What will Dad say?'

The sound of the back door latch made Sarah start in alarm, her heart beating wildly, fearing that Frank Bass had arrived to continue his bullying.

'What the bloody hell's the matter with the lass?'

'Jim,' his wife said, a frown warning him to remain silent for a minute. She held Sarah close to her. 'Now, start from the beginning and tell me what's up.'

'I went back to the Co-op for my purse round the back over the wall and went into the storeroom at the back of the shop and I saw them . . . Mr Bass and Dolly.'

'Yes?' Joanna stiffened slightly, half-guessing what her innocent daughter had seen.

'They were on the floor and Mr Bass was on top of Dolly and . . . oh, Mam, I can't say any more.'

The veins in her father's neck were standing out red and angry as he fought to obey his wife's unspoken order to remain silent. Like a massive statue sculpted out of black marble, he stood filling the doorway as his daughter struggled to go on.

'Dolly didn't have any knickers on and Mr Bass's trousers were round his ankles.'

'I'll kill the bastard!'

'Your blouse, how did that get torn?'

'It was Dolly, Mam. She grabbed me and said I had to keep me mouth shut and then Mr Bass said I was sacked and he'd tell everyone that I'd been stealing and Dolly would say I had too. So I just ran out and I've left my purse there . . . and that's why I went back . . . to get the money for the wool.' She took a deep breath. 'Miss Potter at the wool shop'll tell you I hadn't got any money and that's why I had to go back to the Co-op.'

The White Rose Weeps

'Jim! Come back!' It was too late to stop him now, already out of the front door, up the street and hammering on Miss Potter's door.

Miss Potter, after her second cup of tea was dozing off with her cat comfortably settled on her lap, when the noise made her throw her arms up in the air, tipping the poor animal onto the floor.

'Miss Potter! Come down, now!'

First groping for her dentures and then struggling to push them into position, took almost a minute.

'Just a moment.' She pushed up the heavy sash window in order to look out and see who was down below at her shop door. A face streaked with coal dust told her it was one of the local pit workers, and as the face was turned up to her, she recognised the man as being Jim Mulvey, the father of that Sarah who had tried to fool her into parting with the ball of wool.

'Did my Sarah call here for wool just now?'

For a moment Miss Potter feared that she was to be blamed for not giving the girl the ball of wool. 'Yes, but, I . . .'

'Never mind the buts, what did she say to you? For God's sake woman, don't stand there looking so bloody gormless, what did she say?'

'She said she'd left her purse at the Co-op and was going back to collect it, but the next thing I saw was her running past here crying.' She was about to add that she'd stayed open specially, but even as she thought better of it, he had gone.

'Now listen, my girl. Sit there and do as I tell you.' Frank Bass was in his office with Dolly, now afraid that the story of what Sarah had seen might even now be circulating round Colethorpe. She'd had enough good hidings off her father, and news of her goings-on with Frank would give him a good excuse to rip the hide off her.

'It's all very well—' she began.

'Look here, if we stick to our story that she's making it up because you caught her stealing from the till and that I had just sacked her, then we'll be in the clear. For God's sake girl, stop snivelling, Go and tidy yourself up while I finish clearing up here.'

'What if your wife gets to hear of it and your chapel people?' Dolly was sharp enough to realise that he would drop her, even sack her, if there was any likelihood of his reputation as a good husband and a God-fearing man being put at risk.

'They won't,' he told the girl, in a threatening snarl. 'And if I have any suspicion that you've been opening your mouth, you'll get sacked an' all.'

His neck swivelled round sharply as a splintering sound from the direction of the front door alerted him to Jim Mulvey's arrival.

'Keep your mouth shut and do as I say,' he muttered.

A crowd, gradually increasing in number, had gathered in front of the Co-op, where Jim was hurling his massive shoulders against the woodwork.

'Come out, you filthy bastard! Bring your whore out with you!'

There were those in the crowd who had had their suspicions about Frank Bass and Dolly, and now it seemed that big Jim Mulvey was about to expose the two of them.

Prepared to face his accuser, the white-faced manager unlocked the door. 'Any more damage and I'll call the police. I've a good mind to call them anyway after what your daughter's been up to, thieving from the till after I—'

He did not get a chance to finish, as two firm fists gripped him round the throat, threatening to throttle the life out of him.

'You lying bastard! My lass just came back for her purse and found you and that whore in there half-dressed on the floor.'

Frank Bass twisted his head struggling to escape from the huge hands almost choking the life out of him.

'Come inside, Jim,' he gasped. 'Let's talk it over in my office.'

'Oh no, you're not bloody coming that one. Call Dolly Redmile out here, now!'

A frightened Dolly appeared in the doorway. Seeing some of her mother's neighbours, she knew it was only a matter of time before the news of what had been going on between her and her boss reached her mother's ears.

Self-preservation being Dolly's number one priority, she turned on her boss. 'You deserve to rot in hell, pretending to be so bloody holy and all the time the only way a girl could keep a job was to let you do what you wanted. I'm not the first,' she told Jim, 'just you ask poor Effie Farnton.'

'What?'

Jim's astonishment and subsequent relaxing of his hold on his victim's throat gave the man the opportunity to twist and duck. He lunged forward clawing at Dolly's face and screaming obscenities at her.

'You enjoyed every minute of it, you little trollop, couldn't get enough, could you?'

There was the sound of bones cracking as Jim's right fist came up to connect with Frank Bass's chin.

'Right, get inside, you snivelling little bastard. I'm

going to make bloody sure that you tell your bosses that you've finished with Colethorpe. We don't need your sort round here messing about with girls.'

There were a few sly grins and muttered comments, most of them unflattering concerning Dolly's morals. Not many believed her tale that she was an innocent victim, only surrendering her virtue to keep her job. More likely that she agreed to do willingly what poor Effie Farnton had been forced to do.

'You mucky cow!' one outraged woman called out, a cry which was swiftly taken up by others, crowding round the now petrified Dolly, whose earlier defiance had been replaced by a fear of being physically attacked by the mob.

'That's enough! Leave the lass alone!' thundered a voice from the back of the crowd. 'Anybody'd think some of you hadn't ever sniffed where you shouldn't.'

One or two of the men exchanged knowing glances on seeing Harry Wilby push his way through the crowd to seize hold of Dolly in a protective gesture.

'Come on, I'll take you home, before these bloody hypocrites lay a finger on you.'

'Fancy her yourself, Harry, do you? She won't need any lessons from her mam,' shouted one man.

His laughter was cut short as a massive clenched fist connected with his jaw. 'I said leave it and that's what I meant. Any one else got anything to say?'

'Get her out of here,' Jim agreed, 'while I sort this little bleeder out.'

With Dolly being led away and Jim hustling Frank Bass inside the Co-op, there was nothing of further interest to be seen, and soon there was quiet once again in the High Street. Only two watchers remained standing at their front gate well away from the action.

'Thank God, your dad didn't kill him.'

But Sarah did not hear her mother's words. Her eyes were on the couple approaching the alleyway leading to the backs of some of the houses in the High Street. The man had his arm round the waist of the girl, who turned at the last moment before entering the alley. Her triumphant grin faded to be replaced by one of vindictive hatred.

Whatever the result in the short term would be of what Sarah had done, there was no doubting of what the long-term effects would be. Grieving inwardly, the bitter truth of the matter struck her that she would be better off well away from Colethorpe, Dolly and Harry forever.

Chapter 8

Infuriated at being unable to find work locally, Dolly had been forced to travel to Barnsley each day where the manageress of a cheap fashion store had taken her on, shrewdly assessing her manner of dress and slightly common appearance as not intimidating the class of customers she catered for. Although the wages were slightly better than those paid by the Co-op, Dolly had to get up earlier, pay her bus fare and spend more than she could afford on being correctly dressed as a fashion salesgirl. More than once she cursed that prissy little Sarah Mulvey. If only Sarah had agreed to keep her mouth shut, Frank Bass could have been persuaded to rescind his threats and all could have been settled quietly with no one any the wiser. The memory of his calling her a whore who had been only too willing to have sex with him still filled her with fury. Her mouth twisted in a triumphant grin. He'd be squirming with unfulfilled cravings now with his wife refusing to sleep with him. Serve him right.

Harry Wilby was a different kettle of fish. Dolly had tried to convince him that Sarah had fabricated the whole story. 'Something wrong with her if you ask me.'

'There's nothing wrong with Sarah, so don't talk about her like that,' he had said. His blazing blue eyes, which could have melted an iceberg at fifty paces, warned her that Sarah was not to be criticised.

'Sorry,' she had replied meekly. If Harry were to be got to the altar, she would have to make sure that Sarah's name was never mentioned. The brooding look he had whenever they passed the Mulvey house was enough to alert her to the fact that the young girl had some sort of hold on his heart. However, now that Sarah was out of the way in service in Blackpool, according to Iris, the coast was clear for her to work on Harry. She'd had enough of being made use of. If that pasty Iris Webster could get herself nicely settled, then so could she.

Sarah clutched her coat tightly around her neck. In spite of the bright sun blazing down, striking a myriad of diamonds on the sea surface, a cold breeze struck through the thin fabric of her coat. She was tired after the long bus journey, the first she had ever taken alone, in fact the only one she had ever taken. Her tears at parting from her family had long since dried, leaving in their place a numbness. It was as if her heart had been frozen in ice ever since the day she had found Dolly and Frank Bass on the floor of the Co-op storeroom. She had been right in guessing that Dolly would become an implacable enemy once her liaison with Frank had been made public.

'Come on girl, if you're coming, I've got a houseful to be waited on this evening and at the rate you're walking we'll not be back in time to get them fed. Shift yourself.'

'Yes, Mrs Scatesburn. It's just that my case is a bit on the heavy side.'

'Never mind the explanations. I thought your dad said you were strong and healthy, so a little case like that shouldn't slow you down.'

Sarah took a deep breath and strode out purposefully, determined not to let this middle-aged woman get the better of her. Their meeting had not been auspicious with Sarah's bus arriving late at Talbot Road bus station and then Sarah missing Mrs Scatesburn. The letter had said that she would be wearing a navy blue coat and hat and carrying a red umbrella. Unfortunately the description of a slender lady in her early forties was out by at least one decade and several stones, with the result that Sarah had not noticed the large red-faced woman in the cheap navy coat who was anxiously scouring the buses disgorging their passengers.

Heads had turned as Sarah walked past and following their admiring glances, the woman had caught sight of the tumble of red curls cascading over the collar of the girl's coat and had proceeded to call her name, chasing her breathlessly.

'You stupid girl making me run after you! Didn't you read what I said? Isn't this a navy blue coat I'm wearing? And what's this I've got on my head?'

Sarah thought it might be cheeky to answer that question. Better by far not to smile at the sight of the tatty velvet hat with the bedraggled feather wobbling up and down in perfect synchronisation with Mrs Scatesburn's double chin.

Little had been said as the two made their way out through the buses seemingly parked willy-nilly and reversing with little regard for alighting passengers, except for Mrs Scatesburn to remind Sarah that she wasn't made of money and that the tram fare to the boarding house would be deducted from her first week's wages.

The White Rose Weeps

'I really ought to deduct mine as well seeing as it's up to you to get yourself to your place of employment. I've wasted good time and money having to meet you.' She tucked a few stray, wispy, dyed brown hairs back under the brim of her hat.

Sitting beside Mrs Scatesburn on the tram, Sarah made up her mind that she was not going to be intimidated by this ill-tempered woman. Today was the start of a new life and a new adventure, filling her with the thrill of anticipation. So many tears had been shed having to leave home that she was determined that they would not have been shed in vain.

At first her mother had been astounded at Sarah's announcement that she wanted to go away into service once the gossip over Frank Bass and Dolly Redmile had died down.

'But why, luv? Why go away? You've done nothing to be ashamed of. If anything you've done everyone a favour getting rid of that rotten man and, well, as for that Dolly, she ought to have been stoned out of town.'

Sarah had clung to her mam weeping. 'I don't want to leave you and Dad and our little Maureen, honest I don't, but I've got to try something different. Can't you see that getting a job round here's not going to be easy for me? I might be the one that's in the right, but folk'll still connect me with that rotten pair.'

Surprised at the perspicacity shown by her fifteen-year-old daughter, Joanna gently brushed back Sarah's flaming locks and kissed her forehead. She did not want to lose her, but had to admit that there was a lot of truth in Sarah's summing-up of the situation. Being the innocent party did not automatically confer immunity from gossip. How long would it be before Dolly spread rumours that Sarah had been stealing from the till? There would always be someone to believe her and embellish the tale further.

'Perhaps you're right,' she sighed. 'Just as long as it's only for a season and then you'll come back, promise?'

The letter she had received from Lizzie was full of praise for the way that her younger sister had stood up to Frank Bass's bullying. Sarah had laughed at Lizzie's light-hearted style, even managing a smile at the memory of Frank Bass's spotty backside pumping up and down. Trust Lizzie to see the funny side of things. The postscript, however, revived bitter thoughts of the day when Harry had walked down the alley, cuddling Dolly Redmile and whispering words of comfort. It was me he should have felt sorry for, not her, she told herself, crumpling Lizzie's letter in her tight fist.

The tram took them first along the promenade where Mrs Scatesburn softened enough to point out the Blackpool Tower, not that anyone could miss it.

'We had a Big Wheel once, a great attraction for our visitors,' she announced, a touch of pride in her voice, 'but it had to come down a couple of years ago. The council's always talking about improvements, but they never happen,' she concluded on a sour note.

'It's lovely here, Mrs Scatesburn.' Sarah was enchanted with the wide promenade flanking the sandy beaches glowing warmly in the late sunshine. All she had ever seen had been the narrow Colethorpe streets, crowded cottages and surrounding them all, the pit and huge slag heaps. In comparison Blackpool was a paradise. 'I'm so glad I'm here. I do hope you'll be pleased with me.'

The woman was touched by the naivety of the young girl, relenting sufficiently to remark that on her day off she would have a chance to go out and see the sights of Blackpool.

'There's a nice park, Stanley Park, if you want a walk. Very pleasant it is too.'

The tram stop was a few minutes' walk away from the boarding house, a large double-fronted late Victorian villa with bay windows and a wrought iron sign with the name 'Rosewood House' swinging in the pleasantly warm light breeze. Net curtains, crisp and white, shrouded all the windows. Hanging baskets with scarlet geraniums hung on either side of the front door, which was made of dark imposing oak. Sarah paused to gaze up at the building. There were three floors with large net-curtained windows and a fourth attic storey with tiny high windows. She wondered where she would have to sleep, praying that she would not have to share with a stranger.

Once the older woman had stepped over the threshold of her domain the earlier gentler mood shown to Sarah on the tram journey was replaced by one of stern authority.

'Wipe your feet and follow me.'

A wide curving staircase led to the first floor with its four bedrooms and a bathroom. Staring all around her, trying to take everything in, Sarah was urged to get a move on and follow her boss to the second floor. This had three bedrooms and a bathroom at the end of the corridor.

'This room is mine and Mr Scatesburn's.' She pointed to a narrow staircase next to their room which led to an attic floor and two further rooms, one of which was opened. 'This is your room. It's quite nice, looks out on the garden. There isn't a lavatory up here, so you'll have to use the chamber pot in the night or the guest bathroom on the first floor. You're not allowed to use my bathroom, remember?'

Sarah couldn't believe her good fortune in not having to go to the bottom of the yard to a cold outdoor lavatory. This was luxury indeed.

'There's your bed. You get fresh sheets each Friday. I think you'll find the cupboard and chest of drawers adequate. Now get unpacked and come down to the kitchen. There's some back stairs just along from your room – they're for the staff. I'll give you ten minutes to settle in and then I want you downstairs.'

The back stairs, narrow and uncarpeted reminded Sarah of home, giving her a sudden twinge of loneliness and regret, which she hastily suppressed. I'm going to make this work if it's the last thing I do, she muttered fiercely to herself before straightening her skirt and entering the kitchen.

Mrs Scatesburn without her hat seemed less forbidding, although very much in charge. A man aged about fifty was standing by the sink peeling potatoes and dropping them into a huge pan of water that was boiling on the gas stove. Sarah was fascinated by the array of pans, cooking utensils and crockery, but even more so at the sight of a man actually doing some cooking. Her father and brothers would have been shocked at the mere hint that they might help with the household jobs.

'This is Mr Scatesburn, my husband.'

Sarah felt she ought to curtsey or something, a handshake being out of the question with Mr Scatesburn's hands deep in cold water.

'How do you do?' seemed to be appropriate in the circumstances.

'Well, well, so you're our new skiv, I mean our new housemaid. You're a bonny lass and no mistake. Where did you get all that lovely red hair from?'

Sarah wasn't sure whether he was being polite or whether there was anything more sinister in his interest as his pale eyes gleamed. Wary of men since catching Dolly and Frank Bass, Sarah turned away from him, unease growing inside her. His wife's eyes had narrowed, giving her a spiteful appearance.

'What can I do to help, please?'

'Nothing yet until I show you the ropes. This is the kitchen. I do all the breakfasts. Mr Scatesburn gives a hand with tea at six o'clock sharp. If it's cold, he lights the fires, but it'll be your job to clear out the ashes and keep the fireplaces in the dining and sitting rooms clean.'

She led the way to the dining room where four tables had been set for the evening meal.

'I'll show you how to lay the tables and clear away before you do the washing up.'

'What about the mornings?'

'Right, you get up at six and report to me in the kitchen at six-thirty sharp. If you want hot water for washing in, you can come down at six and take a kettle up. You can have a quick cup of tea and then lay the tables. Guests start coming in at eight, so it's all go until they've been fed. We do have some regulars and also one or two gentlemen travellers who need to be out to business early, so we do their breakfasts first.'

Sarah was beginning to wonder when she would be allowed to eat.

'Now, while the guests are getting ready to go out, we

have breakfast in the kitchen. All guests have to be out by ten-thirty at the latest and that's when your next jobs start. All the beds have to be made and chamber pots emptied and washed out. Sweep and dust and generally do as I tell you. We do have a woman who comes in to do the rough work once a week on changeover day, but there's not much time to waste, I can tell you. Of course during the light season in the winter, we just have our regulars, so you'll be expected to do the rough work as well.'

'I'm not afraid of hard work, Mrs Scatesburn,' Sarah affirmed, anxious to gain approval.

'That's to be seen.' Hilda Scatesburn was not one to be won over with soft words. She fixed Sarah with a stern gaze, her small dark brown eyes filled with unspoken threats. 'This is a respectable establishment, so there'll be no visitors allowed in your room. Your day off will vary according to how busy we are, but you can generally count on having Sunday off. Remember though, you'll be expected to be in no later than ten-thirty so as to be up in time in the morning. If we're not too busy, I may be able to let you have a few hours off on Wednesday afternoons, but you'll have to be back to help with the tea at six. Is all that clear?'

Sarah could think of no appropriate answer to this list of requirements, merely nodding her head in acknowledgement.

'As for manners, I expect you to address me at all times as Mrs Scatesburn, none of your noddings or "OK", is that understood?'

'Yes, Mrs Scatesburn. There is just one thing please.'

'Yes?' The woman frowned fearing unacceptable demands were to be made.

The White Rose Weeps

'When do I get to do my washing?'

'There's an outhouse at the back of the kitchen with a copper and everything you need. We do the sheets on Saturday once the guests have gone and you'll be expected to see to the beds, towels and tablecloths, so you can fit yours in then. I'll see to mine and Mr Scatesburn's on Mondays, but you can do the ironing.

'Last but not least, either get your hair cut or have it well tied back with a black ribbon.' There was venom and jealousy in her glare at the sight of Sarah's abundant fall of shining red hair. Her own sparse hairs scarcely needed the black hairgrips she used to keep them in place. 'Right, back to the kitchen and I'll give you your pinnies, then you can give me a hand to lay up the tables.'

Sarah was longing to get back to her room and write a long letter home. Flying around after Mrs Scatesburn, a picture kept flashing across her mind of her mother bending over the range seeing to her father's dinner and little Maureen cooing in her cot. The clock in the hall striking five echoed the old Viennese Regulator hanging in the front room at home and forced a tiny sob which she choked back, afraid of annoying her new boss.

Under the eagle eye of her instructor, Sarah laid out the silver, the cruets and glasses.

'You're a quick learner, I'll give you that, my girl.'

Grateful for having passed the first test, Sarah went into the kitchen where she was told how to fill the tureens with vegetables and how many chops to allow for each table depending on the number of guests. She was not prepared for the sudden hush that descended when she walked into the dining room.

'My, we 'ave got a pretty lass to wait on us tonight haven't we, Nora?' A kind-faced man in his late sixties addressed the remark to his wife.

'Where are you from, luv?' she asked.

Blushing and stammering, Sarah told them she was from Yorkshire.

'Ah, a white rose from Yorkshire.' He winked. 'We're from Preston. My wife's a Lancashire red rose. Whichever one shall I choose?'

Nora nudged him, apologising for her husband's teasing. 'Be quiet, you daft fool, can't you see you're embarrassing the lass.' She put a friendly hand on Sarah's arm. 'Don't take any notice of him.'

'Sarah!' Mrs Scatesburn was hovering in the doorway, her thin lips pursed. Once in the hall, Sarah was told not to spend too long with one couple. 'It makes the others feel that they're not getting enough attention. Remember to keep moving. Be pleasant, but don't stop.'

Later that night when she finally got to her bedroom, Sarah pulled out the cheap notepaper to write home.

> Dear Mam and Dad, and Maureen,
> I think I'll like it here. Everyone is really nice to me and I've got a nice room all to myself. It's a lovely house and Mr and Mrs Scatesburn have been showing me what to do. I've got so much to learn. I do miss you all and wish I could see you soon. Just as soon as I can save my fare home and get some time off I'll be home.
> Give our Maureen a big kiss from her big sister and tell her I love her. I'll write again soon.
> Your loving daughter
> Sarah

The White Rose Weeps

She still had to write to Lizzie and Iris, but that would have to be for another night. Before Sarah had left for Blackpool Iris had surprised her with her tearful farewell. Over the months the two had become close with Iris confiding her secret fears about becoming a mother, wondering if she would manage.

Sarah had reassured her. 'You'll be the best mam in the world and our Bernard knows that, so stop worrying.'

Iris had smiled through her tears. 'I'll miss you so much. You've been my best friend. Please write to me and Bernard, and please come and see me as soon as the baby's born. You will be its godmother, promise?'

Sarah had finally released herself from Iris's embrace after agreeing to all her demands.

Walking home from King Street, she had deliberately chosen the route that would take her to the far end of the High Street, through the side alley and along the backs of the houses. It was getting on for six o'clock and if she dawdled long enough she might just catch Harry on his way home from his shift. Coal-blackened men wearily cycling along the back alley recognised Sarah and called out greetings. Most had heard that she was about to leave Colethorpe and wished her luck. Sarah thanked them, her eyes anxiously scanning the street, desperately wishing that Harry would appear.

'Sarah!' Harry's voice came from somewhere up above her head.

Her stomach churning with excitement at hearing his deep voice, she looked up to the back window of his house. Struggling to put on a clean shirt, his thick mop of blond hair was tousled and still wet from his bath.

'Wait for me a minute, I'll be down in a second.'

Flushed and animated, Sarah was in turmoil at this

unexpected meeting. Harry actually wanted to speak to her!

Still struggling to pull a comb through his wet hair, Harry had never seemed so handsome in Sarah's eyes.

'Your Bernard told me you were off to Blackpool to work.' He looked at her thoughtfully. 'Why go away?'

Anger at his insensitivity wrenched an angry reply from her. 'Why? Because everyone knows what I saw and I . . . I just want to get away.'

The light blond hairs on his forearm brushed against her skin as he held her arm tightly. 'But you belong here where all your friends are. How are we going to manage without you?'

'I'm not a child, so don't speak to me like that.' Sarah's spirited reply made him flinch.

'No,' he said quietly, 'you're more than that, but it just came out all wrong.'

She looked carefully at his saddened face searching for what she hoped would be some indication that he would really miss her if she went away.

'You could write to me and tell me how you're getting on.' He turned as a shout from his mother telling him to come in for his dinner interrupted what he was about to say next.

'Well, I don't know, I suppose so,' Sarah began, affecting a studied casualness.

Harry thrust his hands into each of his pockets in turn. 'Trust me not to have a pencil or a scrap of paper just when I need them. I don't suppose you have. Oh damn!'

Thrilled that she was not going to be totally out of Harry's life, she was just about to say that she could always drop it in to him later, when a familiar voice called out.

'See you later, Hal.' Dolly's shrill cry could be heard

from the back gate of her house. 'Bit late tonight, missed me bus.'

The scene at the Co-op flashed into Sarah's mind, only this time in her fevered imagination, it wasn't Frank Bass who turned round in horror, but Harry with Dolly smirking at her conquest. Nausea brought bitter bile into her throat robbing her of speech. How could she be so stupid to imagine that Harry could think of her as anything other than a child, someone to be humoured, the daughter of a respected workmate? Unable to form any words in reply to Harry's suggestion that she might write, Sarah turned and fled. Tears spilling down her cheeks, she ran, desperate to reach the safety of her home and only vaguely aware of Dolly's evil smile as she passed number sixteen.

Mrs Scatesburn had given Sarah an alarm clock. 'We can't afford to let you lie in my dear and this sea air does tend to act like a sleeping pill if you're not used to it. And remember, the house rules are lights are out by ten-thirty, so make sure you are down for your cocoa by nine at the latest.'

Sarah had felt quite comforted by her late night drink even if the cocoa was made with water and very little milk. She had drunk hers quickly, asking to be excused so that she could write a letter. Her first priority had to be her parents, with one letter a night being all that she could possibly manage. Later on in the week she would write to Lizzie, then Iris and Bernard. Iris would be missing her so, especially with her baby due. The thought of not being there when her first nephew or niece arrived filled her with a momentary gloom, questioning whether she had made the right decision in crossing the

Pennines to get away from bitter memories.

Mr and Mrs Mulvey. The names on the envelope remained imprinted on her mind as she lay in her new bed, but the face that tormented her dreams all night long was that of Harry Wilby.

Chapter 9

'Egg and bacon for Mr Palmer and he doesn't like marmalade so make sure he has a pot of raspberry jam to go with his toast. Oh and Mr Stevenson has to be out by eight sharp, so serve him first, never mind what the others have to say. Our regulars are our bread and butter.' Mrs Scatesburn's instructions were uttered with military precision leaving Sarah in no doubt that she would be in trouble if any were misinterpreted.

Weaving her slim body between the tables, as she bore trays loaded with identical breakfasts for each of the guests, requests for more tea or more milk to go with the cornflakes seemed to assail Sarah from all points in the dining room. Fortunately, the first day had dawned hot and sunny putting everyone in a good mood with the prospect of a nice restful day on the sands snoozing in a deckchair.

Calls for her attention were more often than not an excuse to engage the pretty girl in conversation until at one point, Mr Scatesburn stepped in to fob off a couple of young men from Liverpool, who saw Sarah as a possible conquest in their week of freedom from the insurance office.

'Back to the kitchen, Sarah. Tell Mrs Scatesburn we need four more slices of toast and another pot of tea.'

The White Rose Weeps

Once she had gone, the young men were told politely that staff did not mix with guests at a social level. Mr Scatesburn then winked conspiratorially, tapping his nose and whispering that if they were to take a walk along the promenade they would no doubt meet no end of friendly girls who would appreciate their company, 'if you know what I mean.'

Having been made to feel like men of the world, the two ventured forth to try their luck.

'You do cook lovely breakfasts, Mrs Scatesburn,' Sarah hazarded.

Her boss's face already flushed with the heat from the gas stove, reddened even more if that were possible.

'That's very nice of you to say so, Sarah. Mind you, food is important to our guests. The sea air does give them such an appetite. I always hope and pray that they eat a good dinner of fish and chips before they come back here in the evenings, otherwise I don't know how I'd manage with so much to do.'

Sarah's eyes brightened at this remark.

'I like cooking so you've only got to ask if you want me to do more for you, really.'

Thinking that the conversation had already become too cosy between hotelier and maid-of-all-work, Hilda Scatesburn dismissed her with a curt reminder to clear the tables before returning to the kitchen for her breakfast.

Mountains of greasy dishes and cutlery had to be washed and put away while one by one the guests collected their belongings preparatory to the long day ahead. Once out of the house, there was to be no return until the evening meal.

Sarah thought it a bit mean, asking what happened to

the children if it poured with rain.

Clearly astonished at such an ignorance of the delights Blackpool had to offer, Mrs Scatesburn raised an eyebrow.

'My dear child, this is Blackpool, plenty of things to do and places to visit come rain or shine. I ask you, whatever would they want to do in here when there are so many more interesting things outside?'

The rest of the first morning went by in a mad flurry of making beds and emptying chamber pots. Sarah could not understand why the guests used them when they had only to walk along the corridor to a proper indoor bathroom. Keen to try out the modern lavatories the previous evening, Sarah had put on her coat before going to bed, crept down the back stairs, through the kitchen and up the front stairs to the landing where the guest bathrooms were. Tiptoeing so as not to disturb anyone, she had returned by the same route.

If the thought struck her that it was so unfair that miners who slaved all day getting filthy black had to have a bath in front of the fire in the kitchen, whilst this house in Blackpool had proper bathrooms, she did not voice it.

'You can come out shopping with me,' she was told, once Mrs Scatesburn had inspected the bedrooms and found them to her satisfaction. 'My husband has the gardens and windows to see to. A neat clean appearance is the key to success in all things.'

There being no answer to that, Sarah trotted along obediently taking hold of the baskets, which were slowly filling with meat and vegetables, the handles cutting into her tiny fingers.

'I'm giving them mutton chops to start with followed by tinned fruit and custard.'

Not very interesting, Sarah thought, not when you're

away from home and fancy something a bit different. She had never forgotten the menus outside the posh hotel in Barnsley with the names of all kinds of exotic dishes written in a foreign language, which her Mam had told her was French.

'Sometimes I start with soup if there's enough vegetables left over from the night before, but it does make a lot of extra running about, not to mention the washing-up.'

'Mam taught me how to make a good soup with scrag end,' Sarah volunteered, not sure if she ought to make a contribution to Mrs Scatesburn's observations.

'I see.' Did her nose turn up ever so slightly at the mention of scrag end, Sarah wondered?

'You've picked up things very quickly, Sarah. Our guests have all been most appreciative,' Mrs Scatesburn said, stretching her thin lips in what passed for a smile. She handed over a small brown envelope. 'And here are your first week's wages.' Without waiting for Sarah's thanks, she disappeared into the kitchen, returning with a letter.

'This came for you a little while ago.'

'Oh? Oh.' Sarah could have sworn that she had seen the postman call before breakfast.

'We were all so busy that it escaped my mind. Now, you take the afternoon off and go off and enjoy yourself. Just be back for six o' clock to help with dinner.'

'Oh, I will and thank you ever so much, but I must read my letter first.' The writing was familiar. Only her Mam put twirly endings on her letters.

She raced up to her bedroom, eagerly tugging at the flap on the envelope which surprisingly opened without tearing.

Dear Sarah,
We miss you already and so does our little Maureen. She keeps on crying. I think she's got more teeth coming. We are all well and very pleased that you have been so lucky. Your Mrs Scatesburn sounds very nice and I am relieved that you are in such good hands.

The house sounds lovely too with all those bedrooms and bathrooms. People keep asking me for your address so I expect you'll be hearing from Iris and one or two of your old friends before long.

I hope it won't be too long before you can get time off to come home for a day or two.

Dad sends his love as well as Maureen.
Love Mam

Her joy at hearing from home had her dancing around her room hugging and kissing the letter. Exhausted with excitement, she collapsed on her bed, re-reading the letter, going over the mention of old friends wanting her address. Could it have been Harry who had asked for it and if so, would he write soon?

With indulgent smiles on their faces, Mr and Mrs Scatesburn were standing at the bottom of the stairs in the back kitchen.

'I expect you're pleased to hear from your mother so soon. I said to Mr Scatesburn only the other day that I knew you had come from a good home.'

Puzzled at this remark, but still ecstatically happy at the thought that Harry might get in touch with her, Sarah skipped down the back garden path and out into the alley

The White Rose Weeps

that ran between the two rows of houses. It wasn't until she had been walking for ten minutes or so that she suddenly realised that Mrs Scatesburn had known the letter was from her mother without having being told. Surely she hadn't opened it and stuck it down again! Unwilling to consider that a possibility, Sarah concluded that perhaps she had noticed the postmark and put two and two together.

Sitting on one of the seats provided by the corporation and gazing at the gently rolling waves, Sarah began to feel as if she too were on holiday with the thousands thronging the beach. A slight sadness tinged her joy as she watched the families and young couples. Suddenly overwhelmed by homesickness, she could not hold back the tears, and she sobbed quietly into a tiny handkerchief.

'Wotcher! Mind if I join yer?'

A tall skinny girl with light brown hair that looked as if it had been attacked with a blunt pair of scissors, sat down on the bench next to Sarah. Sarah wiped her eyes, embarrassed that this stranger should have seen her crying.

'My name's Flo, what's yourn?'

'Er, Sarah.'

'Pleased to meet yer, gal. You don't look too 'appy. What yer doin' 'ere?'

The directness of the inquisition startled Sarah, having the effect of drying her tears. 'I've just started work here, in a boarding house. I come from near Barnsley. Where do you come from? You don't sound as if you come from round here.'

The girl thrust a bag of toffees under Sarah's nose.

'Go on, take one.' While Sarah chewed, she went on,

'Nah, I'm from good ol' London town, except there ain't much good about it when your dad's down the boozer every night and your Mum clears off with the lodger and there ain't two bleedin' pennies to rub together. I come here for work two years ago and I ain't looked back. There's always summink to do if you're prepared to roll your sleeves up.'

'Don't you miss your mam and dad?' Sarah ventured, fascinated by this girl who was so brash and confident.

Flo threw her head back and laughed, a loud roar of astonished amusement, which had passers-by turning their heads at the commotion.

'I don't care if I never set sight on either of 'em ever again. They can rot in 'ell for all I bleedin' care.' Her sharp, angled features softened. 'Sorry, mate, I didn't mean to shock yer. I can see you're new to all this, being away from your people and all that. How old are you?'

'I was fifteen in May.'

'No wonder you ain't too 'appy. I'm seventeen.'

'Have you got any friends in Blackpool, Flo?'

'Oh yeah, the people I live with are OK – a bit odd, but goodhearted enough.'

'Is that where you work?'

'Nah, I've got a room over a caff. I don't pay much 'cos the old lady who lives with her son 'as a bit of a job getting about, so I give a hand to dress her in the mornings. Then she sits in her wheelchair at the till raking in the cash while her son does the cooking. Right little goldmine it is with the visitors coming in all day for cups o' tea and fish and chips. When I get back from the hotel where I do the cleaning, I sort 'er out for the night.'

'How old's her son?'

'Thirtyish I reckon, not interested in girls as far as I can make out, so I'm safe.' She gave another of her screaming laughs. 'Mind you, 'is mum'd kill any girl who tried to get 'er 'ands on Fred.'

Flo linked arms with Sarah pulling her to her feet.

'Come on, let's go and 'ave a cuppa and I'll show you a bit more of Blackpool. We'll go down the Pleasure Beach and 'ave a go on the Big Dipper and the Virginia Reel.'

'I've got to be back by six to help with the evening meal,' Sarah half-protested, yet keen to get to know this cheerful girl better.

'Don't worry mate,' she reassured her with a wave of her hand. 'We'll be back in time.'

At first Sarah had difficulty in keeping up with Flo's long loping steps, finally gasping, 'Please, not so fast.'

'Sorry mate, I keep forgetting you're only a little titch.'

Sarah couldn't take offence at this gentle teasing. A friend was what she needed, and she couldn't help liking Flo.

Still suspecting that the Scatesburns were monitoring her letters from home, Sarah decided that it was time she took more control of her life. Her father had spent his working life having to suppress his pride. She was damned if she was going to do the same.

'Cheeky sods!' Flo had said, when they met the following Wednesday afternoon.

'You're right. I'm buggered if I'm going to be treated like a servant girl,' Sarah responded, picking up her friend's defiant attitude to life.

From then on, Sarah watched out for the postman, nipping into the hall to gather up the mail and extract any letters addressed to her.

'And what do you think you're up to handling private

letters? Our guests would be highly offended.'

Sarah straightened herself up on hearing the rebuke. Mrs Scatesburn's pursed lips and angry frown intended to intimidate the young girl did not have their usual effect.

'I'm not handling private letters. I just took the one addressed to me, Mrs Scatesburn,' Sarah answered with a studied casualness that came off better than she could have hoped for, her heart thumping at her temerity in defying her boss. She waved the envelope under the woman's nose just long enough to allow her a glimpse of 'Miss Sarah Mulvey'. Sensing that she had won a battle, Sarah went on, 'I didn't think you'd mind if I took what's mine.'

'No, why should I?' Her yellow skin was suffused with dark patches as she tried to conceal her anger.

Burning with curiosity, Sarah kept fingering the envelope wondering whose the writing was and longing to open it far away from curious eyes.

> Dear Sarah,
> I managed to get your address from Iris. She told me about your new job. Is it OK? I hope you don't mind me writing to see how you are getting on. I didn't get a chance to say goodbye to you and I keep on wondering about you. Why did you run away when I asked for your address? If you like I could come to see you one weekend if you get any time off. There's a bus from Barnsley. Write to me and let me know.
> Love Harry

The only person she could share the news with was

Flo. She could hardly wait for Wednesday afternoon to come.

'Harry wants to come and see me.'

'Is 'e your fella?'

'No, he's just someone I know from home.'

'Who are you kidding?' Flo grinned, nudging Sarah's arm. 'Go on, admit it, you're daft about 'im.'

'Well, I do like him, only he's older than me and I don't think my dad'd want me going out with him.'

'What's it got to do with your dad, you daft 'aporth? You're old enough to leave home and live with a lot of strangers so you're old enough to sit in the back row of the pictures and 'ave a little kiss and cuddle.'

There was something irresistible about Flo's logic, conjuring up images of Harry's lips on hers releasing the pent up feelings she had fought to suppress since starting her new job. The Scatesburns kept her so busy that sheer exhaustion prevented her from indulging in flights of fancy. Once in bed she fell into a drugged sleep that was just about long enough to prepare her for the hard work of the following day.

One night she half-woke up to hear the creaking of her door as if it were being opened. Too tired to fully rouse herself, she dismissed it as being in her imagination and immediately fell asleep again. The sound of someone breathing deeply, increasing to a crescendo of agonised rasping ending with a moan, woke her again. She felt her arm being flung back across her chest. As she struggled to sit up, whoever had been holding her hand had fled.

'It must have been a dream, Flo,' she told her friend when they next met. 'Who would want to come into my room?'

Flo pursed her lips. 'Listen to me, gal. That was no

dream. More likely some dirty old man trying it on.'

'Oh Flo! Who?'

'Take my advice mate and get a lock on your door before some dirty old bugger frightens the life out of you.'

Mrs Scatesburn glared at Sarah when she put the suggestion to her. 'Of course you don't need a bolt on your door, you silly girl. What if you took ill and we couldn't get to you?' Filled with self-righteous indignation, she had continued, 'Anybody would think we had riff-raff in this establishment. Really Sarah, I'm surprised at you.' She had gone back to the kitchen sniffing loudly, but Sarah had the feeling that evening that Arthur Scatesburn's hunched shoulders over the kitchen sink gave a hint that he and his wife had had an argument. No doubt Mrs Scatesburn had told him that as the man of the house it was up to him to make sure that the male guests were respectable.

Perhaps a chair placed under the doorknob would secure the door. At least, if someone tried to open the door, she would be woken up and ready to deal with any intruder. Several weeks went past with no repeat of the strange event.

'I'm beginning to think that it was just a dream,' she confided in Flo on their next afternoon off.

'More likely 'is wife told 'im exactly what she'd do if she caught 'im with 'is pants down. You've gotta learn to look out for yourself a bit more, Sarah.'

'You mean, it might have been him?'

'Why not, he's a bloke, after one thing just like they all are. Take my tip and keep your 'and on your 'apenny when 'is sort are about.'

Looking out for herself was a novel concept for Sarah, but after three months of hard work, mixing with people from all over Lancashire and Manchester, she was beginning to acquire a confidence more in keeping with that of a much older girl.

Although not consciously rude to her employer, which would have resulted in instant dismissal, Sarah shook off the appearance of a meek and mild servant girl. She was damned good at her job and if the Scatesburns did not want her, she could always find another boarding house to take her on.

More than once lately, the reflection in the mirror over her dressing on table showed a young woman with a perky outlook on life, shoulders set back proudly, face upturned to challenge whatever the day might bring.

A challenge presented itself in an unexpected form one Monday morning.

'Oh, my God!' Arthur Scatesburn greeted Sarah with a face filled with doom. 'Mrs Scatesburn's gone down with something, I don't know what. I've sent for the doctor for what good that'll do.' He rushed around the kitchen picking up pans then putting them down. 'I'm no cook. I might manage a bit of toast and peel a few potatoes, but it's the wife who's the boss in the kitchen.' With his head in his hands he sat down at the kitchen table.

From the redness of his nose and bloodshot veins in his yellowing eyeballs, Sarah surmised that he'd been seeking an answer to his problems in the whisky bottle. She rolled up her sleeves and tapped him on the shoulder.

'Come along now, Mr Scatesburn, just you go and lay the breakfast tables and leave the cooking to me. We've got ten in for breakfast including our regulars – I'll do them first. Oh and when you've done that, you'd better get someone in to do the bedrooms. I can't cook and clean as well.' Her turned-up nose wrinkled with delight at this opportunity to show her worth as something more than a dogsbody.

Her air of calm confidence had the effect of galvanising the man into action. A woman in charge – now that's what he was used to.

'You're sure you can manage?' This was merely a formality. All women could cook, but the only misgivings he felt concerned Hilda's reaction to the news that the maid had taken over her domain.

'I'll send a message round to Betty to come in.' She was the woman who came in once a week to do the 'rough'. 'You stay here and see how you get on.'

Singing away merrily, she snipped the rind off the rashers, cracked eggshells and popped toast under the grill. The miracle of keeping more than one ball in the air was child's play to Sarah, who had the knack of perfect timing when it came to cooking. Breakfasts were produced in rapid succession with Sarah having to call Arthur Scatesburn back out of the dining room only once when he spent too much time gossiping.

'Lovely breakfast, best yet,' was heard more than once as the guests waved farewell before tackling Blackpool's attractions.

'See, what did I tell you? I'll take over this for as long as Mrs Scatesburn is ill.' Her confidence faded briefly. 'That's if Mrs Scatesburn agrees of course.'

The first crisis over, Arthur puffed out his chest. Tapping his nose he added, 'I'm in charge while the missus is laid up. In case it's escaped your notice, it does say Mr as well as Mrs Scatesburn over the front door. Just you carry on here while I check up on her.'

'I think you might get a better reception if you went up with a tray of tea and toast, Mr Scatesburn. Oh, and before we go any further, do you want me to shop for tonight's tea? If so, I'll need some money.'

'Well, I don't know about that.' Panic at what Mrs Scatesburn would say to money being doled out to Sarah filled his eyes with water and Sarah stared in fascination at the huge dewdrop forming on the end of his nose.

'If I don't get going soon, all the best veg in the market will be gone.' She changed her tone to one of wheedling. 'I know just what to buy to make a tasty meal out of next to nothing. You can trust me.' Then in a sharper tone, 'It's either that or give the guests their money back to buy a meal out.'

The sour smell of fear caught her unawares. Whether it was fear at losing money or at not running the boarding house efficiently in the absence of his wife Sarah could only guess. She held out her hand.

'There you are now, and I'll expect some change and a list of what everything costs.' He glanced anxiously towards the stairs. 'I'd better just go and check with the wife.'

Mrs Scatesburn's high-pitched voice calling her husband a fool gave Sarah a fit of the giggles. Never mind, her ambition to be in charge of organising a menu and doing the cooking was enough to make her heart swell in pride and self-importance. She was going to make a success of her first venture into catering and be damned to Mrs Scatesburn.

'Best apple pie since me old mam died. I don't suppose

there's second helpings?'

The wistful request was relayed to the kitchen where Sarah was busy dishing up huge platefuls of casseroled lamb and vegetables for the latecomers.

'Is there enough, Sarah? Some of your helpings look a bit on the generous side already. If the missus finds we've overspent, I mean . . . well, we're in trouble.'

A broad smile dimpling the corners of her mouth lit up Sarah's pink cheeks.

'There's plenty, really there is, Mr Scatesburn, stop worrying. See, I did what me mam does. The cheapest scrag end's lovely if you cook it long and slow. Besides that me mam showed me how to render the fat down to make the pastry. I got the apples off the market just as the man was packing up to go, and I picked up some that had fallen off his barrow, so the pie cost next to nothing.'

Filled with relief that there was change from Sarah's shopping expedition and culinary efforts, Arthur beamed and chatted to the guests as he bore the steaming platefuls into the dining room. At least tonight there would be no beatings from Hilda's hairbrush when he reported how happy everyone was with the arrangements. The bruises from the last onslaught had only just begun to fade leaving yellow patches on his arms and shoulders.

Why Mrs Scatesburn did not share her husband's euphoria was a mystery to Sarah. Now partly recovered from whatever had struck her down, she was standing by the open kitchen door. Her illness had done nothing to improve her sallow, blotchy skin or her peevish expression.

'I shall be well enough to take over now. Don't think I'm finding fault with what you did, but the guests do expect a certain standard.'

Hesitating by the kitchen door, she pulled an envelope from her apron pocket. 'This came while you were out. I don't want to know who you are writing to, but I feel that as you are so young, I have a duty to your mother to keep an eye on you.'

It was on the tip of Sarah's tongue to ask, if that were the case, why could she not have a lock on her door to keep out intruders. Instead she galloped up the stairs to tear open Harry's letter.

> Dear Sarah,
> As I promised, or threatened, I'll be coming to see you for an afternoon on Sunday. You said you had the day off and if I get the bus from Barnsley I should be in Blackpool before dinner-time. Can you meet me at Talbot Road bus station at half-past eleven? Even if you don't notice me in all the crowds, I certainly won't miss your lovely red hair shining above the rest. You'll have to tell me where you want to go and what you want to do. The day is yours.
> Love Harry

Writing a reply to Harry took her hours. She was finally satisfied with her third attempt, which she decided did not give an impression of being either too formal or too forward.

When Sunday came there was no way that Sarah was to be put off seeing Harry whatever the sour face of Hilda Scatesburn conveyed and the mention of her recent illness and really needing an extra pair of hands.

'I've done some extra cooking while you were poorly, Mrs Scatesburn. There's pies and cakes in the tins as well as a big pan of soup on the stove, so I'll see you later.'

A quick brush through her unruly curls and Sarah was out of the door. If she took a tram she would be at the bus station in no time. Better to be early than miss Harry altogether.

Chapter 10

Harry's strong arms lifted her up in the air, swinging her round, much to the amusement of the passengers milling about either getting on or off the buses.

Sarah caught her breath feeling his hard muscles against her breast as he clutched her to his chest.

'Stop!' she managed to gasp.

'Aren't you pleased to see me?' Laughter turned the cerulean blue of his eyes into a myriad of sparkling silver.

'Oh, you know I am. I haven't seen anyone from home for three months and it seems like forever.'

His wide generous mouth turned down at the corners. 'Oh, I see, so anyone would have done, is that right?'

Sarah pulled herself away from him, aware and half-afraid that everything was moving too fast between them. 'I didn't mean that,' she replied quietly, 'but you know what I mean.'

They walked in silence away from the hordes of people pushing and shouting.

'I didn't tell anyone I was coming here today, Sarah.'

She did not have to ask why. Apart from the fact that she was only fifteen, her parents would not have been happy that she was seeing a man whose name had been linked with that of Dolly Redmile.

The White Rose Weeps

'Well, you couldn't, could you? And what about Dolly?' Spite and jealousy sharpened her tone.

He gripped her shoulders and turned her to face him. Anger and a bitter frustration narrowed his eyes, emphasising the indelible charcoal grey lines, the legacy of hewing coal and absorbing its dust for years on end. The master branding his slaves, was what her father called it.

'Sarah, I came to Blackpool because I couldn't live another day without seeing the red of your hair and the green of your eyes and the way your dimples come and go when you laugh and . . . oh, just you.' His mouth widened in a huge smile as he shook her. 'And stop laughing at me, Sarah Mulvey!'

'Oh, Harry, I'm not making fun of you, I'm just ever so happy.'

'Fair enough, so long as that's understood,' he told her with mock solemnity making her collapse in a fit of giggles.

Wedged close together on the tram that took them along the water's edge, Harry linked her arm through his.

'I'm going to wake up in a minute and find that this is all a dream.'

Sarah peered up at him through her long golden lashes.

'It is really, isn't it? I mean I'm still only fifteen and Dad won't want you to come here to see me again, will he?'

Harry stared straight ahead without answering. How could he lie to the man he worked alongside every day in the pit, the man he respected above all others?

Rides on the Big Dipper, tea in a café full of chattering children and their parents, walks along the

Promenade in the blazing sunshine of a golden Sunday afternoon — all were memories to be stored and brought out to be lovingly remembered in the weeks to come.

It was not until his bus disappeared, with Sarah waving frantically, that she realised that he had not kissed her goodbye. Just a gentle caress of her cheeks and, 'Goodbye my little Sarah.'

'So what did you expect, you soppy 'aporth?' Flo asked her later on at the café where they had arranged to meet. 'You did say he's a lot older 'n you and your dad would be wild if he found out.'

Sarah swirled the orange-brown liquid in the bottom of her cup, gazing into it as if it could give her the answers to her problems. 'Yes, but it's funny isn't it? When I came here I felt as if I was more like twelve than fifteen and now I feel at least seventeen.'

A red hand roughened by hours in soda water scrubbing and cleaning covered hers. 'Look cock, time'll pass and if your Harry is as soft on you as he sounds, he'll wait.'

Walking back to the boarding house, Sarah pondered on her friend's advice. It was all very well hoping that Harry would wait, but would he? Her body was now that of a young woman and she was beginning to feel longings stirring within her, passionate desires which sprang into life whenever an image of Harry's masculine frame came into her mind. How did Harry feel? Would Dolly manage to talk him into marriage? The earliest that Sarah would be home would be Christmas and anything could happen between August and December. Desperate at her situation, Sarah wished that she could run after Harry, beg him to take her away and hold her close to him forever. Wild silly impulses, she recognised, mentally railing against the fact that she was still not even sixteen years old.

From now on, her only breaks from the drudgery of the Rosewood Boarding House would be her afternoons out with Flo, unless Harry came to Blackpool again. She gulped hard trying to stem the tears threatening to fill her eyes. Hadn't Harry said that he didn't want to lie to her father? No, he would wait until she got time off at Christmas. No doubt, that horrible Dolly Redmile would be all over him between now and then.

'What if he marries her? What if she gets pregnant and he has to marry her?'

Sarah voiced her fears over and over again when she met Flo on her next Wednesday afternoon off. Flo listened patiently.

'From what you've said, he's not that daft, and in any case, that Dolly knows how to keep out of trouble.' A strong hand pressed Sarah's shoulder reassuring her that all she had to do was wait patiently. 'Think about it, you daft cow, 'e'd 'ardly come all this way to see you when 'e knows yer dad'd 'alf kill 'im if 'e found out!'

'Perhaps you're right,' Sarah agreed.

'Now, I want you to come round the caff and see where I 'ang out. You can meet Fred and his old girl and I'll show you my little room. Not much, but better'n what I 'ad in Bethnal Green.'

The café, uninspiringly named 'Fred's', had a prime position on the front with seats hard to come by in the high season. Cups of tea and fish and chips were dispensed in a steady flow from breakfast until late evening with Fred's Mum presiding over the counter whilst Fred did the fry-ups in the kitchen which opened off the main part of the café. This way he could keep a wary eye on customers who had come in for a cup of tea to escape from the rain and who were occupying seats too long.

'Right little goldmine they've got 'ere. Once the old girl pops 'er clogs, Fred'll be worth a bob or two, a right catch for someone.' She paused, eyeing Sarah speculatively. 'That's if 'e fancied girls.'

'Don't all men?' Sarah's worldy-wise air didn't fool Flo.

'Well, there are some fellas who fancy other fellas instead of girls.'

Sarah spun round, staring at Flo.

'S'right. Dunno exactly what they get up to but there you are.'

In a quiet mood, she entered Fred's Café to be greeted by a kindly-looking man probably in his early thirties. Sarah had never found pale sandy hair and eyes the colour of boiled gooseberries particularly attractive, but there was no mistaking his friendly attitude. Perhaps appearances weren't everything.

'You young ladies, sit yourselves down and I'll bring you a nice cup of tea and some of our best scones with strawberry jam.'

Flo nudged Sarah as Fred turned to go towards the tiny kitchen to fetch the promised tea.

'Blimey girl, I reckon I might've read 'im wrong. You've clicked with our Fred.'

Both girls giggled at the prospect of the older man fancying the fifteen-year-old Sarah.

'Shh, he's bringing the tea,' Sarah warned anxiously.

'Where's yer mum then?'

Fred set the tea and scones in front of the girls before sitting down with them and replying. 'She's not as young as she used to be, but she just won't give in. I've made her go and have a lie down before we get the next rush.'

'What you need is someone to help you, Mr Connolly,' Sarah ventured. Colour flooded into her cheeks as the realisation of what she might have been hinting filled her with embarrassment.

'Call me Fred, everyone else does.' He grinned. 'And if you're looking for a job, a pretty girl like you would bring in even more customers.' Still smiling, he rose. 'Enjoy your tea, girls.'

'You could do worse,' Flo advised, nodding sagely.

'Oh, no, don't be daft. I'm fine where I am. Mr and Mrs Scatesburn are all right and I've got a nice room and the food's OK.'

'Yes, but you don't want to stay there forever.' Flo's usually broad grin faded. 'I'd better come clean wiv you girl. See, I've met this fella, Sid 'e's called, and well, I think 'e's keen on me. I know it's looking ahead and I don't wanna count me chickens, but I don't reckon on staying on in the caff if Sid pops the question.'

Sarah squeaked in excitement, 'You mean you're getting married?'

'Shh, I never said that.' Flo's grin returned. 'I've gotta work on 'im yet.'

'Why haven't I met him?' Sarah was a little hurt that Flo had left it so long before telling her the good news when she had confided everything about Harry to her.

'Don't get it all wrong, you daft 'aporth. I've only been to the pictures with him twice. He works at the Tower Ballroom and don't get much time off.'

Placated by this explanation, Sarah's imagination began to be filled with a happy picture of herself and Harry enjoying a fun-filled day with Flo and Sid.

'Wouldn't it be lovely if we could all work in Blackpool together?'

'Not so fast,' Flo warned. 'It may be lousy work down the pit but at least your bloke's got work in the winter. Sid ain't sure what's gonna 'appen when the summer season's over. There ain't no dole for seasonal workers, you know.'

Sarah didn't know and stared gloomily into her tea cup, all happy surmisings floating away with the steam off her tea. It was no use hoping for life to fulfil her expectations. Better just to get on with it and pray that you could bear the disappointments.

'I'll just say thanks to Fred for the lovely tea and then I'd better get back to give a hand with the visitors' tea. I don't want to upset Mrs Scatesburn.'

Flo waved goodbye to a downcast Sarah, whilst she stayed on offering to help her landlord with the next influx of visitors.

Bloodshot eyes and breath wafting strong waves of whisky greeted Sarah on her return. Arthur Scatesburn was in his usual place at the sink endeavouring to peel potatoes. Sarah shrank back as the vegetable knife described a wide circle in front of her face.

'Poor old Arthur, stuck here like a kitchen maid while Hilda gives all the orders.' Unaware that his wife was just entering the kitchen, he lurched towards the terrified girl and pressed her against the kitchen table.

'Arthur! Get on with what you've been told and stop frightening the poor girl.' Hilda Scatesburn's face was purple with fury at her husband's drunken appearance. She stood behind him, one bony hand kneading her fingers into his shoulders until he cried out in pain.

'Mind my bruises, Hilda,' he begged. 'I'm black and blue already!'

Hilda slapped him gently on the back, at the same time

attempting a feeble grin. 'Just our little joke,' she explained. 'Now, you go and lay the tables while I cook the tea.' She nodded in the direction of the clock on the kitchen mantelpiece. 'Six already. No time to waste in silly games.'

Sarah was glad to escape from the weird exchanges between husband and wife, her instincts telling her that there were sick hidden depths in the relationship. Serving the meals to the visitors and making suitable replies to their observations on the day and the meal, left her no time to surmise further on what had gone on in the Scatesburn household while she had been out with Flo. Hilda's false gentility and Arthur's half-drunken attempts to act the convivial host made Sarah force down her meal untasted in order to escape from the charade.

'We'll call you down in half an hour or so to do the washing up,' she was told.

Once in the safety of her room, she was free to daydream about Harry and the precious hours they had spent together the previous Sunday. Flo's confidences concerning her latest swain had filled Sarah with apprehension. What if Flo and Sid did get married? That would leave her alone once again with no one to turn to. Perhaps if she suggested to Harry that there were jobs going in Blackpool, he might leave the pit – and Dolly Redmile – and come and work here. If only! Thoughts of Harry taking her out on her days off were interrupted by Mrs Scatesburn hammering on her door.

'What on earth is wrong with you, you stupid girl? Are you deaf or something? I've been shouting for you to come down for the last five minutes to get on with the washing-up. Come on, shape up,' she concluded, lapsing into the local vernacular.

Sarah felt Arthur's eyes boring into her back all the while she was standing at the sink working through the enormous piles of plates and saucepans. Anger and fear filled her as she felt his hot breath on the back of her neck. Right you've asked for it, she thought, turning round with a saucepan raised high above her head ready to floor him.

'Arthur!' His wife stood in the doorway. There was no doubt that she had read the scene correctly, a scene that had been played out many times with other kitchen maids. 'Come along, Arthur, I've got a nice cup of tea waiting for you upstairs. And Sarah, stop waving the pans around before you have an accident.'

The hotelier's fingers dug into Arthur's shoulders as she steered him out of the kitchen.

Relieved that Arthur was safely out of the way, Sarah soon demolished the mountain of washing-up and was able to go back to her room to write to her darling Harry. Curiosity led her to the Scatesburns' bedroom door where Arthur's plaintive cries of, 'Not the hairbrush, Hilda, please,' were punctuated by Hilda's, 'One more smack, you snivelling little worm!'

> Dear Harry,
> It was so lovely seeing you again. I hope
> you enjoyed being in Blackpool.

Sarah sucked her pen for a moment. Should she ask him how he felt about coming to work in Blackpool. Why not?

> It's really nice working here. Why don't
> you come and get a job here?

Perhaps that was going a bit far, but there was no harm in trying. She went on to tell him about Flo and her bloke, Sid, hoping that Harry would guess how lonely she would be if anything came of the romance.

A further suck of the pen and she launched into a description of the goings-on between the Scatesburns.

> I'm sure she hits him with her hairbrush from what I've heard and he does complain of sore shoulders. I've never heard of a woman hitting a man before.

There were so many things she wanted to say to Harry and here she was writing about uninteresting, silly folk like the Scatesburns. Better get to bed and finish it off the next night. She'd have to warn him not to say too much in his letters as she did not put it past her employer to steam open envelopes.

Exhausted after her afternoon off followed by the hours spent at the sink, Sarah soon floated off into a deep sleep, dreaming of Harry and herself owning a large hotel in Blackpool and spending every afternoon riding on the Big Wheel.

The click of the door handle was the sound of the door to their bedroom in their grand hotel being opened in her dreams.

'Come here Harry,' she murmured, stretching out her arm, and was not surprised to feel her hand held tightly. Drunk with sleep, she put up no resistance to the kiss at first. It was not until she was shocked into wakefulness by the foul odour of Arthur Scatesburn's breath that she began to kick and try to scream. His hand clasped over her mouth took away her breath preventing her from crying out. In spite of her frantic struggling and kicking, she was no match for the man. He finally released her as a spurt of liquid covered her hand.

Weeping and whimpering, Sarah managed, 'I'll tell—'

'Now, if you say one word about this, I'll tell Mrs Scatesburn that you asked me to come here to your room. And if she sacks you, you'll never get another job.' He bent over her and kissed her again before wiping her hand dry. 'Sorry about this, my dear. It's all Hilda's fault really. It's the hairbrush you know,' he snivelled as he crept out of the room.

Nauseated at the smell of his body, which pervaded the room long after he had gone, Sarah struggled to control her trembling. How would she have been able to fend him off if he had got into bed and made her do even worse things. Memories of Dolly and Frank Bass writhing on the floor filled her with shame at what she, too, had nearly been unwittingly forced to do. Swallowing hard in an attempt to force back the bile rising in her throat, she threw back the sheets and blankets, staggered over to the washstand and poured the cold water from the jug into the china bowl. In a trance, she scrubbed herself all over with soap and the icy water to cleanse herself thoroughly. How could such filth exist between men and women? As she stood cold and naked, the room lit by a flickering candle, Sarah forced herself to acknowledge what was in her secret heart. If Harry had come to her in the night and held her in his arms, she would have clung to him willingly, such was her love and desire.

When her alarm clock shrilled through the room, Sarah had slept for barely an hour. The tiny mirror over the washbasin reflected a white-faced young woman with black smudges under her eyes.

After dressing, Sarah sat on her bed and thought through the events of the previous night. I'm buggered if I'm going to let that miserable little worm get away with it, she told herself. I can't walk out right now, or else I'd end up on the streets with nowhere to go. A plan, which would require careful organisation, was beginning to form in her mind, but first of all, she had to face Arthur Scatesburn downstairs in the kitchen.

Clumping down the back stairs as loudly as she could to signify her defiance, she reached the kitchen door, turned the handle and strode in. A quick glance at the sink showed a flustered Hilda Scatesburn struggling to wash up teacups and keep an eye on the frying pan at the same time. The wispy hair looked as if it had been hastily clipped back and her face was devoid of even the faintest hint of her usual pink powder. The lace collar of her navy dress was grubby and wrinkled as if she had grabbed it out of a pile of unwashed clothing. Sarah looked at the woman's disarray and concluded that it was just as well that the guests would not be seeing their landlady.

'Come along girl and give a hand. You're five minutes late already.' Her voice pitched several tones higher than normal carried the beginnings of an hysterical screeching. 'Mr Scatesburn is confined to our room with a sprained ankle.'

Sarah pursed her lips in a vain attempt to hide a smirk at Mrs Scatesburn's pathetic attempt at lying. Had Arthur been caught coming down the stairs from her attic room and helped to the foot of the stairs by his wife? If the untidy appearance of her boss's hair was anything to go by, Mrs Scatesburn must have broken her hairbrush on the obnoxious Arthur's shoulders after she had helped him to their room.

'I'm sure Mrs Scatesburn knows what he gets up to,' Sarah told Flo.

Flo's indignant cries of, 'The filthy little bleeder!' caused more then one surprised summer visitor to turn round and stare at the two girls sitting on a bench on the promenade.

'I've made up my mind, Flo, I've got to get out of there as fast as I can. I've been thinking.'

'Yeah?'

'What about your Fred? Do you think he might give me a job in the caff? I can cook, clean, do anything.' Sarah kept quiet about what was really in her mind. She had seen the workings of a boarding house and now she wanted to get more practice in actually cooking meals for large numbers. After her one-off opportunity at cooking the meals when Mrs Scatesburn had been ill, Sarah had been kept firmly away from the cooking side of the establishment.

'You mean you wanna work in the caff?' Flo was puzzled at Sarah's suggestion, but a faint smile of pleasure broadened into a grin of delight as the full implication struck her.

'Yes, I wouldn't have asked otherwise, would I?'

'Cheeky cow!' Flo's grin changed into an expression of thoughtfulness. 'Good idea. You could squeeze up in my room. I ain't got much and I don't suppose you 'ave either. And you could give a hand with Fred's mum. Tell you what, I'll 'ave a word with Fred and see if I can twist 'is arm.'

Excitement at a new future opening up before her gave Sarah the energy to run all the way back to

Rosewood. Quieten down, she told herself, before the Scatesburns get wind of what you're planning.

'My, you've caught the sun and no mistake.'

Sarah lowered her eyes, half-afraid that her boss would be able to read her guilty secret. Better have everything cut and dried before handing in her notice.

'I've been running, didn't want to be late,' she muttered breathlessly, turning away to run up the back stairs to her room. 'I'll be down just as soon as I've got my pinny,' she promised.

The evening went by in a whirl with Sarah desperately hoping that Flo would have good news for her the following Sunday.

On changeover day on Saturday, Mrs Scatesburn announced that she and her husband had to go into the town centre on business and that Sarah could get on with changing the sheets and putting them in the copper to boil.

The floor of the steamy outhouse was covered with piles of soiled sheets and towels.

'Blast! What's her ladyship's pinny doing amongst this lot?' Sarah bent to pick it up, at the same time noticing an envelope sticking out of the pocket. Something familiar about the writing made her scrutinise it more carefully.

'Harry!' The envelope addressed to Miss Sarah Mulvey was barely stuck down.

Her anger turned to horror as she opened the letter and read what Harry had written on the underside of the flap, 'Mrs Scatesburn, you're a nosy old bugger.'

So Harry had written again. She didn't know whether to be pleased or angry that he had upset her boss, then reasoned that if Mrs Scatesburn hadn't steamed the letter open she would not have read the accusatory words. Just wait until I tell Flo tomorrow, she thought, giggling silently.

Flo greeted her with a huge hug, lifting her tiny friend off her feet. 'Come on. Fred wants to see you right now. The job's yours and you can bunk up with me.'

'Just a minute, Flo, I can't keep up with you.'

Half running behind her friend and gasping for breath, Sarah finally reached the café.

'Come and see Mrs Connolly,' Fred said, nodding in the direction of his mother who was sitting in her wheelchair carefully counting out change to a customer.

Although not yet sixty, the ravages of her paralysis, which had robbed her of her mobility some fifteen years previously, made her appear much older. Her once handsome features were deeply lined, her brown eyes faded and dull.

'So you're the little girl our Flo's told us about, are you?' She leaned forward, peering deep into Sarah's eyes. 'You look honest, but then appearances are often deceptive. How do I know that you won't murder us all in our beds and run off with money out of the till?'

'You don't,' Sarah told her, encouraged by the glimmer of a smile round the old lady's lips, 'but Flo's my best mate and I'd never let her down.'

'You'll do,' Mrs Connolly told her. 'Go on Flo, show her where she'll have to sleep.'

Flo led Sarah through the kitchen at the back of the café to a passageway with two doors. She pointed to a door on the left.

'That's the old lady's room and there's the parlour,' she said indicating the other brown painted door.

'What does Mrs Connolly do for a lavatory?'

Flo showed her the outhouse at the back of the café.

'Fred's built on a bathroom for his ma so as she can get the wheelchair in and out.'

Sarah's eyebrows raised in two perfect arcs. 'He must think a lot of her then.'

'Yeah, I reckon. But never mind them, come on up.'

There were two more bedrooms on the first floor, one of which was Fred's and the other Flo's. One single bed and a camp bed filled nearly half the room. A tiny wardrobe and dressing table took up the rest of the space. Pink curtains splashed with a decoration of perfect pink roses hung at the window overlooking the back yard.

'It's really very good of you . . .' Sarah began.

'Now don't start that. It'll be a lark 'avin you 'ere. Just mind you keep the place tidy, that's all. I can't stand a mess.'

There were so many things that Sarah had to sort out now that the job at the café had been settled. She would receive all meals, a better wage than that given by the Scatesburns and a share of the tips.

'You can make quite a few bob if they like you,' Fred told her. 'And I'm sure they will.' He winked at Flo as he said this.

Now was the time to hand in her notice to Hilda Scatesburn, something she rightly dreaded.

'You selfish girl,' Hilda Scatesburn ranted. 'After we took you in and taught you everything.' Lank brown-grey hair escaped from restraining hairgrips as she shook her head at Sarah. 'I've a good mind to write to your mother and warn her about the unsuitable company you've been keeping. No daughter of mine would be allowed out with men at all hours.'

How had anyone known that Harry had been to see

her? The letters, that was how.

'I haven't done anything wrong, Mrs Scatesburn and I'm grateful for being given a start here, but the time has come for me to better myself.'

'Better yourself!' she screeched. 'A fish and chip café better than my establishment? Arthur, did you hear that?'

Arthur had heard and his raddled face wore an expression of deep sadness. 'Well, if the girl wants to go, it's up to her. She's not the first and she won't be the last.' He sighed, turning back to resume his chores at the kitchen sink.

Sarah made for the stairs to her room, glad to escape further tirades.

'And whose fault is it that they leave?' Sarah heard, followed by a plaintive, 'No Hilda, please, you're hurting.'

A letter home to tell her parents the good news and give them her new address, then a quick note to Harry to let him know not to write to Rosewood again.

> . . . And no more cheeky remarks to Mrs
> Scatesburn, even if she is a nosy old
> bugger. I nearly didn't get your last letter,
> because she hid it in her pinny after what
> you called her.

That'll make Harry laugh, she thought, as she got on with packing her few belongings.

She had arranged with Flo to take most of her things to the café on the Wednesday afternoon, bringing the rest with her on the Saturday morning.

Unpacking her small case and hanging up her clothes in the half of the wardrobe allotted to her, she told her fears to Flo. 'It's Mr Scatesburn. He's still giving me funny looks and ... er ... touching me.'

'What?' Flo was scandalised. She flopped down on her bed, her eyes screwed up in a sudden serious expression. 'I don't like the sound of this, not one little bit.'

'You think he might ... do something before I leave?' Sarah's cheeks were stripped of colour in her terror. 'What should I do, Flo? You know they wouldn't let me put a bolt on my door.'

Flo leapt to her feet and burst into loud laughter.

'What's so funny about that horrible man?' Sarah was puzzled and upset at Flo's finding the situation at all funny.

'There'll be something very funny about him if he tries anything on again,' she screeched. 'Listen, if he's going to try anything, it'll be the last night, Friday. Right?'

Sarah nodded.

'So, do you think you can sneak me into your room on Friday night?'

'You mean you'll be there to help?'

'Oh yes, just you leave it with me, young Sarah.'

Sarah did not know whether to trust Flo in this mood.

'Never you mind why, just get me in quietly.'

The best time had to be as the guests arrived at the front door, returning to Rosewood for the last meal of their holiday week in Blackpool. Mrs Scatesburn would be busy preparing the evening meal, leaving Sarah to lay the tables and open the front door. Sarah would keep an eye open for returning guests, letting them in and then engaging them in conversation in the hallway. Meantime, Flo would nip up the front stairs to Sarah's room and wait there.

Fortunately, just before six o' clock, a group of six

happy holidaymakers, weighed down with buckets, spades, sticks of rock and dozens of souvenirs, all converged on Rosewood at the same time.

'Lovely day, we've had.'

'By, it's been a scorcher today,' one red-faced Mancunian announced.

'Here, let me give a hand,' Sarah offered, as his wife dropped several packets on the floor.

Flo was lurking in the porch, carefully weighing up the situation. A frantic nod from Sarah warned her that now was the moment to make a dash for it.

'What's the matter, luv?'

'Nothing, everything's fine,' Sarah told the woman. Flo's long legs, taking two stairs at a time had swiftly carried her out of sight. Sarah beamed happily, confident that if Arthur Scatesburn came into her room on her last night, he would have two tough young women to throw him out.

With the tables all laid and dinner ready to be served, Sarah spoke to Mrs Scatesburn.

'Could I have my wages now please?'

'You'll get them in the morning, and don't be so cheeky young woman.'

'I've done my week and I'd like them now,' Sarah persisted. 'That's if you want me to stay.'

A crumpled brown envelope was thrust into Sarah's hand with, 'If we did not have all these guests to wait on tonight, I'd let you go right now.' She began throwing piles of mashed potatoes onto plates. 'Here, start serving and be quick about it.'

Arthur Scatesburn followed her into the dining room, whispering in her ear, 'You won't go until tomorrow, please, Sarah.'

Safe in the knowledge that she now had Flo to protect her, Sarah dimpled and reassured him that she would not leave until after breakfast.

All the time she was serving and later eating her meal in the kitchen with the Scatesburns, Sarah could not help wondering how Flo was managing upstairs. The problem of getting some food up to her was her main worry. Her chance came when her boss told her to get on with the washing-up.

'As you know, Mr Scatesburn and I like to have a word with our guests and offer them a cup of tea in the parlour on their last evening. Make sure everything is put away before we return.'

Grabbing a plate, Sarah piled up vegetables and a lamb chop, then dashed up the stairs.

'Thank God for that. I've been dying of starvation up here. It's been hours. Besides that, it was a good job you'd got a jerry up here otherwise I'd 'ave wet meself.'

Sarah clamped a fist over Flo's mouth before she let out one of her ear-splitting laughs.

'Look, here's a book for you to read. It'll be at least another hour before I get done in the kitchen, so be quiet!'

The hands of the clock on the kitchen wall barely seemed to move as Sarah struggled through the mounds of greasy dishes.

'Set the tables for breakfast and then you can wait and wash up the cups and saucers. Quite a few of our guests have accepted our offer of tea.'

No point in complaining. She'd be out of it by tomorrow, she thought, as she set about placing the cutlery on the tables for breakfast.

'A little birdie tells me you're leaving,' the elderly

Mancunian's wife whispered. 'Here, don't tell that landlady anything.' Finger on lips, she pushed two shillings into Sarah's palm.

Within minutes, this scene was repeated until Sarah had more money in her pocket than she had earned in weeks. More for my post office savings, she thought. One day I'll have enough to buy somewhere better than this.

'You can take your cocoa up to your room. Mr Scatesburn and I wish to converse in the kitchen after we've said goodnight to our guests.'

Sarah wasn't sure whether she ought to give a little curtsey after this pompous announcement, but nodded her head meekly, only poking out her tongue at the woman's retreating back.

'As you wish, Mrs Scatesburn.' At least this would give her the chance to make a cup of cocoa for Flo as well, but she'd have to be quick. A last minute dive into the biscuits and she was on her way back up to her room.

It was a bit like having a midnight feast with the two girls trying to muffle their giggles as they dipped their illicit biscuits into the scalding cocoa.

Organising the sleeping arrangements was Flo's prerogative.

'Now, listen to me and do exactly as I say.'

Flo's deadly serious expression frightened Sarah.

'Why, what do you think is going to happen?'

'Perhaps nothing. Remember, I'm here just in case. Now, if mucky Arthur comes in, lie still. We'll both be dressed and you've got the last of your stuff in that bag. Bung it under the bed with me. Promise not to make a sound whatever 'e does until I give the signal, or else you'll spoil everything. He won't get far with me 'ere as well. Wait 'til I shout "Run!" and then we'll both scarper down the back stairs and out the back door. Got it?'

Lying in the dark with Flo under the bed, Sarah felt so safe she was even beginning to doze off when she heard the telltale squeak of the door handle. Flo reached up to give her a reassuring squeeze of the hand. The rasping breathing she had heard on previous occasions got louder as the man approached Sarah's bed. Pretending to be asleep was almost more than she could manage with her heart beating so fast she could scarcely breathe.

'Don't be afraid, Sarah. You've been so good to me,' he whispered.

She could smell whisky on his breath as he bent over her and began to stroke her face.

'I'm going to show you what a big man I am tonight.'

The first noise she heard was that of a metal buckle being unfastened, followed by a rustling of clothes as he unbuttoned his trousers. Sarah could sense that he had dropped them to the floor and waited desperately for Flo to give the command. My God! Now he's taking off his drawers!

'Open your eyes, Sarah and see what I've got for you.'

Still pretending to be asleep, Sarah peeped through long lashes to see him standing naked, his penis erect. What was Flo waiting for?

A howl of agony as a sheet of flame shot up from under the bed was swiftly succeeded by Flo's shout to Sarah to get out of bed and run for it.

Sarah threw back the bedclothes to see Arthur clutching his genitals and trying to put out the flames licking his shirttails.

'Never mind him!' Flo hissed, dragging Sarah to the door, down the stairs, out of the back door and out over the garden wall. Once clear, they paused to see lights going on in all the rooms, every guest being woken by the screams of pain emanating from the attic room.

'I've got the filthy bugger's trousers here,' Sarah said, slinging them over the neighbouring garden wall.

Flo was lost in admiration. 'You crafty monkey. How's 'e goin' to explain this to 'is old woman.' She grabbed Sarah's arm. 'Blimey, a cop, watch out.'

A policeman on a bicycle was on patrol round the corner from the boarding house.

Before Flo could stop her, Sarah ran up to him, nearly pulling him off his bike. 'Quick, Officer, there's a terrible fight at Rosewood Boarding House. Someone's going to get killed if you don't get there soon. My friend and I were just passing when we heard it.'

The policeman listened solemnly to Sarah's tale. The poor mite seemed terrified.

'You'll need help, it's really terrible. Please don't go on your own.'

'Just you get along home and leave this to me,' he advised. A long loud blast on his whistle summoned three more policemen who ran, truncheons drawn, to investigate the disturbance at Rosewood.

The girls did not wait to see the outcome of the police visit, running until they were gasping for breath outside Fred's Café.

'It's OK, Fred's given me a key,' Flo managed to get out between huge gulps of air.

Sitting on their beds they went over the events of the evening, Flo showed Sarah the workings of the lighter which had caused such damage to Arthur Scatesburn's manhood.

'Sid found it in the Tower Ballroom. Some posh geezer must have dropped it. See, you can make the flame come up as big as you like.' Flo demonstrated the wonders of the new toy several times, reducing Sarah to hysterics as they recalled the would-be rapist's screeches of agony.

'The guests had a nice show to end their holiday. I bet they'll be talking about it for months to come.' Sarah frowned, a moment of panic seizing her. 'There's only one thing. I mean, what if the police come after us for burning his wotsit?'

'I don't think there's such a crime as cock blistering,' Flo told her, still laughing at the memory of what she had done. 'Can you really see his missus telling the police what happened?'

'No, but I can just picture him in court.' Sarah stood up, her head drooping in imitation of Arthur Scatesburn. 'Your Honour, there I was standing in the young lady's bedroom and all of a sudden, a flame came from underneath the bed, nearly burned my balls off. I've never felt pain like it. Right little minx she is.'

Flo's screech filled the tiny bedroom.

Sarah sat down on the bed again. 'I bet he'll get a going over with the hairbrush as well, and serves him right.'

That night, Sarah slept better than she had done for months. Tomorrow would be the start of a new life learning the workings of a popular café. With Flo as her friend, nothing could go wrong.

Chapter 11

Sitting on the bus as it left Talbot Road bus station, Sarah clutched her new imitation crocodile handbag tightly. The previous day she had been to the post office to draw out some of her savings to take home for Christmas. Although she had bought some Christmas presents in Blackpool, mainly plates and cruet sets decorated with a picture of the Tower for her mother and Iris, her plan was to take her mother to Barnsley and buy her something really extravagant.

Working for Fred had been a time of high earnings and savings for Sarah with generous tips from the customers and very little in the way of outgoings. Even after withdrawing some of her savings, she now had over fifty pounds tucked away. Her hotel money, she called it — her big secret.

Sharing a room with Flo had not turned out as well as they had expected after the excitement of exacting revenge on Arthur Scatesburn. For one thing, Flo's hours at the hotel were variable, with her free evenings being taken up with her beloved Sid. More than once Sarah had been woken up by a cheerful Flo eager to tell Sarah how the romance was progressing.

It was Fred who came up with the solution.

'There's a lumber room, well more of an attic really,

but it's full of all sorts, mostly rubbish. If you want to have a go at clearing it out, you could have that as your room. I expect you girls have been a bit squashed up in the one room. I won't charge any rent, seeing as both of you have been a great help with Ma, so it's yours if you want it.'

Flo had been full of remorse for her unthinking behaviour and had set to with a will to turn out the rubbish, scrub the lino and help hang new curtains at the tiny window.

It was true what Fred had said. Sarah had fallen into the habit of getting old Mrs Connolly undressed and into bed whenever Flo was working late at the hotel.

'You're a right little wonder, you are. I just wish my Fred could find a lass half as lovely as you and settle down.'

Sarah never knew what to reply to such confidences. If Fred had wanted to marry, girls weren't that hard to find, surely, and Fred would make quite a catch with his thriving business. It was doing even better now. He had not taken much encouraging to allow her to make apple pies to follow the fish and chips the customers consumed in huge quantities.

'As for these scones you buy in,' she had told him, 'they taste like sawdust and cost three times what I could make them for. And don't you think it's time we offered them something else besides fish and chips.'

She had been surprised when he had allowed her to buy the ingredients for her meat pies and try out her recipes on the customers. Before long, Fred was laughing and pretending to complain that the café wasn't big enough. His expression of amazement at her suggestion that he buy up the rundown knick-knack shop next door and expand was accompanied by a half-serious 'I'd need a partner to do that.'

Alarmed at the implication of what he might be thinking, Sarah had shrugged her shoulders and told him not to take any notice of her daft ideas.

She did not turn down his offer of higher wages when her deft hand in the kitchen resulted in higher profits. At fifteen, she was earning as much as her father.

Sarah looked out of the bus window watching the rolling sweep of the moors, cold and dark in the early December morning, and wishing that she were already home.

She smiled as she pictured Flo's expression on opening her present on Christmas morning. Would Flo realise that the pair of matching pillowcases, the first item for Flo's bottom drawer was intended to give Sid a bit of a nudge in the direction of the altar?

Sarah's biggest problem was going to be whether she ought to get something for Harry. He had written to the café several times, chatty, non-committal letters, in which he told her which films he had seen in Barnsley, how many times he'd seen Barnsley football team play, about a day out at Doncaster races with his mates, but nothing more intimate. Cold, icy fingers seized hold of her heart whenever Sarah studied his letters closely. Was he patronising her? The news he passed on was not what she wanted to read. Who was he spending his evenings with? Did he wish that he could be in Blackpool with her? No mention of Dolly Redmile, but that was hardly likely, not after what Sarah had seen her doing with that horrible creepy Frank Bass.

Perhaps she might just send him a Christmas card on the quiet, or else her parents might wonder what was going on in her mind.

The White Rose Weeps

She woke with a jolt, as several stops and some hours later, the bus pulled into Barnsley bus station. Some crumbs from a hastily eaten sandwich prepared by Fred's mother for the journey threatened to mar her immaculate appearance. She stood up, smoothed down her smart new green coat, ran a quick comb through her tangled curls and pulled on her gloves.

'Let me give you a hand, luv,' the conductor offered, recognising that the young girl's worldly-wise appearance was only a facade.

He handed down her small suitcase and the two parcels containing the breakable ornaments.

My, but she was pretty!

'Going home for Christmas?'

'Oh, yes,' she breathed, hardly able to speak for the tears choking her suddenly. 'Home, I'm so happy.'

A sharp wind nearly took her by surprise, making her thankful that she had spent money on a good warm coat. She and Flo had spent hours in the big shops trying on first one then another. Sid had been with them and it was his advice that had made her choose the green one, which so very nearly matched her eyes.

Leaving Flo and Sid alone at Christmas had worried her until Sid had announced that they were to spend it with an uncle and aunt who had brought him up after his parents had died in the big influenza epidemic during the Great War. Flo had winked at Sarah and whispered, 'Do you think I'm being inspected to see if I'm suitable?'

At first Sarah could not see the number of the bus that went to Colethorpe. Please let there be one soon, she begged, tired out after her early morning start and the long bus journey. If only Harry were here, but no deity answered her prayers, leaving her to travel the last few miles alone until the bus deposited her outside her home.

The welcome was enough to break her heart with her mother and father vying to give her a big hug.

'Oh, and just look at our Maureen.' Sarah ran to pick her up out of her pram, which now occupied one corner of the kitchen.

'Oh, Mam, she's beautiful.'

'Aye, and she's ever so good, hardly makes a muff all night now, so your dad can get some sleep before he's off down the pit.'

Sarah rocked the baby back and forward in her arms, trying to fathom the colour of her eyes.

'You can't tell at this age, but she's so like you, I reckon I'm going to think I've had twins fourteen years apart.'

Amidst the laughter, Sarah asked if Lizzie would be home for Christmas.

'No, she's on duty.' Joanna's mouth turned down at the corners. 'She's hoping to get away for New Year, but I expect you'll have to leave before then. It would have been so nice to see you together again.'

'But I will see her. Oh Mam, that's wonderful!' Still cradling the baby, Sarah danced around the room. In response to her father's query about her job, Sarah told him that Fred always took his mother to a hotel in Harrogate for Christmas and the New Year.

'He must have some brass then.'

'Well, his parents had the café first, then after his father died, he carried on running it with his mother. They don't go anywhere all the year round. Fred would never leave his mam on her own — she's a cripple, in a wheelchair.'

'He's not married then?'

Sarah did not notice the exchange of glances between

her parents when she replied to her father's question that her friend Flo said that she didn't think he liked girls.

'But he's ever so kind to me and Flo, so I think she's got it all wrong.'

The few days left before Christmas Day went by in a blur with the frantic preparations.

'Bernard and Iris are going to her mam's for Christmas but they're coming here for Boxing Day, so we'll cook a chicken for them and we'll have the beef.' Joanna paused, smiling at her husband. 'Your bit of money has made all the difference in the world, luv, you've no idea.'

Her mother refused the offer to go with Sarah to Barnsley, pleading that she could not take Maureen out on the bus.

'She's getting to be such a handful now.'

'In that case, Mam, you'll have to put up with whatever I choose.'

It seemed strange at first in her old room. The old familiar wallpaper was peeling off in one corner and the pattern on the lino was almost worn right away. The runner for the dressing table, which she had embroidered with such care, had been freshly washed and starched, but the whole room bore witness to the poverty of her childhood.

Lizzie was right. You had to get away to see how the rest of the world lived, or else you'd begin to think that there never could be anything better. Anger rose within her breast at the thought that her poor mother would never know how convenient it was for a woman to have a proper bathroom with a lavatory and hot running water in the taps.

She swore there and then that if it took her ten years, she was going to make sure her mother had some of the comforts of life before it was too late.

What she saw on glancing out of the window made her gasp, and sick at heart, cling to the brass bedstead for support.

She could not mistake the proud confident stride, the thick thatch of hair the colour of corn in July, but her delight at seeing Harry Wilby was swiftly turned to despair when she immediately realised who was chatting to him with such familiarity and animation.

What else could she expect? Dolly Redmile, with her inviting smile and aura of experience, lived only a few doors away from Harry and could see him every day, while she was now living miles away on the other side of the country. How could her child-like letters compete with that? Sarah was mature enough to rationalise that there was no contest; Dolly had all the advantages.

Putting away her new skirts and jumpers in the newly polished oak wardrobe and chest of drawers, Sarah did not hear her mother's voice the first time.

'Really, Sarah, how many more times do I have to call you. Are you deaf or what?'

'Coming.' It took a great effort to sound enthusiastic after seeing Dolly Redmile talking to Harry. Why was it that her dearest dreams always seemed to flare brightly for a brief moment then die away leaving a tiny, sad heap of ashes.

'Can I do anything, Mam before . . .' The words faded to a whisper.

'Well if it isn't Sarah.' Harry strode across the room to give Sarah a brotherly hug. 'You're looking well, I must say.'

Emotions tumbled over her one after the other like waves beating on the rocks, depriving her of the power of speech.

'Oh, that's our Maureen crying. Make Harry a cup of tea, luv, while I change her nappy.'

Left on their own, Sarah was able to calm the wild beating of her heart, making the most of the ritual of filling the kettle and getting out all the tea-making paraphernalia.

'Never mind that, Sarah. Just let me look at you.' He scrutinised her slowly from head to toe, his blue eyes as deep as the ocean on a summer's day. 'You get prettier every time I see you.'

For one mad moment, Sarah prayed that he would take hold of her and kiss her on the lips. So strong was this longing that she took a step towards him ready to part her lips and be gathered up in his arms.

'Whatever's up with you, Sarah? Come on with that tea will you? Harry will think we've got no manners in this house. Mind you, how you can see what you're doing in the dark, I don't know. Don't tell me you've forgotten how to put the light on. Here, sit yourself down Harry.'

'No, really, Mrs Mulvey, I just called by to see if Jim was about. I expect he's already over at the club.' He winked at Sarah, then, as her mam's back was turned, placed a finger on his lips and blew her a kiss. Then he was gone.

'That was nice of him to call by for your dad. He often calls in since he was best man to our Bernard. Probably made him think he's one of the family.'

Christmas Day and Boxing Day went by in a blur. Joanna was delighted with the plain black skirt that Sarah had bought for her. 'Wherever did you get all that money from?' she gasped, recognising that the material was a good worsted and not a cheap wool and rayon mixture.

Sarah's unfeigned delight at seeing Iris again thrilled the young wife, whose plain looks had taken on a bloom with approaching motherhood. The two had embraced affectionately.

'You don't write half often enough,' Iris admonished her.

'Not surprising,' Jim told her. 'Didn't she tell you she's too busy earning plenty of brass?'

'Dad, don't exaggerate!'

It was partly true, Sarah had to admit to herself. She was obsessed with the idea of making money and, no matter how hard she had to work, was determined that one day she would be her own boss.

For the first time, Lizzie's arrival on New Year's Eve did not overshadow Sarah's presence. No longer the little girl expected to jump up and wait on her older sister while she held court, Sarah's newfound confidence had Lizzie surveying her speculatively. Curious to know what had made her so much in charge of herself, Lizzie came into Sarah's room early on New Year's morning with a cup of tea and a questioning look in her eye.

Sitting on the edge of the bed, Lizzie demanded to know every detail of Sarah's life in Blackpool. She nodded approvingly when told of Flo's devotion as a friend. The story of Arthur Scatesburn's blistered genitals had Lizzie helpless with laughter. When the laughter had died down, Sarah leapt out of bed.

'Can you keep a secret?'

'Depends.' Lizzie slanted a quizzical look at her young sister.

'Promise.' Lizzie's nod was enough for Sarah to continue. 'Harry Wilby came to Blackpool and took me out for the day.'

'What?' Lizzie's voice nearly hit high C.

'Shh, you promised!'

'But Sarah, he's far too old and besides—'

'Besides what?'

'I don't want you getting into trouble.'

Sarah's cheeks flushed bright scarlet as she denied that Harry would ever do anything like that to her.

'Ah, you say that now, but what happens if you're alone with him and it all starts with an innocent little kiss, then what? How far will it go?'

Sarah's anger at her sister's implication that Harry would ever take advantage of her made her bang her cup down hard on her saucer.

'You see little sister,' Lizzie explained, carefully choosing her words, 'it isn't just the men who take advantage, it's the girls who want it just as badly as the men.' It was with a shock that Lizzie realised from the defensive look in Sarah's eyes that her words had hit home.

As Lizzie left for London the following morning, she hugged Sarah closely, making her promise to be careful.

'I know what you mean,' Sarah said, solemnly acknowledging Lizzie's concern as having substance.

She stood watching the departing bus until it turned the corner at the bottom of the hill by what they used to call the Proddy Dogs' church. Much as she loved being at home with her mam, dad and Maureen, there was little to do other than help in the house and mind the baby. Since moving to Blackpool, she had become used to a life full of bustle, meeting new people every day in the café, exchanging bright remarks amidst laughter.

'Mind if I pop round to see Iris and Bernard?' she asked her mother the day after Lizzie had gone.

Joanna had sensed a restlessness in her daughter ever since the first day she had arrived home for Christmas. Gone was the quiet self-effacing Sarah, but the new Sarah, confident as she was, seemed to be still finding her way, searching for something.

'No, go on. Do you good to get out.' Joanna busied herself with plugging the squawking infant's mouth. Smiling down at her baby, she hardly noticed Sarah's departure.

Iris was only too delighted to have her bridesmaid call on her, busying herself with getting out her best cups and saucers.

'Put the kettle on for your sister,' Iris ordered, so occupied with loading the tray that she did not see Sarah's look of astonishment on seeing her brother actually doing something to help in the house.

Bernard spent the evening lost in the Green 'Un, not that he would have dared put any bets on the horses, but at least he could see who would be turning out for Barnsley's First Team.

Iris was full of her pregnancy and asking Sarah for the hundredth time to ask for time off to be godmother at the christening.

It was with a shock that Sarah realised that it was nearly ten o'clock.

'What's the worry, Sarah, after all no one can check how late you stay out in Blackpool. Anyway, Bernard can walk you home.'

Bernard was almost asleep on the sofa and grunted agreement to his wife's request.

'Don't be daft, Iris, I have to get myself home often enough in Blackpool, and in any case, Bernard's got to be up for work in the morning.' She gave her brother a gentle pat on the arm. 'Thanks all the same, I expect I'll see you again before I go back.'

Outside the moon was hidden by a thick covering of dark cloud. There were no lights in any one of the row of terraced houses with all the occupants in bed, sleeping in order to gather strength for the next agonising day's struggle down the pit. Sarah paused briefly to get her bearings, standing still to absorb the peacefulness of the moment.

'Sarah! I've got bloody frozen hanging about here for the last three hours waiting for you to come out. You women certainly know how to talk.' Harry crossed his arms and thumped his shoulders in an exaggerated pantomime of seeking to get his circulation going.

Sarah gasped in astonishment. 'Harry! What are you doing here?'

'Waiting to walk you home, what do you think?'

He linked her arm firmly through his, pulling her so close to his side that she could hardly breathe.

'Please Harry, I can't keep up with your long steps,' she pleaded, her face turned up to his.

Before she could protest, his lips were on hers, firm yet tender. Just as swiftly, he pulled away.

'I didn't intend that to happen,' he said quietly. 'I came to take care of you, because that is what I want to spend my life doing, just looking after you.'

They walked on in silence, neither daring to speak in case a word might break the fragility of the moment's magic.

It was Sarah who finally whispered, 'We're nearly home, Harry.'

'Right, I'll watch you into your back gate,' he told her in such a matter-of-fact tone that Sarah thought she must have imagined his kiss. 'Oh, and don't forget to keep writing, will you?'

She ran the last few yards, turning to wave just as she reached her gate. Harry's tall, broad figure was silhouetted briefly as the moon made an appearance from behind the clouds.

Her parents were seated at the kitchen table eager to hear the latest news of Iris and Bernard, and were pleased at Sarah's lively description of what had, after all, been simply a pleasant visit to the family.

'Our Bernard's certainly taken to the life of a married man. Why, he even makes the tea and washes up.' She could not resist exchanging a conspiratorial grin with her mother when both caught sight of Jim's disapproving frown. A man should be a man in his house and not do women's work was his philosophy.

'I bumped into Harry Wilby on the way home,' Sarah called out from the hallway, as she hung up her coat. At this safe distance from her parents' eagle gaze, she could affect a nonchalance that she was far from feeling. 'He walked a little way with me.'

'Oh aye,' was the only comment from both her father and mother.

Sarah took advantage of the fact that no further questions were forthcoming to escape to her bedroom, where she lay for hours drifting in and out of sleep dreaming of Harry's promise to spend his life taking care of her.

Saying goodbye to baby Maureen and her parents was even harder after such a long spell at home, but once back in the café, Sarah was soon back into the routine of getting up early, helping Flo with old Mrs Connolly first thing in the morning and starting work in the kitchen.

Flo had been full of the Christmas she had spent with Sid's aunt and uncle. 'They was really nice to me and when I showed 'em the pillowcases you gave me, you should have seen the way they teased Sid.'

'What did Sid say?'

Flo could hardly restrain herself from shouting out loud. 'We've started saving for the wedding!'

Hugging one another and dancing around Flo's room, the two girls finally collapsed on the bed.

'And your bloke, this 'Arry, what about 'im?'

Her eyes shining, Sarah described her last meeting with Harry. 'I'll be sixteen in May, so perhaps Dad'll let him take me out properly when I go home again.'

If Flo thought that no man would wait years and years for a girl to grow up and be old enough to marry, she did not voice her opinion. Much as she did not want Sarah to pin her hopes on a man who was more than likely to marry a girl nearer his own age, she knew that in her present euphoric mood, Sarah would not listen to her.

The grey January mornings were alike in that few visitors to the town ventured as far as the promenade to pit their strength against the vigorous north-easterly winds which whipped up the cold, grey-green sea.

'We mustn't overdo the cooking,' Fred warned her. 'We don't get much in the way of passing trade in January and February. It starts to liven up a bit at Easter, then after that we're rushed off our feet.'

Sarah was sitting at a table in the window of the café looking out at the empty promenade and beyond to where the sea burst on the shore creating ever-changing lacy patterns with each wave.

'How can we get people to come here in the winter?'

Fred ran his hands through his sandy hair, shaking his

head at the impossible idea. This young friend of Flo's was certainly a funny lass with odd ideas.

'Have you ever thought of offering cheap meals, say on a Monday, you know, advertise in the paper? I bet lots of people like sales reps would jump at the chance to get something better than they get in those miserable little boarding houses. Besides, I'm not pulling my weight, Fred.'

'Don't be daft, lass, it's worth a hundred pounds a week to have such a pretty lass as you around. Mam thinks the world of you, says you're really gentle with her.'

Sarah blushed at this unusually long speech from Fred. His devotion to his mother was such that he would have paid Sarah double to have her keep the old lady happy.

'I'm serious about what I said, you know.' Sarah jumped to her feet. 'Tell you what, you advertise cheap fish and chips and if no one comes and you lose money, you can stop it out of my wages.'

Mrs Connolly, who had just manoeuvred her wheelchair into her usual position behind the cash desk, heard Sarah's offer and roared out laughing. 'Well, son, that's a fair offer, but I hope it works for Sarah's sake or else she'll be well out of pocket.'

'I won't,' Sarah told her, 'in fact, it'll be so popular, I'll be expecting a share of the profits.'

'You cheeky monkey,' was the reply.

It was midnight before Sarah heard Flo's footsteps on the stairs. She rushed down from her attic room to tell Flo about the offer she had made to the Connollys.

'Honestly, Sarah, I thought I was barmy, but you take the biscuit. Ain't you satisfied with 'aving a comfy little job like this with your money coming in regular?'

There was no way that Sarah could get Flo to

understand what she wanted out of life. 'But I want to be the boss, Flo, can't you see?'

Flo shook her head. 'My, you're a rum 'un, but you're still the best mate I've ever 'ad.' She gave Sarah a friendly poke on the shoulder. 'Tell you what, can I come and work for you when you're the boss?'

'Hmm,' Sarah preened, pretending to consider the question. 'I don't know about that. I'm very choosy about my staff. I'll let you know.'

The two pressed their fingers to their lips on hearing Fred's, 'Don't you girls ever shut up?'

Nothing more was said about advertising cheap dinners and Sarah felt too embarrassed to ask Fred if he had made up his mind one way or the other. Perhaps she had been too free with her advice and overstepped the boundary between employee and employer. Living under the same roof tended to breed the kind of familiarity that would not have been tolerated in other jobs. Lizzie would hardly have dared tell the matron how to run her hospital. If Lizzie were to be believed, nurses were trained to obey orders without question.

It was towards the end of January on a bitterly cold Monday morning that Fred seemed more preoccupied than usual. His pleasant freckled features had taken on a worried frown, causing Sarah to speculate on the reasons for his mother's raised voice earlier on that day.

The puzzle resolved itself when she saw several sacks of potatoes and half a dozen boxes of cod piled up in the kitchen, enough to last them throughout January and February with business the way it was.

'Well, Sarah, get cracking on the chips while I see to the batter for them cod.'

Quick colour came into her face as she realised what

Fred Connolly had done, gambling her month's wages on cod and potatoes.

'You're expecting a lot of customers?' she whispered.

'No, you are, Sarah. It's your idea remember?' His eyes were cold and hostile. His look told her that if the food were wasted, she need expect no pity and would be the one to pay for the losses.

The two worked together in silence, Sarah rightly deducing that much of his hostility was a direct result of his mother's opposition to the scheme.

'Fancy letting a bit of a kid talk you into such a daft idea,' Sarah had heard Mrs Connolly berating her son.

As midday approached, Sarah raised her head. The café was still empty with not a soul to be seen out defying the cold wind . Fred had begun to fry a third of the potatoes she had chipped and was tossing the portions of cod into the fat, now sizzling and giving off a blue haze.

'I'll lay a few tables, just in case,' she said feebly.

Fred made no reply, nor did his mother. Sarah could feel both of them watching her back as she bent over the tables, putting out salt, pepper and vinegar.

Their lack of faith in her abilities began to stir feelings of resentment. Damn it all, she told herself, I'm the one that's going to be the loser. I'll have to draw some money out of the post office if I have to pay back the Connollys for this lot.

It was with relief that she heard the welcome sound of the door being pushed open with loud voices cursing the cold wind, at the same time making appreciative sounds as the aroma of fresh fish and chips activated their salivary glands.

Some half a dozen men, all in their late thirties or early forties greeted Fred.

'Well, let's see what you're giving away then,' they called out to Fred.

Although the summer season was several months away, there were still many men out at work all day in Blackpool, on the buses, trains, public utilities and those engaged in servicing the rides to ensure their safety for the paying passengers. A cheap, hot meal in the middle of the day was proving to be more of an attraction than even Sarah had envisaged in her most optimistic moments.

Slowly Fred allowed his manner to thaw as the huge quantities of chips swiftly disappeared under the gargantuan appetites of the men appreciating the 'threepence off' offer.

'Everywhere else is closed down apart from the posh places and we're not paying their prices,' was the oft-repeated comment as Sarah went round collecting the plates and handing out cups of tea.

'And they haven't got such pretty waitresses,' one of the younger travelling salesmen called out to Fred.

Clearing up after the last of them had gone, Sarah avoided the speculative gaze of old Mrs Connolly. Something in her gaze told Sarah that, although she was pleased at the money rolling in, she had not relished being made to appear wrong in her business judgement. Or was it more? Fred was so much under his mother's influence, was it that Mrs Connolly feared he might slip from her grasp? Stirrings of half-knowledge in the depths of her mind told Sarah that this was not a normal mother and son relationship.

Not for the first time, Sarah felt that she had made a mistake in antagonising the older woman. It did not take the wisdom of Solomon to deduce that Fred was as subservient to his mother as she was.

'So far so good,' Mrs Connolly said grudgingly. 'We'll see what the rest of the week brings.' She turned her wheelchair round. 'Here Fred, give me a hand. I'm sure Sarah won't mind doing the washing-up being as all this were her idea.'

In fact, the influx of customers during the rest of the week mirrored the first day's success.

'There's not much profit being made, Sarah, with such low prices, but we're ahead and that's what matters,' Fred managed to whisper when his mother was out of earshot. His freckly face seemed plainer than ever, as he hung his head sheepishly. 'I doubt if we can give you any bonus.'

Clearly his mother speaking, Sarah guessed.

'I didn't ask for any and I don't expect any. So long as the extra business means my wages are safe.'

No point in stirring up trouble for herself, she told Flo later.

'I mean, I only suggested it as a way of keeping the caff open. I've got a nice little room, a decent enough wage and I can send me mam something every week, so I didn't expect a rise.'

Flo, clearly troubled by the hostility of the proprietress, shook her head. 'What's got into her? She don't usually mind what Fred does. Perhaps she thinks you're gonna take 'im away from her.'

This ludicrous suggestion sent them both into fits of giggles once more and the incident was forgotten.

As if anyone could take her Harry's place. He had kept his promise to write every week, and even if the letters were not romantic in any way, Sarah kept every single one, holding them to her lips, knowing that Harry's hands had touched each page of the cheap, lined writing paper. Besides, he had promised to come and see her soon and take her out for the day.

Flo had turned down the suggestion that she and Sid should spend the day with them.

'Honestly, I do wonder about you sometimes. Your fella ain't seen you in months, so 'e's 'ardly gonna want me and Sid watching what you get up to now, is 'e?'

Sarah blushed. 'We're not going to get up to anything,' she protested, desperately trying to fend off Flo's teasing.

'Says you! Just you wait until he gets you in the back row of the flicks.'

Chapter 12

'Come here, let me hold you a bit closer.'

'Stop it Harry, people are looking at us,' Sarah protested breathlessly, her lips parted in laughter as she clung to him.

'I'm only checking to see if you've grown since I last saw you,' he claimed, his blue eyes twinkling. 'After all, you're a whole year older today, so there's bound to be a big difference.'

Sarah pulled herself away from him, still hardly daring to believe that Harry was actually hers for one whole day. He took her arm, pressing himself to her.

'We'll find somewhere quiet where we can talk. No, don't worry,' he said, picking up her anxious look. 'I told your mam and dad that I was coming to Blackpool.'

'What did they say?' Sarah was terrified that her father would be furious.

'Well, your dad laid down the law a bit about you being only sixteen, but I reminded him that you'd been here in Blackpool for nearly two years and nothing had happened, and you certainly weren't going to come to any harm from me.'

'What about Mam?' Sarah knew that her mother would have misgivings, especially since his name had been linked that of Dolly Redmile.

He frowned, remembering Joanna's green eyes piercing right through him as if reading his intentions. She had clearly not been keen on the idea and her look had warned him that he had better be careful.

'I have to be honest, Sarah, I don't think she was really pleased with the idea, but,' he shrugged, 'she knew I'd come whatever anyone said.'

They walked in silence for some minutes until they reached a vacant bench on the promenade.

'Come on, let's sit here.' Harry took her hand, gently drawing her down beside him.

It was still early on in the season, too early for the holidaymakers to have arrived in their thousands, and the two sat for a while enjoying the sound of waves slapping on the pebbles and watching the gulls circling and swooping in search of delicacies.

Sitting holding hands, Sarah acknowledged the immense change in their relationship since that stolen kiss at Christmas. She had been just a child then, terrified lest a neighbour might have seen Harry Wilby kissing her. Now she felt as if there was a deep understanding between them that did not need putting into words.

She turned to contemplate the hard planes of his face, the deep line etched from his narrow nostrils to his full lips. How could anyone have such deep blue eyes and such long dark lashes? Sarah longed to stroke his face with her fingers. As if reading her thoughts, Harry took hold of her hand, laying her fingers across his cheek, allowing her to run the tips gently in a circling movement until he could kiss the palm of her hand.

'My dear sweetheart.'

Sarah shrank back, suddenly shy. 'Am I really your sweetheart?'

'Why else would I be here?' he laughed. 'You don't

think I'd take that bus ride on my day off just for the fun of it, do you?'

He began to delve into his overcoat pockets, pulling out a tiny parcel. 'This is from your mam, and this one,' he said, producing a second packet, 'is from Iris and Bernard.'

The first contained some prettily embroidered hankies and the second a scarf with a pattern of green and white flowers. The sudden, unexpected reminder of home brought hot stinging tears to her eyes.

'Here, come on sweetheart, you're not supposed to cry on your birthday.' He smoothed back a stray red curl before brushing his lips on her forehead. 'If you go on like this, I'll have to take my present back home again.'

He opened the box containing a dainty silver necklace with a heart-shaped pendant. His strong fingers struggled with the catch as he tried to fasten it around her slender neck.

'Oh, damn it!' he muttered as the delicate clasp eluded his efforts. 'I hope you're not going to be as difficult to manage as this is,' he finally said with a laugh.

Sarah took the pendant from him to look at it again, before she fastened it herself.

'I didn't expect anything at all from anyone, being so far away. This is my best birthday ever.'

He stood up, pulling Sarah to her feet and placing his arm round her shoulder.

'As if I'd let my best girl be on her own on her special birthday.'

The rest of the day was one to cherish for many months. It was as if they walked for miles, talking and laughing, with Harry teasing her and reminding her that she had to wait for him.

'No running off with this Fred you keep talking about.'

'I keep telling you that he's not interested in girls,' Sarah insisted.

Harry shook his head. 'There's something odd about him then. Are you sure you're safe to be under the same roof as him? I don't know what I'd do if anyone hurt you,' he said, his voice taking on a deep, almost savage timbre.

'Oh, stop worrying. I've got Flo and even if she does marry her Sid, there's Fred's mother in the place as well. I've got a good job and I'm learning all the time.' She was just about to add, 'You wait and see, one day I'll have my own café and perhaps later a boarding house,' but bit her tongue. Harry would surely have laughed at her impossibly ambitious dreams.

Clinging to Harry at the bus station, Sarah wept as he kissed her goodbye. 'I wish you didn't have to go. Couldn't you come and work here and be with me?'

'One day, Sarah, one day, but not yet. Be patient please, for me.'

She watched the bus gather speed until it was lost from sight, carrying her Harry further and further away from her. The long, hot summer stretched out in front of her, days slaving in the kitchen, clearing tables, washing mounds of greasy plates and cutlery, all the while putting on a great act of being cheerful to keep the customers happy.

'They only get one week's holiday a year, and it's up to us to make sure they come back to us again,' old Mrs Connolly reminded her whenever the heat in the kitchen made her sigh as she wiped away the perspiration running down her cheeks.

It was true. People struggled hard all year, scrimping and saving to spend one week at the seaside, pretending that the life of luxury was there for the taking and that one day life would be one long holiday. Sarah smiled and laughed at the teasing remarks as she moved amongst the tables. The memory of the beautiful green-eyed girl with the wild red curls would haunt the memory of many a young male once he was back on the bleak factory floor.

It was at the end of September that Flo burst into Sarah's room late at night. She bounced on to Sarah's bed with a loud whoop of excitement.

'I'm getting married!'

Sarah hugged her friend, who by this time was half-laughing and half-crying with joy.

'Calm down and tell me all about it. When is it going to be?'

After a few gulps and blowing her nose, Flo managed to explain that Sid had been offered a job at the hotel where she worked as a chambermaid. Being the biggest hotel in the town, it remained open all the year round, so he would be paid winter and summer, unlike most of the jobs catering for summer visitors.

'He's seen a little flat not too far from the hotel and if I can keep working for a while, we can afford the rent. Just imagine, me and my Sid in a proper little home of our own. I keep thinking I'm dreaming it and I'll wake up and it won't be true.'

Sarah guessed that for Flo, who had never known the comfort of a loving family as she had, marriage to Sid promised to bring her the kind of happiness she had only ever seen on the cinema screen.

'And we want you to be a bridesmaid, so no excuses,

Sarah Mulvey.'

'Who's going to give you away. I mean, will you write and tell your dad?'

Flo's bitter rejoinder, 'I don't know where the drunken sod is and I don't care,' shocked Sarah. ''E's never done nothin' for me, and I don't want my wedding day ruined. Sid's best mate at the Tower's gonna stand with him and look after the ring.'

She got up and walked over to the window, staring up at the night sky. 'Since I come to Blackpool, I've 'ad you, the best friend a girl could 'ave, I've met Sid, I've 'ad me own little room with no one to bother me and I've never bin so bleedin' 'appy.'

'Then why are you crying, you soppy old thing?' Sarah asked, tears rolling down her cheeks in sympathy with Flo.

'I dunno.'

At this, both girls giggled. Flo explained that Sid's uncle would give her away and his aunt would put on a bit of a do at the newlyweds' flat for a few people.

'Knowing her, it'll be a good spread. Sid wants to invite some of the blokes he's been working with, and there's one or two nice girls from where I work. There'll be you and I'll have to ask Fred and Mrs Connolly, of course, so there'll be about twenty of us altogether.'

'Sounds wonderful,' Sarah agreed, painfully trying to conceal her envy at her friend's happiness.

Flo stared hard at her. 'I bet you're wishing it was you and your 'Arry, ain't you? Come on, it's no good shaking your 'ead at me. This is Flo you're talking to. Now, listen here. I'm eighteen and I've 'ad to wait, so even if the next couple of years seem like a 'undred, you know your bloke will be waiting for you, so just you remember that.'

A feeling of shame at making Flo feel guilty about her happy news swept over her. 'We're going to make this the best wedding in Blackpool. Tell you what, Flo, I'm pretty good at sewing, so if you want me to make your dress, you've only got to ask.'

Flo's jaw dropped in admiration. 'Blimey, and there's me can't even mend a pair of socks.'

'Well, you'd better learn before Sid finds out,' Sarah warned her. 'I won't tell him how useless you are, promise.'

Flo's screech of delighted laughter provoked a warning shout from Fred's bedroom and a few muttered remarks implying that he must have been out of his mind to let two girls like Flo and Sarah into his house.

Sarah lay awake long after Flo had finally taken herself off to her room. Sid and Flo did not have much in the way of material possessions, but they loved one another with the kind of devoted affection that would sustain them through whatever misfortunes life had to throw at them. She mused about her own relationship with Harry, perceiving it to be on a different plane from that of Flo and Sid. There was an undercurrent of deep passion, an emotion that would brook no interference. Perhaps it was just as well that fate had kept them apart for much of the last two years, as there would have been trouble if her parents had known the extent of her feelings for Harry Wilby. The prospect of her parents' opposition filled her with dread. What if they made her wait until she was twenty-one? Would Harry wait all that time?

The day of the wedding was fixed for the last Saturday in August, which gave Sarah just under three months to make Flo's wedding dress and her own bridesmaid's dress.

The White Rose Weeps

At first, Flo had insisted that she would look silly in a white dress, but Sid had supported Sarah's vehement insistence that Flo should look like a proper bride. Finally, they had compromised on a calf length dress with a scalloped hem. It had taken Sarah many hours of patient sewing to achieve the exact copy of the dress she had seen in a newspaper advertisement for the brides' department of a large London store. Her own simple cream muslin dress with its tiny pattern of pink rosebuds was designed so that she could wear it later for special occasions.

On seeing the two dresses finished, Flo had hugged and kissed her, tears spilling down her cheeks.

'I never dreamt in my whole life that I'd be walking down the aisle in such a beautiful dress. Oh, Sarah, tell me it's not just a dream and I'm gonna wake up and find myself back in that rat hole in Bethnal Green.'

'Come on, try it on,' Sarah urged her, not satisfied until she had made a few adjustments. 'There,' she said, beaming at her efforts, 'you look beautiful. Sid'll fall in love with you all over again.'

It was true. Love and happiness had softened Flo's strong features, giving her a glow that no cosmetic could improve on.

'It's a pity 'Arry can't make it,' Flo said, reading the sadness in Sarah's eyes. 'Still, if 'e wants to get out of the pit, I suppose 'e's got to 'ave a good look round.'

'I suppose so,' Sarah agreed ruefully, 'but I wish he'd chosen a different weekend to go down to Essex or wherever it is to see what jobs are on offer.' At the back of her mind was the fear that he would move South and she would lose him. Being near London could provide a young man with so many diversions that visiting her in

Blackpool might prove to be an unwelcome chore. She could always move South as well, Flo reminded her, but could she? Her parents would want to know what it was that she and Harry Wilby had planned. It was different with Lizzie, who had lived in a nurses' hostel and therefore, her parents assumed, was subject to some kind of supervision.

The tiny church was surprisingly full of friends who had managed to escape from work for an hour or two to see Flo and Sid get married.

Sid stood at the altar, his newly-cut light brown hair giving him the appearance of a raw recruit whose sergeant had ordered a short back and sides. The off-the-peg navy blue suit with its knife edge creases was just a fraction too large for his spare frame, but bespoke tailoring was far out of the range of his meagre wages.

'Come on, this is it, Flo. If you want to change your mind, you've only got to say so.' Sid's uncle was carrying out the duties of a father as instructed by his wife.

He needed no answer, as Flo grasped his arm firmly and stepped out to the strains of 'The Wedding March'. Sid turned to see his bride, his eyes widening at the unexpected vision of Flo in her white gown, looking more beautiful than he had ever imagined.

Sarah did her best to keep her mind off Harry, remembering that this was the second occasion she had been a bridesmaid. What was it they said? Three times a bridesmaid, never a bride. She'd better turn down any more requests or Harry would never be hers.

It was almost midnight before she was back at the café and in her bed. Things would never be the same now that Flo had moved out. Sarah had refused Fred's offer of Flo's old room, although it was larger than her small attic room, feeling happier to be on a different floor from Fred. Lately, she had noticed that he was watching her every movement, following her with his eyes as she worked at the tables, chatting to the customers. Surely he would not be like Arthur Scatesburn. Sarah trembled with fear whenever she heard him coming up the stairs to his room, relaxing only when the sound of his door shutting reassured her that he was safely in his own room. If only Flo were still here, but Flo was ecstatically ensconced in her own home, happily enjoying her new status as a married woman, and Sarah did not want to worry her with her problems. In the early morning, attending to his mother, Sarah told herself that she was simply imagining Fred's intense gaze and that her fears all arose from the fright she had had at Rosewood with Arthur Scatesburn.

Full of descriptions of his trips down South, Harry came to see her late in September. 'The money's twice as good and they're building really decent houses with proper bathrooms and little gardens for the workers. Since Dad died, Mam's wanted to get away. She's really thrilled at the prospect of moving.' His blue eyes shone with such enthusiasm that Sarah hesitated to share her misgivings with him. 'Here, why so miserable? Anyone'd think I was going to the moon.'

Unable to stem the tears, Sarah managed to blurt out that if he went so far away, she'd never see him again.

Harry stroked her hair, twisting her curls lovingly through his fingers, finally burying his face in her wild, tumbling locks.

'Do you think I'd ever let you go after all this time?

Look, there's nothing planned for certain yet. More than likely it'll be after Christmas.' He kissed her lightly on her forehead. 'You'll be getting on for seventeen come Christmas, and I'm going to tell your mam and dad that I want to take you out properly, none of this half-pretending that I'm just an old friend of the family.'

'Sort of almost engaged?' Sarah's shyness at daring to put into words what she was hoping reduced her voice to a whisper.

'No sort of, I want to shout it from the housetops that I love little Sarah Mulvey and she loves me.'

'So, I'll see you at Christmas?'

'I'll be with you every minute I can. And stop worrying about me going down South. If and when I go, I'll find a place to rent with Mam and then you can start looking for a job near me.'

After seeing him off at the bus station, Sarah pondered on his words. It was all very well saying she could pack up and move down South, but her parents would not want her so far away before she was married. Why couldn't everything be as simple as it had been for Flo and Sid?

Harry kept his word about speaking to her parents at Christmas and indeed, when he met her at Barnsley bus station, he greeted her with the news that he had obtained their permission to take her out to the pictures.

'Really? They don't mind about us?' She spun round, staring him straight in the face. 'You're not telling the truth, Harry, I can tell by the way you're not looking me in the eye.'

Harry affected an air of complete bafflement at her lack of trust. 'How can I look you in the eye when you hardly come up to the middle of my chest?'

Sarah pummelled his chest with her tiny gloved hands, daring him to mock her. 'Did Mam have anything to say . . . I mean did she mention Dolly?'

They walked along in silence, Harry pretending to be fully occupied in searching for the Colethorpe bus.

'Answer me at once,' Sarah ordered.

Harry put her case down on the ground at his feet between them. 'OK, it wasn't as easy as all that. Your dad thinks I'm too old for you, or rather you're too young for me, which is a bit different. Your mam doesn't like the fact that I've been seen with Dolly.'

'Can't say I do either, if it comes to that.' Sarah pouted.

Palms facing upwards, Harry sighed, struggling to find the right words. 'I've known Dolly since we started at Colethorpe Mixed Infants together and we've lived a few doors away from one another all our lives. OK, so I've taken her out now and again, but so have plenty of other fellows.'

Sarah had enough feminine good sense not to ask him to define exactly what he meant by taking her out. If Harry had made some progress with her parents, this was no time to start quizzing him about his past. All the same, she relished the thought of walking out on Harry's arm for Dolly Redmile to see.

'Glad to see I've brought a smile to your face, young lady. For one minute there, I thought I was in trouble.'

Sarah reddened, ashamed of her desire to humble Dolly and relieved that Harry had not guessed the true reason for her smile. This was going to be the best Christmas ever with Harry able to call on her and take her out.

'Do you remember last Christmas when you waited

outside Bernard and Iris's house for me?'

'Do I remember?' Harry laughed. 'Here feel my fingertips, they still haven't thawed out.' The smile faded as he took her hands in his. 'I remember the girl of my dreams letting me kiss her, making me the happiest man on Earth.'

Harry delivered her to her doorstep just long enough to greet her mother before waving goodbye with a promise to call when he got home from work on the Monday. Much as she loved him, Sarah longed to see her family, cuddle little Maureen who was now over two years old and a lively toddler. Sarah's disappointment when Maureen shrank from her, brought home to her what she had sacrificed in living so far away.

'Just give her time, luv,' her mother told her, seeing Sarah's distress.

'A whole week off before Christmas! By, you're a lucky lass and no mistake,' her dad's pleasure at her long holiday was evident. 'That Fred and his mam gone off again to Harrogate?'

Sarah explained that the café was closed for a few weeks as usual, but that she would have to be back soon after the New Year.

'I get a bonus for thinking up the idea of cut-price fish and chips in the winter season, and I don't want to miss out on that.'

'Right little moneybags, aren't you? Who'd have thought it of our little Sarah?'

He was right, no one thought she had it in her to make something of her life, like Lizzie in London and Patrick in the army in Egypt, but she intended showing them.

Her first outing with Harry did not go as smoothly as

Harry had led her to believe.

'I can't say that your Mam and I are best pleased at this arrangement, but as you're only home for ten days, we'll allow you to go the pictures with him this once, but you're to be home by eleven at the latest.'

Harry listened to Jim Mulvey's instructions as to what bus he was to catch and when he expected Sarah in. The young man acquiesced, bowing his head meekly. He would comply with whatever conditions were laid down in order to get Sarah to himself for a few blissful hours.

The back row of the cinema was a favourite spot for courting couples with the darkness affording a cover in the warmth for their cuddles and caresses. Harry and Sarah were no exception.

'Don't you think we ought to watch the film in case someone asks us how it ended,' Sarah whispered.

'I've seen it before, so I'll tell you later.' Harry tugged at her arm. 'Come on, let's get out of here, before that usherette shines that bloody torch on us again.'

There was an urgency in Harry's voice that half-frightened Sarah. Didn't he like kissing her any more?

'We'll get the bus as far as Dinsdale, and then we'll walk.' His face was grim. 'Look, I need you to myself for an hour. All we ever seem to do is meet with the eyes of half the world on us.'

Sarah could not understand him in this mood, having only ever seen him cheerful and teasing her. No doubt he would tell her once they go off the bus at Dinsdale and started walking.

Dinsdale was a small village that still retained its rural aspect, no mines or slag heaps disfiguring its fields.

No one else dismounted at Dinsdale, there being only one small public house, a church and one main street consisting of a row of Victorian cottages leaning drunkenly against one another for support.

'We can cut across the fields and through Purley Woods. It won't take long and we'll be home long before your dad said.'

The evening was beginning to take on the air of something of an adventure as, clinging together, the two picked their way through the long grass. Every so often Harry stopped to kiss her, each kiss deepening in intensity, until she could hardly breathe. She found herself pressing ever closer to him, avid for more kisses, even as he attempted to gently disengage himself from her.

The night was dark, and Sarah struggled to see where she was placing her feet, afraid of twisting her ankle in a rabbit hole.

'Stop worrying,' Harry tried to reassure her. 'You're such a tiny delicate thing that if I had to I could carry you all the way home. Here, let's stop for a rest. I'm a thoughtless idiot, letting you walk all this way.'

Thankful for the rest, Sarah leaned against the trunk of an age-old oak. All around them was the silence of the night, broken only by the call of a fox, or the rustling of a small creature as it sped to its den to escape its predators.

Sarah felt as if they had left the normal world and were now inhabiting some magic place meant for lovers only. It seemed so natural for her to respond to Harry's more demanding kisses that she scarcely noticed that he was gently pulling her down to the ground. They lay close together, each lost in exploring one another with caresses increasing in intimacy. She made no protest when he began to push against her, her need as great as his. Her first cry of pain was forgotten after Harry entered her a second time, bringing her to climax in a frenzy of delight. Sarah lay for some time in a state of disbelief at what had happened. This had been the most wonderful experience of her life. No wonder Flo was so blissfully happy. She was roughly brought back to reality with Harry dragging her to her feet.

'Oh my God! What the hell have I done?' Groaning and cursing, he turned away from Sarah. 'Oh, Sarah, this shouldn't have happened. I promised your dad I'd look after you and now, look at me. If your dad were to find out, he'd take a horse whip to me and serve me right.'

'Please Harry, it wasn't your fault,' Sarah whimpered, afraid that she had disappointed him in some way.

Harry began very carefully to brush Sarah's coat and skirt. He took off her shoes and polished them with his clean white handkerchief.

'We'll walk back to Dinsdale and get the next bus home. That'll give me a better chance to make sure that you look tidy before you go in. Your dad isn't daft, he'll soon put two and two together if sees mud on your shoes or grass stains on your coat.'

Anguish and guilt lined his rugged face. 'What the hell have I done?' he kept repeating as they waited for the bus in Dinsdale.

Sarah wanted to bring back the happy, carefree mood of earlier in the evening, but that had gone irrevocably. Deceiving her parents, committing a mortal sin, and what was even worse, perhaps getting in the family way. No, she comforted herself, that wasn't possible. Flo had definitely told her, that you couldn't get pregnant, not on your first time.

It was fortunate that her parents were in bed when she let herself in at the back door soon after half past ten, a whole thirty minutes before she was due in, giving her the chance to run up to her room. She needed time to undress carefully and examine her body to see if she looked any different. No, she was still the tiny, innocent-looking Sarah Mulvey who had gone out earlier that evening with Harry Wilby. She lay awake for several hours debating whether she ought to tell Lizzie, who was due to arrive the next morning, but embarrassment and shame mingled with a desire to hug the wonderful experience to herself, decided her. Not even Flo would be told.

Amidst all the Christmas preparations and hearing Lizzie's latest news about her nursing exams, which had gone very well, and the hint that a certain doctor was taking more than a professional interest in her, the focus of attention was shifted from Sarah. She was filled with a vague unease that Harry had not contacted her since making love to her, leaving her wondering if he had regretted making such a commitment to her. There was some comfort in the thought that he too had to conform to the conventions of remaining with his family over the Christmas period.

It was Iris who raised the subject when she and Bernard called round on Boxing Day.

'Fancy Sarah going out with Harry Wilby.'

They were all seated at the kitchen table except Sarah, who, keen to establish a bond between herself and her baby sister, was playing on the rug with Maureen.

'What's this?' Lizzie's sharp query carried more than a hint of censure.

'Oh, he just took me to the pictures once.' Sarah's pretence at nonchalance did not fool Lizzie, who wasted no time in interrogating Sarah once she managed to get her on her own.

'He's a man, not a boy, and far too old for you. Surely you don't need reminding that men want one thing only and once they've had that, they'll throw you on one side.'

'Oh, don't be silly, there's nothing like that, he's just a friend.'

Lizzie was not to be put off so easily. 'Just you listen to me. Don't let him do anything, you know what I mean. You don't want to end up like Effie Farnton.'

'I won't, so stop fussing will you? I've managed to look after myself for nearly two years without anyone worrying about me so I daresay I can manage a bit longer.'

Seeing Lizzie's unhappy frown, Sarah relented and assured Lizzie that it was nice of her to be concerned, but really there was nothing to worry about.

But there was. Harry did not call again until the day she was due to catch the bus back to Blackpool, simply dropping by to wish her all the best, before he left with the excuse that his dinner was almost ready and that he had better not keep his mother waiting. Sarah's frantic unspoken plea that he spend a little time with her, see her off on the bus did not appear to register with him. From his cheerful, casual demeanour, no one would have guessed that he was saying farewell to the girl he had promised to love forever.

'You will write, won't you?' she whispered, shocked at the coldness of his goodbye.

He nodded, still smiling over her shoulder at her mother. Desperate with fear that he had found her wanting since that magical time he had made love to her, Sarah watched him stride down the path. He turned briefly, smiled and waved goodbye.

Chapter 13

'You're not looking your usual cheerful self this morning, Sarah. That's twice you've managed to button up my cardigan the wrong way.'

'Oh, I'm sorry, Mrs Connolly, I didn't sleep too well last night, that's all.'

'Missing your young man, I bet.' The old lady grinned knowingly. 'Never mind, you're still young, plenty of time before you think of settling down. You don't want to rush into things.' She pulled the rug up over her knees. 'Now push me into the café, there's a good girl.'

It was one of those bitingly cold, late February mornings when summer seemed as if it would never come. The café would warm up later once Fred lit the gas burners under the fish fryers, but at the moment, Sarah's fingers felt icy as she swept the floor and dusted the windowsills.

'You do look pale, Sarah, doesn't she Fred?'

'Honestly, I'm fine,' Sarah insisted, uncomfortably aware of Fred's scrutiny. 'Just a bit on the cold side, but I expect I'll soon warm up once we get busy.'

Laying the tables gave her the opportunity to keep an eye out for the postman. Harry had written to her just the once since Christmas, a strange letter that had filled her with fears for their future. His explanation for not calling round again was that he felt it would be safer if they were not alone together after what had happened. He still loved her and would come and see her as soon as his plans were clear.

Sarah had been shocked at the way he could quite coldly decide that they should not see one another for a while, although in his favour, she remembered how horrified he had been in allowing their longing for one another to have led to their making love that night.

Mrs Connolly sniffed loudly, calling Sarah to fetch her a hanky from her room. 'This cold is making my nose run like a tap. Come on, Fred, be quick and light that gas.'

On her return, Sarah was handed a letter with the familiar handwriting.

Mrs Connolly poked Sarah in the ribs, gently teasing her with the remark that this would bring the roses back into her cheeks. Sarah stuffed the letter into the pocket of her apron with a casual remark that she would read it later.

It wasn't until the last customer had left and Mrs Connolly had been helped into bed for her afternoon rest that Sarah had a chance to read Harry's letter.

> My darling Sarah,
> It's no good, I can't wait until your eighteenth birthday for us to get married. I need to be with you all the time. I've made up my mind. I'm going away soon to find work and then I want you to come with me. If we can get away from Colethorpe, we can start a life together as we planned.
> Your loving Harry

Sarah did not know whether to be thrilled at Harry's proposal or not. Was he expecting her to live in sin? Surely he knew that she would never agree to live with him until they were properly married. But her heart sang with happiness at the love in his letter. Somehow everything would work out fine. Their love for one another would find a way to overcome any obstacles.

There was one niggling thought which had not quite taken shape in the back of her mind, until the third week in March when she woke up feeling violently sick. Even after vomiting, the feeling of nausea persisted throughout the day, leaving her feeling weak and scarcely able to cope with lifting Mrs Connolly in and out of bed.

'Look here, Sarah, it's none of my business and you can tell me I'm an interfering old besom, but I think it's high time you took yourself off to the doctor. You've been sick every morning this week and there's got to be a good reason for that. I've told Fred we can manage without you this afternoon, so don't put it off any longer, do you hear me?'

Ignorant as she was, Sarah was not entirely taken aback by what the doctor announced. He glanced at the bare third finger of her left hand.

'You'd better get the young man concerned to marry you as soon as possible,' he told her, saddened at the girl's obvious immaturity. 'The baby's due towards the end of September. You won't be showing for a month or two yet, so there's time.'

Harry's baby! Her reaction to the news fluctuated between delight and abject terror. In a dream, Sarah left the surgery, not knowing where to go or what to do. How could this have happened after what Flo had told her? She sat for a while on a low garden wall, desperate for someone to talk to, for someone to reassure her. How could she tell her parents? They'd never allow her in the house after bringing shame on the family. What would her father do when he found out that the man he had been working with had seduced his daughter without caring for the consequences? The irrational thought struck her that Dolly managed to do all the things she did without having a baby.

She let herself into the café, going straight up to her room. First of all, she had to write to Harry. If she got her letter into the post that evening, he would be sure to reply by return, or even better, he might get the first bus to Blackpool. He'd realise that they would have to organise a quiet wedding as soon as possible. For a moment, the excitement of being Harry's wife sooner than they had planned made her wildly happy. It was a wonderful stroke of fate that Harry wanted to leave Colethorpe to work down South. That way, her parents could be a little vague about dates when telling people that she was married and, later on, expecting.

Tiptoeing out of the back door, she raced to the post box. There was a late night collection, so Harry would get her letter by the time he came in from work on the Friday. Feeling more content now that she had faced up to what had been frightening her since the end of January, she intended to keep it secret from the Connollys until the time came for her to hand in her notice.

'Just something that's disagreeing with me, the doctor said,' was all that Sarah said when quizzed by Mrs Connolly. If that lady had her own ideas, she did not enquire further, simply nodding and suggesting that Sarah should avoid tea and fried foods in the morning.

There was an unprecedented rush in the café on Saturday morning with a coach party passing through. The weather having turned out to be one of those pleasant sunny spring mornings with just a hint of a cold breeze, the party had decided to stop for lunch in Blackpool and 'get a breath of the briny,' as one wag put it.

'Wake up Sarah,' Fred called out, 'take these plates over to the couple next to the door. I don't know what's got into you the last few days.'

By the end of the day, it was clear that Harry was not coming, but Sarah consoled herself with the thought that he had not received the letter. If he didn't come on Sunday, there would certainly be a letter on the Monday or Tuesday. An agony of waiting followed, with each succeeding day filling her with panic. She wrote again, telling Harry how frightened she was and please would he answer and tell her what they ought to do.

With no reply to her fifth letter, all hope of Harry's marrying her faded completely. Lizzie had been right about men. All they wanted was one thing and if they could get it without being tied down, then so much the better, but she had been fool enough to think that Harry was different.

Sarah had never expected life's plums to be thrown in her lap, but with Harry she had felt secure and loved. Now that dream was shattered and she would have to find a way to fend for herself and her baby.

'When did you say the baby was due?' Flo was all sympathy as well as full of practical suggestions. 'If only you'd told me sooner, we could have sorted something out. One of the girls I work with knows a woman who can—'

Sarah put her hands over her ears. 'No! I don't want to hear about it.'

Flo's rueful, 'Well, you're too far gone anyhow,' pacified her.

Her friend's suggestion that she should go home and tell Harry to his face seemed to be the best solution. 'You never know. I reckon it might be that 'is mum's opened the letters and 'e ain't never seen them.'

Sarah's gloom lightened at this obvious explanation. Of course, that was it. Harry had not had her letters.

'Oh, Flo, trust you to have the answer.' Reassured that Harry had not abandoned her, Sarah's eyes sparkled with new hope for the future. 'I'll ask Fred if I can have this weekend off, tell him my mam needs me for a day or two. Once I tell Harry about our baby, he'll be so happy, wanting us to get married just as soon as we can arrange everything.' Oblivious to Flo's worried frown, she continued with her litany. 'I'll have to tell Mam and Dad, but if Harry and I move away, no one will know I had to get married. I can't believe that everything's going to be fine.' She kissed her friend on the cheek. 'What would I do without you?'

'Probably fall flat on your face, I wouldn't be surprised,' Flo said. 'Now, it's like this, I've got three days off my job. Sid won't mind if I cover for you at the caff, you know, 'elp out with the old lady and that.'

With a letter in the post to her mother to let her know that she had a few days off to come home for her seventeenth birthday, Sarah was on her way, hope rising in her breast at the thought of the wonderful reception she would get from Harry when she told him her news.

She was still dreading the first meeting with her

parents, afraid that even her loose flared skirt would not conceal her now more rounded belly from her mother. Apart from commenting that the extra weight suited her, the fact that Jim was in hospital with a broken leg after a fall at work was uppermost in her mother's mind.

'Oh Mam, why didn't you let me know?'

'Well, I didn't want to worry you luv. I've got Bernard and Iris to help and they've been ever so good. Iris looks after Maureen at her house while I go on the bus with Bernard to the infirmary.'

She was suddenly most apologetic. 'Oh, we're off in a couple of minutes and I haven't even given you a cup of tea.'

Sarah concealed her relief at this unexpected opportunity to go and see Harry while there was no one about. She reassured her mother that all she wanted was to rest after the journey and to be sure to give her love to her father.

Impatient at the time it took for Bernard and her mother to get ready to catch the bus, Sarah finally waved them off. Excited at the prospect of seeing Harry, she flew out of the back door, along the lane to his house. A sudden fear gripped her as she pushed open the back gate to number twelve. Her hand on the gate, she tried to fathom out what it was that made the house seem so unfamiliar. The curtains at the kitchen window were a different colour. Still, Harry's mother might have decided to have a change she told herself, not permitting herself to consider any other explanation. At the sound of the gate being opened, a dog began to bark. Had Harry got a dog since she last saw him?

It was a stranger who opened the door. No, she didn't know any Wilbys. The woman explained that she had moved in after the previous tenants had left and she did not know where they had gone.

'There's been some letters come, from Blackpool according to the postmark, but we chucked them on the fire.'

So Harry had disappeared with no forwarding address, and without writing to her. She had still one more avenue open to her. Bernard would be sure to know where his best man had gone and would let her have his address, but she would have to be careful how she broached the subject in order not to arouse suspicion.

Back from the hospital, Sarah insisted that Bernard should sit down and have a cup of tea while he told her all his news about Iris and their baby son.

Her question, 'Still enjoying working down the pit then?' elicited the information she was seeking.

'Oh, aye, but you'll never guess what; Harry Wilby has packed it in, gone to work somewhere down South, so he said.' He laughed. 'You'll never believe it, but he just told his mam they were off and that was that.'

Sarah chose her next words carefully. 'That's a pity for you losing your best mate and not knowing where he is.'

'That's right, but he said he'd let me know where he was once he got settled. I believe he's had one or two moves since starting work down South.'

'Well, if it's as good as it sounds, perhaps you and Iris might follow. Where's he working, by the way?' Her attempt at throwing in a casual question while pouring out the tea made her mother ask sharply why she was so interested.

'Well, it might suit Dad as well if he can get a better job than slaving underground down the pit. I mean, we're not all tied to Colethorpe, are we? Patrick and Lizzie have gone and I'm doing fine in Blackpool now, even though I never thought I would.'

'Perhaps you're right, Sarah,' Bernard agreed. 'All I know is that he's trying for work in one of the factories somewhere in Essex. He'll be sure to let us have all his news and then we can make up our minds. There's no rush, we'll all have to wait and see how he gets on.'

Except I haven't got time, Sarah agonised. Another month and her condition would be obvious to everyone. Her slight build would soon show the tell-tale bulge. If Harry didn't write with an address, she would have to tell her mother. And what about her father? He'd never have her in the house again. Her reply, light in tone, elicited no inquiring looks this time from her mother.

'Well, let Mam and Dad know when you do hear, and we can all start making plans to follow suit.' She gave a brittle little laugh.

The effort of appearing carefree left her worn out, so much so, that for the first time, she was glad to catch the bus back to Blackpool.

'Your holiday hasn't done you much good,' Mrs Connolly commented, her sharp eyes missing nothing.

'No, it was all a bit worrying with my dad in hospital and all the trips back and forth and our little Maureen to look after as well.'

Her one visit to her father had passed off quite smoothly. It had been a wintry day with a biting wind, and therefore she had worn her thick coat which, as well as keeping out the cold, hid the recently acquired curves.

As the days passed, the burden of her knowledge was threatening to overwhelm her. Her letter to Iris asking about Harry had been her final hope. Dear, kind Iris had guessed the reason for the inquiry and had tactfully replied to the effect that she would let Sarah know as soon as they had any news. She had ended her letter with the promise that she would do anything at all to help, even to the extent of having Sarah to stay with her and Bernard if she could not go home.

Sarah wept at this kind-hearted offer. Iris's mother would have been mortified at her married daughter harbouring a single girl who had brought shame on her family. Much as the offer touched her, Sarah had to accept that she could not return home.

Telling Mrs Connolly had to be the first hurdle to overcome. Flo had promised to give Sarah a roof over her head if the Connollys threw her out.

'I guessed as much,' Mrs Connolly said. 'We're not going to put you on the streets, don't you worry. Just you work as long as you can and then we'll have another think about it.'

At least that was some respite, giving time for Harry to get in touch. His next letter was a note scrawled in haste to say that he had changed his job and that he and his mother were having to move out of their present rooms. Again the promise that he would send for her as soon as he had a permanent address.

July was one of the hottest on record with Sarah barely able to cope with the back-breaking work in the café in the summer rush. At seven months pregnant, she should have been resting and making preparations for the birth of her baby. Instead, she had to wait upon the wave after wave of hungry holidaymakers who descended on the café from soon after ten in the morning until after six in the evening. Exhaustion stripped her already pale face of the last vestiges of colour, leaving her looking as if she was on the point of collapse.

It was Fred who finally broached the subject of her situation one evening after he had locked the front door.

'Look, me and Ma have been having a little chat, Sarah. It's getting plain that the café work is too much for you. I'm sorry, but we need to think about hiring someone to take your place.' His plain, freckled face wore a blank expression. 'I don't know what to suggest really I don't, Sarah, except I think you'll have to go home to your family.'

She took a deep breath before replying. 'I haven't told them.' The sheer hopelessness of her situation hit her hard, leaving her with no more strength; she sank into the nearest chair. Her misery was so great that the great fountain of tears inside her remained unshed, filling her with desperation.

Fred stared at her for a moment, unable to comprehend the depth of her unhappiness. Sarah returned his gaze, reading with shock his total inability to cope with emotion of any kind.

'I'll speak to Ma. She'll think of something.'

It wasn't until the following week on the Bank Holiday Monday that Mrs Connolly summoned Sarah into her room.

'Right, now Fred tells me that you've not told your parents and that you've got nowhere to go. I want to make it clear to you, sorry as we are for you, that you're not our responsibility.' She thumped her walking stick on the floor with each word as if to emphasise her point. 'You understand that, don't you? However, I'm not daft. I do know that you're a damn fine cook and some of your ideas have brought in more money and customers.'

Sarah waited, hardly daring to guess what the old lady

had in mind, but flabbergasted at her next words.

'Once the baby's born you'll be able to work again, I'm sure of that. On the other hand, this is a respectable establishment and I can't have you here without a ring on your finger.' She leaned forward, poking Sarah in the chest. 'Listen to me, because this is the only chance you're going to get. My Fred will marry you to give the child a name. No, don't interrupt and try to give me all that rubbish about love. Look where it's got you.' Her sneer stabbed Sarah to the heart. 'Where's the young man who did this to you? Run off, left you to manage as best you can?'

'Oh, no, he says he's sending for me just as soon as he's settled. There's no need for Fred to be forced to marry me.'

Sarah was sickened at the thought of having to share a bed with Fred Connolly.

'Oh, I know what you're thinking, but don't let your imagination run away with you. This is only a business arrangement, no bedroom nonsense. My Fred can't abide women near him, that's apart from me of course.' Her lined face creased in a parody of a flirtatious smile, the implications of which were lost on Sarah. 'You'll have your own room as before and be treated as an employee.'

'Can I have time to think about it?'

'Yes, OK. I'll give you a bit of time until tomorrow morning. If the answer's no, then you can pack up and go right away, no argument.'

All night long, Sarah weighed up the hopelessness of her situation. Her savings would not be enough to live on for very long with rent to pay and a baby to clothe and feed. Besides, where would she find somewhere to stay long-term in her condition? The only glimmer of hope would be if she could buy some time. Accepting the bizarre offer would keep a roof over her head and in the meantime, perhaps Harry would write with an address, sending for her.

'You'll have to write and get permission off your parents to marry, being as you're only seventeen, so get on and do it right away. We'll want the wedding settled by the beginning of September,' Mrs Connolly told her. 'I don't want Fred to look too big a fool.'

There was no easy way that she could explain the full extent of her predicament to her parents without causing them pain. In the end she decided to write as simply as possible, saying that she was to marry the owner of the café and needed her father's permission. That they would read between the lines went without saying, she knew. There would be no questions asked, no offer to attend the wedding, no present and no congratulations. The misery she had heaped on her loving parents would never be forgiven either by them or by herself.

Her last hope of escaping the act of desperation that this marriage represented lay in writing to Iris privately to find out if there had been any further news from Harry. The reply ripped out any last remaining hope she might still have been harbouring in her heart.

'No news,' Iris wrote. 'Bernard is very disappointed that his best man has lost touch with us. The only news is that Dolly Redmile has disappeared. She told her mam that she'd heard there were good jobs going down South and simply cleared off.'

So, that was the kindest way that Iris could let her know what everyone was guessing about Harry and Dolly. Bitter tears stung her eyes. How could Harry have been so deceitful? He had let her go on thinking that he was going to wait for her, when all the time he was practically inviting Dolly to move down to be near him, Dolly who was nothing better than a whore. Again she recalled what Lizzie had warned her about men. Once they get what they want, they'll throw you aside like a worn shoe, that's what Lizzie had said and she had been right all along.

The letter giving permission for the under-age marriage arrived, Sarah recognising her mother's handwriting on the envelope. There was nothing else, just the barest requirements of the law, no best wishes, no recriminations, no invitation to visit. A line had been drawn under that part of her life and now she would have to face the future with Fred and his mother as her only relatives.

'I've fixed up with the registrar for a nine o' clock wedding, so we'll be back in time to open up for ten,' Mrs Connolly announced. 'No need for any fancy dress or parties, seeing as Sarah won't want to advertise her shame.'

Sarah reddened, making no reply. She was indifferent to whatever arrangements Fred and his mother wished to make for this sham of a wedding. If their only concern was to keep a good cook and carer for Mrs Connolly at the cheapest possible price, she was quite content with the arrangements. All that mattered was that her child would have a name, and she would have a roof over her head until she was able to leave Fred and set up on her own.

With her usual stoicism, Sarah accepted that she had hit a low point in her life, but she was damned if it would always be like this. Her father had found her first job. Her mother had set an example of living in poverty with no hope of betterment. If it had not been for that weasel Frank Bass and Dolly Redmile she would not have been driven to leave Colethorpe for Blackpool. And now, the ultimate degradation of a shotgun wedding was to be heaped upon her.

So be it, but her experience of life so far had taught her that, in the end, she would have to look after herself. This marriage was simply one way of doing that for the time being. Ambition still burned deep in her, and neither Fred nor Harry would grind her into the ground. One day, she promised herself, one day she would rise and show every one of them, including her parents, that Sarah Mulvey would be her own woman.

If she shut out all thoughts of Harry and the wedding she dreamed of in the Catholic church in Colethorpe, she would be able to get through the mockery of this civil marriage ceremony. Sarah was relieved that the registrar had been forewarned not to invite the groom to kiss the bride. Fred's mother had thought of everything.

A brisk walk back to the café, followed by a cup of tea and it was a day like any other day.

'Of course, you can't expect wages now that you're a married woman and just helping your husband,' Mrs Connolly gloated, a triumphant grin splitting her wrinkled mouth.

'Fine by me,' Sarah smiled back at her, pulling off her overall. I'll behave like any other pregnant, married woman then, shall I? I'll just go and put my feet up. Oh, and I won't be doing any lifting, so Fred will see to you in the lav and get you to bed later.'

'Exactly what do you mean, you ungrateful girl?' the woman screamed, the mask of affability cast aside.

'What I say. If you think that you've got yourselves an unpaid cook and nurse, then think again. Don't treat me as if I'm simple. I might need help now, but so do you, so the first time my wages are missing, I'll be straight out of that door. I've got friends who'll give me a bed until I get myself straight.'

This new, defiant Sarah came as a shock to the old woman who looked as if someone had dowsed her in ice-cold water. Her eyes narrowed to black slits. 'Half-wages until you start work full-time again,' she countered.

'Sounds fair to me,' Sarah conceded, half-admiring her mother-in-law for not capitulating completely. 'My baby's due in three weeks or so, and I'll need another four before I can really pull my weight, but during that time I won't be idle. I'll do what I can to earn my half-pay.'

'You're a hard nut and no mistake,' was the muttered reply.

'I wish that me and Sid could've done more. You didn't 'ave to go and get married to Fred.' Flo shuffled uncomfortably. 'I mean, I know 'e wouldn't 'arm you, but there's something funny about 'im and 'is ma.' Flo carried on pouring out tea for her friend, at the same time struggling to find the right words to say what was on her mind. 'Look, there ain't much room in this flat, but I reckon that if mates can't 'elp one another out, then they can't call themselves mates. If you ever feel that that you can't put up with Fred and 'is ma, you've got to come straight round to us. We can always make room for you and the baby.' She grinned, disappearing into the bedroom before reappearing with a tiny garment. 'You told me I'd gotta learn 'ow to use a needle. What do you think of my knitting?'

'You've knitted this?' Sarah's eyes filled with tears. 'My baby's first present.' She hugged the pink matinée jacket to her. 'How do you know it's going to be a girl, Flo?'

'It'd better be, 'adn't it, now that I've knitted in pink.' Her loud, high-pitched scream of laughter made Sarah realise how much she had missed Flo's company the last few months.

Suddenly serious, Flo tried to put into words what had been on her mind for some weeks. 'Once you start getting pains, tell Fred to come and get me. You'll need someone to give an 'and and Fred and 'is ma won't be no bleedin' use.'

Memories of her mother's agonised groans when she was giving birth to Maureen suddenly reminded Sarah that the joy she had experienced at the rapturous moment of conception would be long forgotten as she struggled to bear the pangs of labour.

'I'd like that Flo. You're all I've got, you and Sid.'

Still clutching the pink matinée jacket, Sarah took the way back to the café past some of the big stores. One store was having a special baby equipment event, pride of place being given to a luxurious pram advertised at only eight guineas, but sold at nine and a half guineas in London, so the blurb said. On impulse, Sarah entered to find herself ignored by the superior salesman engaged in talking to a pregnant woman dressed in a specially-made maternity suit.

'But I do assure you, madam, that this price is most competitive.' He continued to hover round the woman, hoping to persuade her to buy the pram and ensure him a decent commission on sales in his Friday pay packet.

Sarah's anger mounting at the attention being paid to

the sulky woman who clearly could not afford the expensive pram, she approached the sales assistant and tapped him on the shoulder.

'Kindly wait your turn, madam, as you can see, I am engaged in selling a baby carriage to this lady.' His ugly sneer tipped the balance of Sarah's temper.

'You're wasting your time with her then, anyone can see she hasn't two pennies to rub together. I expect she wants to buy it on the never-never.'

Pulling a fistful of pound notes out of her bag, she thrust them under his nose. 'I'd come in here specially to order that pram you have on display in the window, but as you are so lacking in manners, I'll go elsewhere. And I'll see the manager before I go, just to let him know you can't recognise a genuine customer when you see one.'

Feeling decidedly perky at her newfound confidence, Sarah tossed her head and made for the door. The threat to inform the manager of his subordinate's mistake was not carried out. It might have resulted in his dismissal and jobs were not easy to come by in 1933. Whatever Harry had done to her, at least she had a roof over her head and money in the post office.

The walk round the shops after visiting Flo had proved to be more tiring than she had calculated and the thought of resting in her little attic room gave her the incentive she needed to struggle on the last few hundred yards.

Flo's warning concerning the weird behaviour of Fred and his ma was vaguely disquieting, leaving her wishing that she had asked Flo exactly what she meant. Sarah dismissed it from her mind, concluding that Flo and Sid had been spending too much time watching the latest Hollywood films such as *Dracula* starring Bela Lugosi and

Boris Karloff's *The Ghoul*, with their far-fetched, if chilling plots.

The sound of an ambulance's siren distracted her from concentrating on the effort of putting one foot after the other. Someone's had an accident, she thought, mentally praying for whomever it was who was suffering.

'Oh, my God!' Running to the café was out of the question, but she forced herself to walk more briskly than she had been doing.

The ambulance had stopped outside the front entrance, and as she drew nearer, she saw Fred bending over the form wrapped in a blanket on the stretcher.

'It's Mam, she's had a heart attack,' Fred blubbered. 'Mam, wake up, it's me, Fred, don't die Mam, please.'

Sarah was moved by the desperation in his voice; she had never seen a man crying. No matter how weary she felt, Sarah knew that Fred had forgotten all about the café and that she would have to take charge.

'Now, don't you worry, Fred, just you go with your mam to the hospital, while I see to things here.'

The anticipated word of thanks did not materialise. Instead, he turned on her a look of hatred and loathing, which was not missed by the ambulance men who were heaving the stretcher into the back of the ambulance. They exchanged surprised glances.

'You look as if you ought to go and sit yourself down, young lady,' the older of the two men advised. 'We don't want to have to come back for you.'

The last few customers were finishing off their meal and one or two were no doubt hoping to slip out in the confusion without paying. Sarah hastily went round all the tables, her practised eye assessing what food had been on the now clean plates.

The White Rose Weeps

'Right, you can pay me now that I'm here, and that includes you,' she shouted to a couple of youths that were about to sneak out of the door. 'Don't think you can put one over on me.'

Abashed, the two turned back and handed over their money. Sarah was enjoying her moment of power, the heady feeling of being in charge, knowing exactly what was going on in every corner, giving orders and being obeyed. If only this were all mine, she thought, all weariness draining away.

Once the door was locked for the night, she was overwhelmed by a feeling of hunger for the first time in weeks. There were still a few portions of plaice and chips keeping hot over the gas cooker enticing Sarah to pile a generous helping onto her plate and make herself a cup of tea to wash it all down. Perhaps she ought to keep something for Fred for when he got back from the hospital.

It was almost eleven o'clock when Sarah heard a taxi draw up outside the café. She rushed to the door to see a white-faced Fred paying the driver. There was no need to ask him how his mother was; his tear-stained cheeks and wild eyes told her.

'Get out of the way.' He pushed past her roughly. 'She's dead, Ma's dead.'

'Oh, Fred, I'm so sorry.' Sarah's pity for the strange man was genuine. There had never been any doubt in her mind that Fred's love for his mother had been the most important thing in his life. Inadequate as her response was, she was totally unprepared for the savagery of his reaction.

'Sorry? Sorry? What do you know? My ma was an angel. She even took pity on you, made me marry you.

What did I need a wife for when I'd got Ma? She was the only woman I ever needed.' He lumbered past her into his mother's room, brushing aside all Sarah's words of condolence. Long into the night, his cries of pain echoed throughout the house only ceasing as dawn broke when, exhausted by grief, he fell into a deep sleep.

Sarah rose early to start on the day's preparations. She began by dragging in a sack of potatoes from the outhouse and peeling them ready for the chip fryer. A sharp pain in her side left her doubled up and gasping for breath. Please God, not the baby, not just yet, she prayed!

By ten o'clock, Fred had not emerged from his mother's room and there was still the batter to make. He would be too busy with the funeral arrangements to have time for cooking meals, the responsibility for which would fall on her. Perhaps he might consider closing the café for the day as a sign of respect.

'Right, you can get on with the tables now. There was no need for you to do the chips, that's my job.' Fred's red-rimmed eyes showed no emotion. It might have been a day like any other day.

Sarah hesitated, not sure what reaction she would get to her suggestion that he should close up for the day.

'There's things you've got to do, Fred,' she reminded him gently.

He stared at her uncomprehending. Sarah felt a cold chill grip her stomach; the blankness of his gaze showed no glimmer of emotion, as if he had cut himself off from normal human interaction.

'The death certificate, the hospital, the funeral, Fred, you've got to see to all that.'

'Yes.' His tone was matter-of-fact. 'Perhaps I'll go out after we've done the dinners. First things first.' Whistling

The White Rose Weeps

quietly, he turned to the fryer and lit the gas. 'Just make us a cup of tea, will you? If I don't get a move on, we'll never be ready for the rush. Ma will think I'm useless, and we don't want that, do we now?'

If this was his reaction to grief, then she would have to comply with whatever he wanted until he was in a more normal state of mind. With no Mrs Connolly to help at the till, Sarah had to cope with serving meals, taking money and clearing tables. As the day wore on, it became clear that Fred's lack of comprehension that his mother was not there was going to lead to greater problems unless she did something positive.

Not only were her ankles swollen to twice their normal size, she was in agony from the stabbing pains in her back. She called Fred into the scullery.

'What's the problem?'

'The problem?' she screamed at him. 'Either you close this café now, or I will. Your mother is not here and I cannot and will not pretend that she is.'

For one dreadful second, Sarah thought that Fred would strike her. Instead, he stood staring into space, at the same time rocking himself back and forth, whimpering like a whipped puppy. Finally, his eyes focussed on Sarah.

'Yes, you're right, I've got to see to things.' With that, he put up the 'Closed' sign on the door, went to get a jacket and left without another word.

Her body was screaming out for rest, but the need to talk over with Flo and Sid her realisation that Fred was not capable of functioning without his mother, overcame the pain.

Sid was still at work, his days off not coinciding with Flo's rest days.

'Just as well, or I'd never get on with me cooking and cleaning with 'im, I mean "him", around.' Flo was trying, not too successfully, to improve her diction in the hopes of getting promotion at the hotel. 'Here, listen to me going on when you look as if you're fit to drop. Sit down while I get the kettle on.'

It all poured out, the story of her fears for Fred's state of mind, the approaching birth of her baby, whether she could stay under the same roof as Fred.

'If only I could hang on a bit longer, I've saved up a tidy sum. All I need to do is wait until I can get some job that'll have me with a baby.'

Flo pursed her lips, shaking her head. 'Not many of them about. Look, wait and see how he shapes up once the funeral's out of the way. I'll pop round tonight and tell 'im I can give a hand on me days off, but he's got to get someone in.'

Another of her loud whoops of delight echoed throughout the tiny flat. Sarah gulped her hot tea wondering what it was that Flo was planning this time.

'Of course, Doris Sibthorpe! She's just packed up at the hotel, the shift work was too much for her, but I bet she'd be glad of a part-time day job,' she explained. 'Leave Fred and her to me.'

Having been forced to go back to the hospital, register his mother's death and see the funeral directors, Fred had come to accept that his mother was indeed dead. His reasonable attitude to Flo's suggestion that Doris Sibthorpe should come in part time to help until Sarah was back on her feet, met with a half-smile and a nod.

'Send her round tomorrow.'

'First thing,' Sarah put in promptly. 'We'll want her to start right away if we're thinking of opening.' She addressed Fred directly. 'I can do your ma's job of sitting at the till and generally keeping an eye on the café, so long as this Doris can serve and clear away. I don't mind sitting down to peel the potatoes for the chips, but you'll have to do all the cooking, Fred. If Doris is OK, we can get her to do the potatoes for the next day before she goes home. While I'm laid up with the baby, the two of you will have to manage as best you can, but as I told your ma, I'm not idle and I don't intend to see this café shut down.'

Flo's astonished reaction to Sarah's proprietorial air was quickly disguised with a cough. 'Right Fred, I'll get her to come round tomorrow first thing.'

Doris turned out to be a cheerful, capable woman in her late forties, well built, with slightly greying, short wavy hair. She cast one look round the café, eyed Sarah up and down and said, 'You look as if you need a strong pair of hands to help out here, my love. I've had three of my own and it's no picnic trying to work and keep an eye on them an' all.'

'That's settled then, what do you say, Fred?'

He nodded, then beckoned Doris into the parlour to discuss wages and hours. Sarah smiled to herself at discovering how easy Fred was to manage now that his mother was dead. She would insist on keeping Doris on for good, leaving her to concentrate more on the fancy cooking and assisting Fred with the management side. If she still wept into her pillow for Harry, longing to feel his touch again, her practical nature told her that Harry was a part of her past, even though it was a beautiful part that she would never forget.

For the time being, the café and the money she could save would provide the passport for herself and her baby to build the future she was determined to achieve.

Chapter 14

Flo's reaction on seeing the tiny bundle wrapped up in the cot beside Sarah in the hospital was one of rapturous delight.

'See, good job I knitted the matinee jacket in pink. I just knew it had to be a girl. Wotcher gonna call 'er?' Flo's resolutions to improve her diction were all forgotten in the excitement of the baby's birth.

'I thought Rosie for a first name and perhaps Joanna after Mam.' She intercepted Flo's disapproving look. 'I know she's not been to see me or anything, because of Dad, but look what she's sent me.' She pulled out a pair of pink bootees. 'I expect that's all she could afford.'

'Yeah, you're right, she's your mam after all. You did right dropping her a line telling her about her little granddaughter.' Flo bent over the cot to gaze at the tiny miracle sleeping peacefully. 'Did you ever see such fair hair, just like a film star she's gonna be.'

There was a stirring from the cot and a muffled cry as the object of all the admiration opened her eyes and stared unseeing at the stranger leaning over her.

'Her eyes! Did you ever see such a colour blue?' She looked at Sarah. 'Yours are green, so she don't take after you.'

Sarah fought back the tears. 'She takes after Harry. Oh,

Flo, you've no idea how hard it is, what with the other mothers asking when my husband's going to visit and the nurses wanting to know who she takes after. How can I tell them the truth? I just want to get out of here as quick as I can.'

'Right, I'll collect you tomorrow first thing, never mind what they say. I've got some 'oliday due, and I've got nuffin' better to do than spend it with my best mate. Don't you worry, I'll tell that old sister, the one sitting at her desk looking as if she's got barbed wire in her drawers, that I'll be here at ten to fetch you.'

There were a few knowing looks exchanged between the mothers who, being respectably married, had decided that Sarah was no better than she ought to be. With no visit from her husband, it was clear that he did not exist in spite of her excuses that he was too busy with the café. As she left next day with Flo, one or two wished her good luck, reckoning that she was going to need it.

'A taxi! Have you gone completely mad, Flo?'

'Well, it's not every day I get to escort my best mate's baby home.' Flo was quite unrepentant about her extravagant gesture. 'Sid said it was time someone spoilt you a bit, so stop complaining.'

Nothing more was said as the taxi negotiated the unfamiliar parts of the town, Sarah's thoughts being firmly fixed on how Fred would react to having a baby in the house. It would be fine during the day with the motherly Doris there, but Fred would hardly appreciate being woken in the night by a squawking infant. Perhaps if she asked him, she could have a gas ring in the attic bedroom to heat the baby's bottle in the middle of the night.

His indifference was noted by Doris, who had guessed

that something was not entirely normal in the household. Although they recognised that caring for a baby was women's work, even the worst of fathers made some fuss of their offspring. Fred had not looked at Rosie once, acting as if she did not exist. Sarah's request for the gas ring was acceded to with a curt nod and a muttered suggestion as to where she could obtain one.

It was while Fred was at the fish market that Sarah finally decided that Doris ought to know the background to this unorthodox marriage. They were sitting in the café sharing a pot of tea before they opened to admit the hordes of holidaymakers.

'I know you've not asked, Doris, but I want to tell you why Fred is as he is.'

Doris did not even bother to object to Sarah's confidences. Something was very wrong and she wanted to satisfy her curiosity if she was to remain working in this strange atmosphere.

When Sarah reached the part of the narrative where she lost touch with the father of the baby, Doris leapt up from her chair.

'Come here, you poor little love.' All sympathy, she hugged Sarah to her, all the while murmuring words of consolation.

'So you see, I had to have a name for my baby, even if it is Connolly and not Wilby as it ought to be.'

Doris nodded, her worn, wrinkled cheeks creased in sympathy. 'You've had a rough old time of it, love, but if ever you need a hand, just you give me a shout and I'll come running.' She gave Sarah's hand a friendly squeeze.

One of Doris's jobs when the café was quiet, was to tidy up the downstairs rooms. The parlour was hardly ever used and apart from a little light dusting, needed no cleaning, but she had noticed the unmade bed in Fred's mother's old room, wondering why it was that he slept there in preference to with his young and beautiful bride.

'His mam said that there wouldn't be any, well, bedroom stuff, so it seemed the only way to keep a roof over my head.'

'I don't understand,' Doris persisted, 'what benefit are you to him?'

Sarah burst out laughing at the memory of his mother's disappointment when she told her that being married did not mean that she was to be an unpaid slave for Fred and his mother.

'So you see, Doris, it's a business arrangement.'

If Doris was saddened at the tragedy of a lovely young woman who, if married to the man she loved, would make a wife the envy of all men, she saved those opinions until later when she went round to her married daughter's for tea. All that love and beauty gone to waste, she thought.

The promise to Fred's mother was fresh in Sarah's mind, leading her to remind him that she would be back working four weeks after the birth of the baby and would be back on full pay.

'But we've got Doris now,' he protested.

'But we haven't got your mother and if you think I'm going to work all day down here as well as keep the place clean, think again, Fred Connolly.'

'Yes, but you'll expect time off to look after the child.'

'Right, and I'll make up that time in the evenings when Rosie's asleep. Don't you worry, I'll do the hours as fixed with your mam.'

So far she had managed to avoid dipping into her savings, which she guarded jealously for the day when she could escape from the drudgery of café work and having to live under the same roof as a man who could only be described as an emotional cripple.

The letters from Lizzie and from Iris brought her some cheer. Iris sent some baby clothes and wished that she could see little Rosie, but explained that she did not dare upset Bernard and his father. Lizzie was overcome at the idea of being an aunt, insisting that she would have to be Rosie's godmother.

'I can always plan my holiday to fit in with whatever date you arrange, so no more secrets, little sister or I'll personally inflict something really horrible on you. For example I do an absolutely thorough enema!'

Lizzie's light-hearted letter was so typical of her that Sarah did not know whether to laugh at her jokes or weep for the tragedy that had separated her from her loving family. Harry was the one who ought to bear the blame for her wretched situation, she told herself, at the same time choking back a sob at the recollection of his wide smile. Whatever he had done, no one could ever take his place in her heart.

Christening Rosie was going to present problems as her marriage to Fred had taken place in a registry office. It would have to be a proper baptism in a Catholic church for Rosie; she would not compromise on that point.

The priest at the nearest Catholic church was more liberal in his outlook than Father Kelly had been, surprising her with his jolly attitude to life.

'She's the prettiest baby I've ever seen,' he said, smiling at Sarah's obvious pride in her little daughter. 'I'd be pleased to welcome her into the family of God.'

Relieved that one problem was out of the way, Sarah now had to convince Fred that he would have to play his part. His reluctance, verging on terror, at having to enter the house of God gave Sarah the first inkling of what was buried in the depths of his tortured mind.

'I promise you won't have to do much except just stand there and say one or two words. The priest and the godparents do most of the talking. We'll come back here afterwards for tea in the parlour. You can always make the excuse that you've got to serve in the café so you needn't stay with the rest of us.'

His grudging agreement to the plans encouraged her to tell him that Lizzie would be staying overnight, leaving after breakfast on Monday morning.

Meeting Lizzie off the train brought back such poignant memories of their childhood that Sarah clung to her older sister afraid to let go.

'Come on now, let me have a good look at you and my little goddaughter to be. Let's see who she . . .'

Her vibrant voice trailed off into a gasp, as she peered into the pram, gently turning back the pink blanket to reveal the baby's face. This time it was her turn to grab hold of her sister, hugging her and stroking her red curls.

'Oh, Sarah, why didn't you let me know you were in trouble?' Her mood changing, she glowered, tossing back her brown glossy mane, wild amber glints lighting up her eyes. 'That swine Harry Wilby! What happened to him? Tell me Sarah! It was at Christmas wasn't it?'

'It's all over now, no good going back on what can't be changed. Here, bung your case on the pram and you can push.'

The threatening rain had not materialised, the black-bellied clouds having taken their load away over the Pennines.

'It's not too far to walk and we can talk before we get

back to the café,' she continued. Lizzie marvelled at her courage; this tiny girl who had once seemed to be so fragile was now possessed of the mature determination of an older, worldly-wise woman. 'Simple really, I lost touch with Harry and Fred offered to marry me and give Rosie a name — that about sums it up.'

Lizzie stopped and stared hard at her young sister. Comprehension at the sheer physical and mental torture that Sarah must have suffered, having to marry a man she did not love in order not to end up in the gutter, choked her, strangling her reaction. Finally, she managed to bend over the handlebars of the pram and continue pushing.

'If only I'd done more to help,' was her anguished response.

As Sarah had hoped, Flo and Lizzie formed an immediate bond. Lizzie gratefully recognising that Sarah had found a true friend who would stick by her.

'You're to let me know at once if anything crops up and I'm wanted,' she told Flo. 'You know what I mean, don't you?' It had not taken long for Lizzie and Flo to confide in one another their misgivings about Sarah's marriage.

'I will, no fear,' Flo assured her. 'I dunno what it is about Fred, but he's different since his ma died, sort of weird, if you know what I mean.'

Lizzie did and tackled Sarah once they had settled Rosie down and had gone to bed, sharing a big double bed as they had done when they were children.

'That's the arrangement, just business. I get a proper wage and a home for me and Rosie.'

'What if he decides he wants, you know, a proper marriage?'

'That's not the agreement,' Sarah replied coolly. 'Now,

stop mithering and let me get some sleep.'

Lizzie's visit had given Sarah's spirits a boost, forging links with her past and her family, yet it filled her with longing. If only she could persuade her mam to come and bring little Maureen to Blackpool. Lizzie had painted a graphic picture of the now three-year-old baby sister, suggesting that Sarah write and invite her.

'Blast it, girl, you're a respectable married woman with a husband, a baby and a share in a little goldmine.'

In spite of Lizzie's optimism, Sarah did not feel equal to risking a refusal, instead putting the idea to the back of her mind. Perhaps she would, one day.

Doris was very taken with Lizzie, making her tea and toast before she set off for the bus station on the Monday morning. This lively, bright young woman may not have had the striking red-gold hair and ocean-green eyes of her younger sister, but she had an indefinable magic.

'Bet you've got all the men patients eating out of your hands.'

'Yes, I keep telling them to use the plates provided, but they're mostly too daft.'

'Oh, gerraway with you,' Doris laughed. 'I bet next time we see you, you'll be married to some wealthy surgeon.'

'Me? Not likely. They're all old and have bad breath.'

The protestations came too quickly, raising suspicions in Sarah's mind that there was something going on in Lizzie's private life that she intended should remain private.

'Perhaps we can forget all this rubbish about babies and church and get on with some work.' Fred's mood one morning not long after the christening did not reflect his usual non-committal attitude to life. 'I'm beginning to get fed up.'

Sarah pondered carefully before replying. It did not suit her plans to quit the café just yet. She had the use of all the upstairs rooms since Fred had taken over his mother's old room and she had turned one bedroom into a sitting room and sewing room. Having her own flat was a luxury she could never afford and she was well aware that with Rosie just a couple of months old, lodgings and employment would be hard to find. She needed at least two more years before she could leave Fred and start a new life. Somehow, Fred would have to be humoured.

'I'm not surprised,' she agreed. 'You do nothing but work all day and half the night. At least I can go and see Flo when I want a bit of a break. Why don't you take yourself off out for a pint, play a game of darts, whatever it is men do at the pub?'

'Mmm, I'll think about it,' he said, his mood lightening. 'Yes, I'll definitely think about it.'

While he was in a more positive frame of mind Sarah decided it was the right time to tackle him about a new project for raising money.

'The parlour, it's doing nothing but gather dust. We're paying Doris to clean a room that's not being used.'

Fred made no comment on her use of 'we', merely observing that there wasn't much he could do about the empty room.

'But there is,' she insisted. 'Come and have a look.'

The room was surprisingly large and if the heavy sofa and armchairs were to be removed, they could seat at least eighteen to twenty diners.

'Don't you see, Fred, we could use it for private

functions, for business people who need a quiet room for a talk over a meal. It'd have to be booked in advance of course.'

Fred stared open-mouthed. 'I've never heard anything so daft in all my life. What would we do with the three-piece suite?'

'Right, listen to me. We'll get rid of the sofa, buy you a smaller one if you like to put in your room, and then we'll advertise. Don't forget,' she silenced him, 'that the cheap winter dinners were my idea and they worked. With Christmas coming up, there might be some small firms who would appreciate somewhere reasonable to organise a small do.'

Faced with her enthusiasm and driving ambition, Fred was forced to capitulate. Doris backed her up, seeing the continued prosperity of the café as her guarantee of future safe employment.

While Fred was at the market, Doris gave her a hand to move the heavy desk, which had belonged to Mrs Connolly and where she had kept all the accounts.

'If we shift this, we can put a small armchair for Fred along this wall.'

With the old oak desk scarcely budging an inch, Sarah realised that much of the weight was lodged in the drawers. One by one she pulled them out as Doris watched, not sure that they should be interfering in what were, after all, private papers. Sarah grunted at the effort of pulling out the bottom drawer, swearing as it jerked out, scattering the contents over the worn Axminster carpet. She ended up seated on the floor surrounded by ancient bills, some over twenty years old.

'I'll get these into some order while you go and make us a cup of tea,' Sarah giggled, wishing that she had not started on such an impossibly difficult job without Fred.

A page from a letter, tucked into one bundle of bills, fluttered onto her lap. If the writing struck her as familiar, she assumed it to be that of Mrs Connolly, and was about to stuff the page back into the bundle of bills, when the sickening truth sent wave after wave of nausea over her.

The letter was dated two days before her wedding to Fred and although it bore no address, Harry had written to tell her his joy at having found a house to rent just for the two of them.

'I can't believe that we'll be together soon in our own little house. I'm getting the keys next week, so I'll send you the address to write to.'

It went on to tell her how much he missed her and how he longed to be with her.

'Here's your tea, love,' Doris called out, almost dropping it in her horror at seeing the tiny figure slumped in a dead faint.

As Sarah slowly came to, realisation of the old woman's cruel, calculating actions tore rasping sobs from the very core of her heart. It had been planned all along that Sarah would marry her Fred and thus provide a cheap extra pair of hands in the café. The cunning old woman had feared that if Sarah had received the letter, she would have left to join Harry, foiling her carefully laid plans.

'Harry must have thought I didn't want him any more,' she wept, clinging to the kindly woman who for once could find no words of consolation. 'Now I expect he's married to someone else.'

Gradually, the mood of utter despair gave way to one of grim determination to work herself into the ground if need be in order to escape from a man who was still as firmly fixated on his dead mother as he had been when she was alive. The sooner she got her new project off the ground, the sooner she would start making more profits for herself. With that in the forefront of her mind, Sarah brushed away her tears and set to work with renewed energy on converting the parlour into a private dining room.

'The first part of the profits will have to go towards paying for the new tables and chairs.' Sarah's mouth turned down at the sight of the dingy wallpaper with its faded pattern of roses and ivy leaves. 'I'll get someone to come in and strip this off, then I'll choose a pale apricot paper and cream paint to give the room a lift and make it look bigger.'

Fred's blank, dead cod eyes remained fixed on the chips he was dropping into the fryer. His only acknowledgement was a barely perceptible nod of the head.

'I'll write round to some of the local small businesses as soon as I've costed the rent of the room, heating and food. We'll need to be competitive to start with, but believe me, once word gets round, we'll make a fortune. That'll cover the slack period before Christmas and then we can start on the cheap dinners after Christmas. No point in paying rates on unprofitable premises.'

The planning of her new project helped to fill the void in her aching heart. It was only after Rosie had been fed, bathed and put down for the night, that Sarah lay wide-eyed in the dark as the tears coursed down her cheeks. Harry came to her in her dreams, sometimes so vividly that she called out his name, only to wake to the cold cruel emptiness of her bed.

The new project turned out to be even more profitable than she had dared to dream with bookings taking up every day from the beginning of November until two days before Christmas. Although the main course was always fish, Sarah had devised some interesting puddings, both filling and attractive. With the aid of a cookery book loaned from the library, she had concocted a delicious apple dessert with a sponge base and a meringue topping. Word soon got round that the young cook at Fred's Café was a dab hand in the kitchen, with the result that Sarah felt encouraged to try out a variety of dishes from the cookbook.

Groups of anything from ten to twenty arrived full of Christmas spirit. Mostly they were young factory workers, who in spite of having very little spare cash were determined to enjoy the festive season. Doris was delighted with the extra hours she had to work, helping Sarah to make some cheap decorations with paper chains and artificial mistletoe and holly.

'The room looks absolutely beautiful,' Doris said, admiring the result of their combined efforts.

They certainly had succeeded in creating the right setting for the Christmas parties. Hearing the carefree laughter of the customers reminded Sarah all too often of the last Christmas she had spent at home – the last time she had been truly happy, safe in the knowledge that Harry loved her.

All these changes Fred endured with indifference, offering no opposition to the innovations or to Sarah's half-share in the profits. One more year of this, then I'm off, she told herself, when the long, lonely nights threatened to overwhelm her with the barrenness of her existence.

As Christmas approached, Sarah remembered that Fred had always spent time away with his mother, and wondered whether she ought to broach the subject of Christmas. She had no need to, as Fred told her that he was off on the morning of Christmas Eve to the hotel in Harrogate where he and his mother used to stay.

'Lots of her old friends will be there. You can have this place to yourself.'

His indifference to her plans did not cause Sarah any misgivings; their living under the same roof was simply a business matter. In any case, she and Rosie were to spend Christmas Day with Flo and Sid, whilst they in turn were coming to the café on Boxing Day. Sarah had rearranged the furniture in the new dining room so that they could all sit comfortably round the tiny Christmas tree, which had pride of place.

'Cor! A present from your mam and dad for Rosie. That's a turn up for the book, ain't it?'

Sarah's pleased smile was answer enough. A parcel from Iris and another from Lizzie had been added to the number under the tree. Give it time, they seemed to tell her, and it won't be long before we come to see for ourselves this little Rosie. Perhaps time would erode the feelings of blame attached to Sarah for getting pregnant and having to find a man to marry her. No doubt chins would still wag as the harpies in Colethorpe did their mental arithmetic, concluding that Sarah Mulvey was no better than that Frank Bass and Dolly Redmile whom she had made such a fuss about.

Cradling her beautiful Rosie, not yet four months old, Sarah longed to show her off to the rest of the family. She could just picture her mam cuddling her and exclaiming over her lovely fair curls and eyes the blue of a tropical sea.

New Year's Eve, a momentous event at home, with

coal and salt being brought over the threshold by a dark-haired man, went by with no comment from Fred, who, since his return from Harrogate, had appeared to be more morose and detached from reality than before.

'I'm going round to see Flo and Sid. They said you could come as well if you like.'

A shake of the head was his response to the invitation.

Sarah wrapped Rosie up in the new shawl sent by Iris and tucked the sleeping baby up against the cold winter flurries of snow just beginning to cover the pavement with a dusting of white.

She had barely gone out of the café when she remembered that she had left the back door key on the kitchen table and Fred would not want to be disturbed once he had retired to his room. Fortunately, the door was still unlocked, but the key was not on the table where she thought she had left it. Damn! I'd better ask Fred where it is, she thought, mentally fearing his reaction.

The door to his room was ajar, but a sixth sense stopped Sarah from going in. The sound of a woman's voice singing a lullaby gave Sarah an eerie feeling that she ought not to look any further, but curiosity overcame her scruples and she peered through the crack in the door.

With a sense of shock she realised that the figure dancing around in front of the dressing table mirror was not old Mrs Connolly, but Fred dressed up in his mother's clothes. As he danced, he picked up his skirts like a young girl at her first ball, swishing them to and fro.

'I'm a pretty girl, aren't I, Mummy? Please say I am.'

Sarah registered with horror the scarlet lipstick painted in two broad stripes across his mouth giving him the appearance of a clown. So this was what he did when locked away in his room.

The White Rose Weeps

Her problem now was to get out without his having seen her, but he was so much wrapped up in his fantasy world that she had no difficulty in locating the key, which had fallen on the floor, and creeping out of the back door.

''E's going off 'is bleedin' rocker!' was Flo's reaction.

Sid was equally concerned at the prospect of Sarah's return to the café, begging her to move in with them.

Sarah was touched at her friends' worries about her situation, refusing to accept their offer.

'He's odd, I'll grant you that, but he's never laid a finger on me and he lets me get away with all sorts of ideas, never contradicts or complains. Don't you worry yourselves.'

Her brave speech concealed her terror at facing what was to her an unknown phenomenon. Why should he want to dress up in his mother's clothes? Only kids did that kind of thing. That's it, she told herself, he's just a kid at heart, convincing herself that he was perfectly harmless.

Chapter 15

The cheap fish and chip dinners still pulling in the customers after Christmas meant that Sarah was kept busy. Even though the work was hard and not as profitable as her pre-Christmas venture had been, the money was mounting up in her account.

She had not forgotten Fred's aberrant behaviour, dressing up in his mother's clothes, and continued to watch him carefully for traces of lipstick.

'See, he's all right, I told you so,' she assured Flo on one of her friend's regular after-work visits. 'He just gets on with his job and I get on with mine. I reckon I can put up with anything so long as the money comes rolling in.'

Flo frowned at this new tone of hardness creeping into Sarah's outlook. She and Sid were so happy in their marriage, notwithstanding their small wages and the tiny flat which they had made their home, that she grieved for Sarah deprived of a normal, loving relationship.

'Money ain't everything,' she dared to suggest.

'Well it is for me,' came the vehement retort. Sarah's pretty face was contorted into one of hate and resentment. 'I've spent most of my life with damn all money and a load of hard work and what have I got for it? A man who loves me? No! And I don't suppose I ever will. It'd have to be somebody bloody good before I make a fool of myself again.' Seeing the hurt in Flo's big eyes, she relented, running over to hug her friend. 'Oh, I know you and Sid are happy, but things don't seem to work out for me.'

Flo took hold of her in her arms, rocking her gently back and forward as if Sarah were a baby.

'One day, one day, just you wait and see. At least you got your little nipper.' A pink glow spread across her cheeks. 'Sid and me keep trying, but it ain't 'appened yet, so count yourself lucky.'

It was now Sarah's turn to comfort her friend and assure her that it would happen one day. 'Perhaps you're trying too hard,' she said with a tiny smile dimpling the corners of her mouth.

'You cheeky monkey!' She stood up, still laughing. 'Come on, I'll give you a hand to clear away these tea things and bath Rosie before I go.'

Long after Flo had gone, Sarah pondered on what her future would hold. When would the day come when she could be independent? Perhaps one more good summer season would give her bank balance a boost.

With May over and Blackpool bracing itself for the next influx of summer visitors, Sarah suggested to Fred that they ought to open up the dining room previously used for the special Christmas dinners.

His bulging eyes filled with tears, but Sarah quickly realised that these were tears of fury not of grief. Although not huge, he had a solid physique with muscular arms and now with his sleeves rolled up, as he advanced towards her, she knew real terror.

'I don't want strangers in there again,' he shouted. 'Next thing you'll want Ma's room as well, you'll want to go poking about in there as well.'

By now, Sarah was pressed up against the kitchen door with Fred leaning against her, breathing down into her face. Just as suddenly, his anger subsided, giving way to a leering smile. His hand cupped her breast, as he bent to kiss her.

'No! Get away from me!' She twisted her body, ducking under his arm to escape into the hallway. 'You promised!' she yelled, sobbing in her fear of what he had in mind.

Two strong arms grabbed hers, pinning her against the door in the hall. Shouting at him to leave her alone, Sarah turned her head to bite his bare left arm. With a cry of pain, he let go of her, hanging his head in shame and bursting into tears.

Astounded at this sudden change, Sarah stopped at the foot of the stairs and turned to face him.

Huge tearing sobs were shaking his chest. One arm over his eyes, he leant against the wall.

'I'm sorry Ma, I'm sorry Ma, I won't do it again, I promise.'

In spite of her fear, Sarah crept towards him, but he was entirely oblivious to her presence, continuing to sob and beg for forgiveness.

Later when she tried to raise the subject of his violence, he stared at her blankly. 'Don't be silly, Sarah. As if I would do anything to hurt you. Don't talk like that.'

When the summer rush began in earnest, Rosie was coming up to nine months and displaying an inquisitive nature. She was now crawling, eager to seek out areas previously beyond her reach.

On one occasion, Sarah was horrified to find her being bounced up and down on a customer's knee and being fed Fred's thick chips.

'What a little beauty she is,' the middle-aged woman cooed, delighted at the friendly response of the baby.

Sarah cuddled Rosie, now reluctantly separated from the culinary treat. It was true; Rosie was becoming even prettier with each passing day. Her fair curls were thicker, tumbling down over her forehead and giving her an impish air. The brilliant blue eyes twinkled, reminding Sarah's aching heart of the way Harry used to tease her, his eyes sparkling with concealed laughter. She consoled herself with the thought that wherever Harry might be, there was still a precious part of him with her day and night.

After that incident, Sarah worried about having Rosie around while they were working. The only alternative was to leave her in her cot upstairs, but that was too far away for her to hear if Rosie cried. It was Doris who came up with the ideal solution.

'We're not using the parlour, so why don't you rig up a playpen and put her in there? We could take it in turns to pop in and keep an eye on her. Fred won't mind, will you Fred?' she called out.

Too late, fearing another outburst from Fred, Sarah tried to warn her that it was out of bounds at the moment.

'Yes, if you like,' was his expressionless reply, being more concerned with the consistency of the batter he was mixing in a huge metal bucket.

With the aid of a wooden clothes horse and some strong string to tie the makeshift playpen to the dining table in the parlour, Sarah reckoned that she could restrain her little daughter during working hours whilst at the same time having her near enough to supervise.

It was almost two o'clock and most of the diners had gone with just a few stragglers coming for a late meal. Fred and Doris being able to cope, Sarah returned to the task of constructing the playpen.

'If you don't want to lose Rosie, you'd better come quick.' Doris's gruff laugh echoed through the hall as she called out to Sarah.

Impatient at having to leave what she was doing, Sarah rushed into the café, calling for Rosie.

'Wait till I catch you, I'll . . .' Her voice trailed away at the sight of Rosie sitting on the man's knee.

The two fair heads were close together, the man holding Rosie as if he would never let her go. The look of reproach as he turned to face her tore at her heart. She clutched the counter, desperately holding on to it as the scene blurred in front of her. Voices drifted into the distance.

Gradually tables, chairs and people began to take shape as Doris's solid arms enfolded her. 'Come on, love, sit down,' she heard her say.

'I'm OK, don't worry,' Sarah managed to whisper. Right up to the very moment when she had been forced to marry Fred, she had dreamed of the day when Harry would walk through the door and take her away. As the waves of shock faded, the harsh anger on the man's face brought her back to reality.

'So, you're married then? Done all right for yourself I see. Pity you hadn't the decency to let me know.' His voice was low. No one in the café was aware of the fury and desperation in his words.

He shook his head, almost as if unable to believe what was so obviously true. He threw a scornful look towards the kitchen, before turning to face Sarah again. 'The

The White Rose Weeps

money was it? You always did have ideas. I thought you loved me more than that.'

Sarah shook her head. How could she make him understand? 'Harry, Harry, I had to . . . I . . .'

A woman at the table nearest to Harry nudged her husband. 'She's crying, poor kid. That big bloke looks like trouble.' She gave a disapproving cluck. 'You'd think her husband'd chuck him out.'

'I've a damn good mind to take her with me, she's mine!' Harry roared. 'You had no right.' He was holding Rosie so tightly, that for one moment, Sarah thought that he was going to carry out his threat.

'No!' she screamed, leaping forward to grab the hem of Rosie's dress.

'Time to go, now, right now,' the woman with him muttered.

'Shut up!' Harry turned on the woman. 'What do you know about it?'

His anger subsided giving way to one of concern for Sarah's distress. 'I'm sorry, I didn't mean . . .' He kissed the top of Rosie's head before reluctantly placing her in Sarah's outstretched arms.

Until then, Sarah had taken no notice of his companion. Although it had been a while since she had seen Dolly Redmile, Sarah recognised the plump, rouged face with its sharp, spiteful expression.

'So, you're nicely settled. Glad to see you're married.' Dolly might have added, 'So Harry's mine,' it was written all over the sneering droop of her cheeks. 'Come on Harry, time to get back. I'm sure that Sarah is too busy to stand around talking.'

At that moment, Fred came out of the kitchen, pausing at the sight of Sarah's distress and the stranger who looked so like little Rosie. He gave no indication that he had any inkling of the scene that had just taken place. 'Can you come a minute, Sarah? I need a hand.'

'Better do as you're told,' Dolly smirked catching hold of Harry's hand.

His angry response was to wrench his hand free and place it on Sarah's shoulder. Before Sarah could protest, he bent to kiss her cheek, whispering in her ear,

'She's mine, how could you?'

Knowing that she would never see him again, Sarah watched in an agony of despair as he pushed open the door with a savage heave of his massive shoulders.

Doris broke the suspense with her usual kindly offer to make a cup of tea and suggest that they all had a break and a bite to eat.

Still holding Rosie, Sarah dragged herself up the stairs to her room. Within minutes, Rosie was asleep, unaware that she had been held for the first time in her life by her father and that her mother was sick at heart at hearing his reproaches. So he had married Dolly after all, or else why would they have come to Blackpool together? Her head thumping with the beginnings of a migraine, she stumbled downstairs. The smell of the frying threatened to bring on an attack of nausea, something she had not suffered since before Rosie's birth. At least she would never have to go through that again.

'Come on, love,' Doris coaxed her, 'just have a bite of bread and butter. It'll help stay you.'

'You sound just like my mam.' Uttering those words brought back so many memories of her childhood in Colethorpe with a loving family, that the tears flowed, staining her pale cheeks.

Finally, her grief finding no further solace in weeping,

Sarah forced herself to drink the tea and eat the sandwiches prepared by Doris.

'See you tomorrow, love. Don't let things get you down too much.'

The trite advice was echoed by Fred once Doris had departed.

'You made the choice and you work here, so I don't want to keep hearing about what you could have done. We're paying Doris to work, not keep minding you.'

Nothing more was said. It was just as Sarah was feeding Rosie before putting her down in her cot that she heard the door slam, signalling Fred's departure for the pub, something he had taken to doing with increasing regularity. More than once she had heard him struggling to find the keyhole to open the door, followed by sounds of unsteady footsteps as he made his way to his room.

Sleep did not come quickly, with thoughts of Harry burning into her mind, filling her body with an aching longing to have him here in the bed beside her. It was two in the morning before exhaustion finally claimed her, calming her tortured mind. She did not hear the sound of her bedroom door being opened, nor did she feel the man getting into bed beside her.

By the time he had grabbed hold of both of her hands with one of his, she was powerless to prevent him from forcing himself upon her. The smell of drink, nauseating though it was, was bearable compared with what followed. Her flimsy nightdress was ripped and thrown to one side, brutal hands tore at her body until finally the sickening episode was at an end and Fred sank back with a grunt of satisfaction, muttering his mother's name.

Terrified to move, Sarah lay there until Fred left. Trembling with cold and fear, she dragged herself out of bed, put on the light and surveyed her body in the mirror. Pale bruises were beginning to show on her breasts and stomach. Please God, don't let me get pregnant. She fell on her knees, muttering prayers learnt in childhood. 'Holy Mary, Mother of God,' she repeated in quiet desperation.

Fred, the kind man who had given her a roof over her head, who had offered to marry her to give her child a name and a home, had turned into a monster since his mother's death. The chill thought struck her that perhaps he was always deranged, his mother's presence keeping manifestations of his disorder in rein.

The most pressing need at this moment was to get away before he could do any more damage to her or to her precious Rosie. She began to pull clothes out of the cupboards and drawers in a frantic desire to be doing something positive about her situation. The pile of underwear, half a dozen pairs of knickers carefully mended, two slips and some stockings, did not take up much space. Apart from the outfit she had bought for Rosie's christening, the new blue dress and matching jacket, which had never been worn again, her wardrobe consisted of three dark navy skirts and a few plain blouses and jumpers for working in. One pair of sensible black shoes, the high-heeled courts which matched her best outfit, and a pair of well-worn bedroom slippers lay on the floor beside the bed.

Pushing the heap to one side to make room for her aching body, she sank back on the bed beside her possessions. A plan of action was what was required, not lying down full of self-pity. Her savings account stood at one hundred pounds, just enough to rent a room for a few months and keep herself and Rosie until she could find work. And then what? Who would care for Rosie while she worked? Even worse, who was to say that any future job would be any better? She could just as easily be considered fair game for any man in the house, seeing her as a lonely, defenceless woman with no man to look out for her.

I'm not going to give in, not yet, just when I've got so far, she decided. The most practical solution for the time being would be to remain in the café until she could find the kind of live-in post where Rosie would be accepted. A careful eye on Fred plus a strong bolt on her door would not cover all eventualities, but he was not likely to harm her while Doris was about in the daytime. If she retired to her room with Rosie soon after tea, she should be relatively safe.

It was the first meeting with Fred in the morning that would decide how soon she would have to move out.

'You're late this morning,' he grumbled. 'Oh, well, never mind,' he relented, 'just get a heave on with the tables and then you'd better sort out the counter.' He gave a grin in an attempt to appear amiable, and went back into the kitchen.

Sarah stood still, her heart thumping, as she steeled herself to tackle him. Angry that he was treating her as if his savage attack had not taken place, she pursued him into the kitchen.

'So, what the hell do you think you're playing at, Fred Connolly?'

He put down the bag of flour he was about to tip into the bucket he used for mixing the batter and stared at her, puzzled? 'Playing at? What do you mean?' The blank eyes showed no comprehension of the reason for her anger.

'Last night, don't you remember or were you too drunk?'

'Sorry if I made too much noise and disturbed you. I must have fallen over when I came in. I did have a fair skinful at the pub.' He hung his head like a naughty boy caught stealing sweets. 'Won't do it again, promise.'

Sarah opened her mouth to confront him with the details of his unwarranted sexual attack, but a sixth sense told her that she would be better advised not to try to make him remember something which he had pushed to the depths of his strange, tortured mind.

Doris's arrival gave her the opportunity to slip out to buy a bolt for her bedroom door. Fitting it took a matter of minutes, giving her a feeling of security.

'You look tired, love,' Doris commented. 'Why don't you put your feet up for half and hour while I clear the tables and wash the floor. Fred'll be shutting up soon and then we can all have a nice cup of tea.'

'No, I want to check the till first, make sure we've got a decent float for tomorrow.'

'I dunno,' Doris sighed, 'right little businesswoman you are. You ought to be a landlady.' She laughed at her little joke, pleased that Sarah had responded with a cheerful smile.

Oh, yes, Sarah thought, one day I'm going to show the lot of them.

The next few days Sarah watched Fred's every move, monitoring his goings and comings, and carefully driving home the bolt on her bedroom door. She had brought Rosie's cot into the room with her so that she too would be safe. A length of rope looped through two hooks that she had screwed into the skirting board was stretched across the top of the stairs each night before she retired.

The White Rose Weeps

If Fred ventured upstairs whilst blind drunk, he would trip, not only giving her warning, but with a bit of luck, knocking himself unconscious.

The usual pattern had been re-established. Doris left at six, Sarah fed Rosie and had her own tea, while Fred finished in the kitchen, preferring to eat alone later. This gave Sarah the chance to go upstairs, set up the trap, and bolt herself into her room.

Gradually the strain began to result in sleepless nights, as she listened fearfully for his step on the stairs, until one night when he had not returned from his drinking session at the pub, she went downstairs to make herself a cup of tea to take back to bed with her. Engrossed in watching the kettle, willing it to hurry up and boil, she did not notice the sound of the key being turned in the lock.

'Worra you doing in Ma's kitchen?' Bloodshot eyes, wild and angry glared at Sarah.

Feeling that it would be better to calm him down rather than have a confrontation, Sarah forced herself to stop shaking and offered him a cup of tea.

'Tea? What do I want with tea?' He lunged at her, punching her full on the mouth, knocking the teapot out of her hand.

Rather than escape upstairs to where Rosie lay sleeping peacefully, Sarah ran into the old parlour.

'Come here, you. Don't you go into Ma's parlour.' Stumbling and swearing, he pursued her into the new dining room, kicking over chairs and tables.

Sarah's pleas for him to try to think what he was doing met with no response. He went on to pick up furniture, hurling it across the room, finally seizing the terrified girl by the hair and savagely pushing her against the fireguard.

His momentum caught him off balance, and as Sarah managed to wriggle out of his grasp, he fell heavily against the fireguard. Seeing her chance to escape, Sarah fled upstairs, rapidly bolting the door.

Fred's reaction next day was what she had half-anticipated; total amnesia regarding what he had done while he was drunk. Doris raised a quizzical eyebrow on seeing the chaos in the parlour, saying nothing as she began to set the room straight. Apart from the broken fireguard, only one chair had been damaged, a flimsy light wooden chair of a cheap, easily replaceable design.

A week went by with Fred remaining in every night, staying alone in his room. Sarah still remained wary, retiring early to the sanctuary of her own bedroom. For some days now, she had been checking the calendar. There was no denying it; she had to acknowledge that the recent swelling of her breasts and early morning nausea were all symptoms of pregnancy, the result of being raped by Fred the night he had come into her bedroom.

The thought of giving birth to a child who might inherit Fred's madness horrified her. Clutching Rosie tightly, gazing into the beautiful innocence of her blue eyes, Sarah wept. How could she have been so naive as to think that she could cope on her own with Fred Connolly?

She was astounded one Friday late in October, when Fred announced his intention of going on a pub outing for the day.

'There's plenty of fish and chips ready. Doris can see to the tables.'

Sarah tried to conceal her delight at the prospect of having the café to herself for the day, planning to ask Flo round for an hour in the evening. She was the only person she could turn to.

'Been avoiding your old mate, 'ave you?'

There was no hiding the truth from Flo, who, before long, had extricated every last detail of Sarah's anguish. Her distress at being kept ignorant of the extent of Fred's mental deterioration led her to give Sarah a severe ticking-off.

'You mean you think he's got you pregnant? Oh, Sarah, what am I gonna do with you, girl?' She stared into space, struggling to put into words what she feared might offend Sarah. 'You remember that girl I told you about, the one at the hotel? Now don't jump down me throat, but, well, you don't 'ave to 'ave it if you don't want.'

'You know I don't want this child,' Sarah wailed, 'but what you're suggesting is all wrong, I know it is.'

A harsher tone crept into Flo's voice. 'I know bloody well that you've 'ad enough wrong done to you, girl, and it's time you put yourself first.'

Silence hung between them for a while, each wondering if the other were right. Finally Sarah sighed deeply. 'You're right. How soon can you fix this up? I just want to get it over with quickly.'

Flo leaned over and grasped Sarah's hand in hers. 'You won't regret it, 'cos I won't let you. If no one else can look after you, you've got to let me and Sid take over.' Her look of concern was replaced by her usual wide grin. 'Of course, why didn't I think of it before?'

Her plan was that she and Sid would find a bigger place to rent, Sarah could work the opposite shifts in the hotel to Flo, and between them they could care for little Rosie. Sarah's rent and contribution to the household would mean that they'd all be better off.

'We could afford a proper 'ouse with a garden for the

kids to play in.' Her eyes widened with excitement at the prospect of being with her friend.

Sarah was touched at this offer. 'But what about Sid? He's not going to want me there in your house with Rosie as well.'

'He might think it a bloomin' good idea to 'ave the two of us there bein' as there's gonna be two nippers to look after.'

'Flo! You mean you and Sid? Oh, Flo, you should have said, instead of listening to me and all my misery.' Sarah jumped up and down in her excitement, weeping, then kissing Flo. 'Even better, I'll be able to go out to work while you stay at home with Rosie and your baby.' She clapped her hands at the prospect of escaping from Fred and having a proper home for herself and Rosie.

A loud wail from upstairs alerted the two girls to the fact that their excited laughter had woken Rosie.

'Go on, bring 'er down, let me see 'er,' Flo begged.

Rubbing her eyes with a podgy finger, Rosie gradually woke up, treating them to one of her dazzling smiles, the blue of her eyes like the promise of a summer's day.

'Give 'er to me. Oh, Sarah, do you think mine'll be as pretty as your Rosie?'

'Not if it's a boy, I hope,' Sarah teased, knowing that Sid's plain, homely face and Flo's strong features could not combine to produce a child with Rosie's promise of beauty.

'Perhaps it'll be a boy and then if they get married, we'll be related.' Flo's screech of laughter at her own joke started Sarah off into a fit of giggles.

Sitting in the parlour in front of the fire, the two chatted and planned. Rosie, now wide awake, played contentedly on the floor and for the first time in a long

The White Rose Weeps

while, Sarah felt almost happy.

It was gone nine before Flo leapt to her feet, declaring that Sid would be out looking for her if she didn't soon make a move. Sarah, too, realised that she would have to get herself and Rosie back into her bedroom with the door firmly bolted, before Fred returned from his drinking session.

Closing the café door behind Flo, she gathered up the teacups and plates to take into the kitchen to wash. If previous evenings were anything to go by, she had at least an hour, probably more to get herself and Rosie ready for bed, but she wasn't taking chances.

She went into the kitchen to boil some water to wash up the crockery, clattering about in her haste to be upstairs. At first the whistling kettle drowned out the sounds of Rosie's cries, and even when she was aware, Sarah called out, 'Won't be long, darling, Mammy's getting your milk and then you'll soon be going to bye-byes.'

A frisson of terror seized her when she realised that the cries were real screams of pain, which suddenly stopped.

'My God! No!'

Sarah and Flo had let Rosie crawl around the floor as they chatted, intermittently picking her up for a cuddle, and Sarah had left her to play with her favourite teddy bear while she did the washing up. In their excitement, Sarah had forgotten the fireguard, broken by Fred in his violent drunken attack on her. It lay tipped on its side.

The baby, now silent, lay partly in the dying fire, the stench of burning flesh and singed hair filling the room.

Chapter 16

The white-coated doctors whispered, one of the younger ones casting sympathetic glances in Sarah's direction. So far, no one had told her the extent of Rosie's injuries. Please don't let her be scarred for life, not my beautiful little girl, she prayed, her eyes not leaving the conferring doctors.

The nightmare of finding Rosie unconscious in the hearth with no one at hand to help, had sent her running out into the street, where a policeman patrolling on foot had found her screaming for help. His first summing up of the situation was that the lovely young woman with the red hair was the victim of a domestic dispute, and had wondered if it might be politic to ignore her. Once he had managed to calm her down, however, he was able to make some sense out of the phrases Sarah was gasping out in her terror.

His first sight of the injured baby now wrapped in a clean white shawl, was one he would never forget to his dying day, he told his colleagues later. 'I knew she couldn't live, not with her little body all burnt like it was.'

Three short blasts on his whistle and more policemen arrived, one delegated to phone for an ambulance.

'You'd have thought they'd have a phone here,' one of them complained, desperate to see the tiny child taken to

The White Rose Weeps

hospital and away from its mother who, cradling the poor burnt body, was frantically trying to revive her baby. 'Please don't die, Rosie. Please don't die, you're all I have in the world. Please God, don't let her hurt.'

The arrival of the ambulance was a relief not only to Sarah but also to the policemen whose elementary medical skills were of no use to the child.

Sitting on the cold, hard chair in the hospital corridor, Sarah went over and over in her mind every second of that frantic half-hour, the moment she had first heard Rosie's screams, then calling for the policeman to help her, and the pitying looks of the ambulancemen.' It was all my fault,' she kept muttering to herself, castigating herself for leaving Rosie in the room with the broken fireguard.

'Come this way, Mrs Connolly,' said a voice with a southern Irish lilt which sounded so much like her mam, that Sarah was disorientated for a second.

The strong arm of the nurse supported her, taking her to a side ward, where two doctors stood beside Rosie's cot.

'My baby!' Sarah screamed, rushing at the cot to pick up Rosie.

'We're so sorry, Mrs Connolly,' one of the doctors said, gently restraining her, 'we did everything we could, but your little girl's burns were too extensive. I promise you, we didn't let her suffer.'

'I'll wake up in a minute, won't I? This is just a bad dream, isn't it?' she begged the nurse, who was standing close by Sarah.

'No, my dear, your little girl is dead.'

Her beautiful little Rosie with her fair curls and laughing blue eyes, the mirror image of her darling

Harry. At least Harry saw her and held her just once, and now no one will hold her again.

'Sleep in the arms of Jesus, my little darling,' she whispered, making the sign of the cross on Rosie's forehead, before speaking calmly to the nurse. 'I have to find my husband,' she said, 'then I'll be back. There'll be things to see to.'

Nurse O'Mahoney had seen grief manifested in so many different forms that she did not think that she could ever be disconcerted, but Sarah's sudden change of mood, from disbelieving dismay to a calm discussion of practical matters, worried her. Still, the young woman had a husband and no doubt he would help her through this terrible time.

What Sarah had in mind was clear. If it had not been for Fred's wild drunken attack on her in the new dining room, destroying furniture and rendering the fireguard useless, Rosie would be alive. If it had not been for his mad obsession with his dead mother, Rosie would be tucked up safely in her cot, sleeping peacefully.

Leaving the hospital grounds, she walked for what seemed like hours, but what was in reality only thirty minutes or so. The wind had not yet died down, making the air bitterly cold, cutting through the thin jacket she had pulled on quickly when the ambulance had arrived. Looking straight ahead, seeing nothing but Fred's face, she walked with a determination that caused the few people who crossed her path to leap out of her way.

She passed the café. No lights on, so Fred must still be at the pub, getting drunk and ready for another violent outburst. So much the better, she would be ready for him this time. By now, all sensation had left her icy fingers. A damp, cold breeze from the sea had begun to spring up, as she approached the Duck and Feathers.

A slight detour to pick up a piece of driftwood lying on the beach and she was almost at her destination. The familiar figure staggering out of the door must have been the last to leave. She heard the publican closing the door behind Fred and warning him to watch what he was doing.

Sarah hung back ready to follow him, but he had seen her and lunged towards her, snarling like a rabid dog.

This was not what she had intended. How stupid she had been to imagine that she would win in a physical battle, even if she were armed with a wooden bar!

In her fear, she ran down to the sands, where she felt he might have difficulty in running, thus allowing her to escape. She was wrong. Even above the roar of the wind and the swooshing of the waves as they broke on the shoreline, she could hear Fred's manic threats to kill her. At this late hour, the Promenade was deserted with no possibility of help. Her thin cries were lost on the breeze.

Sobbing and gulping for air as she struggled to evade Fred's murderous grasp, she stumbled and fell against a groyne. Fred hurled himself at her, missing her, but striking his head against the wooden structure. Thankful for the brief respite, she ran up the beach and back to the promenade.

Flo, she had to see Flo and tell her about Rosie. Fred could get himself back to his café and rot for all she cared, she would never set foot there again.

Her hair wet and straggling over her face, her jacket soaked and clinging to her thin body, Sarah was barely recognisable as she stood on the dark doorstep begging Flo and Sid to let her in.

Great wrenching sobs shook her frame so that her words were unintelligible even to Flo, who struggled to calm her distraught friend.

'Where's Rosie, what is it, Sarah? Come on, tell me.'

Sarah who was now rambling and barely coherent, muttered, 'With Jesus. Mary's looking after her. Hospital.'

Flo and Sid stared at one another in horror.

'Quick, Sid, round to the caff and see if you can get any sense out of Fred, that's if 'e isn't still down the pub. If 'e ain't back, phone the 'ospital and be quick about it.'

Rocking her friend back and forth in her arms, Flo managed to soothe her, gradually extracting the story of the broken fireguard and finding Rosie in the hearth. Flo could not accept that the lovely, smiling child she had held in her arms only a few short hours previously was dead. She must be in hospital and perhaps very poorly. As soon as Sid got back she would know the truth.

'What about Fred? Is he at the hospital?'

Sarah frowned, then began to shiver. 'I don't know where he is. He tried to kill me, Flo.' Recollecting the terror she had felt as he pursued her along the beach, her voice rose. 'He tried to kill me, Flo.'

'Now hush, my girl. I'm gonna get you a drop of brandy. Sid keeps some by in case, and then I'm gonna undress you and put you to bed with a nice hot water bottle.'

The brandy had the effect of putting Sarah into a drugged sleep with her friend watching over her, dreading Sid's return. Something had to be very wrong for Sarah to be in such a state.

It was midnight when Sid returned, his sad expression telling Flo that what Sarah had said, was true. Little Rosie had been burnt to death, he had been told when he rang the hospital, pretending to be a relative. He had called at the café, but it was in total darkness and he could get no reply.

'Drunken sod's sleeping off the booze.' Flo had seen enough of her father to know how deeply a drunkard could sleep.

Sid slept on the couch, while Flo held Sarah close to her, dreading the moment when Sarah would awake to the recollection of the night's horrendous events.

At six next morning, Flo felt Sarah stir, gradually returning to consciousness, her eyes opening, then closing. She began to moan and sob miserably, 'No, no, not my Rosie, please not my Rosie.'

All that Flo could do was to hold her until the sobbing ceased. Once she had calmed, she was able to drink the hot, sweet tea Sid had brought into the bedroom.

'I've got to go back to the café and get my things and I've got to go up to the hospital and see about . . .'

'You're doing nothing without me and Sid, so just you get yourself up and washed and we'll go round to the caff, but not before you've 'ad a bite of breakfast, just a bit of toast, that's all.'

As Sid had seen the night before, there was no sign of life at the café. With Flo and Sid to support her, Sarah summoned up enough courage to unlock the back door and venture into the kitchen, calling Fred's name. Now that he was sober, he would have forgotten his drunken pursuit and threats of the night before.

Getting no reply, Sarah knocked on his bedroom door. She knocked louder, finally pushing open the door and walking into the room.

'He's not here.' She clasped her hand to her mouth, remembering where he had fallen by the groyne. In her desperation to escape, she had not looked back to see if he had stood up again, assuming that he had seen her run away and had returned to the café as usual.

Flo and Sid were puzzled. 'Where the bleedin' hell can 'e be?' Flo said.

A loud hammering at the front door of the café made them jump. Flo peered out to see two policemen standing outside.

''Alf a mo', just coming,' she called.

'Are you Mrs Connolly?' one of them asked.

'What is it?' Sarah had just emerged from Fred's room, having searched under the bed to see if perhaps he had rolled there during the night.

There then followed some questions about when she had last seen him.

'Just before he went off to the pub. I know that for certain, 'cos I was here with Mrs Connolly until nine and he hadn't returned then.' Sensing there was something seriously amiss, Flo had pulled out all the stops to speak correctly to the policemen.

One of them had heard the story from his colleague about the child being burnt to death in the fire, and was quick to connect Sarah with the child.

Flo explained how soon after she had left the café and gone back home, Sarah had arrived to break the news of the baby's death.

'Come straight from the hospital to us, she did, 'cos she knew 'er 'usband wouldn't be back. He never cared about 'er or the baby.' In her efforts to assure the policemen that Sarah had not set eyes on her husband since soon after tea, Flo's diction suffered.

A warning hand silenced her, and Sarah was asked to sit down.

'The body of a man has been found on the beach not too far from here. He appears to have fallen down and drowned when the tide came in. One of the men who found him was the landlord of the Duck and Feathers and recognised him as being Mr Connolly. Apparently, your husband was very drunk, and the last that was seen of him was as he left the pub. Seems as if he fell down drunk. Looks as if he hit his head on the breakwater, probably knocked him out, that's if the drink didn't, and then he got caught by the tide.'

A few murmured condolences and something about identifying the body and they had gone, shaking their heads at the double tragedy that had overtaken the lovely young wife and mother.

'It's my fault, I should have stopped to see if he was all right,' Sarah moaned.

Flo sat her down firmly. 'Now, you're the religious one, not me, but 'aven't I 'eard you say something about God's will be done and all that?'

Sarah was in no state to enter into a theological argument concerning God's will and free will, but let Flo and Sid take over, tidying Fred's room, clearing out the fireplace in the old parlour and putting up a sign on the door to say that the café was closed for a week due to a double family bereavement.

Doris's arrival at that point meant that explanations had to be given. Shocked and distressed as she was, her innate common sense told her that practical help was what was needed, not more murmured words of pity.

'I know where Fred got his fish from down the market. I'll go and get one of the men to come and pick up what's in the kitchen, perhaps just leave a few pieces for meals for a day or two.'

Sarah was scarcely aware of what was going on around her, wrapped up in a kind of numbed state of grief, half-knowing that she should be doing something, but unable to summon up enough strength to stand up. Rosie's cot and clothes had to be packed up as did Fred's — she would do that later, perhaps. Staring into space, hearing voices that seemed to come from far away, she sat for most of the morning, overwhelmed by the blackest of all moods, a total and utter sense of loss.

Flo prepared a lunch of steamed fish with a parsley sauce, hoping to tempt her into eating something to give her the strength to battle with the coming challenges.

'Come on, luv, just try a bit and then we'll go off up the 'ospital. It's gotta be done, you know.'

Slowly and deliberately, Sarah ate a few mouthfuls, putting her knife and fork down on the plate between each one. Finally, she took a deep breath and stood up to face Flo and Sid.

'Right, I've made up my mind, so listen. There'll be no double funeral, got it? Fred will be buried in the Congregational cemetery where his mother is. The business people can attend if they wish. That will be the day before my baby is laid to rest in the Catholic churchyard.'

Flo and Sid nodded, not sure what to make of this sudden change in Sarah.

'My family will all come the next day and will stay, so we'll need to make up beds in Fred's old room, and the two bedrooms upstairs. I'll sleep in the little attic room. That way, Mam and Dad, Lizzie, Bernard and Iris can all stay as long as they like. I'll get started on them once I've been to the hospital and seen the undertakers, I'll put an announcement in the paper straight after.'

Sid, desperately trying to be his usual dependable self, suggested that he might telephone the priest in Colethorpe, so that the news could be broken gently to Sarah's parents.

'No, while I'm out I'll send telegrams to all my family to let them know all the details and . . .' The brave facade disintegrated. 'Harry, Harry,' she wept, 'our baby's dead and I don't even know where you are.' Her head on her hands, she wept, huge heaving sobs tearing her tiny frame.

Before the day was out, everything had been settled as Sarah had planned.

'Now, you two have got jobs to go to,' she told Flo and Sid, firmly ushering them out of the door, 'and I don't want you losing your jobs on my account. I've got Doris here to help out, so between us we'll get everything done.'

'Not so bleedin' fast, young Sarah,' Flo protested. 'You needn't think I'm letting you sleep 'ere all by yourself. I'll be round later, so you'd better let me in, right?'

Fred's funeral was a very quiet, low-key ceremony, attended by some of his cronies from the Duck and Feathers and a few of the fish and vegetable merchants with whom he had traded. The latter, no doubt anxious to remain on good terms with the widow. Whispers as to whether she would carry on the business reminded her that she would soon have to make a decision. It was as Fred's coffin was being lowered into the grave that she made up her mind. I've bloody well earned that café, she told herself, and I'm not about to throw away a perfectly good business.

She felt no obligation to invite anyone back to the

café, sensing that those present would have accepted more out of curiosity than respect for the dead man. They've paid their respects and I've given Fred a Christian burial and that's that.

The taxi she had ordered to pick up the family at the bus station pulled up outside the café soon after three o' clock.

'Mam! Dad!' Sarah dashed outside the minute it drew to a halt. 'You've come,' she cried.

'Of course, love.' Her mam held her close, stroking her hair. 'My poor little girl,' she whispered.

Sarah stood back eying her dad. Had he forgiven her?

'Come here then.' Not one to show his emotions – that was for womenfolk – her father gathered her in his arms. 'There now, love.'

Little Maureen, now nearly four, danced around excitedly. Sarah ruffled the curls of her baby sister. 'You don't remember me, do you? I'm your big sister.' Maureen smiled shyly and hung behind her mother's skirts.

'Iris! Bernard!' Once again, Sarah was comforted by loving arms enfolding her.

'And here's our little Joe.' Bernard held up his son, now two-and-a-half years old.

'Quick, come on in, it's freezing out here,' Sarah urged. She went to pay the taxi driver, but was restrained by her mother with a warning look.

'Let your dad see to that.'

It was an emotional reunion, all past rifts forgiven in the grief intermingled with guilt for allowing the bitterness to continue for so long.

Sarah showed them the latest photographs of herself and Rosie, taken on the beach. Sarah had built a huge sandcastle and the photographer had managed to catch Rosie's mischievous expression as she raised her little spade intent on knocking it down.

Iris, always the considerate one, took Sarah to one side.

'This must be hard for you, I mean, having little Joe and Maureen, what with …'

Sarah's response was to embrace her, 'Of course not,' she assured her. 'Just look at them playing together. If anything they've made me feel better.' It was true; their presence was a healing one.

Ordinary practical decisions, such as what the children would have to eat and where they would sleep, took away some of the bitter memories for a brief while. Sarah could not bring herself to sit in the room where Rosie had died, so Bernard and her dad brought out the armchairs from Fred's room and turned the café into a big sitting room.

There was a sudden hush as Sarah stood up to peer out of the window. 'Here's Flo now. She's offered to help keep an eye on the children, so we can all go down to the undertakers and say a last goodbye to my Rosie.' Her fierce gaze did not brook any refusals or excuses, each one silently rising to fetch coats and follow her out of the door.

It did not need saying. An innocent seventeen-year-old, she had been cast adrift amongst strangers to cope alone with the birth of her baby, at a time when she should have expected to be cared for and protected. Instead, she had had to settle for the protection of a poor, demented man and his scheming mother. They all had some responsibility for Rosie's death and they would have to bear some of the pain with her.

Her father began to mutter something about the

children not knowing Flo and that perhaps, after all, he and her mother ought to stay.

'Everyone — and I mean everyone,' she told him, daring him to deny her request.

Iris chipped in with, 'Don't you worry, we're all going.'

A quiet, weeping procession filed past the baby's tiny coffin, only her father pausing to frown, then wipe away a tear.

Sarah bent to kiss the cold forehead still partly covered by a bandage hiding the dreadful injuries. She gently touching a golden curl, before turning to summon her family away.

Lizzie had been unable to leave London early, arriving later that night, looking older and more tired than Sarah had ever seen her. In spite of her own grief, she sensed that there must be a reason, other than the grinding drudgery of her nursing job, which had robbed her sister's complexion and hair of its lustre, and her whole being of its animal vitality. Clinging to Sarah, her tears seemed to be more for herself than for Rosie's death.

Sarah had arranged for Doris to look after Maureen and Joe while their parents left for the church. There were to be no absentees at this funeral.

All through the Mass, Sarah gazed fixedly at the tiny coffin covered in white roses, her only stipulation concerning flowers. *My pure little white rose.* Sarah stored up every detail in her mind, determined that one day she would find Harry and tell him how their darling girl had left this world.

Crowding round the open grave, she listened to the priest saying the final words of committal.

'Here, Sarah,' Iris whispered, handing Sarah a box full of moist earth. 'To throw on her coffin, from Yorkshire.'

This plain girl's compassion was noted by everyone, each in turn taking a little of the precious soil to sprinkle on the coffin.

It was her father who faced her with the question that had been on everyone's mind. 'So what will you do now? If you want to come home, you know you've . . .'

'Oh, Dad, can't you see that I've made my life here now? There's nothing more I'd love to do than be with you and Mam and our Maureen, but things have changed and I've got this business to run. I'm not sure yet quite how I'll start off, but it's all mine, every brick and every stone, not a penny owing.'

All eyes were on her. Little Sarah Mulvey, who used to work at the Co-op, and then got sent away into service, got into trouble and had to get married before she brought disgrace on her family. Sarah, still only eighteen years old and the owner of a big café in Blackpool. Oh, yes, Sarah guessed rightly what was going through their minds.

'And there's a tidy sum in the bank coming to me,' she threw in.

Her mother kissed her, managing to utter a husky, 'You deserve everything good, luv.'

'Besides, you'll all be able to come here and spend your holidays and it won't cost you a penny.'

Flo recognised the slightly hysterical tone creeping into Sarah's voice and cut in with a suggestion that it was time for a nice cup of tea. 'Dunno about you lot, but I'm gasping.'

It had taken more than a little effort on the part of Sarah's parents to understand this brash, lively Cockney girl, but Joanna Mulvey recognised that the ungainly exterior contained a heart as big as Yorkshire, and that while she was around, her Sarah would never lack a real friend.

The farewells next day were sad, Sarah insisting on seeing them off at the bus station. Joanne, unable to stem the tears and holding her daughter to her, desperately begged her forgiveness for not insisting that she came home when she knew she was pregnant.

'Oh, Mam, I couldn't have done that, you know I couldn't.'

Lizzie had been able to take some of her holiday entitlement in order to be with her younger sister for a few days. Besides, she was in great need of a rest, and with Sarah having closed the café for the week, she still had the weekend to lie late in bed and try to relax.

'There's nothing wrong, honest, just some rat of a junior doctor, who's gone off and married the daughter of 'Mummy's best friend'. And she's got pots of money, not like poor little me.'

'Well, he wasn't worth having then, if money's all that he's interested in.'

Lizzie gave a lopsided grin. 'Quite the little comforter, when it's me that should be comforting you.' She looked round the café, a thoughtful frown creasing her broad forehead. 'Has it occurred to you, that you're quite a catch now? You'll have to be careful, Sarah.'

'And has it occurred to you, that it's once bitten twice shy as far as I'm concerned? No bastard of a man is going to get within a mile of me and my money, not if he wants to keep his manhood intact.'

Her vehemence astonished Lizzie. This new Sarah was made of steel, no doubt about that. The best thing Lizzie could do would be to take a leaf out of her book and sod the junior doctor!

A more cheerful Lizzie having departed on the Monday morning, Sarah put a notice in the café window to announce that she would be opening as usual for business on Friday. She would need until then to negotiate terms with the local suppliers. She knew to the nearest farthing what Fred had paid for fish, fat and potatoes, so the first trader who tried to put up the charges would be soon told that she was taking her business elsewhere. There'd be no second chances given. Once the word got round, she would be respected as a formidable businesswoman.

One further important matter had to be cleared following the letter she had received from a local firm of solicitors requesting her attendance at their offices. On presenting herself to a thin grey-haired spinster who presided over a noisy typewriter in the outer office, she was invited to take a seat. From time to time, the secretary peered over her spectacles to stare at this girl, who didn't look old enough to be a widow inheriting what she knew to be a tidy sum.

In fact, it was more than just a tidy sum. The elderly Mr Farnby, who had handled the business arrangements of Mrs Connolly and then those of her son, took a deep breath, rustling a pile of yellowing documents on the desk in front of him.

'You see, Mrs Connolly was left very comfortable on the death of her husband, who, with a little advice from this firm, invested very wisely.' He preened, dusting down his grey striped trousers.

'I don't know anything about Mrs Connolly's husband, she never mentioned him.'

'Well, that's as maybe, of course.' He gave a little

cough, signalling he was about to continue.

'How much money are we talking about?'

The direct question caught him off balance. He had been looking forward to making a little drama out of announcing the sum that was to come to Fred Connolly's widow, and now she was spoiling his innocent fun.

'Fifteen thousand pounds,' he said, enunciating each word deliberately and slowly.

He was not to be robbed of his fun after all. It was warm in the office, the heat heightening the colour in Sarah's cheeks, but this news stripped her of all colour as, with her breath coming in short gasps, she swayed in her chair, gripping the arms tightly.

'Miss Smith, quick, the sal volatile, and a cup of tea I think,' Mr Farnby called. That'll teach that young miss not to be so sure of herself, he thought.

Chapter 17

'You're sure it was just the shock of hearing that you'd come into Fred's money and the caff that made you pass out?'

Flo's piercing gaze reminded Sarah that she had been putting to the back of her mind one horrific event, the memory of which had had to be suppressed.

'You can't put it off any longer.' A look of surprise passed over her face. 'Surely you're not, I mean, 'cos of losing Rosie and that.'

'God! No!' Faced with the suggestion that a child fathered by Fred could in any way make up for her precious Rosie, Sarah shrank back in her chair. 'You said you could fix it up soon, so how soon?'

'Well, I did speak to that woman I told you about at the hotel only yesterday and if you like, I could take you there in the morning. You'll need to rest after, so you'd better close up for a day or two.'

'Why?'

'Blimey Sarah, surely you don't need me to tell you that.'

'I don't want to lose good paying customers.' Sarah frowned. 'Still, so long as it's just for the day. If I have it done Monday morning, and then have a rest, I can open as usual on Tuesday.'

The White Rose Weeps

This cold detachment, so unlike Sarah's usual sensitive reactions, frightened Flo. It was as if Sarah had distanced herself from her decision, almost as if it were happening to someone else.

Sarah's cool attitude deserted her the minute she and Flo got off the bus and began to walk. This was certainly not the prosperous side of town. Run-down terraced houses with peeling paintwork and dingy net curtains, front doors opening on to the street and the sound of a squalling infant accompanied by obscene shouts from the unfortunate baby's father, made Sarah wish she had not agreed to this illegal abortion.

'Not far now,' Flo assured her, gripping her arm firmly. 'No need to panic. It's above the chemist's shop just down here.'

The thin man with the straggly moustache who was serving behind the counter gave a furtive glance towards the doorway to check that no one was listening. 'Mrs Cartwright, oh yes, a friend of mine.' Another furtive glance and then he seized hold of Sarah. 'Quick, no time to hang about, my girl.' He turned to Flo. 'And when you've done, there's a way out the back. Don't come through the shop, understood?'

Sarah found herself at the foot of a steep staircase.

'Go on,' Flo urged in a stage whisper, as she followed behind.

A man appeared at a doorway at the top of the stairs. He beckoned to Sarah inviting her to enter the tiny room.

'I thought it was going to be a nurse.' The thought of this fat, greasy man touching her made her feel as if she wanted to vomit over the threadbare carpet.

'Don't be scared. I'm a doctor, just had a little problem

with the police. Always ready to help unfortunate girls like you.' The smile was replaced by a cold hostile glare. 'Got the money, have you?' The room was filled with the whisky fumes from his breath.

Sarah handed over the twenty pounds and approached the bed. Dried bloodstains remaining from the butchering of the previous woman's unborn baby at the hands of this man decided her. 'No! No! I can't murder my baby!'

Firm hands gripped her. 'Oh no you don't. You've made the booking. You needn't think you're wasting my time.'

Sarah turned to Flo. 'Tell him he can keep the money.' As the man showed no signs of releasing his hold, Sarah bit him hard on the arm, forcing him to let go.

Flo gave him an extra shove before following Sarah out of the room. 'It's OK, Sarah, wait for me!'

It was too late. Blinded by tears and sick with guilt at the thought that she had been about to murder an innocent unborn child, Sarah flung open the door and ran down the stairs. A loose stair rod and a hole in the carpet were all that was needed to cause her to lose her balance and be hurled forward.

When she woke up in hospital, a middle-aged woman doctor was standing by her bed. Getting no reaction from the patient when told that she had lost her baby, she concluded that Sarah was like so many of her pregnant women patients who inflicted dreadful injuries on themselves rather than be forced to have an unwanted child. She cursed the fact that there was so little that she could do.

'I don't know if it is any consolation to you, but I have to tell you that the baby was not formed properly and you would not have carried it to full term in any case.' She gave a weary smile. 'Perhaps next time.'

'There won't be a next time, believe me,' Sarah promised. 'And don't look at me like that either,' she warned the surprised doctor. 'How soon can I get out of here?'

'I've told your friend to come first thing tomorrow morning.' She gave Sarah a gentle push on to the pillow. 'Just rest for now.' She paused. 'And don't look at me like that either, young lady,' she retaliated.

Sarah lay in a drugged sleep until five o' clock the following morning when the clatter of hospital routine — voices, trays, trolleys, the rustle of starched aprons — reminded her of where she was. The first thing she remembered was the words of the doctor. She would never have borne the child. Perhaps God had been merciful this time, taking pity on her.

Apart from a slight feeling of dizziness when she tried to sit up the first time, Sarah found that she could get herself to the bathroom and back with no problems. Once Flo got her home, she would open the café and start up in business once more.

'It's my business and I mean to make it the biggest in Blackpool,' she told a surprised Flo who arrived at ten on the dot to take Sarah home. 'I love you, Flo, and I don't know what I'd have done without you, but don't you see, I've got to build up some sort of a life for myself. I've got to stand on my own two feet.' Seeing the dismay on Flo's face, she added. 'In any case, it's my turn to help you.' She stroked her friend's cheek. 'Dear Flo, don't forget your baby. I want to be its very favourite aunt.'

'You soppy 'aporth,' Flo grinned, taking Sarah's arm. 'Come on then, back to the caff.'

Although Flo and Sid begged Sarah to spend Christmas with them, Sarah refused. 'No, it's time to start rebuilding bridges. I've promised Mam and Dad that I'd go back and spend it with them.' She realised that she had not said she was going home. So many things had happened to her that she felt that she had no 'home', in spite of her wealth and owning her own business.

Going to Colethorpe for Christmas no longer filled Sarah with the delicious sensation of being wrapped up in the warmth of a loving family. To begin with, her baby sister Maureen viewed Sarah more as an intruder making demands on her mother, thus depriving her of the attention to which, as an only child now, she was accustomed. It caused Sarah pain, having to convince this little mirror image of herself, that she was her big sister. Buying Maureen's affection with expensive presents was looked on with frowning disapproval by her mother and father. An unspoken guilt hung in the air between them and Sarah, the death of Rosie having reproached them with too many memories of what their duty should have been towards their daughter. Instead of giving her the love and help she needed, they had let pride and religious narrow-mindedness prevent them from helping.

There was also a wariness of this daughter, widowed and apparently the owner of a thriving business. With her comparative affluence and indefinable air of being in command, the lines defining the roles of parents and child had become blurred, almost to the extent of the parents deferring to their daughter. Advice had to be offered tentatively, as they were discovering. Sarah realised that they were bewildered, no one in the family ever having been in the position of power money brings. Even so, hearing some of her plans, her father had to voice his misgivings.

'Go easy, love, I know you think you're doing fine at the minute, but you're not used to running a business, are you? Hang on to your pennies, you never know when you might need them.'

Sarah had debated within herself the problem of how much she should tell people about the fortune she had inherited, but had finally decided that her parents should be told, with the proviso that no one else was to know.

On Christmas Eve, her mother was struggling with the last minute preparations for Christmas morning, filling Maureen's stocking and wrapping one or two small presents to put on the Christmas tree bought by Sarah on Barnsley market.

'Sit down, Mam, and you Dad.'

Jim had been about to go out to the club for a drink, and sighed impatiently. 'Out with it then, lass.'

'It's about money.'

Joanna and Jim exchanged worried glances. Both were thinking that perhaps the café wasn't to be Sarah's after all, and that she was in some sort of trouble again.

'What is it love, are you all right? You know we'd do whatever we could to help you. You've only got to ask.'

Her Mam's concern soon turned to indignation at Sarah's amused reaction.

Sarah put an arm round Joanna's shoulder. 'I know you would, both of you, but it's me that should be helping you.'

The amount of money she had been left as Fred's widow was more than a miner could earn in a lifetime, and was almost beyond the comprehension of her parents.

A long silence hung between them, with Sarah wondering why her father's still handsome face wore such an expression of ineffable sadness.

'You're a wealthy woman.' His eyes travelled round the shabby kitchen, taking in the worn lino and rag matting, the best he had been able to provide for his wife and children after years of toiling in dark and danger.

Sarah read rightly his sensation of despair at a lifetime of failure, a stabbing pity making her go over to him and take hold of his arm.

'I didn't work for that money, remember, it was chance.'

'Or the will of God,' her mother said quietly, 'to help you in some way for your terrible loss.'

Her words released the emotions all three had been struggling to suppress ever since Sarah's arrival. She and Sarah, both weeping, clung together, comforting one another's pain.

'Come on you daft buggers, this is no way to spend Christmas Eve.' Sarah's father hugged her briefly. 'I expect you're trying to think of a way to tell us your next plans, is that it?'

Sarah waited till they were all sitting down again, her parents promising not to say a word until she had finished.

Sarah's first announcement that she intended selling the café and buying her own boarding house, which she would run with the help of Sid and Flo, did not come as a shock. They had often wondered how Sarah had managed to survive, living in the café, seeing every day the room where her Rosie had died.

'I've already got someone interested, and I've seen the ideal place I want to buy. It's got an empty house next door, which I'm going to buy as well.'

Jim's promise not to interrupt was broken at this last

piece of news. 'Steady on, lass.'

He was silenced by Sarah's reminder that he wasn't to interrupt.

'Now, you and Mam,' she said, aware of their unease. 'I've had one or two ideas, but it's up to you.' She took a deep breath. 'I don't know if you'd like to come and live in Blackpool and help me run my new boarding house.' She paused, but there was no reaction, both Jim and Joanna too stunned at the speed of events. 'On the other hand, if you don't want to leave Colethorpe, you could always come and spend your holidays with me. Maureen would love the seaside and the lovely sand.'

Her pause gave the signal that some reaction was expected.

'By, you certainly have been doing some thinking, Sarah. Your mam and me'll have to have a long talk.'

'If you decide to stay . . .' Sarah recognised the look of relief on her dad's face, 'there's no reason why you have to stay in this house. I've taken a walk up the Cadworth road and they're building some really nice houses, all with proper bathrooms and gardens, just the thing for Mam and our Maureen.'

'Hold on, lass, your mam and me are quite happy where we are.'

Joanna's stricken look stirred Sarah into retaliating angrily. 'Oh, yes, it's fine for you, just opposite the club and with nothing to do round the house and no garden for you to look after, but what about Mam? No one else outside mining would put up with no proper lavatory and a back yard covered in coal dust. Do miners' families always have to live worse than any other working-class families? Has working down the pit taken away all your pride? Have the mine owners got you so beat?' Sarah's green eyes were flashing the colours of a sea whipped up in a storm. Fingers running through her hair ruffled her red curls, recently carefully cut and combed back in a sophisticated style.

Joanna closed her eyes waiting for Jim's black fury, born of desperation and frustration, to descend on them all, and for Jim to shout abuse, closing his ears to further persuasion, before leaving for the club. What was Sarah thinking of, upsetting her father like this and just before Christmas?

Jim shook his head, then smiled ruefully at his wife.

'I remember a long time ago, it was late at night as I recall, meeting a beautiful Irish girl with long red hair and green eyes. When I appeared, she was berating her poor brother, who had fallen off his bike and was lying in the ditch begging for help. You know she left him there half-dying of cold while she told me exactly what she thought of me. Called me a traitor, she did.'

'I did not!' Joanna protested.

'Oh, yes, you did. And you know, no one's ever argued with me since that day.' He smiled again. 'And our Sarah puts me so much in mind of her mam and the way she told me a few home truths that night.'

'Well?' Sarah asked, not sure where all this was leading.

He answered quietly. 'I'd never have wished for you to have got money by marrying the wrong man, Sarah. I never meant that to happen.'

Sarah recognised and finally understood with a maturity which surprised herself, that each generation acts according to patterns of behaviour inculcated from birth, and is bound by the moral codes of the community. She had been wrong to lay any blame on her parents for having any part in Rosie's death. They had loved her and still did, just as deeply as she had loved Rosie.

Jim went on, 'But it has happened and we can't turn the clock back, no matter how much we wish we could, and no one wishes that more than me and your mam, so if you want to set us up in a decent house, it's no more than your mam deserves.'

Christmas morning arrived and her mam had never looked happier. At last the New Year would bring some hope and joy. In her excitement, Sarah forgot to put the potatoes on to cook, something that would previously have met with recriminations and sulks. Instead, her father joined in the laughter and actually set to, offering to give a hand.

Bernard and Iris arrived at one o'clock for dinner with their son, Joe, and were greeted with the news of the house that Sarah was buying for them.

Iris's eyes filled with tears. 'You're a lovely girl, so kind, you didn't deserve . . .' She wiped her eyes, forced herself to smile and to wish everyone a happy Christmas, while Jim poured out drinks for everyone.

In spite of telling herself that she would not ask either Bernard or Iris whether they had had any news of Harry, she raised the subject as she and Iris were putting young Joe down for an afternoon sleep in her old bedroom. Iris stroked her little son's hair, gently murmuring the while until his breathing became more even, and he fell into a contented sleep.

'You don't have to tell me why you want to know, Sarah. Harry Wilby could never have denied Rosie, if he'd wanted to. The truth is we haven't heard a word from him. He seems to have disappeared into thin air, ever since he left to go South for work.'

'I saw him once, he came to the café with Dolly Redmile. He held Rosie for a minute.' Choked and unable to say any more, Sarah struggled to stem the tears threatening to well over.

'Hush, love, we don't know anything about Dolly Redmile. There were rumours that she'd found work down South and that she was getting married, but we never got to hear who her husband was.' Iris stroked Sarah's hair just as she had stroked little Joe's dark brown curls. 'Try not to live too much in the past, you've got to plan for the future, make the best. Me and Bernard, well, we're not well off, but we're happy. You will be one day, you're still not nineteen, remember, and look what you've got.'

'I'd live in a hovel if I had Harry and Rosie, you know that, don't you Iris?'

Iris nodded, blinking back her tears. 'I know, I know. Come on, let's go downstairs and face the others.'

'I can't wait to write to Patrick and tell him,' Joanna was saying to Bernard. She paused, the lines on the bridge of her nose more pronounced, as she frowned. 'I wonder what he's doing this Christmas. His last letter was full of some foreign girl he'd met, talked about her being really beautiful.'

'You'll get a shock if he marries a foreign girl,' Bernard laughed.

'Well, it's no more than I did,' Jim laughed.

There had been no visit from Lizzie, who had written to say she would be on duty in the wards over Christmas and, in any case, had very little holiday allowance outstanding.

Leaving Colethorpe was not the wrench it used to be.

The White Rose Weeps

This time her parents were smiling, eyes full of anticipation of their move. Before she said goodbye to them, she had paid a visit to the bank and one to the builder and her mother was free to choose her new home.

Sarah opted to walk from the bus station instead of taking the tram. In spite of the cold wind blowing off the wintry sea, she felt warm and even exhilarated. Now that her plans had been voiced to her parents, more ideas began to take shape in her mind. Filling her lungs with the frosty air, far from encouraging her to get indoors as quickly as possible, gave her the heady sensation of being reborn. The plan to buy her own boarding house was as yet in the embryo stage and would need careful costing. She was not about to fritter her wealth on wasteful schemes.

It was true, she had seen a boarding house for sale with an empty house next door. On the face of it, it seemed to be a profitable proposition, But why was it up for sale and why was the house next door empty? Some surreptitious investigations would need to be made. Good old Doris! What she did not know, her daughter and son-in-law would find out.

Sarah relished her fight against the fierce buffeting of the wind, finding it heightened her sense of adventure and optimism for the future. No more saving every penny. She was now her own mistress ready to achieve her ambition of running her very own establishment.

Memories of Rosewood and Mrs Scatesburn's ideas on what constituted adequate menus, reminded her that, although she could produce more exciting meals than that lady, she needed some professional training. The local college probably ran evening classes, which she could attend after closing time at the café.

Time for change, she thought, turning her steps away from the seafront and further into the towncentre. Flo and Sid would be at home, having decided to stay put at Christmas. Sarah guessed rightly that they would not have much cash to spare for luxuries with Flo having to give up her work at the hotel and the baby due in March.

It did not take long, therefore, to read what they were trying to hide behind their cheerful New Year greeting.

'They've put the rent up and now Sid's been told they're all on 'alf time until the season picks up again. And 'ere's me at home doing bugger all to 'elp.' Suddenly contrite, she went on, 'Just 'ark at me, after all you've 'ad to go through. You must think I'm a right misery guts.'

'You're right, that's exactly what you are,' Sarah said, squeezing her friend's hand affectionately, 'and there's me needing someone just to sit at the till and take in the money. Surely a great, idle lump like you could manage that easily.'

It was a joy to hear Flo's screeching laugh echo through the flat, and see Sid smiling at his wife's change of mood.

'I don't know about you Sid, but I could do with a man's hand as well. There are some of the heavier lifting jobs I can't manage on my own. If you could do me two or three days, you know, fit them in when you're not needed at the hotel, I'd be really grateful, otherwise it means taking on someone else, and I don't fancy letting strangers work in my café.'

A spirit of friendly co-operation made the café a warm, welcoming place with everyone prepared to pull their weight, even Flo whose increasing size was making it difficult for her to sit behind the till. As March approached, Sarah suggested that Flo and Sid should come and live at the café.

'There's two bedrooms upstairs as well as Fred's old room. Think of the rent you'd save with so much to get for this nipper of yours.' She silenced Flo's protests. 'I'm perfectly happy enough in my little attic room for the time being. Besides, you shouldn't be on your own when the baby starts to make a move. We can call an ambulance and I could come with you to the hospital.'

Flo's look of relief was a joy to see. 'Blimey, girl, you're a pure godsend, you really are. You've no idea 'ow much I've been dreadin' bein' on me own.'

'That's settled then,' Sarah told her, delighted to have company in the café at night. Although she kept it to herself, she dreaded the nights alone, hearing Rosie's screams in her wild imagination. One night, the screams had seemed so real, that she had started down the stairs, shouting, 'Mammy's coming, don't cry.' It wasn't until she was half-way down, that the finality of Rosie's death overwhelmed her, and she was left sobbing, clad only in her thin nightdress on the cold, draughty staircase.

There still remained the problem of who could sit at the till and keep an eye on the takings, once Flo was out of action.

'My Cynthia could come and give a hand, while her little 'uns are at school,' Doris offered. 'She's pretty quick at figures.'

Sarah was apprehensive about allowing someone else to handle money, but as Flo pointed out on the quiet, she'd be around as well and could help Sarah count up at the end of the day. It would not take long to spot if there were shortfalls.

Cynthia reminded Sarah of Doris with her short

dumpy figure and no nonsense attitude. It soon became obvious that she had a sharp mind. With her at the till, there was no surreptitious sneaking of buns while no one was looking, because Cynthia could smell out dishonesty at a hundred paces. With the profits still mounting, Sarah kept adding to her already substantial bank balance. She had taken Fred's elderly solicitor's advice to hire an accountant.

Although still in his early thirties, John Hume had built up a thriving practice, his success founded on his brilliant mathematical mind and his knowledge of every inch of his hometown. His delight when this gorgeous young woman walked into his office was written all over his round, cheerful face. He was flattered that she should seek his advice about diversifying by buying a boarding house. The one she had seen had been on the books of an estate agent well known to John Hume.

'Leave it with me and I'll see what I can find out for you.' His eager expression disconcerted Sarah. She would have been stupid not to admit that she noticed how men's heads turned as they passed her in the street. Comments from the young men who came into the café were just loud enough for her to hear, no doubt hoping for some response. Her determination to ignore all men was just as strong as it had been when she swore to Lizzie that no bastard man was going to be part of her life ever again.

His advice that she ought to have a man with her when she went to view property or enter into negotiations, and that he would be only too pleased to be of assistance, was met with a cool acknowledgement.

'That's most kind, but I do have someone to escort me.'

But who, she asked herself later? Perhaps Sid would do at a pinch, so long as he did not actually have to say anything. Her natural instinct for business led her to take the next step and divulge her plans to Flo and Sid.

'You mean you're giving up the caff?'

'Yes, now listen first and then you can tell me what you really think, right?'

Sarah went into a detailed description of her plans.

'I'll need help in the kitchen, someone to wait on tables, good workers to clean out the rooms and see to the laundry, and a reliable man to generally keep the place looking smart. Of course, it would be perfect if I had a husband-and-wife team who would be prepared to live in. There'd be a nice flat for them and a garden for their children, that's if they had any of course.'

Flo's grin had been getting wider and wider, as it dawned on her what Sarah was offering.

'Well, don't ask me to wait on tables, I'm too bleedin' clumsy, I'd drop everything.' Suddenly serious, she went on, 'You know that's just the kind of job me and Sid could do with, don't you? You're not just takin' pity, honest?'

'You'd be the ones taking pity on me,' Sarah insisted. 'It's all going to be new to me remember, and I need you and Sid to be with me every step of the way. Who else would tell me where I'm going wrong? Who else would I want to be with me?'

Sarah knew that Sid was not the sharpest knife in the drawer, as her mother would have said, but he was thorough, and there were few odd jobs that he could not tackle. The paintwork, the gardens and upkeep of the property would be safe in his hands, and would spare her the expense of calling in outside tradesmen. As for Flo, she had plenty of experience of hotel work. With someone to help with the rough work, Flo could organise the beds and the laundry plus giving Sarah a hand in the kitchen. With Flo in charge, the bedrooms would be immaculate and would meet with the demands of the most exacting guest. Doris would be useful waiting on tables and keeping the dining room looking clean and inviting.

All that needed to be done was to go and see John Hume again to find out if he had any more information on her proposed purchase.

'Good news, Mrs Connolly. Nothing sinister at all about the sale of the boarding house. The couple who ran it just decided that it was getting too much for them and had bought the house next door to retire into. Unfortunately, the lady died suddenly, so her husband has gone to live with his son in Morecambe.'

'That still doesn't answer my question. Why haven't either one of the properties sold?'

'The old boy is a bit difficult and wants to sell them as one lot, which is really out of the question, but neither his son nor his estate agent can convince him.'

Time for decisions. 'I'll go and take a look with my gentleman friend and if, and I mean if, the properties are suitable, I shall expect a reduced price for buying the two.'

'Leave it with me,' he beamed.

Sarah guessed rightly that between John Hume and his friend, there would be a nice commission for them to share if they could push the sale through.

She might have added, 'Right, but understand, Mr Hume, that I'm not paying over the odds for a property that will probably need a great deal of refurbishment. So you and your mate had better think again, if you're looking for a pushover.' She did not need to say it in so many words, John Hume reading them in the cold green of her eyes.

Doris had also done some ferreting and had come up with a friend who had known the previous owners of the boarding house. It appeared John Hume and the estate agent had not been trying to unload an unsaleable pair of properties, after all.

The front gate was rusty, opening on to a crazy paving path through whose cracks grass and weeds had found a foothold. The dark front door was solid enough but needed a new letterbox, the old one now dull and spotted with rust. Sarah's first sight of the interior of the Glendale Private Hotel filled her with gloom. Whoever had done the decorating, and that must have been many years ago, was singularly lacking in inspiration, deducing that a good coat of dark brown paint and varnish would not need replacing for generations to come.

In the end, Sarah had succumbed to John Hume's insistence that she needed a professional man with her, but reminded him that if his advice proved to be wrong, she would sack him, and furthermore she would let all her business associates know why.

'I'm damn glad she didn't accept my invitation to dinner and the theatre,' he told his friend later. 'She'd make an iceberg feel warm in comparison. Pity any man that ends up with her.'

It was true. She had closed her heart to any future relationship; all the love she had ever known was enclosed in a capsule in her heart reserved for her Rosie and Harry. There was no room, and never would be, for any other man.

The dining room was surprisingly large with enough

space to sit twenty guests, possibly more if the tiny parlour adjoining it were incorporated. With a larger sitting room at the back, this small one could easily go into the dining room.

'Oh, my God!' she exclaimed when she saw the kitchen. 'This is something out of the ark.' A wooden draining board, bent and cracked, must have harboured enough germs to kill off the guests in their dozens. Cupboard doors were hanging off their hinges and everywhere exuded a stale, indefinable odour.

'Just needs a bit of tidying up, that's all, Mrs Connolly.'

'Shut up, I don't pay you to talk nonsense,' was her terse reply.

Similar to Rosewood, there were two flights of stairs, one leading from the front door and one from the kitchen. At least the stairs and banisters seemed solid enough. The bedrooms, six in all, were arranged on two floors with a bathroom on each. There were also two tiny attic bedrooms.

'I'll need more living space than this. I must have ten bedrooms for the guests, and living space for my live-in staff.'

The empty house next door would provide what she needed for herself as well as Sid, Flo and the expected baby. A careful examination of the house showed that the downstairs was large enough to give Flo and Sid a spacious flat with two bedrooms, a sitting room and a bathroom. The kitchen would not have to be shared if she could have a tiny one installed in an attic flat. At first glance, she reckoned that the attic flat would provide her with sufficient room to install a bathroom. An alcove off the room designated as her living room would provide some basic cooking facilities.

The first floor provided three more double bedrooms for guests. It would be a simple job to knock down part of the wall between the properties. This would give nine bedrooms of any size, catering for eighteen guests.

'Not quite as big as I should have liked, but they might do if the price is right.'

She had carefully concealed her delight at the gardens behind both houses. Although the lawns needed mowing and the flowerbeds weeding, they had obviously been planned and tended by a genuine garden lover. Flo would be ecstatic at the prospect of being able to put her baby out in its pram in such beautiful surroundings.

'I'd like to show it to some trusted friends before I make up my mind. I'll put in an offer as soon as I've had a word with them.'

'You'd like me to arrange a survey first, I expect, Mrs Connolly, just to make sure there's no dry rot.' A pink flush spread over his chubby cheeks at his temerity in suggesting anything to this self-possessed young woman. He got his reward in seeing her lack of comprehension at this advice. 'I shouldn't want you to make any offers until you've checked out that the structure is sound and that you can start knocking down walls.'

'Oh, oh, yes, of course, Mr Hume, I was just about to ask you how soon that could be arranged.'

Two bright scarlet spots appearing on her pale creamy face told him that she was trying to hide her inexperience in buying property, but you had to hand it to her, he thought, she's a fighter, and she's going to learn fast.

Chapter 18

'Don't worry, Flo, I said I'd stay and that's what I'm doing. Sid'll be here the minute he gets off work at the hotel, probably just in time to see his son and heir enter the world.'

Flo was in bed in the general ward of the infirmary along with seven other women. The screens had been placed round her in anticipation of her imminent removal to the labour ward.

'You never told me it was gonna 'urt as much as this,' Flo complained, her forehead damp with sweat.

Sarah held her hand tightly. 'You never asked,' she grinned.

'Cheeky cow,' Flo gasped, a sudden spasm of pain twisting her face in a grimace.

'You'll have to go now, I'm afraid.' A nurse in a stiffly starched uniform and cap, put her head round the screen.

'Best of luck, love,' Sarah whispered. A quick squeeze of the hand, a wave of encouragement to Flo and she left the ward to sit on a hard, narrow bench in the corridor and wait for news.

Was it really only last year that she had sat here, tense and afraid, waiting for news of Rosie from the grim-faced surgeons? Closing her eyes, she went over every second of the horror of being taken into the side ward, where Rosie's burnt little body lay in crisp white sheets.

'You OK, Sarah?' Sid's anxious question brought her back to reality.

'Oh, Sid, you've got here.' She was so relieved that he had arrived before his child was born. 'Flo's fine, won't be long now, so sit down and I'll get you a cup of tea.'

Her optimism that it would not be long, was short-lived. Sid had waylaid one of the staff to be told that it would be at least another four or five hours, which would take them into the early hours.

'They want me back at the hotel by six,' Sid grumbled, an anxious look creasing his thin cheeks. 'Seems they've got some unexpected bookings.'

Sarah suppressed her anger at the way he had been treated by the management of the hotel. He had had to be prepared to work part-time when it suited them, and now he was at their beck and call.

'Well, if they don't like it, they can lump it. You're going to be here with Flo.'

'But . . .'

'Later, don't worry, Sid.' This was not the time to expound on her plans to open her boarding house. Instead, she kept his attention by talking about the latest film he had taken Flo to see, before it became too uncomfortable for Flo to sit for very long.

'She really enjoyed Myrna Loy in that film; you know the one I mean.' He paused. '*The Thin Man*, that was it,' Sid said, valiantly trying to sustain his part in the conversation.

'What was it she said about Shirley Temple in that film, what was it called?'

'*Girl in Pawn,* I believe. If we have a girl, Flo wants to—'

He was interrupted by a smiling nurse inviting Sid and Sarah into the ward to see a tired but elated Flo nursing her newborn son.

'He come all of a sudden at the end,' she told them proudly. 'Took us by surprise, 'e did.'

Sid was speechless, gazing at his son, unable to find the words to tell Flo what a wonderful baby she had produced.

'Go on, give her a kiss,' Sarah whispered.

Shyly he leant over his wife, kissing her on the lips.

'I'm glad it's a boy. Guess what Sid wanted to call it if it was a girl? Only Marina after that new Duchess of Kent. I wasn't having no baby of mine called after a toffee-nosed duchess.'

Sid caught Sarah's eye and winked. Flo went on, 'We're gonna call 'im David, that's what we've decided. You ain't said a word, Sarah. What do you reckon? I done all right, didn't I?'

'He is beautiful, Flo.' Sarah was not trying to please her friend, the baby really was a handsome little boy. His round face held the promise of resembling his mother later on. The elements of Flo's strong features were there, the planes too masculine and defined to be accepted as beautiful in a woman, yet fine and handsome in a boy. 'Is he going to break some hearts when he grows up!'

She stood up to leave, promising to visit the next evening. 'Some of us have got work to do, can't stay in bed all day like some people.'

Flo's raucous laugh echoed throughout the ward, bringing a tight-lipped nurse in to tell Sid also that he had stayed long enough, and that the new mother needed her rest. Relieved that he would be able to be up in time for work next morning, he left with Sarah to return to the café.

The White Rose Weeps

With all the excitement of young David's birth, Sarah had not had time to prepare for the following day in the café, and consequently had to get up at six, having had three hours' sleep. Still tired, she struggled to tidy up the kitchen, mix batter and make a fresh batch of scones. When Doris appeared half an hour late with a young girl in tow, Sarah was ready to explode.

'I'm ever so sorry,' Doris explained, 'but my sister's had to go away to look after her father-in-law for a week, he's ever so poorly, and I'm keeping an eye on young Pearl here. I don't like leaving her on her own while there's no school, so—'

'How old are you, Pearl?' Sarah interrupted.

'Nearly fourteen, Miss, I'll be leaving school anyway in the summer.'

'Fancy earning your keep? You can give a hand with clearing tables and washing up, if you like, instead of getting under everyone's feet.'

Pearl's face was a picture of delight. 'You bet!'

Doris tapped her arm. 'Less of those silly expressions, my girl. It's all these American films making you talk like that. Just you remember your manners.'

Pearl was small for her age, with a pert face and turned-up nose, and a perpetual smile on her face. Just as willing as the other members of the family to work and do whatever needed doing, it did not take her long to get into the routine of the café with her Aunt Doris and cousin Cynthia there to guide her.

Sarah's weariness dissipated with so many helpers. Watching Pearl skipping around, quick and nimble, clearing tables, washing up, looking for what needed to be done next, Sarah gave a sigh of satisfaction. No need to look further for her live-in girl at the boarding house.

Pearl would be leaving school at exactly the right time.

Flo's arrival home with little David brought back memories that Sarah had thought she was able to cope with, but at the first sight of the baby wrapped in his fluffy white shawl she felt the tears starting as her throat tightened.

'Get him into the warm, Flo. Doris will make a cup of tea. I'd forgotten I had to go out this afternoon; won't be long.'

With that, she ran upstairs, put on the first coat that came to hand, and fled out of the back door, as the tears coursed down her cheeks. How long she walked, uncaring whether her grief was attracting curious, if sympathetic stares, she did not know.

The walk to the cemetery where her Rosie lay took her a good half-hour. The tiny grave was under a tree where a bench had been placed to the memory of a long dead alderman. Sarah sat down gazing at the mound of earth over the unmarked grave. She had firmly resisted the undertaker's offer to arrange for a suitable headstone to be erected with Rosie's name tastefully carved.

'No stone and no name,' she had told the mystified funeral director, who had been astounded at this lack of feeling. Most parents ordered elaborate memorials to remind them of the saddest loss of all, that of a child.

'But, I do assure you—'

'No headstone and no name. I don't need any reminder of where my baby is buried.'

Her baby's name was Rosie, beloved daughter of Sarah Mulvey and Harry Wilby. An inscription that the church authorities would never allow. The grave would remain unmarked, yet, in her mind, hopeless as she knew it to be, she prayed for the impossible to happen.

A few murmured endearments to her sleeping child and she was gone, heading back towards the promenade and a seat overlooking the beach. There she remained for over an hour, looking out at the sea. The relentless lapping of the waves on the shore had a calming, almost soporific effect on her. What was it she had been told about an old king called Canute, who had demonstrated that no one could hold back the sea? He had been right. Time, like the sea, goes on, no matter how much one tries to cling to the past.

A sense of shame overcame her. How could she have been so unwelcoming to her best friend? Flo would understand, she felt sure. What was clear was that she had to get out of the café as soon as its sale and the purchase of the boarding house could be finalised. The renovation work on Glendale would have to be put in hand at once.

With a renewed sense of purpose spurring her on, she found a telephone kiosk and rang John Hume, fixing an appointment with him and the estate agent regarding the purchase of Glendale.

Flo said nothing about Sarah's abrupt departure, accepting her explanation that she had business to attend to.

'Won't be long before we're all at Glendale, so you'd better make the most of your little rest here, my girl,' she told a beaming Flo.

Flo had guessed rightly from Sarah's stricken look that staying in the café, especially with a new baby, was too much for her to bear. The sooner they all got out and started a new life, the happier Sarah would be.

'Won't be long before I'm back on me feet, so no need to wrap me in cotton wool.' Flo cuddled her baby son, then handed him over to Sarah. 'Go to your auntie for a minute while I pop into our bedroom and get your cot ready.'

Sarah held the warm little body next to hers, stroking his round cheeks with the back of her fingers. She looked up to see Flo smiling.

'You'll meet someone one day, and 'ave more babies, Sarah.'

Her voice hard, Sarah told Flo, 'No time for that, Flo. I've got a café to sell and a hotel to get ready in a couple of months to be in time for the summer. We won't make the early part of the season, but I want to be up and running by July.' She wagged a finger at Flo. 'So just you tell Sid, no more babies for a while. You'll have to put your foot down.'

'Blimey, Sarah, I ain't got over 'avin' this one yet. Give us a chance.'

Laughing at the prospect of telling Sid what Sarah had said, Flo disappeared to put David down in his cot.

Flo meant well, thought Sarah, trying to reassure her that she was not yet nineteen and had plenty of time to meet the right man and settle down with a family. I have met the right man, the only man I'll ever want, and if I can't have him, I don't want any other man. The pain, the longing were at their worst when she stopped to think; it was a blessing that Fate had stepped in to preserve her sanity by keeping her occupied with planning and working to achieve a feeling of satisfaction.

Her first meeting the following day was with John Hume who advised her on the procedures required to purchase Glendale. Her next was with the solicitor, Mr Farnby, instructing him to go ahead with drawing up the documents for the sale of Fred's Café and the purchase of Glendale.

Michael O'Leary, the estate agent friend of John Hume, proved to be an unpleasant over-effusive man in his late thirties, who saw the lovely young widow as the means of making an exorbitant profit and also as a possible conquest. Even with John Hume present, he leered and ogled, suggesting that they discuss the business deal over dinner, until Sarah, exasperated and offended by his behaviour, stood up, leaned over the desk and poked him hard in the chest with her forefinger.

'Now, you listen to me, you bloody idiot. I've had just about enough of you. I've told you my price and that's it. I've no desire to mix with you socially, nor do I wish to prolong this meeting any more than is necessary, so you'd better give me a straight answer this very minute, or the deal's off. There are other agents and other hotels, such as the Conway. That's got fifty bedrooms and it's going for six thousand pounds. Any more mention of upping the price on the Glendale, and you can keep it.'

She resumed her seat, gratified to see the man redden and splutter his apologies. 'You've misunderstood me, Mrs Connolly. It's just my manner, no offence meant,' he babbled.

Sarah glanced at her watch, then stared pointedly out of the window. 'Get on with it, will you?'

It wasn't until later that she realised just how much she had enjoyed being in control, putting this obnoxious man in his place.

'All agreed, Mrs Connolly, I'll be in touch with your solicitor at once.'

Sarah ignored his outstretched hand, spinning round on her heel and marching to the door. John Hume rushed to open it for her, the thought running through his mind that he was having to earn every penny of his share of the commission on this transaction.

'I did warn you,' he told a deflated Michael O'Leary that evening.

'Pity any poor sod married to her,' he sighed. 'But, Christ! Isn't she the most beautiful woman you've ever seen?'

'Well, you're not going to get her into your bed, so forget it,' John Hume advised. 'In any case, would you really want a block of ice in your bed, man?'

The two men laughed, congratulating one another on their lucky escape.

Sarah was right about the Conway Hotel with its fifty bedrooms, but saw that as the next step in her career. To own a large hotel with a comprehensive staff needed experience. The Glendale would do very nicely to begin with, but she did not intend staying there forever. It struck her that a look over the Conway might not be such a bad idea. As a prospective buyer, she would see not only the accounts, but also the structure of the business, how many employees were needed plus the cost of employing them. A look into the kitchens might also give her some useful tips for Glendale.

Without telling Flo or Sid, she made an appointment to view the Conway with the agents acting for the owners, a London-based group. But first, there would be no repeat of her experience with Michael O'Leary. She pulled her hair back, pinning her curls firmly down to her head with strong hairgrips. With a neat brown hat matching her sensible winter coat, she had achieved the near impossible task of adding a few years to her age. Satisfied with her efforts, she smiled at her image, thus immediately destroying what she had set out to do. It was only when her features were in repose that the sadness behind the eyes betrayed the heartbreak she had suffered, making her appear to be older than she was.

It took her a while to find Nicholas and Sandis, an old established firm, situated at the opposite end of Blackpool from Michael O'Leary's office, and managed by a quietly spoken Scot called Fergus Robertson. Probably in his early forties, Sarah guessed, and a better class than that clod O'Leary, he invited her to sit down, pulling out a chair for her first.

'I understand that you are interested in my client's hotel, Mrs Connolly.' A slight lift of the black, well-shaped eyebrows signalled disbelief that this young woman could be a serious buyer.

'That is so.' Sarah was curt, sensing what was causing him to have reservations.

'I do have to tell you that the asking price is six thousand pounds.'

'I know that. Do you have a problem with that, Mr Robertson?'

His square jaw tightened at this implied criticism. 'No, no, of course not.'

'So, when can I view? I must warn you that I have other establishments in mind.'

There was a pause, as Fergus Robertson deliberated. Who was this gorgeous young creature who could not be much more than twenty, but had all the sharpness of a man twice her age?

'Of course, Mrs Connolly. I'm just thinking when the best time to visit might be.'

'I think now would be as good as any other, don't you?' She smiled, daring him to deny her. 'I'd like to see the hotel as it is, not as someone would like me to see it.'

She gave him five minutes to arrange for his assistants

to take over for the rest of the afternoon, before leading the way out of his office.

'It is quite a way, but I do have my car.'

Sarah was impressed, although she wondered how much money he was making on commission to buy himself a car. Not a top of the range model, but the small Austin was comfortable enough. She watched him changing gears, not always smoothly, coming to the conclusion that if he could drive, then so could she.

A little way out of the town, the Conway Hotel occupied a large site with ornate gardens to the front and a smaller garden at the back.

'Nowhere to park cars,' Sarah commented.

'Not needed, surely, Mrs Connolly.'

'How do the visitors get to the beaches and the amusements, then?'

'There are trams and buses, and besides, anyone staying here would either not want to spend time where there are crowds, or would take a taxi.' He smoothed his dark, abundant hair. She really was a difficult client.

Sarah spent the next hour being treated as if she were a princess. Doors were opened for her, seats pulled up, and tea provided on a silver tray with tiny iced cakes. So this was what a big, expensive hotel was like.

On a tour of the empty bedrooms, her eye took in the shabby carpets and sagging mattresses. Although the décor may have been originally designed with curtains to match the bed covers, some rooms now had cheap, non-matching covers put on the beds. The linen cupboards told the same story with worn sheets and towels, fit only for the ragbag or dusters in Sarah's opinion. The housekeeper had an unenviable task with the whole place needing an expensive refurbishment. Glendale was similar but on a much smaller scale. The mischievous thought that she had no intention of buying the hotel, in any case, made her feel a little guilty at dragging this nice Mr Robertson out of his office.

'The kitchens, please,' she commanded.

The rush to prepare the evening meal had not yet begun, so that the chef had time to explain the menus to her. His fingernails, half-mooned with grime, revolted Sarah, as did his greasy, lank hair. In one corner of the kitchen stood a large refrigerator, something that Sarah had not seen before. She opened it, taking in the contents.

'Wouldn't be without the fridge, a real godsend that is. I can put stuff in there to use the next day or even the day after that. Doesn't half save chucking food out, I can tell you. Besides,' he said, anxious to please this prospective buyer, 'I can get a good deal buying in bulk in advance, and I never run out of stuff if we get a rush on.'

'Excellent,' said Sarah, doubtful that the problem would ever arise. She suppressed a smile, noting the relief on Fergus Robertson's face at her favourable comment. He had not missed her turned-down mouth during the inspection of the bedrooms.

The visit to the manager's office was a real eye-opener for Sarah, with accounts for every aspect of running a hotel.

'The details are with Messrs Armworth and Cornish, our accountants, and they will be able to give you the full story, of course.'

On the way back to the car, parked in the road, Sarah thanked the charming Mr Robertson for his time, then told him that she had never seen such a dreadful dump in her whole life. She omitted to tell him that she had never set foot in anything grander than the Rosewood Boarding House.

'Whoever buys the Conway is going to have to close it down for a season for a complete re-fit.'

'I'm sure we can—'

'Forget it, Mr Robertson, I want something better than that. Now if you'll just drop me off along here, by Woolworths, I'll say goodbye.'

Sensing that he had been taken for a ride, Mr Robertson opened the door to let her out.

'Sarah! You never made that poor sod take you all round when you had no intention of buying!'

A cheeky grin lit up Sarah's face. 'I might have done, but how could I run that fine place with the staff I'm lumbered with?'

Flo yelled, threatening to throw a milk-sodden baby's bib at her.

'Seriously, though, I got lots of ideas, like buying a refrigerator to store the food that's likely to go off in hot weather. Buying in bulk would save money, too. Besides that, I liked the idea of having radiators to heat the rooms instead of having to light fires. I reckon those Crane boilers would be just what we need for Glendale.'

Flo shook her head, her broad mouth split in a disbelieving smile. 'To think, when I first met you, you was a lonely little scrap of a thing, sitting all by yourself, an' lookin' as miserable as sin.'

Sarah's huge hug embraced Flo and young David. 'Where would I have been without you?'

'I dunno, but, you know, sometimes . . . well . . . I think it was my fault you got all that grief. I mean, it was me what introduced you to Fred.'

'You idiot,' Sarah hastened to reassure Flo, 'how could anyone have known how he'd turn out once his ma was dead?' Suddenly very solemn, she went on, 'There are some things in life you can control, and there are others that happen to you that you just can't help.'

'Honest?'

'Yes.' There was a determined set to Sarah's jaw now. 'What I can control is the purchase of Glendale, and getting it ready for a July opening. I can't control how soon this café sells, but that is not important to my plans.' She did not respond to Flo's questioning look. The large sum that Fred had left her, sufficient to buy Glendale before selling the café, was her secret.

In the event, luck was on her side, with two middle-aged Mancunians, a Mr and Mrs Britten, showing a genuine interest in purchasing Fred's Café almost as soon as it had been put on the market. Having run a successful fish-and-chip shop in Manchester, they had thought that a change of scene, with a chance to enjoy the attractions of Blackpool, was just what they were looking for.

Mrs Britten was impressed with Sarah's scones and teacakes, seeing their continued sale as giving her the opportunity to make use of her talents as a good cook.

'It'll make a change from the everlasting fish and chips,' she laughed.

The only drawback for Sarah was the exchange date. 'If you could just hang on for six weeks or so, that would be more convenient.' She did not go on to explain that her proposed new home was, at the moment, uninhabitable.

With the Brittens quite happy to settle for a date in the middle of May, Sarah shook hands with them both.

At that point, Sid came in, proudly carrying his baby son.

Mrs Britten rushed over to have a look at the handsome little boy, cooing over him and thrusting a half-crown piece into his little palm. 'What a lovely baby, and aren't you lucky to have such a pretty mam and such a clever dad.'

Before any explanations could be given, she was out of the café, explaining that they were on their way to see the agent and their solicitor.

Sid gave an embarrassed laugh. 'I'm sorry, Sarah.'

'Don't worry,' she reassured him. 'In any case, it's just as well that they think I've got a man behind me. They won't try to beat me down on the price.'

Things couldn't be better, except that it was now urgent to start organising a builder to carry out the structural alterations to Glendale, before Sid could start decorating. They needed to be able to move in by the third week in May.

Much as it went against her feeling of independence, she had to ask Sid if he would come with her to see a local building firm, which had been recommended by Doris. 'I'll do most of the talking, Sid. You act the part of the hen-pecked husband.'

'That won't take any acting.'

Flo, who was meant to overhear the remark, pretended to box his ears.

'Now, you two lovebirds, no fooling around, there's work to do, if we're going to have a roof over our heads by May.' Sarah's words were said only half in jest. It was all her responsibility to make sure that Glendale would be ready by the agreed date.

The White Rose Weeps

Insisting that the builder did exactly what was wanted proved to be a battle of wills which Sarah intended winning. By the end of the second week in April, he came to the conclusion that life would be simpler if he did as this headstrong young woman decreed.

There were days when Sarah doubted the wisdom of having bought two properties which needed such extensive alterations, but by the end of April the main structural alterations had been completed and Sid had started on the decorating. The plumber who was installing the boiler and radiators was an old friend of Sid's uncle, and even if they did waste some time in chatting about mutual acquaintances, at least they were able to co-ordinate the tasks.

'We can do without the refrigerator for the time being,' Sarah told Flo, but we need furniture for your flat and for mine.'

'But there's plenty 'ere already. What do we need to buy new for?' Flo protested. 'I don't mind 'aving second-hand. I've never 'ad new in me life.' She was horrified at all the furniture in the café going to waste.

'Not one stick, not one vase, not one pot or pan, Flo.'

Sarah had been brought up to be thrifty, but she was not carrying any baggage from the past with her to Glendale. It might be Fred's money buying her new future, but that was all.

By the end of May, Fred's Café existed no more. The signwriter had erected a new sign bearing the name, Tom and Flora's Café. A board announced that it was under new management, and that homemade cakes were a speciality.

The little party that had vacated the premises had needed only the smallest of vans to transport them to their new home. Flo, full of excitement had kept looking back at the café.

'You don't regret coming to live and work with me, do you?' Sarah asked, detecting a faint look of regret in Flo's eyes.

'Course not. You're the best thing that 'appened to me in my whole life, I mean apart from Sid and my little David.'

'And Ginger, our old tom cat, and—'

'Oh, shut up, Sarah, you know what I mean.'

One more chapter in her life was over. Soon she would be running her own private hotel with no time for brooding on what might have been.

Rarely did she admit to herself that there were some parts of the past that tugged at her heart, catching her unawares, bringing salt tears to her eyes.

Chapter 19

The next few weeks went past in a mad flurry of activity. Sid soon proved that he was well worth the trust Sarah had put in him. Although possessed of a small frame and, in Sarah's eyes, had been undernourished in childhood, he had unexpected stamina, working at decorating the rooms from early dawn until late. Flo never complained, insisting that they were only too grateful for what Sarah had done for them.

'But I don't want you to be grateful,' Sarah insisted. 'You're my friends and I'm the one who should be grateful to you for helping me out.'

'OK, if you say so.' Flo was partly pacified. 'But we ain't sponging, and I ain't taking no wages until I can pull my weight.'

This was the first time that the two friends had disagreed over something as fundamental as status and wages and Sarah realised that, unless these problems were settled, resentment could arise later on. It would be useless to insist that Flo drew wages and yet ordinary tact and diplomacy would not be enough.

'Right, do you want to hear what I did about wages when I was at the café with old Mrs Connolly?'

Flo nodded, her sulky mood still showing no signs of lifting. 'If you like,' she said, staring at a spot above Sarah's head.

The White Rose Weeps

'Well, I knew that I couldn't work full-time with Rosie to see to as well, so we worked out some part-time hours when I could work and I got paid for that.'

A grin gradually spread over Flo's face. 'Whose idea was that?'

'Mine. The miserable old cow didn't want to pay me anything.'

At this, Flo exploded into fits of uncontrollable laughter.

'Honestly girl, you take the biscuit, you really do.' Then more seriously, 'That'd suit me, Sarah. I want to work, but . . . well, you know what I mean.'

She got up to go to attend to David, but Sarah gently put a hand on her shoulder, making her sit down again.

'Promise me that if ever you feel that something isn't right, you'll tell me. I need you Flo more than I can ever tell you, and you're the only one who's likely to come out with what you think, so you've got to be honest with me.'

'Promise,' Flo said, loping off in the direction of David's hungry cries.

As each room was finished, Flo and Doris set to work hanging curtains and lining wardrobes and drawers, while David slept peacefully in his pram in the garden. Doris had asked to do the same hours as she had done in the café, which suited Sarah, who in spite of having more than enough cash in the bank, did not want to squander it. Her ambition was to see her capital grow until she could buy the hotel she had set her heart on.

They agreed that once Glendale was up and running, Doris would make an earlier start so that she could help serve the breakfasts. Her niece Pearl would be there to help Flo in the evenings.

Pearl had been overjoyed at being offered the chance to be a live-in maid, starting at the end of July. After having to share a room with two sisters, she was thrilled at the prospect of having her own room. Being told that she could have Wednesday afternoons and Sunday off suited her, giving her the opportunity to go home to see her family, who lived only a couple of miles away. Not like me at her age, Sarah thought, miles from home and from my darling Harry, and with no one to watch over me.

The reply to a tentative letter to Iris to find out if Bernard had heard any more from Harry, settled once and for all any hope she might have had of seeing him and telling him about Rosie's death, and that with Fred dead, she was now a free woman. Since the day when he had come into the café with Dolly, and seen that she was married, he had cut himself off from all contacts in Colethorpe. She would never be able to explain how Fred's ma had hidden his letters, which meant that he would go on thinking for ever that she had preferred Fred to him. This longing to see him again and explain, burned into her heart, creeping up on her so many times when she was least prepared for it.

The team of workers quickly settled into a routine. Soon after Doris left at five, Sarah prepared a meal for herself, Flo and Sid, which they shared at the kitchen table, discussing and planning the next day's chores.

The printers had delivered the brochures for Sarah to include in replies to prospective visitors. She had been too late to advertise in time for those who preferred to book up early, and had been forced to pay out for publicity in the newspapers covering the north west of the country.

The White Rose Weeps

'Seems you're 'avin' to spend out an awful lot without getting anythin' back,' Flo commented, as they sat round the table talking.

'Ah, well, you've got to speculate to accumulate.'

Flo put down her cup of tea. 'Gordon Bennet! I ain't heard that since I left 'ome. Me dad used to say that just before 'e went down our street to catch the bookie's runner and lose all 'is money. I dunno if 'e ever won. If 'e did, we never saw any of it. It all went down the boozer.' She sighed at the memory of a childhood spent in poverty. 'I dunno 'ow we managed.'

'There's no need to worry about what I'm spending. I've got all the money from the sale of the café.' She did not add, 'and more besides.'

The only misgivings expressed by Sid concerned the garden. He had cut back the rampant roses, tidied up flowerbeds and cut the grass with the brand new mower Sarah had entrusted him with buying.

'A few more weeks and I'd have it tip top,' he promised. 'I wouldn't want visitors to get the wrong impression.'

Sarah had discovered that Sid was a perfectionist, and if the opening date were left until he decided that everything was in order, they would never open. She was beginning to realise that the job of management required not only tact, but also a firm hand.

'But everything looks absolutely lovely as it is. In any case, Sid, it'll be interesting for the guests to see you working. There'll be plenty of gardeners only too keen to have a word and ask your advice, especially when they see what you've achieved.'

A relieved sigh told her that she had said the right thing. It struck her later, that praise was also a prerequisite of good management.

The first inquiries for bookings in late July and onwards began to trickle in, not as many as Sarah had hoped for, but enough to cover the ongoing costs.

A couple in their late fifties and two families each consisting of parents plus two offspring, arrived on the third Saturday in July. Sarah was not immediately taken with one twelve-year-old who was intent on prying into Flo's flat and wandering upstairs into her own private attic area. Catching him trying the doorknob to Pearl's room, Sarah took hold of the astonished lad by the ears and shook him hard.

'If I catch you up here again, there'll be no questions asked, believe me. Your mam and dad will find all their luggage out on the pavement.' He opened his mouth to protest that they wouldn't be able to get a coach back to Liverpool, if she did that. 'Shut up and listen, because I mean what I say, and I don't give a damn if you and your family have to sleep all night at the bloody bus station, got it?' She shook him even harder until he yelled with pain, then she smiled. 'There you are, Paul, I'm so glad we understand one another, and I do hope your parents will be able to stay long enough to enjoy their holiday.'

Rubbing his ears, the lad fled down the stairs. She might be prettier than his mother, but she wasn't half a nasty piece of work.

The incident worried Sarah, remembering her own unhappy experiences with the lascivious Arthur Scatesburn. Paul might just be a silly adolescent, but how was she to know what fantasies some of her male visitors harboured? She shuddered, suddenly ice-cold, seeing again the image of Fred, dressed in his dead mother's clothes and prancing in front of his mirror.

Fortunately Pearl was not at all taken aback by the suggestion that Sid should fit a bolt inside her bedroom door. Quite the reverse, much to Sarah's relief. 'You're right, Mrs Connolly, a girl does need her privacy. I think it's very nice of you to be so considerate.'

Sarah concealed a smile at this prim, old-fashioned reply. Pearl was certainly more worldly wise than she herself had been at fourteen.

Once the families were settled in, Sarah offered them a cup of tea in the parlour.

'This is welcome, I can tell you, Mrs Connolly. We had to wait a while for a bus to get here and it were damned hot,' the middle-aged man complained, rubbing his red neck with a spotlessly white handkerchief, and ignoring his wife's nudge.

'I'm so sorry that you have had such an uncomfortable start, but, as you know, we have only just opened. We hope to have our own car very soon, which will be most useful for picking up our guests from the station.'

Flo had just been pouring out second cups of tea, as this unexpected announcement was made. The teapot in mid air, and her mouth wide open, she stared at Sarah in astonishment.

Sarah ignored Flo's reaction, enjoying the comments that this would make Glendale very popular indeed. She went on to explain how the hotel operated, handing them all a copy of mealtimes and a plan showing where the various rooms and bathrooms were.

'We are not too far from the trams, and you'll find plenty in Blackpool to amuse you during the day.'

Sarah waved goodbye to the last of them as they left to spend their first afternoon eating fish and chips, probably at the newly named Tom and Flora's Café, gawping at the wonders of the Tower and sitting on the beach struggling with dripping ice-cream cornets.

She went into the kitchen, turning the taps on full blast, well aware that Flo's disapproving frown was piercing her back.

'A car? What on earth will you think of next to waste your money on?'

Sarah giggled, 'I don't know, honestly Flo, the idea just came to me suddenly.'

'Who's gonna drive it?' Her jaw dropped again, as Sarah's intentions struck her. 'You don't mean you?'

'Who else? Oh, there's no reason why Sid shouldn't learn as well after me. And then—'

'Oh no, you don't, you ain't gonna catch me be'ind the wheel of one of them.'

The more Sarah thought about it, the more the idea appealed to her. The benefits of having her own transport were listed in her mind, the main one being that she could drive to see her mother and father and be back the same day if need be.

'Who's gonna teach you?'

Sarah had her own ideas on that subject, but kept them to herself for the time being. Monday would be a good day to make a start on that particular aspect of being a car owner.

Once breakfast was over, with Pearl and Flo hard at work cleaning the bedrooms, Sarah told them that she had business to attend to in town and would be back in time to start on the evening meal. They were not to wait for her but were to have their own lunch.

A short ride and Sarah was outside the offices of Nicholas and Landis. Fergus Robertson's secretary pursed her lips on hearing Sarah's request to see her boss as a matter of urgency. The outcome of the abortive visit to the Conway was known to Fergus Robertson's secretary, as she had been the one to write to the owners explaining that the client did not wish to proceed with a purchase. As if that chit of a girl could be in a position to own an hotel.

The disapproving look did not escape Sarah, who was beginning to tire of the raised eyebrows and overt jealousy, whenever the matter of her wealth was in question.

'Yes, now, right now. So if you'd kindly tell him I'm here.'

The door to the inner office opened, and a beaming Fergus Robertson appeared. 'I thought I recognised your voice, Mrs Connolly.' He nodded curtly to his secretary, still hovering in the doorway. 'Some tea, if you please.'

Outraged at the special treatment being afforded to this young woman, Miss Henshaw reminded him that he had an appointment booked in fifteen minutes' time.

'Oh, that's only old Bill Prosser. Ring and cancel it, will you? It's nothing urgent, and besides he'd sooner be out on the golf course on such a lovely afternoon.'

'Yes, Mr Robertson, certainly.' Any attempts to remind him of his obligations fell on deaf ears as he ushered Sarah into his office. His delight at seeing her again encouraged Sarah to begin by apologising for her rejection of the Conway.

'I do hope you don't think that my request to view was frivolous in any way, I really was interested.'

Fergus's fine dark eyes sparkled. 'I'm sure you were.'

'In fact, I've just started in a small way.' Her explanation of her latest business venture took him by surprise. He had been totally convinced that he had been the victim of a hoax.

He nodded his head, expecting more revelations.

'I realised that if I wanted to run a hotel, I'd better start in a small way and work my way up. Who knows? One day you might find me a really good hotel to buy.'

This candour disarmed him, his besotted smile infuriating Miss Henshaw who had just entered bearing a tray of tea and biscuits. Sarah's courage was beginning to evaporate throughout the ceremony of pouring tea. How could she have imagined that this man would be interested enough in her to do what she wanted.

'It's like this, Mr Robertson. You're the only man I know who has a motor car.' She held his gaze waiting for a reaction.

'That's probably true.' Fergus had been rather proud of being the first in his social circle to own a car. 'But why —?'

'I want to buy one and I need advice.' It all came out in a child-like rush to get the difficult part out of the way, and not as Sarah had intended.

He sipped his tea slowly, finally replacing the cup on the saucer with studied deliberation. 'You want to buy a second-hand car, Mrs Connolly?'

'Of course not! What do you take me for? I want a new one and I don't know what to buy. I don't want some sharp car salesman pushing rubbish on to me. I thought with you having a car, you'd know what would suit me.'

Fergus Robertson had been let down ten years previously by his fianceé who had decided that she preferred a certain bank manager and his salary to that of an estate agent whose income depended mainly on commission. The fact that he was now better paid than that bank manager did not compensate for his lonely bachelor existence. At thirty-nine, he had felt that he was destined to remain unmarried, with Miss Mabel Henshaw the only devoted female on his horizon. This lovely girl was now giving him the opportunity to enjoy female company, and actually inviting him to spend time with her.

'How about a run out in mine, then we can go and look at some other makes?'

His eagerness took Sarah by surprise. Her direct approach had certainly borne fruit, but she had to be back at Glendale to see to her guests' evening meal. She glanced at her watch, a present to herself to celebrate the successful opening of Glendale. Fergus Robertson did not need to be told the cost of the elegant gold timepiece with its delicately wrought gold bracelet. No wonder she was not interested in buying a used car!

'At least let me give you a lift back to your hotel,' he begged.

Sarah's cool detachment deserted her. Sensations she thought were long buried, never to resurface, began to stir her body into a sensual reawakening. Fergus Robertson was a handsome man, his hewn features, strong jaw and dark eyes enough to attract any number of female admirers. It was with horror that Sarah realised that she was actually thinking that she could very easily enjoy being in his bed.

'I won't bite,' he said, half-smiling at her discomfiture.

To hell with it, she thought. 'Excellent, Mr Robertson.'

By the time he had taken her on a tour of Blackpool, pointing out the premises of one particular car dealer whom he could recommend, they were on first name terms, arranging a date and time when they could meet to buy her new car.

'I'll soon teach you how to drive,' were his parting words, leaving Sarah feeling that somehow she had lost control of this situation. The last thing she wanted was to embark on a love affair with him. No, that wasn't strictly true. She was reacting to Fergus in a way she had thought was no longer possible. Her body cried out for love, but if it was Harry she wanted, he was out of reach. And Fergus is here, wanting me.

Flushed and out of breath, she ran up the front path to have the door opened by a triumphant Flo, who had been watching Sarah get out of the car of this unknown man. She seized Sarah's arm, dragging her off to the kitchen and sitting her down firmly.

'Come on, let's 'ave it, what've you been up to? Who is 'e?'

She did not believe Sarah's explanation that he was simply a very kind man who was going to help her buy a suitable motor car and teach her how to drive it.

'Gerraway! So you're gonna be off out somewhere down the country lanes with a man you hardly know?'

'Yes,' Sarah beamed, 'and now do you mind if we get on with the cooking. We've got a hotel to run, remember?'

That visit to the offices of Nicholas and Landis was the beginning of a warm relationship between herself and Fergus Robertson. There was an unspoken understanding between them that neither wanted a sudden, ephemeral affair, knowing that it could end only in a sad cooling-off. They restricted their early meetings to business-like appointments during the day, when Fergus took her to various showrooms for her to view cars.

Sarah did not allow the fact that she had enough cash to buy whatever model appealed to her to blot out the early memories of the few shillings a week she had received for skivvying at Rosewood House. Models such as the Armstrong-Siddely with its self-changing gears at four hundred and twenty-five pounds were dismissed as being impractical. She was quite taken with the new Morris Major, especially the coùpé with the folding head, but reminded herself severely that it would have taken four years to earn that amount at the Rosewood Boarding House.

Invariably, she and Fergus would finish by having lunch before he took her back to Glendale. The question of more intimate evening meetings had been carefully avoided by both of them.

Her first visit to a car showroom had made her so angry that Fergus Robertson began to doubt the wisdom of being involved with such a fiery young woman. The salesman's attitude was one of barely-concealed contempt. The advantages of the small saloon on display were explained to Fergus with Sarah being ignored.

'Allow me to show you this Austin Seven, sir, at just one hundred and forty pounds. It is designed to seat four people, yet taking little space on the road. You would hardly notice that it is just under four feet wide and eight feet eight inches long.'

'Yes, but you see—'

'As a man you will appreciate that it has all the attributes of a much larger car. Note the water-cooled engine, the three-speed gearbox and the four wheel brakes.'

He opened the driver's door. 'Perhaps sir would care to sit in the driver's seat and test its comfort.'

'Actually, it's the young lady who is buying the car,' Fergus explained, conscious of Sarah's heightened colour and pursed lips.

Sarah did not miss the suggestive nudge and whispered comment to Fergus. 'I expect you agree with me, sir. Women drivers are a menace on the roads. They're just not capable of understanding the highly technical workings of the modern machine.'

This remark brought Sarah's simmering rage to boiling point. Elbowing Fergus out of the way, she smacked her palm hard on the salesman's shoulder. His leering grin faded at this physical onslaught. He took a step back, not knowing what was coming next.

'You miserable little worm, how dare you treat me like this! I've come in here to buy a car with my money, nobody else's and I expect some respect from the likes of you.'

The manager had observed the scene from behind the glass front window of his office, and afraid that the woman was drawing interested looks from passers-by, hastened to the assistance of his employee.

Sarah immediately switched tactics, giving him the benefit of her most dazzling smile. 'Apparently your assistant here is completely incapable of selling me a car. He seems to think that lady drivers should be banned. I do think that is a pity as there are going to be so many of us wanting to buy cars before very long. I shall just have to go elsewhere with my money. Come along, Mr Robertson.' Without a backward glance, she marched out of the showroom with Fergus at her heel.

He drove in silence for a few minutes, not sure of his feelings towards this young woman who had created such a scene. The car salesman's opinions were shared by the majority of drivers. It was quite reasonable to suppose that a woman's mind was not capable of understanding the mechanics of a car engine.

'You were a bit hard on the poor man,' he ventured.

'Hard! He practically suggests that I'm a whore and that you're buying the car for me, then he says that women shouldn't be allowed on the roads!' Seeing his downcast expression, she relented, adding, 'Perhaps we ought to make it clear from the start, that you are simply there to advise me and that I am the purchaser.'

Fergus stopped the car, turned to Sarah, and said, 'Perhaps we'd better, or you'll never succeed in getting a car.' He put out a hand, tentatively touching her cheek. 'Promise you'll behave yourself?'

They both laughed, Sarah relieved that she had not incurred Fergus's wrath, but declaring that she was not sorry one little bit for putting the man in his place.

The car she finally decided on was a Model Y Ford, big enough to hold herself and three passengers, four at a pinch, yet small enough for her to manoeuvre. Although the manager of the showroom was keen to teach Sarah the rudiments of handling her new purchase, warning her that she would have to pass a test and needed professional tutoring, Sarah refused as tactfully as she could. He wished her luck envying the good-looking man who was to have the delight of spending hours beside her in the car. Concentrating on his work proved almost impossible for the rest of the day, as the image of a beautiful girl with skin smooth as milk and hair the colour of a blazing fire, constantly flitted across his mind.

Thorough in everything he tackled, Fergus made Sarah practise every day, insisting that they made the most of the summer weather to go out every afternoon. He omitted to mention that Miss Henshaw was threatening to resign unless he paid more attention to the business.

'How can I possibly keep telling clients that you are out every single day?'

'Tell them that I am a very busy man with many commitments. That should make them appreciate my proficiency.' He ignored her scornful sniff.

It was true; he was allowing himself to become so much under Sarah's spell that very soon his business would suffer. How to further their relationship without threatening their friendship was causing him sleepless nights. He felt sure that he was not imagining Sarah's awareness of him as a man, and yet on the occasions he had tried closer physical contact, leaning over in the passenger seat to brush her cheek with his lips, she had stiffened, her smile not fading, but becoming fixed. He agonised about his inability to fathom what was holding her back from making a commitment. What would happen once Sarah was a proficient driver no longer in need of his tuition? From the day when she had walked into his office asking for his advice, their meetings had been all to do with the car purchase and learning to drive. Would she respond favourably to an invitation to more intimate meetings?

His reaction to her excited announcement that she had passed her test and did not need him any more, was one of dejection.

'Sorry, Fergus, that's not exactly what I mean. In fact, what I really mean is, I can't think of anyone else I'd sooner celebrate with.' She hugged him with a childlike spontaneity, pulling away, sensing his desire to prolong the embrace.

The heady feeling of being able to drive remained with her throughout the dinner Fergus had booked at a country hotel some five miles out of Blackpool. Fergus had insisted on driving her himself. It was one way of keeping his mind off the dilemma that was tormenting his every waking moment.

The bottle of champagne he had ordered to celebrate her success was noted by the other diners, assuming that the lovely girl and her handsome escort were toasting their engagement.

Sarah's bubbly laughter rang out as she overheard a remark referring to the engaged couple. 'Should we let them think that it's true? Go on, I dare you to kiss me.'

Whether the request was due to the effect the unaccustomed champagne was having on her, releasing her inhibitions, or whether it was simply her mischievous nature, Fergus did not stop to consider. Her warm parted lips were too much for him to resist, and ignoring the raised eyebrows, he leaned across the table to kiss her.

'You realise that your wanton behaviour is going to get us thrown out of here, don't you?'

Sarah responded with, 'Well, let's go then before they do just that.'

During the drive back, she clung to his arm, until he protested that he couldn't change gear with her holding on so tightly.

'God! Sarah don't you know what you're doing to me?'

He slammed on the brakes, wrenched the handbrake and turned towards Sarah, who was staring wide-eyed at this sudden change in Fergus's usually subdued manner. With a groan, he took her in his arms, holding her so tightly that she could not wriggle free. A sudden need, so long suppressed, responded to his, returning his kisses with a passion she had thought she would never feel again. The sensation of being wanted and of returning that want, was making her lose control of the situation. It was not until Fergus murmured in an agonised hoarse whisper,

'I love you, Sarah,' that she pulled back, half-afraid of the violent emotion she had released in him. The brooding look in his dark eyes told her that she had let the excitement of the evening deprive her of common sense. And yet, why not?

'I'm sorry, Sarah.'

She leant over to him again, kissing him gently. 'Please don't say you're sorry, Fergus. It's . . . well . . . it's just that I don't want us to rush things.'

'You don't mind that I love you?'

She kissed him again. 'No, in fact, I think I could get to like it very much.'

Love was an emotion she had denied herself for so long, that she could not tell whether the way she felt towards Fergus was love or simply a kind of loving friendship. Perhaps if she gave it time, she would discover the depths of her feelings. Lately she had concluded that her heart had shrivelled up with losing both Rosie and Harry. It was as if her whole being was afraid of giving way to feelings of love, in case the object of her love might be snatched from her. Far safer to deny that she needed a normal relationship. That way she would never again suffer the pain that had torn her apart for the past two years.

Satisfaction now lay in being her own woman, being in charge of her business operation and turning heads as she drove around Blackpool. She was not blind to her beauty, the mirror telling her that it was not only her vibrant colouring that was so striking, but also an indefinable aura, which men found disturbing.

Flo was agog to hear what had gone on between Sarah and Fergus Robertson.

'You mean you've been sitting up until midnight just waiting for me to come in so you could quiz me? Honestly, Flo!'

Flo gave a sheepish grin. 'No, it was David, woke up half an hour ago, but 'e's gone down quiet enough now. I thought I might as well wait and hear what the latest is. Something's 'appened, I can tell by the look on your face. Come on girl, out with it.'

A solemn expression furrowing her broad forehead, Flo listened while Sarah tried to explain that she did not know how she felt about Fergus.

'He says he loves me, and I know that I'm really happy when I'm with him, but it doesn't seem like it felt when I was with Harry.'

Flo's eyes glistened with tears. 'You loved Harry so much that there just ain't gonna be anyone like 'im, I know that. But I can't tell you to marry a bloke just because 'e's nice to you and because you need someone.'

Sarah gave a rueful smile. Flo's intuitive perception had got to the heart of the matter again.

'I promise I won't do anything rash I'll just enjoy being with Fergus. Knowing I'm loved will have to do for the time being.'

Lying awake in the early hours she prayed that it would be Fergus who would be able to shatter the block of ice that encased her heart.

Chapter 20

With winter approaching, Sarah realised that she was going to be faced with the same problem that she had encountered when running Fred's Café. The summer visitors having gone, other paying customers needed to be attracted. It was Sid who came up with an idea which seemed as if it might provide the answer.

'Remember the travelling salesmen who used to come to the caff for cheap dinners, well, I do know some of them who stay at the smaller hotels on the front. From what I've heard they're not too well catered for. I've met one or two of them in the pubs when I've dropped by for a pint.'

Flo's mouth opened wide. 'Cheeky sod! You never told me! You might 'ave taken me out with you.'

He tweaked her nose affectionately. 'Perhaps I will if you keep quiet a minute, while I explain what I mean to Sarah.'

'Good idea,' Sarah agreed.

'Well, I think we could build up a nice group of all year round regulars.' He paused, frowning. 'The trouble is, they do like a drink with their meals, and you haven't got a bar, let alone a licence.'

Sarah bit her lip, furiously trying to think of a way to overcome this obstacle. Glendale was a family hotel with a parlour for the use of the guests in the evening. Putting a bar in there was out of the question, she knew. Most of the clientele attracted to Glendale were looking for a respectable family hotel, and would hardly appreciate a bar full of loud-mouthed travelling salesmen impinging on their quiet evenings in the parlour.

'We need larger premises.' Sarah closed her eyes.

'Blimey girl, you ain't thinking of moving again, are you? We've only just got this place straight.' Flo stared at Sarah in disbelief.

'Not exactly, but I've had an idea.' Without enlarging any further, she stood up, went up to her flat to get a coat, then disappeared out of the front door.

'She ain't taken 'er motor, so she can't be going too far,' Flo surmised, peeping through the curtains, as Sarah went out through the gate.

It was over an hour before she returned, smiling widely and virtually skipping into the kitchen, where Flo and Sid sat gloomily nursing cups of tea.

'That's settled. Right Flo, take that worried look off your face and pour me out a cuppa.'

'You're up to something, aren't you? I can tell by that look in your eye. You can't fool me, so out with it.'

'OK, I'll tell you what I've managed to arrange so far.' She took a huge gulp of the scalding tea. 'You know Mr and Mrs Bainbridge next door. Well, I've been giving them lifts to do their shopping and I've taken Mr Bainbridge up to the hospital a few times for his appointments.'

Flo nodded. It was typical of Sarah, generous, always ready to lend a helping hand.

'Now, the other day, while Mr Bainbridge was having his check-up, Mrs Bainbridge told me that they really wanted to move to a smaller house to be nearer to her sister, but what with being so frail, looking round suitable houses and then having to organise the move, well, everything is just too much trouble for them. They had decided to stay put and just muddle along somehow or other.'

'Poor old things.'

'Well, don't you see? Their house is exactly what we need.' Sarah clapped her hands in delight, expecting a show of enthusiasm.

'Are you thinking of buying up the whole street, girl?'

'Not yet, but give me time.' Sarah winked at Sid, who was still waiting patiently for Sarah to unravel her plans. 'Their house will be ideal. It'll give us extra rooms, as well as providing an area for a bar well away from our guests' parlour.'

'I bet some of our male guests would like that in the summer, you know, give them a chance to have a pint, and leave their wives nattering in the parlour.'

'I'm glad you think so, Sid, because you'll be the bar steward in charge, extra pay of course.' Sarah did not need telling that Sid often felt that he was the general factotum with no real role.

Not used to showing emotion, his quiet 'I appreciate that very much Sarah,' conveyed what he felt.

She went on to say that she had offered the old couple a fair price for the house, on top of which, she had told them that her estate agent friend would be sure to find them a suitable smaller property.

'I've also told them that that they can stay here while the removal men see to everything, and then we'll give them a hand to settle in, hang curtains and unpack and so on.'

'Is there anything you can't fix?' Flo grinned, shaking her head.

'There'll be an awful mess again, knocking down walls I'm afraid, and more decorating for Sid, but if we can get a move on, we should be ready by Christmas.'

Do you really think that people will want to spend Christmas in Blackpool away from home, Sarah? I mean, I'm getting a bit worried at all the money you're lashing out on spec.'

'I'm positive,' Sarah assured her. Hadn't Fred and his Ma spent every Christmas away from home at a big hotel? A little more scouting round and she could find out what these bigger hotels did to entertain visitors at Christmas. There must be lots of lonely people out there longing to join in with like souls. 'Of course they'll come, and when they've been once, they'll come again, you'll see. We'll have a Christmas tree with presents, lights, a huge Christmas dinner and games for everyone. By the time we've got them in a happy frame of mind, they'll be buying drinks all round.'

Excited at the proposed expansion of her property and business, Sarah could not wait until the next day to see Fergus, contacting him that evening on her newly installed telephone. Although carefully avoided by Flo, it had proved to be the means by which several late bookings had been effected. It also meant that Fergus could get in touch with her at any time, suggesting that they meet for lunch or dinner. The latter was usually out of the question, with Sarah responsible for the cooking, but with the winding-down of the season she had been able to spend more time with him.

Admittedly, much of their time together was in the public eye, in restaurants, the cinema, or out driving. He had never invited her to his bachelor flat, making Sarah curious about why he had avoided the issue.

She was mildly humbled by his serious answer. 'I have to think about your reputation, Sarah. I could never do anything which might cause you harm.'

He had spent some riotously entertaining evenings with her, together with Sid and Flo round the kitchen table, enjoying Sarah's cooking. Mindful of what Flo would say, Sarah had not invited him up to her flat for a meal, restricting his first visit to a tour of the guest rooms with just a cursory glance at her living area. His wistful expression had not escaped her, but Sarah was not yet ready to risk the temptations offered if she were to be alone with him and her bed so conveniently at hand.

Besides, it was hard to explain even to herself the reasons why the proposed expansion of her hotel pumped her so full of adrenalin that she hardly gave a thought to Fergus while all the activity was going on. True, she had to rely on him to find a home for the elderly Bainbridges to move into.

'There are times, Sarah my love,' he said one day, when they were sitting in his office poring over suitable properties, 'that I think you treat me as just a useful member of your staff, ready to jump into action whenever you snap your pretty little fingers.'

Sarah pouted, not sure whether Fergus was being serious or teasing her as he often did. 'Do you mind?'

Fergus's dark eyes narrowed. 'You know I can't refuse you anything, especially when you look at me as you do.'

'That's fine then.' Sarah assumed a matter-of-fact voice, half afraid that he would become serious and mention the matter of marriage. 'Anyway, you can hardly complain at the extra business I'm bringing you with the sale of the Bainbridges' house and the purchase of another for them.'

Seeing his disappointed, hurt expression, she immediately regretted the harshness of her tone. 'Tell you what, Fergus, you get this fixed up in the next couple of weeks and you'll be my guest for Christmas at Glendale.' She kissed him lightly on the forehead. 'And you'll have the best room, and that's a promise.'

'Am I allowed to choose?'

Sarah felt a moment of panic. Perhaps she was giving him too much to hope for. Damn! He was everything a woman could desire, and there were times when she ached to have him in her bed, but there was always something holding her back, preventing her from making the irrevocable commitment. She had made that commitment to Harry, had given birth to her lovely little Rosie, only to lose them both for ever. Was it the fear of having her happiness snatched away once again which made her afraid to give rein to her womanly feelings? The pain of loss had nearly robbed her of her reason, her only defence being to build an impenetrable wall around herself. Or was it that deep down she was hoping for the impossible, that one day she would see Harry again? Time after time, she had told herself that she was being irrational, that Harry was married to Dolly and had written little Sarah Mulvey out of his life for good. How wonderful it would be if Fergus could be the one to break through the pain barrier enclosing her heart in its iron grip.

Having seen the particulars of one house which she thought might appeal to her neighbours, she asked Fergus if she might take the file for them to look at. 'I promise I'll bring it back first thing tomorrow.'

'How can I refuse, when it means I'll see you again so soon?'

As soon as the Bainbridges saw the price of the house and that it was located barely a hundred yards form Mrs Bainbridge's sister, they were keen to view it. Their gratitude towards Sarah made her suffer some pangs of guilt, knowing that it was to her advantage to obtain possession of the house which had been their home for so much of their married life.

Mrs Bainbridge seemed to sense Sarah's disquiet. 'You know, my dear, we've had such a happy marriage and spent such wonderful years in this house, and now we'll be able to look back and share our memories. If we'd stayed, it would have become a burden and we could have come to hate still being in it. This has all happened for the best, and I hope that it does you a lot of good too.'

The speed with which Fergus managed to complete all the legal and financial formalities surprised Sarah. 'Do all your clients get this express service?'

'No, but then none of them has ever invited me to spend Christmas with them.'

The hope and anticipation in his voice caught Sarah off guard. How much was he reading into her invitation? Part of her wanted to become closer to him, and yet when he made a move, she found herself stiffening, afraid to respond. The thought struck her that the romantic Christmas atmosphere might encourage him into trying to push her into agreeing to get engaged. The idea was not unattractive, but in all their business dealings, Sarah sensed an underlying disapproval of her position as owner of a seaside hotel. Would he expect her to sell out and remain at home if they married? If a choice had to be made between Fergus and furthering her business career, which would she choose? Sarah wished that she could answer the question honestly.

Having the elderly couple to stay, and organising their house removal, gave her something to occupy her mind before the structural alterations were to begin. Mr and Mrs Bainbridge were overjoyed at the efficiency with which they found themselves installed in their new home, thanking Sarah over and over again.

'You deserve to succeed, my dear,' Mr Bainbridge told her as he and his wife were leaving Glendale. 'A clever business woman with a heart of gold, now that is something different.'

Flo nodded her head vigorously in agreement. 'You're right there, and I should know.'

Embarrassed at all this effusive praise, Sarah took refuge in rushing out to her car and opening the doors for the old couple. She'd be glad to get this little performance over.

Builders, dust, noise and constant questions as to where various items had to go nearly drove her to distraction, especially when she tried to convince the builder that one area was to be a bar.

'No, I haven't got a licence yet, but it's been applied for, so the sooner you lot get finished, the sooner I'll be able to show the magistrates that I'm running an efficient, respectable business.'

The man did not appear totally convinced, agreeing privately with his partner that there was something decidedly odd about this slip of a girl having so much money.

'I mean, the way she acts, you'd think she was a man.'

'And twice her age,' the other added.

Each night, Sarah threw herself on to her bed, totally exhausted, yet exhilarated at what she was achieving. Once the interior work was completed, Sarah had plans to incorporate the house fronts into one large facade to create the impression of its being one property. The front gardens of the two sections either side of the main building were to be converted into parking space with one drive leading to the back and to her own garage. Once that was done, she would order the printers to produce new brochures advertising the latest attractions, namely the bar and the taxi service provided.

'Well, one thing's for sure, we ain't gonna get all this done for Christmas.' Flo surveyed the piles of rubble outside the door of the Bainbridges' former home.

Sarah poked her friend playfully on the shoulder. 'Well, another thing's for sure, it had better be finished if I'm going to put up all the people who've replied to my adverts.'

Flo's jaw dropped. 'You don't mean to say you've been and gone ahead touting for customers before we've even got the place decorated.' She cast a despairing look towards the back garden. 'Just look at the mess out there. Honestly, you take the bleedin' biscuit girl.'

'Who's going to want to be outside in the garden on Christmas Day, tell me that Flo? We'll stuff them so full of good food and drink, they won't want to stir very far. Perhaps on Boxing Day, we might show them a bit of Blackpool, that's if the weather is fine enough.'

Flo's air of disbelief did not escape Sarah. 'Trust me Flo, I know what I'm doing.'

There was to be no contradicting Sarah when she was in this frame of mind. The builders would be out just in time for Sid and a mate to decorate the new bedrooms.

The White Rose Weeps

Extra furniture and carpets had been ordered to be delivered a week before Christmas.

'Now, our job is to get the puddings and cakes done. A good dollop of brandy and they'll be perfect, nice and mature in time for Christmas.' A glow of excitement lit up her whole being, bringing colour to her cheeks and a spark of fire to her green eyes. This was what she had wanted her whole life through, to be mistress of her own hotel, to plan, give orders, decide on menus which would keep bringing back customers. She remembered with a smile the day she had read the menu outside the smart hotel in Barnsley and had asked her mother what 'pommes frites' were. Ever since that day, they had been called 'posh chips' in her mind.

The dates with Fergus had taken her into some of the best establishments on the coast; nothing had escaped her eye.

'How about paying me a little attention, young lady?' had often been his complaint when Sarah had been astutely assessing the roles of the various staff.

'I am, but I was just wondering what—'

'Well stop wondering and enjoy your meal, or else the next time it'll be fish and chips out of a newspaper.'

With just a week to go before Christmas, the builders had departed, and Sid had wallpapered the last bedroom according to Sarah's instructions. At seven in the morning a huge pantechnicon was parked outside the Glendale hotel with the men ready to start unloading carpets and bedroom furniture.

All the staff were standing in the hallway prepared to move into the rooms immediately the carpets had been laid and the furniture put into place. Doris, together with her daughter Cynthia then polished and dusted every surface in every room, made up the beds and hung the curtains. Doris's young niece, Pearl, ran up and down the stairs doing the fetching and carrying. Sarah never ceased to wonder at Pearl's energy and unfailing cheerfulness.

'Steady on Pearl,' she told her, seeing the girl taking two steps at a time in her desire to deliver new bedding to her aunt and cousin.

'I'm all right, really I am, Mrs Connolly.' She paused, her eyes full of admiration for her boss. 'I hope you don't think I'm being cheeky, Mrs Connolly, but I think you're ever so clever doing all this.' She hung her head, suddenly fearful that her words might be seen as insolent.

Sarah patted her shoulder. 'No, I don't think you're being cheeky, Pearl. This is something I've always dreamt about, having my own hotel.' She wagged her finger. 'Just you watch and learn, and perhaps one day you'll work your way up as well.'

Thrilled at the prospect of being more than a mere housemaid, Pearl danced up the stairs, singing to herself. Sarah watched her, amused at the impression she had made on the girl. Was it really only just over five years ago that she had been the lowest of the low in the Scatesburn household, given the meanest tasks cleaning up after disgustingly filthy guests? Anger burned fiercely in her breast at the memory of Arthur Scatesburn's attempts to rape her. She would never be able to repay Flo for rescuing her from Rosewood House.

She wandered through into the bar where, once the licence had been granted, the shelves had been stocked with the brands of beer and whisky as advised by Sid. Port and lemon for the ladies, plus a sweet sherry for those requiring a drink before dinner had been added at Doris's suggestion.

The White Rose Weeps

Sarah was pleased to be advised by those whose experience of alcohol went beyond downing huge pint mugs of ale. Her only concern was that the bar would not be profitable.

'Of course it will,' Sid assured her. 'Most of the men will be gasping for a drink in the evenings.'

By evening, the last dressing table had been polished, the final bedcover smoothed down, and all the dusters and brooms put away.

'Right, into the kitchen everyone.' Sarah clapped her hands. 'Come on, help yourselves,' she offered, producing a huge casserole filled with a mouthwatering stew. Freshly baked rolls, still warm from the oven, were piled up in a basket and eagerly seized upon by the exhausted and hungry workers.

'Well, you said we'd be done by Christmas, Sarah, and to be honest, I never thought we would be, but you've done it again.'

Sid's praise was echoed by Flo. 'She's a bloomin' miracle worker, that's what she is.'

Sarah beamed, enjoying the friendly camaraderie of her staff. 'We've got a few days before the guests arrive, so I think it would be a good idea if you all had a couple of days' break before Christmas Eve.'

Doris's plump face creased in such a broad grin that her brown eyes were almost reduced to slits. There was no denying it; she was not as young as she used to be, and there was still plenty to do at home.

Pearl had opted to stay on at Glendale, her parents having been invited to spend the holiday season with some dull, elderly relatives. 'They'll all keep on about the old days and how much better everything was, and then they'll listen to the King's speech on the wireless. Next thing, they'll all be snoring their heads off, and I'll be told to do all the washing-up. No thanks!'

It was true; the noisy bustle and laughter, permanent features of Glendale, suited her ebullient nature far better than the staid atmosphere of her elderly relatives' house. Besides, she had become very attached to David much to Flo's relief, which meant that she could play with him and keep him out of mischief while Sarah and Flo were busy cooking.

Half-hearted protests that they would stay if wanted were soon countered. 'I've got Pearl here if anything needs doing.' Sarah grinned at Pearl, whose delight at being considered indispensable, evinced itself in a slow blush which seemed as if it would spread to the tips of her toes.

The calm before the storm was how Flo described the run-up to Christmas Eve. 'You'd better 'ave a night out now, if you're reckoning on getting a bit of a break,' she advised Sarah.

'Have you been listening in to my telephone calls again?' Sarah teased.

Flo faced her friend with a stern look. 'You know what I mean. All you ever do is think about this hotel and landing yourself with more and more work. There's that lovely fella Fergus out there, who'd give 'is back teeth for the chance to marry you.' Her features softened with concern. 'I want you to be 'appy, Sarah.'

'I am happy, really happy, so stop fussing.' She ruffled Flo's untidy mop of hair. 'Just you make sure that you've got everything right for my little godson. I want your precious David to have the best Christmas ever.' She paused on her way out of the kitchen. 'And if it's any consolation to you, I'm going to get ready for a date with

Fergus tonight.'

Flo looked marginally cheered by this news. 'Well, if he asks you to marry 'im, say yes, and put us all out of our misery.'

Still laughing at Flo's advice, Sarah went upstairs to her flat to take a long, hot bath before dressing for dinner with Fergus.

Entering the Grand Metropole Hotel with Fergus as her escort, Sarah could not help noticing the covert, admiring glances cast in her direction. She had made a special effort this evening, choosing the latest style in a figure-hugging gown in shot silk, which clung to her gently full breasts and slim hips, emphasising her tiny waist. Hard work at the hotel nullified the effects that her generous meals might otherwise have had on her figure. Slender strapped sandals and a matching patent leather evening bag completed the simple but stunning outfit.

Fergus clutched her arm in a possessive gesture not lost on the men, whose envious looks threatened to evoke angry responses from their own partners. Exulting in her triumphant business expansion added a brilliant sparkle to her emerald eyes. The heightened, yet delicate flush of colour on her milky white skin, lifted her beauty from out of the ordinary to an incandescent glow.

Fergus had reserved a table discreetly hidden behind a large ornamental plant, well away from the gaze of other diners, yet close to the dance floor. The maitre d'hotel pulled out Sarah's chair in an extravagant gesture of gallantry, before summoning a waiter to advise on wines.

'Champagne, I think,' Fergus ordered.

Sarah smiled shyly. Fergus's handsome, finely chiselled features aroused in her a feeling that she had long since forgotten or deliberately suppressed.

He leant towards her, clasping her hand in his. 'I'm the luckiest man alive,' he breathed, longing and desire in his low, vibrant whisper.

As each course succeeded the other, Sarah was scarcely aware of what she was eating, lost in the wonder of being alive and loved once again. The band struck up a slow foxtrot, and as several couples took to the floor, Fergus led Sarah out, holding her closely, until she could feel every contour of his firm, hard body. He bent low to nuzzle her neck, the heat from his breath making her gasp. It was as if she were in another world, where pain and grief had been banished forever and only love and desire had a place.

'Take me home, please, Fergus,' she begged, when the waiter hovered close by offering coffee. 'It's been lovely, a truly wonderful evening.

The waiter appeared with the bill, breaking the magic thread which had been slowly binding them together all evening.

Fergus was silent as he held open the door of his latest car, a large Buick designed with luxury and comfort in mind. Sarah snuggled down in the passenger seat beside Fergus, moving over towards his side to be closer to him. The engine growled into life, and soon they were heading along the coast road until there were no more lights, just the gentle sound of the soughing breeze and the caress of the waves on the sands.

Sarah knew what Fergus was about to say when he braked, pulled on the handbrake and turned towards her. They clung together, kissing and murmuring until Sarah felt that his lovemaking was becoming too urgent. She pulled away, shy and hesitant.

'I'm sorry. I didn't bring you here to take advantage of

the situation.' He grabbed hold of the steering wheel, his knuckles white in the pale light of the moon. Once again he turned towards her. 'I'm not very good at making fancy speeches, you know that Sarah, but if you'd marry me, I'd be the proudest and happiest man on this earth.'

Sarah stroked his cheek. 'Dear Fergus, I think that was a very pretty speech.'

'Well?'

'Well, it's a big decision,' Sarah heard herself saying. Why was she putting off the decision? She loved Fergus, she told herself, true not with the same passion that had gripped her whole being with Harry, but probably with more passion than many people experienced in a lifetime of marriage.

'Please say yes.' Fergus's desperation made her feel guilty.

'I want to marry you, truly I do, Fergus, there isn't anyone else, and I know we could be very happy together, but . . .'

'But what?'

'I'm a bit overwhelmed by everything. So much has happened to me in the last few weeks, I need a day or two to get back to reality. Look, I promise I'll give you my answer on Christmas Eve. You're to come to supper and give a hand with the last minute touches, and then..'

'And then I'll have the happiest Christmas of my whole life, or maybe the most miserable.'

Sarah kissed him again, this time gently. 'You're a lovely man, and I do love you, Fergus. Just wait and see.'

The morning of Christmas Eve saw Flo and Sarah hastily packing mountains of mince pies into tins and cooking geese ready for Christmas Day. The response to Sarah's advertisements had meant that eleven rooms were booked for nine married couples, a single man on his own and an unmarried lady in her late thirties or early forties. Twenty guests would keep them all busy, if Sarah's promise of providing the best Christmas in Blackpool were to be kept.

As the guests appeared, the smiles on their faces at seeing the bright, newly decorated rooms told Sarah that she had been right in rejecting the sensible, durable qualities of dark, drear colours in favour of pastels and lightness.

Pearl served them tea in the comfortable parlour, chatting to them and getting them to break the ice. 'I wouldn't be surprised if them two single ones don't make a go of it by Boxing Day,' she told a surprised Sarah.

As the clock in the hallway struck three, Sarah left Flo in charge in the kitchen. 'Won't be gone long. I'll be back in time to start dinner. Just get Pearl to peel the potatoes and scrub the carrots.'

Flo did not need to ask where Sarah was going. Every week, Sarah collected a specially ordered bunch of white roses to lay on Rosie's grave. No doubt with this being Christmas, the roses would cost a fortune, but whatever the time of year, and whatever the price, Sarah had never missed.

She had to park her car a little way from the market area, with the crowds still thronging the streets intent on picking up a last minute bargain from the butchers. A chicken, considered a special treat, was all that most could afford to put on the table for Christmas dinner. Sarah pushed her way through, occasionally distracted by the cries of the street vendors offering cheap Japanese dolls and mechanical toys to put in children's stockings along with the nuts and oranges.

'Oh, hello, fancy bumping into you.'

Sarah swung round, as her arm was gripped by a woman whose face she vaguely remembered. 'Oh, yes, it's Mrs Britten. How are you?' Sarah gathered her wits sufficiently to be be polite to the friendly Mancunian who had bought Fred's café and was now running it with her husband. 'All going well with the café?'

'Wonderful, my dear, never been happier. It's nice of you to ask.'

'Good, it's been nice to meet you again. Merry Christmas to you and Mr Britten.'

'And to you. Oh, by the way, I've been wondering if I'd run into you some time, not that it's important. It's just that someone came into the café asking about you.'

'Oh, don't worry, Mrs Britten.' The memory of Fred's café was too painful for Sarah to want to prolong any conversation concerning news of any kind to do with it. Besides, she was beginning to become impatient. It was getting late and darkness had meant that many stallholders were switching on more lights. It would be pitch black by the time she reached the cemetery. A moment of panic seized her at the thought that she might miss her few precious moments with Rosie. She kicked herself mentally for not having started out earlier, and now this woman was wanting to stop and gossip.

The woman was not to be put off. 'Let me see now, oh, it must have been a couple of months back now, come to think of it. A tall, big built fellow, lots of fair hair and a lovely set of white teeth.' Seeing Sarah grow pale, she grasped her arm in support. 'You OK, love? You've gone all white.'

'No, I'm fine, really, just been overdoing it, with it being Christmas. You know what it's like.'

The woman went on. 'He asked about a little girl, but I told him I hadn't seen you with a little girl. Still,' she added triumphantly, 'I told him you were doing fine, what with that nice husband of yours and your dear little baby boy.'

What on earth was she talking about? Suddenly, a cameo flashed into Sarah's mind, of Sid walking into the café when he and Flo were staying with her. He had been holding David in his arms, and the Brittens had assumed that he was her husband and David their child. Sure that they would never meet again, and eager to conclude the sale of the café, Sarah had not bothered to disabuse Mrs Britten of her error.

'He said he was glad to know you were happily settled and then he went off. Funny he wouldn't leave me his name and address, though I did say I'd try to pass on his good wishes. Friend of yours, was he?'

'Someone I used to know years ago, when I was a little girl,' Sarah replied faintly.

'Oh well, I don't suppose he'll come back, not now that he knows you're happily settled. Bye love, and a very merry Christmas to you and that nice husband of yours.' Pleased at having passed on the news of Harry's visit, she disappeared amongst the crowds.

Sarah watched her until she was lost in the melée. A silent scream filling her heart, she stood motionless as tears rolled down her cheeks. Harry would never know that their darling Rosie was dead, nor that she had been left a widow. Because of her stupidity in letting the Brittens assume that Sid was her husband and David her son, Harry had gone away thinking that she was happily married with a baby brother for Rosie.

The glare from the light bulbs framing the stalls hurt

The White Rose Weeps

her eyes now swollen with tears, but she still had to collect her white roses from the florist. Stumbling through the hordes of people, she found the shop, hastily paid for the roses and fled to where she had left her car.

It was fortunate that there were few vehicles on the road, her grief and desperation distracting her from the hazards of driving at night, with last minute shoppers dashing across the road, desperate to get home and paying no heed to the traffic.

'Watch it, missus!'

Sarah swerved, barely missing an angry looking man.

It was as she feared, having left her visit to the cemetery so late in the day. By the light of a small torch she kept in her handbag, she read the sign that the cemetery was closed until nine o'clock the following morning. All alone in the blackness of the winter evening, she clung to the locked gates, rattling them, willing them to take pity on her and open. 'Please, please,' she sobbed.

A gentle tap on her shoulder made her give a little scream. 'Oh, it's you, Father, I, er, I thought . . .' Sarah attempted to calm herself, seeing the kindly face of the parish priest looking at her with compassion.

'It'll be your little girl, Mrs Connolly.' He bent to pick up the roses Sarah had dropped in her frantic clawing at the gates. 'Come along, my dear, I'll let you in and we'll take a walk together. We mustn't waste these lovely roses, now.' He pulled a huge bunch of keys out of a pocket and opened the gate.

Aware that he was humouring her, and yet grateful for his sympathy, Sarah allowed herself to be led through the gates and along the path to Rosie's grave. The priest stood back a few yards while Sarah placed the roses in the vase which bore Rosie's name round the rim.

'Sleep tight, my darling girl, Mummy will never leave you.'

Calmer now that she had done what she had set out to do, Sarah walked back to the gate and to her car.

'Just you come and have a chat any time that you feel you need to,' the priest reminded her before disappearing in the direction of the presbytery.

Alone in the darkness of her car, Sarah came to a decision which she knew would change the direction of her life for ever. Had it not been for the meeting with Mrs Britten and the news that Harry had come looking for her, she would have accepted Fergus's offer of marriage, would even have been able to be happy as his wife. All that had changed with the knowledge that marriage to Fergus would be living a lie. At the back of her mind there would always linger memories of Harry. If she never saw him again, her love was for him alone, the only man she could ever truly love, Harry, the father of her darling child, Rosie.

Having lost all that she most loved in the world, there was only one course left open to her; from now on, she would devote her life to furthering her life's ambition. Perhaps in time, hard work would help deaden the ache in her heart.

Painful as it was to hurt a wonderful, loving man who adored her, and who had every expectation that she was about to accept his proposal, Sarah knew that, as soon as she returned to Glendale, she would have to call Fergus and tell him her decision.

His shocked response told her that she would never see him again.

Chapter 21

'So Fergus ain't coming for Christmas then?' Flo's pursed lips and clipped tone conveyed her disapproval of Sarah's news. 'OK, tell me it's none of my business.' She did not wait to hear whether Sarah approved or not. 'You was getting along fine with 'im, and,' she glared, 'you led 'im on to think 'e was in with a chance.'

'Please, Flo, I know what I've done and I'm truly sorry. You've no idea how ashamed I feel letting him down so badly. You're right, I did lead him on, but only because I honestly intended accepting his proposal.'

'What went wrong, Sarah?' Flo was all sympathy now, sensing that something momentous must have happened. 'When you went out of 'ere a few hours ago, you was 'appy as a lark.'

'I bumped into Mrs Britten, you know, the woman who bought Fred's Café and she told me that Harry had come looking for me.' Sarah went on to explain how Harry had been led to believe that Sarah was happily married and now had a baby son. 'She saw Sid with David and put two and two together.'

'And made five,' Flo finished for her. 'So Harry done the decent thing and went off to leave you in peace, is that it? And you're breaking your 'eart, cos you wish you could 'ave 'im back.'

The White Rose Weeps

Sarah nodded. 'That's about it.'

Flo held her in a cuddle, cooing over her as if she were a baby, while Sarah sobbed great rasping cries which seemed as if they would tear her body in half.

Finally, she stopped weeping and stood up, her chin thrust forward defiantly. 'I've made my mind up, Flo. Harry is the only man for me, and he's gone out of my life.' She gulped hard, forcing herself to stem further tears. 'That's how it is and I can't alter things, so I'll just have to get along. I've got my friends around me and that's enough for me.' She straightened her shoulders. 'And now it's Christmas Eve and we've got a hotel to run. First things first though. I've got something special for my little godson.' She produced a pushalong toy horse. 'And tell him from me, he can shove this into the furniture as much as he likes.'

The sight of the wooden horse poking its nose out of the wrapping paper made Flo smile. 'You're really hopeless when it comes to wrapping parcels, but you're a mate in a million.'

With all the guests gathered in the parlour, Sarah took a deep breath and went in to greet them.

'First of all,' she began, 'I want to thank you all for choosing Glendale.'

'Forgive me young lady,' a stern-faced man in his fifties interrupted, 'but shouldn't your mother be doing the honours?'

Sarah smiled indulgently, repressing the urge to comment that Yorkshire was too far away for her mother to come. 'Perhaps I should have explained; I assumed you all knew. I am Mrs Connolly, the proprietress of Glendale.' A warm glow suffused her whole body as she announced this fact. 'This is my hotel, and I am absolutely determined that you are all going to have a lovely Christmas.' And that includes you, you miserable old sod, she thought.

The man was still not convinced that this slip of a girl with the flashing green eyes and the unruly red curls could possibly be experienced enough to run a hotel.

'That remains to be seen.' His portentous statement was ignored by the other guests, who were only too keen to make the most of their stay at Glendale and who were entranced by this lovely young woman.

'It does indeed.' I'm doing pretty well at keeping my temper, she told herself. 'I certainly trust that you are all going to get on well and join in the fun.' She gestured towards the door. 'Now, if you turn left, you will find a bar for the use of guests. As a welcoming gesture, I should like to offer you all a drink on the house. Dinner will be served at six-thirty, so that should give you all time to unpack, have a drink in the bar and come into the dining-room for a hot meal.'

A buzz of excited conversation followed. Clearly the offer of a free drink had countered the adverse influence of the middle-aged Jeremiah.

'Oh, and by the way, there's nothing worse than feeling cold in a strange hotel, and I've frozen in a few in my time,' she confided in them, the lie tripping unashamedly off her tongue, 'so if your room isn't warm, or you feel the need of a hot water bottle, my staff will attend to your needs.'

She escaped to the kitchen to tell Sid what she had decided to do about free drinks. 'And if that bloody Mr Corbell asks for brandy, offer him a nip of this.' She handed over the cheap brandy she used in cooking.

The dining room had been transformed, with all the

tables put together to form a huge refectory table. Holly, mistletoe and brightly coloured paper decorations set the scene for a festive evening. Only the dour Mr Corbell began to protest at not having a separate table for himself and his wife, a thin, grey-haired woman with a perpetually anxious look.

Sarah took hold of his wife's hands in hers. 'Wouldn't you prefer to join in with the group, Mrs Corbell? We're all strangers here, aren't we? It is Christmas and I do so want everyone to have a jolly get-together.'

Mrs Corbell gave a worried glance at her glowering husband. 'If you put it like that, it does sound as if it might be rather nice just this once for a change.'

Suddenly his mood changed. He grinned at Sarah. 'Anything to please the little lady, I suppose.'

The surprised look on his wife's face showed that her husband's efforts to please her were rare occurrences indeed, leaving Sarah to wonder how much of the cheap brandy had been dispensed by Sid in the bar. Perhaps Mr Corbell needed to put on a show of complaining in order to convince the world that he was a confident man in charge of his life. Probably a sad, frightened little man underneath all that bluster.

Christmas Day and Boxing Day went by in a mad rush of meals, washing up, party games, and attending to one or two guests who had been too enthusiastic in trying out the contents of the bar.

Pearl was highly delighted that her predictions regarding the single couple were coming true. 'He's taken her out for a walk before tea, just the two of them.' She gave a thoughtful, 'Hmm,' adding, 'we'll have to make sure he's got her address before they leave. You know that sort, always too shy to get to the point.'

'Pearl, really!' Sarah protested, while secretly agreeing that Pearl's comments contained some truth.

'Stands to reason, Mrs Connolly, doesn't it? If they weren't both so backward in coming forward, they'd both have been married by now, wouldn't they?'

If only life were as simple as Pearl thought it to be. How could she know that not everyone got to marry the person they loved most? The gods often had cruel sport with the hearts of mere mortals.

'Of course,' Pearl went on briskly, 'that Miss Bixby might have lost her sweetheart in the Great War – she looks the right age. Sad isn't it? My Mam says there's ever so many women left on the shelf because of all the men that got killed. There's not enough men left to go round.'

It was with some relief that Sarah took the last couple to catch their train or coach home. Everyone had declared that it had been their best Christmas ever, promising to return the following year.

'And we'll be bringing friends as well.'

Once the car was shut up in the garage, Sarah kicked off her shoes and collapsed in a chair in the bar. 'Come on, all of you, I reckon we could do with a drink to revive us.'

Sid poured out a sherry for Flo and Sarah, a lemonade for Pearl and a pint of mild and bitter for himself.

'There's plenty of food left over, so I reckon we can put our feet up for the next few days, what do you say boss?' Flo asked, sipping her sherry and cuddling a sleepy David.

'Do you reckon they'll get married?' Pearl mused.

'Oh, Pearl, you're not still dreaming of a romance between Miss Bixby and Mr Dyson, are you? One's gone off to Leicester and the other to Liverpool, so I don't suppose their paths will ever cross again.'

Pearl persisted, 'Perhaps not, Mrs Connolly, but they might write to one another, and who knows what might come of it?'

'That's if they've exchanged . . .' Enlightenment dawning, Sarah glared at Pearl. 'Pearl! What have you been up to?'

Pearl hung her head. 'I was only trying to help. I put her address in his coat pocket and his in hers, so that way they'll both think the other is interested.'

Sarah clutched her forehead, as Flo gave out with one of her ear-splitting screams. David did not stir, accustomed as he was by now to his mother's laugh.

Grabbing Pearl by the arm, Sarah dragged Pearl out of the bar and into the kitchen, where she sat her down hard. 'Now just you listen to me, my girl. If I catch you doing anything like this again, you'll be out on your ear without so much as a reference, understood?'

Pearl burst into tears, promising between sniffs to mind her own business and never to interfere in business that concerned the guests.

'For all you know, Pearl, that Miss Bixby might just have been acting politely towards Mr Dyson and the last thing she might want is an unwelcome letter from him. Right, dry your tears, and from now on, just you remember who the boss is around here.'

They returned to the bar, with a subdued Pearl taking her place beside Flo and offering to hold David.

Once Pearl had gone up to bed, Sarah and Flo mulled over the success of the past few days. Flo raised the subject of Pearl's attempted match-making. 'Come on, Sarah, you can't really blame the girl for being a bit romantic. She only thought she was doing a bit of good, bringing a bit of love into their lives.'

'You think that's what I need, don't you Flo?'

Flo shook her head. 'Whatever I say ain't gonna make a scrap of difference. You still love your Harry, and it seems as if that's all you do want, and you ain't gonna settle for second best. It's no good me telling you what I think, so I ain't arguing with you.'

Sarah was silent for a moment. Her chin cupped in her hands, she stared into space. Flo waited, recognising that Sarah was about to come to a decision and would announce it all in her own good time.

'I've not taken on any bookings for January. We're all due for a break and then the rooms could all do with a spring clean before the Easter rush.'

Flo nodded. Sarah was right; they had all been so busy the whole of the summer season, followed by the building works and the hectic Christmas, that a rest was long overdue.

'I've decided to leave in a day or two to stay with my family. Now I can drive, I don't need to worry about trains or buses.'

Flo looked worried. 'All the same, that road over the Pennines can be dangerous if it gets too icy. Wouldn't it be safer to go by bus?'

Sarah tutted. 'I'll be fine, so stop fussing, Flo. Anyway, why shouldn't I have my car to take my family out in?'

'You rotten old show-off!'

'Maybe,' Sarah agreed, the corners of her mouth turning upwards in spite of her efforts to conceal a self-satisfied smile. 'I haven't seen Mam and Dad and our little Maureen since they stayed here last summer.'

'Wasn't your Dad proud, telling all the other guests

that you were his daughter and owned the hotel?'

'Oh my God, yes,' Sarah recollected. 'I mean, Mam was just as proud, but at least she kept it to herself.'

'Is that the real reason you want to go back to Colethorpe? Could it 'ave anything to do with Harry Wilby's visit to Fred's Café?'

Sarah sighed. 'Are you sure there aren't witches in your family, Flo, or is it that you can see right through me?'

'Right through you and back again, my girl.' Flo's air of triumph at having hit the nail on the head did not trouble Sarah.

'It is just possible, that if he came to the café to look for me, then he might have been in touch with Bernard and Iris.'

'After all this time?' Flo raised her eyebrows in disbelief.

Sarah shrugged her shoulders. 'It's a long shot but I've got to try.' In a whisper, she went on, 'He ought to know that our little Rosie is dead.'

Flo assumed her brisk air. 'Right, off you go and leave Sid and me to look after things 'ere.'

'Pearl can take a fortnight's holiday, then we'll want her back the third week in January to get started on the spring cleaning. You and Sid can have a blessed fortnight's peace.' She clasped her hand to her mouth. 'I'm a selfish idiot, Flo. It never occurred to me to ask if you wanted to go away anywhere. I've just taken it for granted that you'd stay here and keep an eye on the place, while I go off and please myself.'

'Don't be daft. Where do you think we want to go, when everything we want is under this roof? I mean, we're 'ardly likely to want to go off to the south of France like all the nobs do, are we?'

'Well, what about Sid's aunt and uncle? If you'd like them to stay, as my guests that is . . .'

'We'll see. Go and get packed and don't waste any more time natterin' to me.'

A note in the post had already warned her parents that she would be visiting them but she did not know how long the drive would take and had not given them a specific time of arrival. As Sarah began her packing, a shaft of light, warm as the sun, softened her unhappiness and it occurred to her that she did not have to pack every single item, with the back seat of her car free. *My car.* How many young women like her rode around in their very own car? Fergus had told her often enough that she was a phenomenon, a word that she had had to look up in the dictionary in the library, not wishing to appear ignorant in his eyes. *Too right, I am,* she said, when she found the word. *And I mean to be even more of a remarkable person before I'm through.*

Did she detect a sign of relief in Sid's eyes, when he and Flo stood at the gate to wave her off? A feeling of guilt that perhaps she took too much of Flo's time set her thinking furiously about expanding the business further. Maybe it was time for her to consider living out and leaving Flo and Sid to be live-in managers. There was always the possibility that Flo would soon want a baby brother or sister for David.

She took a deep breath, revelling in her freedom, as the outskirts of the town gave way to the lovely open countryside. With Sid's assistance, she had worked out a route through Preston and Blackburn with the intention of skirting the higher moorlands in Lancashire. Sheffield was her next goal, and in spite of Sid's careful poring over maps, there was no way that she could avoid the vast

The White Rose Weeps

stretches of high moors devoid of human dwellings. Mile upon mile of dark, forbidding country stretched as far as she could see, with not one friendly slate-roofed cottage in sight.

Driving round Blackpool, giving way to the clanging trams, was easy compared with negotiating these vast, peaty moors inhabited only by grouse. The higher ground was proving hazardous too, with a damp fog beginning to swirl in front of the windscreen, its insidious chill freezing her bones.

She stopped to get out and wipe the windscreen, and retrieve a rug from the back seat. Flo had filled a flask with soup, which she drank eagerly, cupping the warmth of the cup with numbed fingers. It was no good, she would have to press on no matter how late or how dark. With no villages in sight where she might find an inn offering hospitality, the only way was to keep driving.

It was a very weary Sarah who finally saw the familiar street lights of Colethorpe beckoning. The drive had taken her longer than she had envisaged with the result that her triumphant progress down the High Street was witnessed only by a few cats and a stray dog, every other living creature being sensibly tucked up in front of a blazing fire.

Not to be totally cheated of her moment of glory, she tooted loudly on the horn, and noticing that this gave rise to a number of twitching curtains, perked up considerably.

'Sarah, love!' Her Mam and Dad rushed out, closely followed by the now five-year-old Maureen, the sight of whose round, baby features tugged at her heart, reminding her that Rosie would have been two-and-a-half, no doubt running around after her tiny 'aunt'.

'Just look at this, our lass in her own motor car.'

Sarah shivered, partly with excitement and partly with the cold. Seeing her shiver, her dad said, 'By, lass, you're freezing. Come on in, quick, your Mam and I can fetch your stuff in.' He released his daughter, eager to inspect the smart little car standing by the front gate. He chuckled. 'This'll give t' neighbours summat to gawp at when they look out of the window tomorrow morning.'

'I'll take you all out in it tomorrow,' Sarah promised gaily.

Her mother hastened to put a hot meal on the table, muttering all the while that she still had not got used to this new-fangled gas stove and that her old kitchen range had never let her down.

'Well, at least you don't have to spend half your time stoking it and blackleading it.'

Joanna's face was a picture of contrition. 'Oh, love, I sound so ungrateful after you buying this lovely house for me and your Dad.' She hugged Sarah. 'You've no idea how happy I am here, what with a proper bathroom and a nice garden to hang out the washing and for Maureen to play in.' She held Sarah at arm's length, gazing at her daughter with love and pride. 'There aren't words to tell you how proud we are of what you've done.' She hugged Sarah again. 'And now, it's time to eat. Go and tell your Dad to leave your motor alone and come on in to eat.'

With unopened parcels all over the floor, they sat round the table, all talking and eating at once. Sarah was shocked at the change in her father. There was little black left in the tight, crisp curls, now nearly all iron grey, making him seem every minute of his fifty or so years. Joanna did not miss her daughter's scrutiny, and prayed that Sarah would make no comment.

The White Rose Weeps

It wasn't until later, long after the Christmas parcels had been unwrapped and Maureen was playing happily with the most expensive dolls' house that Sarah could find in Blackpool, that Sarah raised the subject of work.

'Don't you think it's high time that you got another job, Dad? You've done God knows how many years down the pit, surely it's time the younger ones took over underground and you got given a job on the surface.'

His angry response made her regret raising the matter. 'Do you think I'm getting too old, our lass? You might have bought me and your Mam a nice house to live in, but I'm not accepting any more of your charity. It's my job to provide for Maureen and your Mam, so just you stop your interfering.' His grim expression put an end to Sarah's half-formed idea that he should up sticks and come and work for her in Blackpool in a semi-retired capacity.

Only Joanna guessed that her stubborn daughter was not going to leave matters as they were. She just prayed that Sarah would show some tact. She was relieved when Sarah turned the subject to Bernard and Iris.

'They're fine. I've asked them all to come to dinner on Sunday.' She turned away from Sarah, half afraid that her next words would pain her. 'Iris is expecting again. I think she's hoping that this one will be a girl.'

Sarah's eyes were bright, glistening. 'Lovely, let's hope she gets what she wants. I'll pop in and see her tomorrow.' If she could get Iris on her own, she would be able to be honest with her. Iris was a sister-in-law in a million, fully understanding what Sarah had suffered and never once allocating blame. If Iris had any inkling of where Harry was, she would help Sarah with a willing heart.

There was no answer when Sarah knocked at Iris's door the following morning. A head peered out of a neighbour's window. 'Gone round her Mam's for the day, but she'll be back by six, I expect. I'll tell her you called.' She observed Sarah climbing into the driver's seat. That would be something to tell Iris and Bernard.

'Come in, Mam,' a child's voice called out, 'it's unlucky to see a lady driver.'

'Don't talk bloody daft.' The window was closed firmly.

Disappointed at this setback, Sarah compensated by driving up and down the High Street, stopping on impulse at the Co-op.

'Sarah Mulvey!' Charlie was still there, now promoted to deputy manager. His spots had disappeared, but his ginger hair was just as unruly as ever. He shook her hand fervently, demanded to be shown the new car, calling a shy girl to leave the counter and come and meet his old workmate. 'This is Marjy, my fiancée,' he announced, bright red spots of embarrassment high on his cheeks. 'We're getting married in May, that's if we can save up enough money.'

Sarah surprised them both by giving them an all-embracing hug. 'Charlie was a good friend to me when I needed one,' she told Marjy, 'and now it's my turn.' She fished in her handbag for a card and a brochure containing details of Glendale. 'Let me know the date and I'll book you in for a week. That'll be my wedding present to you.'

The two young lovers stood open-mouthed. Marjy looked as if she was about to burst into tears, just managing to whisper her thanks. Charlie shook his head in disbelief. 'We never thought we'd be able to have a honeymoon. Well, you know what they pay here. Honestly Sarah, you've no idea how happy you've made us.'

Sarah gave him another hug. 'Now, promise you'll let

me know the date and I'll even come and pick you up at the station.'

Feeling more and more like Lady Bountiful and enjoying every moment of it, she continued making stately progress through the village. Heads turned at the sight of little Sarah Mulvey driving the posh new car.

She thrust her chin forward. 'I'll show you buggers,' she said, 'laughing at me behind my back because I found Frank Bass and that Dolly Redmile with their drawers down, and I was the one who had to leave Colethorpe. Well, bloody laugh on the other side of your faces.'

Niggling at the back of her mind was the haggard appearance of her Dad. Something had to be done, but what? 'Why won't Dad just ask for a different job?' she asked her mother that evening.

'Because he's got too much damned pride, that's why. He'd sooner drop dead than admit he's had enough of working day in and day out without a sight of God's good daylight. It breaks my heart when I see him come home every night worn out. That Dan Forest could easily find him a place tomorrow, but he'd like to see your Dad crawl, and that's something he'd never do. Look, that's him going past now, he lives just round the corner with his ugly wife and lump of a daughter. It stuck in his craw seeing us move here to the posh part of the village.'

Sarah watched him, a small skinny man with a face like a weasel. 'He looks a nasty little sod,' she agreed with her mother.

'Two-faced little swine, on his knees at Mass every Sunday. If there was any justice, he'd be struck down dead at the altar.' Joanna tapped Sarah on the shoulder. 'Never mind standing there looking at that pig of a man, come and give me a hand with the tea.'

A bitter cold Sunday morning dawned, with Sarah already up and dressed by half past seven. She carried a tray of tea into her parents' bedroom, announcing her intention of going to eight o'clock Mass. 'I'll have my breakfast when I get back.'

Surprised, yet pleased that his daughter was still practising the faith instilled into her from childhood, Jim said as much to his wife. Joanna agreed absent-mindedly, having seen the look of grim determination in Sarah's eyes, and wondering what lay behind it.

Although the Catholic church was in walking distance, it was still further than it had been when they lived in the middle of Colethorpe, and Sarah decided to drive. She revved up the car engine for the benefit of the neighbours.

'A right sparky little sod she's turned out to be and no mistake,' Jim commented with a grin, as he lay beside his wife, enjoying the luxury of a cup of tea in bed.

Sarah was early, just a few devout worshippers arriving well before eight o'clock. She sat in her car looking and waiting.

Dan Forest, his face red and angry, scowled at his wife, who was having difficulty keeping her balance on the treacherously slippery pavement. A well-built girl, probably fourteen or so, was clinging to her mother's arm.

'Get a move on, woman, it's getting late,' he grunted.

Sarah followed the family into the church, taking a place a couple of rows behind them. With several minutes to go before the priest entered with the familiar ritual of sprinkling the congregation with holy water, Sarah was able to look around and absorb the atmosphere of the church where she had spent so many hours as a child. She focussed on the altar rail, where she had seen herself and Harry exchanging marriage vows so many times in her dreams.

The old Latin Mass had been instilled into her by Father Kelly, so there was no forgetting the responses. The familiarity of it all, the childhood memories when life had been so uncomplicated, threatened to bring tears. Her eyes misted over, but she told herself sternly that she must not allow sentiment to get in the way of what she had set out to do.

'Ah, good morning Mrs Forest, and Mr Forest.' Sarah accosted them immediately the service was over. Ignoring Dan Forest's puzzled look, she went on, 'Perhaps you don't remember me, I'm Jim Mulvey's daughter.' As if suddenly noticing how cold it was, she pointed to her car. 'May I offer you a lift, Mrs Forest?'

The woman's eyes lit up. 'That would be lovely, I'm frozen right through.'

Sarah laughed. 'The old church hasn't got any warmer since I used to go there when I was little. And what's your name?' she asked the girl.

'This is our Eileen, she's thirteen, nearly fourteen, leaving school in the summer, but what she's going to do then, I don't know.'

Dan Forest glowered. 'There'll be summat for her.'

Intrigued by Sarah's affluence, Mrs Forest asked tentatively about her present situation. 'Working in Blackpool, I hear.'

Sarah smiled to herself. 'Not so much working as managing. I don't know if you've heard, but I have a hotel.'

'You mean . . .' Dan Forest was beginning to take an

interest in spite of his ill-temper at having to accept a favour from Jim Mulvey's daughter, 'you've got a job as a manageress already?'

Sarah did not answer at once, savouring the moment. 'You'd better tell me where you live first, Mr Forest.' She waited for directions, then added, 'Actually I've bought a hotel with the money left me by my husband when he died. I'm very fortunate that it has been so successful.' God! What do I sound like, and me only five minutes ago on my knees praying for humility?

The exchange of glances between husband and wife was not lost on Sarah. 'And what do you want to do when you leave school, Eileen?'

A sweet, ingenuous smile spread across her plump face, giving the promise of a gentle beauty once her puppy fat had melted away. 'I want to be a cook, I love cooking, but Mam and Dad don't want me to work in a café in Barnsley. I wouldn't mind though, just so long as I could learn.'

'That's enough, Eileen,' her father admonished.

Sarah helped Mrs Forest out of the car, waving away her gratitude, but accepting her offer of a cup of tea. 'Mustn't stop too long. I promised Dad I'd take him out for a run in my car later on. He doesn't get much chance of getting out in the fresh air.'

Dan Forest's eyes narrowed as he stared at her. He ignored the reference to her father. 'Tell me a bit more about this hotel of yours.'

His abrupt tone angered Sarah, but she maintained her air of cool superiority, handing him a brochure and her card. 'As you see, we can accommodate twenty guests at the moment. I am looking to expand and take on more staff.'

'You train them, of course?'

Sarah pretended that a sudden thought had just struck her. 'I say, I don't suppose Eileen would like to give it a try. I'm always on the look-out for keen, clever girls. She'd have her own room and I'd give her lessons in cooking and running a hotel.'

Eileen squeaked in delight, grabbing her father's arm. 'Please say I can, Dad, please.'

'Just a moment,' Sarah laughed. 'If your parents agree, I suggest that you come as soon as you leave school, say for a trial period in the first instance.'

'Oh, yes, that would be lovely.'

'Not so fast, young lady,' Dan Forest told his eager daughter. 'Your Mam and I will have to have a little talk first.'

Sarah stood up to leave, thanked Mrs Forest for the tea, then paused in the doorway. 'There is only one thing. I don't want to raise Eileen's hopes too much. As I said, I'm very concerned about my father still working underground. I feel he deserves a change after the years he's put in. In fact, I was only saying to my mother last night, that if he soon doesn't get moved to a surface job, I'll move them both to Blackpool to work for me. Mam can help with the cooking and Dad can run the bar and drive the guests around. Of course, I wouldn't have an opening for Eileen then, and she'd be so disappointed, I'm sure.'

Mrs Forest opened her mouth to speak, but was silenced by her husband. 'You're a good business woman, Sarah Mulvey, and I wouldn't want our little Eileen missing out on the chance of a lifetime, would I?'

The two protagonists eyed one another. 'I'm sure you wouldn't, Mr Forest. I look forward to hearing from you when Eileen has finished school, and, I must emphasise, if there is still a vacancy.'

She swept out to her car, well aware of the excited conversation which erupted the moment the door was closed behind her.

'You've been long enough on your knees, lass.' Jim was on the front path scattering salt. 'Nearly measured me length just now and that was before I'd had a pint at the Club.'

Sarah could see he was in a hurry to get to see his mates and boast about his Sarah's wealth. Her offer to run him down to the Club was rewarded by such a smile of delight that Sarah was filled with love for this man who had slaved all his life in the dark, dank misery of the pit to provide for his family.

It was getting late by the time she returned to help her mother with the Sunday dinner. Joanna chided her gently. 'I thought it was our Lizzie who was good at getting out of the hard graft. Taking a leaf out of her book, are we?'

'Mam!' Sarah grabbed the vegetable knife out of her mother's hand, and picked the bag of potatoes off the floor. Dinner had better be on time with Bernard and Iris coming round. How she was going to get Iris on her own to quiz her about Harry occupied her thoughts as she attacked the potatoes.

'You're quiet, our lass. Anything the matter?'

Sarah shook her head, thankful that she was facing the window over the sink. 'Everything's fine, really it is. I'm making so much money with the hotel, to tell the truth, I just can't believe it's turned out so well.' She knew from the silence that followed, that her answer did not satisfy Joanna.

'That's not what I mean, so stop trying to pull the wool over my eyes. It's your mother you're talking to. What happened to that nice Fergus you said was going to spend Christmas with you?'

'Nothing, Mam. I'm just not ready to settle down.' She spun round to face her mother. 'You might as well know the truth, Mam, I've no intention of ever getting married. My life is my hotel and making a success of that. My only ambition is to own the biggest hotel on the Lancashire coast.'

Joanna swallowed hard. She brushed a stray hair back off her forehead with her forearm, as she continued to beat the batter for the Yorkshire pudding. Sarah felt a twinge of sorrow, seeing her mother's once abundant red hair now streaked with more grey than it had been in the summer.

'Why Lancashire? Why not Scarborough or somewhere nearer to us? What with Lizzie talking about getting a job on a cruise liner and going off all over the world, and Patrick only happy when he gets a posting miles away, I feel as if I'm losing all my children.'

The enormity of her remark did not strike her until Sarah's choking sob and agonised cry rang through the kitchen. 'I've lost mine, Mam, and I can't leave her all alone in Blackpool in that cemetery with no one to go and visit her every week.'

Joanna dropped the fork she was using to whip up the batter, and rushed to her daughter. She hugged her, crooning words of comfort until Sarah's sobs subsided.

'I'm all right now. It just hits me every so often. I'll just go and splash my face with cold water and then we'd better get a move on with this dinner.' On her return she was smiling, holding a huge clockwork car. 'Do you think

Iris will approve of this for young Joe? I've got to admit that I've tried it out and it goes really well.' Her eyes were shining with laughter.

Not for the first time, Joanna recognised that this daughter of hers was tough enough to take whatever life had to throw at her, spit it out, and start over again. 'I'm sure he'll love it,' she said, forcing herself to smile back.

The noise and fuss generated by the arrival of the three-and-a-half year old Joe and his excitement at seeing the clockwork car whizzing across the lino on the kitchen floor, had everyone laughing and talking at once.

'Come on upstairs,' Sarah told Iris, once the rumpus had died down a little. 'We'll put all the coats on my bed and make a bit of room for this family of yours.'

Iris's relief that Sarah was still her treasured, friendly sister-in-law was written all over her face as she kissed and hugged her. 'We've heard all about your car, and now Bernard says we've got to save up for one. Fat chance with the littl'un on the way.' Pleased to have the opportunity of talking to Sarah on her own, she instructed Bernard to keep Joe with him and amuse him until she came back down again.

The minute they were both alone in Sarah's room, Iris seized her arm eagerly. 'We had a Christmas card from Harry.' She waited to see the effect that this item of news had on Sarah.

Sarah flushed bright scarlet, then a sudden fear that she was to be disappointed once more, stripped the colour from her cheeks. 'He's well?' was all that she could struggle to ask.

'I'm sorry, Sarah, he didn't say anything, the card was signed, 'Harry', that's all I can tell you.'

'But where is he?' Sarah's desperation filled Iris with

guilt at having mentioned the card.

'There wasn't an address on the card.'

'But the postmark, where was it posted?' If she just knew where, she would walk the streets until she found him.

Iris sat down on the bed. 'I'm so sorry, Bernard threw all the envelopes on the fire.'

'Oh, well, it can't be helped. It's nice to know he's not forgotten you and Bernard.'

Her quiet resignation drove Iris to seek some way of consoling Sarah. 'But, listen, don't you see? At least he's got in touch, so he'll probably write soon and let us have his address. Besides, he only signed his name, so I expect he's still single.'

'Dear, sweet Iris, what would I do without you? That brother of mine married an angel, I just hope he realises it.' She held Iris's hand for a moment. 'Come on, let's go down before Mam starts yelling that the dinner is ruined.'

Chapter 22

The newspaper headlines in March 1938, announcing that Austria had now been declared a German Province, and that French troops manning the Maginot Line had had their leave cancelled, fuelled fears that the outbreak of yet another war barely twenty years after the Armistice, was a distinct possibility.

Astute business woman that she was, Sarah was aware that, if war broke out, her holiday trade would be severely curtailed.

During the course of the two and a half years since she had last had news of Harry, opportunities to expand by selling Glendale and moving up-market had presented themselves on a number of occasions, but Sarah had prudently decided against moving each time. It was true that she had thrown herself into a frenzy of work. Not content with having bought the house belonging to the elderly Braithwaites, she had persuaded the owners of the house next to them to move out. Her generous offer had proved to be irresistible, leaving Sarah with a house into which she could move Flo and Sid and their two children, thus releasing their ground floor flat.

'I tell you that my next hotel will either be bang on the sea front and not tucked away down a side street, or else it will be in a location with plenty of parkland. I'd like to have my own swimming pool and tennis court for the guests, and an area where children could be left with a nanny in charge. I'm sure lots of parents would appreciate a bit of peace and quiet now and again.'

Flo rolled her eyes heavenwards. 'I'll be buggered, you think of everything, girl.' With David now a mischievous three year old and a year old baby girl, Jeannie, Flo had her hands full. 'Anyway, what do you want to move for? You've already expanded more than once.'

'That's just it, Flo, you've seen the papers. This is no time to think of buying what could turn out to be a white elephant.' Suddenly weary, she closed her eyes. 'I'll have to think of a way to keep us going, if there is a war, that is.'

Throughout 1939 frightening reports gathered momentum, with a new Women's Voluntary Service being formed. ARP posters calling on women to assist air raid wardens and carry out duties in the event of air raids brought home to Sarah and Flo that their happy existence was shortly to end.

Even before the outbreak of war on September 3, conscription had been introduced. To Flo's relief, Sid was declared unfit due to perforated ear-drums, but there still remained the worry as to what might happen to him.

The inexorable march towards the invetiable did not come until September when German troops invaded Poland.

'Well, what are we gonna do now?'

The few remaining guests at Glendale moved around solemnly, afraid to laugh and let themselves go. Too many of them had seen the horror of the trenches and had been forced to watch good comrades die engulfed in mud and stench.

By the end of the month, Glendale was deserted.

Sarah surveyed her staff, now depleted with Doris's retirement and Pearl's decision to join the Auxiliary Territorial Service.

'Ever since she saw that poster with the girl in uniform blowing a bugle, she's 'ad 'er 'ead filled with dreams of being a girl soldier. If she thinks they're gonna let 'er loose with a gun, she's got another think coming. Cooking, cleaning and running around after the officers, that's all she'll get to do, and without 'ome comforts.'

Flo's portentous expression brought a smile to Sarah's lips. 'If she wants to do her bit, good for her. We've still got Eileen.' She gave the girl an encouraging hug.

Eileen beamed. 'Don't you worry, Mrs Connolly, I'll be here as long as you want me.' Dan Forest's little girl had blossomed into an attractive sixteen year old with a ready, willing nature.

Sarah had been forced to keep back from her Mam the truth about the transaction with Dan Forest, although that lady had had her suspicions. Within two weeks of Sarah's visit to the Forest household, Jim had been moved to a more congenial job on the surface, and Sarah was negotiating with the Forests to employ Eileen. Joanna knew that there had to be a connection somewhere, but she was only too thankful that Jim's health had improved as a result of the move to challenge her daughter on the subject. Fortunately, Jim had not connected the two events. Moreover, it was a source of pride that his daughter was the boss of his own boss's daughter — an evening up of status.

'Right, all of you, sit down.' Sarah's round the kitchen table talks usually signalled that an important announcement was to be made.

The White Rose Weeps

Flo, Sid, Eileen and Doris's daughter Cynthia gathered round, sipping steaming mugs of tea.

'It's a fair bet that our holiday trade will be down, probably non-existent, so we can forget that as a way of earning a living, but I'm not throwing in the towel. You all know me well enough by now to know that I've no intention of losing money. We are going to fight and we are going to survive, depend on it. That Hitler is not going to get the better of me.'

Not bloody likely, knowing Sarah, Flo thought.

'I didn't want to tell you this before in case it didn't come off, but the fact is that I've signed a contract with the Civil Service to provide accommodation for their London staff. I found out that much of their workforce is to be moved out of London and has to be housed. Never mind how I got to hear,' she said, forestalling Flo's question. 'The point is, they're willing to pay one guinea per week.'

Sid whistled. 'And they'll be far from home, so they'll use the bar in the evenings, I wouldn't mind taking a bet.'

Sarah sat back, satisfied that her plans were meeting with approval. She had worked hard and long to make Glendale a going concern, and no jumped-up dictator with a little black moustache was going to make her surrender. Deprived of the man she loved, her darling Rosie dead, and with work motivating her day in day out, she was not prepared to lose what gave her the incentive to live.

'There is just one thing,' Sid obviously was making plans in his head. 'How many of these blokes are going to be single? Will any of them have their wives with them?'

'Mostly single, as far as I can make out, but there might be one or two couples without children.'

Sid scratched his head. 'How about if I put up some partitions in the bigger rooms, divide them into two, so as to give us more rooms?'

Flo grinned, bursting with pride at Sarah's pleased reaction. 'You're an absolute genius, Sid. We'll have our tea and then have a look at ways and means.' She was suddenly solemn. 'Look, I hope you all approve of this. I just wanted to make sure that you all had jobs. There is something else, though.'

For a moment, Flo was afraid that Sarah was on the verge of weeping. 'You OK, love?'

Sarah rubbed her eyes. 'Yes, it's just that I can't help wondering about the children in the big cities. I mean, innocent children being murdered by Hitler's bombs.'

'You mean we ought to take some evacuees, don't you?'

'Yes, Flo, I don't want to fill the hotel simply with paying guests, but could you stand it?'

'Don't be daft, of course we could. I've heard that some of the mothers come as well to help and some teachers, so if we get a mix, we'll be able to manage.'

Sarah nodded, her eyes closed. No one interrupted, recognising that she was planning exactly where each one of the Civil Servants would go and how she would house the city kids so that they would not disturb the peace and quiet of the older guests.

'So long as we have no go areas for the little buggers, we should maintain our sanity. I think we'll have to insist that we get at least one reasonably willing mother and a teacher, that is if we are going to be prepared to take half a dozen or so. I'm not staying up half the night making sure that they're all tucked up and not wandering around the place.' Sarah's kind heart did not stretch to letting herself be made a fool of.

'Right Sid, let's go and have a look and see which

rooms can be made into singles for the duration.'

The last of the summer visitors having departed, Sid set to work on converting some of the double rooms. A plumber was called in to install two extra bathrooms, the expense constituting a good investment as far as Sarah was concerned. Keeping this new class of visitors from London happy and comfortable might well pay dividends after the war, which everyone said would be over very soon.

One by one, diffident young men, all exempted from war service on account of their being assessed as working in a reserved occupation, arrived at Glendale. Mostly shy and polite, they were declared to be good customers by Flo.

'Don't look like this lot's gonna be much trouble. They're pretty quiet and we ain't 'ad no complaints.' She shook her head. 'Mind you from what I've 'eard about the evacuees, we're gonna 'ave our work cut out with them.'

The meeting of evacuees, local committee workers under the direction of a harassed looking vicar's wife, and prospective landladies took place in the nearby school hall. The children carried bags containing what change of clothes they possessed, a gas mask, a tin of corned beef and a bar of chocolate, the last two items provided by the Women's Voluntary Service, so it was said.

Sarah began to wonder about the wisdom of her magnanimous gesture one week after the first group of children arrived. There were four boys and six girls, more than Sarah had intended having; she had been persuaded to agree to the extra numbers, as the authorities had miscalculated the availability of beds. One sad looking mother had agreed to accompany her small son, but instead of the help expected from her, she had proved to be in more need of comforting than the children.

In the end, Sarah had been forced to issue her with a list of duties, which included making sure that they were all tucked up in bed by eight every evening.

'Please, Chrissy, unless you are prepared to give a hand, I'll just have to ask for you to be moved elsewhere and someone else who's prepared to pull their weight can take your place.'

Chrissy O'Mahoney was not as simple as she made out. This was the first time she had ever lived in a posh hotel, a vast change from the tenement flat in Liverpool and the everlasting diet of fatty stew alternated with bread and dripping.

'I think she's got the general idea now.' Flo had gone out of her way to help Chrissy, instinctively recognising in her a kindred soul. 'She's 'ad a tough life,' she told Sarah. 'We'll just 'ave to go a bit easy on 'er.'

Sid was not inclined to be so indulgent towards the woman. Ever since her arrival, the bottles of gin had needed replacing more frequently. As most of the male guests drank beer, with the two wives who had accompanied their husbands preferring sherry, the gin should never have run out. He had tried locking away the gin, but in spite of all his precautions, a phantom drinker was depleting his stocks. Without telling Sarah of his plans, he lay in wait, hiding in the darkened dining-room from where he could observe the bar.

'Gotcha!' he roared, leaping out from his hiding place

and grabbing the collar of the person who was carefully picking the lock of the cupboard where he had hidden the gin.

The figure straightened up, spinning round to face an irate Sid. 'What the bloody hell do you think you're up to, you miserable bugger, stealing my gin?'

The noise of the woman's frightened scream brought Sarah running down the stairs to see what the commotion was all about.

'How dare you!' For one brief second, Sid thought that Sarah was going to smack the woman round the face. 'You thieving little bitch. Right! That's it, pack your things and you can be out of here first thing.'

Chrissy O'Mahoney's thin face was contorted in fury, as she raised her arm to strike Sarah.

'I wouldn't advise that,' Sarah said, seizing her arm and twisting it up behind her back. 'You might think you've been raised in a hard school, but I'm telling you now, mine was a bloody sight harder, so you'd better think again.'

The woman slunk off to her room muttering to herself.

'You don't think she'll try to do some damage to the place before she leaves, do you?' Sid had seen the spiteful look in the woman's eyes. 'She's being turned out of a damned comfortable billet, remember?'

Blast! Why was it when you tried to help some people they got themselves into even bigger messes? Even acknowledging the truth of this, Sarah was not going to be made a fool of. She served Chrissy toast and tea in her room, casting a careful eye round.

'And there'd better be nothing missing or any damage done, or it'll be the police station, not the bus station when we leave here.' She glared at the woman. 'I trust you've got the message.'

An hour later Chrissy O'Mahoney, together with her son, presented herself in the kitchen. 'You can check what you like, there's nothing missing,' she declared defiantly.

Sarah loaded their few possessions into the car. 'Come on, get in Michael, I haven't got all day.'

She drove them in silence to the the bus station. 'Right, get out and wait here while I get your tickets.' She had guessed that Chrissy would be broke as usual.

'We were leaving anyway,' Michael called out as he boarded the bus. 'You can keep your posh old house.'

'Cheeky little bugger,' Sarah told Flo later. 'He won't let life get him down. All the same, I hope he'll be safe in Liverpool.'

As December approached with no sign of any active warfare, many of the noisy evacuees returned to Liverpool, leaving Sarah with the problem of redecorating their rooms to accommodate even more of the Civil Service.

A vague malaise which she could not explain began to trouble her sleep, making her get up and wander about her flat in the dead of night. Sipping tea at three in the morning, she took stock of what she was doing. Looking after her guests was now merely a bread and butter job, with no excitement, no prospects and no incentive to make changes. With a sudden jolt, Sarah recognised that she was becoming bored and that stagnation was beginning to set in. She went back to bed, banishing such heretical thoughts from her mind, but as her head hit the pillow, she smiled with contentment. Of course, why hadn't she thought of that before? I wonder what Flo will say were her last thoughts before drifting off.

The White Rose Weeps

She did not have to wait long to hear Flo's thoughts on the subject. Knives and forks in the dining room remained suspended between plate and mouth as the raised voices in the kitchen carried through the hall.

'I don't believe it, Sarah! 'Ave you gone completely out of your mind? 'Ere, Sid, come quick!' Flo grabbed Sarah by the shoulders, glaring at her friend eyeball to eyeball. 'I've a good mind to give you a bloody good shaking to bring you to your senses.'

At that point Sid came into the kitchen. Taking in the unexpected sight of his wife looking as if she were about to strike Sarah, he shouted, 'What the hell's going on?'

Flo released her grip, sinking into a chair and sobbing noisily. 'It's 'er, the daft cow, says she's gonna leave us to run this place all on our own.' She snatched the hankie proffered by Sarah who was now leaning over her. Blowing her streaming nose noisily, she blurted out, 'She's only gonna join the bleedin' ATS.'

Sid shared an apologetic smile with Sarah. 'I'm sorry, you know how worked up Flo can get over small things.'

That innocent remark galvanised Flo into leaping out of her chair, ready to attack her mild-mannered husband. It took both Sid and Sarah to hold her down in an attempt to calm her. Finally the sobs subsided, allowing Sarah a few minutes to explain her plans.

'Don't you see how I feel, Flo? I need to get away, find a new challenge. You've got Sid and your lovely David and Jeannie. You don't need me any more.' She silenced Flo with a hug. 'Listen, who was it taught me all there is to know about the hotel trade? Without you and Sid to guide and help, God knows where I'd have ended up. You can run Glendale while I go off and do my bit for my country.'

An anxious face appeared round the kitchen door. 'I

don't suppose there's any chance of some more tea and toast?'

'That's what we're 'ere for,' Flo told him, suddenly taking charge of herself and the situation. Busying herself with the grill and the kettle, her mood changed. 'You're right as usual, a right bloomin' know-all. Of course Sid and I can get on with things 'ere while you go off and 'ave a good time.'

Her grin reassured Sarah. 'I don't know about a good time, but I think I might be more use cooking for the troops than for this lot here.' She did not stop to ask what had caused Flo's sudden change of mind. 'I've got to go out. Be back in time to help with dinner.'

'Take all the time in the world. If we've got to manage without you, the sooner we start, the better.' As soon as she heard Sarah starting up her car, Flo turned to Sid. 'Sorry I made all that fuss, love. It was just the way she came out with it.'

'I know, love, you don't ever have to say sorry to me.' He kissed the top of her head. 'But what made you change your mind?'

Flo shook her head in despair. 'Honest, you men 'aven't got a grain of sense. Don't you see? Think of all those lovely fellers she'll be seeing, she's sure to fall for one of them. She can't go on pining for ever for that 'Arry of 'ers. Human nature ain't like that.'

Sid's approval of her philosophy of life led her to continue. 'I bet you it won't be long before she forgets all about that 'Arry.'

Unaware of the reason for Flo's change of mind, yet grateful that her leaving Glendale was meeting with approval, Sarah set about packing away the expensive dresses and outfits which would no longer be needed.

Flo, keen to help, took the lovely gowns off their

hangers. 'It doesn't 'alf seem a shame, but never mind, the war can't last for ever and then you'll be able to get this lot out of mothballs again.' Carefully wrapping a dark blue silk evening dress in tissue paper, she sighed. 'Pity you can't take it with you though. I mean, you never know, there might be dances and things, and you'd want to look nice. There's bound to be lots of 'andsome fellers on the loose.'

Unable to conceal a broad smile which lit up her green eyes, Sarah sat down on the edge of her bed. It was all clear now why Flo had had a sudden change of heart. 'Really, Flo, how many times do I have to tell you that I'm not joining up to find myself a husband? I just want to do my bit for my country.'

Flo pursed her lips in disapproval. 'Well, there's no 'arm in keeping your eyes open.'

Tears, hugs and kisses marked Sarah's departure from the hotel which for so long had been her whole life. A final whispered, 'Promise you won't miss Rosie's white roses every week,' as she brushed away the tears threatening to brim over.

'As if you need remind me,' Flo admonished. 'Sid's found a lovely white rose in one of them catalogues and he's gonna 'ave a go at growing it just for Rosie, so no more tears. Just you get going before we all start blubbering.'

Sid, now the proud owner of Sarah's car, placed Sarah's small suitcase on the back seat and opened the passenger door. 'Right, let's be off before you miss the train, Sarah'.

Sarah stared at the little group outside the hotel until Sid swung into the main street leading to the station. In a few days, all this would be a part of her past. A new phase in her life was about to begin.

Chapter 23

'Right, Connolly, your turn. Straighten your tie and shove that hair of yours under your cap!'

Sarah swallowed hard. Better not start by antagonising the sergeant in charge of the raw recruits, but it was hard having to be a subordinate after so many years of being the boss. She had been standing outside Captain Gordon-Watson's office for over half an hour, as one by one the young women, smart in their new khaki uniforms, were called in for assessment.

Once inside the office, her temper was even more sorely tested at what she considered to be downright rudeness on the part of the officer, who totally ignoring Sarah, continued to peruse the papers on her desk. Typical officer with her tall, slim good looks and clear skin, the result of an upbringing which had known no deprivation.

Without looking up, she said drily. 'Suffering from a cold are we, Connolly?'

Sarah reddened at this astute interpretation of her cough, which had been intended to gain her superior's attention. 'No, Ma'am.'

'Good. Now let me see.' She appraised Sarah from head to toe before returning to the papers. 'I expect the NCO has had a word about your hair.'

The White Rose Weeps

Sarah stared at the officer's smart blond bob. Her hair had not been savaged by an apprentice at the local village hairdresser's. More likely that cut had been achieved with regular trips to London to a fashionable salon.

'Right, I see that you've some experience in hotel work and also that you can drive.' She screwed up her eyes into icy blue slits. 'An odd combination. In my experience, not many chambermaids learn to drive.'

Snooty bloody cow, Sarah thought, waiting for the next put-down.

'Right, tell me what you did in the way of hotel work. Cleaning and kitchen work, I expect.'

'Partly.'

'Well, explain yourself, Connolly, I haven't got all day.'

'Cooking, cleaning, driving, amongst other things.'

'What things?'

'Advertising for customers, preparing the brochures, engaging staff, planning menus, expanding the premises, supervising builders, banking the proceeds.' As she recited this litany with just a hint of pride in her voice, and more than a hint of defiance, Sarah's gaze was firmly fixed on a portrait of King George VI which was hung on the wall behind the officer's chair. Gradually the stony face of Captain Gordon-Watson interposed itself between Sarah and the portrait, as she rose to her feet.

'I'll give you one more chance, Connolly. Now sit down and start from the beginning.' The cold stare was accompanied by a tightening of the jawline and a menacing tone.

'I beg your pardon Ma'am. I thought I'd made everything clear.' The captain's sharp intake of breath made Sarah realise that her insolence would not be tolerated any further. 'I run my hotel in Blackpool.'

The silence hung between the two women for what seemed like an eternity, broken finally by the captain. 'You manage it?'

'No, I own it. It's mine.' It was hard to keep the tone of pride out of her voice.

'I note that you are a widow.' The features softened slightly. 'So, we are very fortunate in having you join up.'

Sarah raised her eyebrows at this sudden change in the officer's attitude. 'Not really, I've got two excellent managers.'

For some minutes more Sarah gazed at the royal portrait while the officer perused her papers. A decision finally having been made, she turned her attention to Sarah.

'Right, now tell me, how would you like to run a billet we have for a group of officers? As you no doubt realise, Salisbury is full to saturation point with the military. Bulford and Tidworth camps are bursting at the seams with personnel. The army has already taken over accommodation in the city. Large properties whose owners have gone away have been converted to house officers. We have been fortunate in commandeering one on the Wilton road.'

A glimmer of a smile lit up Sarah's face. 'You mean you want me to do what I've been doing in civilian life, run a hotel?'

'Exactly. This house will have twelve officers. You will have cleaners and kitchen maids to help you, there are plenty of suitable girls for that,' she added dismissively.

Amazing how one's credibility soars when they know you've got money, Sarah commented when she wrote to Flo to tell her of her first encounter with the officer class.

'If I'm to be in charge of other girls, will that mean I

have a higher rank?'

The captain tapped her even white teeth with the end of her pencil. 'Hmm. Acting Lance Corporal, I think, until I see how satisfactory you are. See Sergeant Pascoe. She'll fill you in on the details.' A dismissive gesture, as the next form claimed her attention, and a bare acknowledgement of Sarah's salute signalled the end of the interview.

The large house referred to by Captain Gordon-Watson was situated behind high walls and was reached through two wide pillars. Only the damaged brickwork bore evidence of the former presence of wrought iron gates, now gone to be melted down to help the war effort. Once the family home of a wealthy doctor with a practice in Harley Street, it now lay vacant, the owner having retired to Canada to live with a married daughter until it was safe to return to England.

Neither the brass lion's head door knocker nor the oak parquet floor in the hallway had been polished since that gentleman's departure. A sour odour of stale cabbage and foul drains caught at Sarah's throat as she entered the kitchen.

'We'll need an army to get this place cleaned up if you want it ready in a week's time,' Sarah told Sergeant Pascoe.

'Mmm, you're right there, Connolly. Officers will be used to something a bit better than this.' Sergeant Pascoe had been one of the first to join the ATS, happily exchanging a boring job as a secretary in an accountant's office for the variety of service life. Her bluff, cheerful manner concealed an implacable insistence on adherence to military discipline, a characteristic which had gained her rapid promotion.

'If it's to be ready in a week's time, then it will be ready. I can let you have some extra help to start with, so no excuses.'

It was clear that extra beds and bedlinen would be required. Most of the heavier bedroom furniture had been put into storage, leaving bedrooms empty and dingy, especially where the wallpaper had been hidden behind dressing tables and wardrobes. Sarah's heart sank. Sid was the person she needed, not a few willing girls, to carry out this work.

'The beds are scheduled to arrive the day after tomorrow, and they'd better, or someone will need to tell me the reason why.'

Sarah felt comforted. This Sergeant Pascoe was a woman after her own heart. 'Right Sergeant Pascoe, the sooner we make a start, the sooner our officers will be able to enjoy home comforts.'

Helen Pascoe at thirty was not exactly plain. There was too much good humour in her plump cheeks and grey eyes. She raised one well-plucked eyebrow. 'Yes, well not too many home comforts, Connolly. You're a pretty girl, so watch it. Any of them takes any liberties, just you let me know, right?'

Relief spread through Sarah's body, warming her to this kind-hearted woman. 'I won't be standing for any kind of nonsense, I promise you.' First one that tries it will soon regret it, she told herself, even if it means I end up in the glasshouse.

Starting on the task of refurbishing Sarum House reminded Sarah of the days she had spent with Flo and Sid building up Glendale. The driving force behind her then had been to satisfy her ambition to run her own hotel, and, she had to admit to herself in her more

The White Rose Weeps

reflective and honest moments, a fear of being idle, lest painful memories left her feeling alone and lost.

Betty Lunsher, a cheerful Norfolk girl with large red hands that looked as if they had been used to hard work, was the first girl allocated to Sarah's team.

'Get out of the way and let me get on with scrubbing this place through from top to bottom,' were her first words, as she put water on to boil and set to work, lugging huge pails up the broad front staircase. Her thick brown hair, as straight as stair rods, had been scraped back and was firmly anchored behind her ears with large black bobby pins. Betty was no beauty, but her bonny features glowing with health would find her the kind of mate who valued good, honest virtues above skin deep prettiness. 'This is child's play compared with our dairies at home, knee deep in cow shit they were sometimes. The men always left the muckiest jobs for me and Ma. Makes you laugh really it does, when you see pictures of us country women in clean white pinnies sitting in clean, tidy kitchens. One day as a farmer's wife or daughter'd kill off your average townie.'

Sarah grinned at the mental picture of Betty's sturdy figure and strong arms sweeping all before her, banishing dirt and lazy dairymen from the dairy. A thought struck her. 'You didn't spend all your life cleaning, now did you? Who did all the cooking for the men?'

The upstairs having been tackled, Betty had returned to attack the kitchen, her fleshy backside swaying from side to side as the scrubbing brush described ever widening arcs over the kitchen floor. 'Me and Ma. Me mostly, I suppose with Ma having to see to Gran. Poor old gel was always wetting the bed, made no end of work for me Ma, so I sort of got stuck with the cooking.'

That snooty officer wasn't as useless as Sarah had thought. Allocating Betty to help had been a stroke of genius. Once Betty had given the house a real going over, she would be invaluable in the kitchen. A rota of girls to make beds, dust and clean the bedrooms and bathrooms, would leave Sarah and Betty free to see to the planning and preparation of meals for the officers.

It had been decided that Sarah and Betty would sleep in Sarum House in order to be there early in the mornings to make tea and cook breakfast. The sight of the two tiny attic bedrooms reached by the back stairs from the kitchen reduced Sarah to giggles, leaving Betty puzzled at this unexpected show of hysteria.

'What's so funny? Come on, spit it out before I get to thinking you're not all there.'

'This is how I started out when I was fourteen years old and absolutely petrified at being sent away from home to live in a strange boarding house.' She sighed. 'God! When I think how I slaved from morn till night for a bloody pittance.'

Betty noted the sudden pallor and the glimmer of horror in her eyes. 'Had some rough old times there, did you gel?'

'Let's say I had to learn to look out for myself,' she said drily. 'We'd better get some bolts put on these doors. Just in case one of the officers and gentlemen loses his way when he's had too much to drink.' The effort it cost her in turning the suggestion into a joke was not lost on Betty.

Two weeks later, with routines well established and the names of the officers fixed in her mind, Sarah was able to take stock of the situation. Weekdays were hectic, but only with the kind of bustle to which she had become accustomed during the summer season in Blackpool. By the weekend, the house was virtually empty with many of the officers wangling weekend passes to get away.

Sergeant Pascoe agreed that Sarah and Betty were entitled to Saturdays off and arranged cover for them. 'Mind you, just you make sure that everything's left ready. I don't want the men who're not on leave complaining about the meals at weekends.' She wandered round the kitchen, reaching up to check for dust on the top of the doors. 'Good so far, let's keep it that way.'

Seeing Sarah's colour rise as she tried to suppress an angry retort, Betty covered her mouth with her podgy hand to hide a smile.

'I know she's a good sort as sergeants go, but trying to teach me how to run a hotel, I bloody ask you!' Sarah exploded the moment the sergeant was out of earshot.

Betty ducked as a dishcloth winged its damp way across the kitchen. 'All I said was, you shouldn't have joined up,' she protested, still laughing.

There was still little sign of action in France, Hitler being apparently content with the occupation of Austria, Poland and Czechoslovakia, although there were rumours that France would be the next country to suffer invasion from his jackbooted armies with their superior weaponry.

'They'll never get through the Maginot Line, not with us there to help the Frogs out,' Sarah had heard Major Fortescue announce confidently to his fellow officers after dinner. 'They learnt their lesson after the last bloodbath. Even Hitler's tanks can't break through those fortifications, the best in Europe.' The authority with which he had made this proclamation had met with nods and muttered agreement round the dinner table. His confident reiteration that the war would soon be over did not somehow ring true. Much as she longed to share his optimism, Sarah feared that many of those enjoying the civilian comforts of Sarum House would be asked to lay down their lives in the service of their country.

'Bloody officers,' Betty moaned one morning, 'all wanting their eggs cooked exactly to their liking. Fussy blooming lot.'

She had been mildly surprised at Sarah's reply, uttered with a chilling severity. 'They may not live to see too many good English breakfasts, so the least we can do is send them off happy.'

The two worked in a thoughtful silence, broken finally by Betty. 'Look, how about a night out for a change? Sarge said we could have Saturday off and I feel like kicking my heels up.'

'Heaven help anyone who gets in the way of your feet,' Sarah laughed, pointing at Betty's comfortable size eights. She carried on slicing the ham for Saturday night's supper. 'You're right, we're not going to win any wars sitting here worrying.'

Later on that evening, staring at the brown-speckled mirror in her attic room, Sarah began to doubt the wisdom of agreeing to go to this dance. Her newly-washed red curls shone in the light of the bright hundred watt bulb with its plain white shade. Away from the every day responsibility of running Glendale and no longer being torn apart by her weekly visits to Rosie's grave, the faint lines which had become etched round her mouth had filled out, almost disappearing. The only lines to appear were laughter lines when she and Betty shared a joke.

'Come on, get a move on, else all the best blokes will be spoken for.'

The White Rose Weeps

'Hang on, nearly ready,' Sarah yelled back. A dash of powder and the faintest hint of lipstick and she was ready. Ready for what? she asked herself.

'Christ Almighty!' Betty gasped, standing in the doorway of Sarah's room. 'There'll be a bulls' stampede when the blokes out there see you tonight. Hope you've got your tin knickers on.'

Sarah blushed, wondering why it was she felt like a young girl about to go on her first date. It was so long since she had had any romantic attachments that the thought of being chatted up by a soldier with one aim in mind was sufficient to make her wish she had never agreed to Betty's suggestion. It had been years since she had thought herself to be in love with Fergus, years since she had so very nearly accepted his proposal. Her guilt at hurting him so badly had been partly assuaged when she read of his marriage to the widow of one of his clients only a month before the outbreak of war.

'Is your heart really set on this dance?'

Betty's response was to grasp Sarah firmly by the arm and march her down the stairs and out to the bus stop.

The Wiltshire and Dorset bus arrived five minutes later.

'Wiltshire and Dorset, wonky and doubtful,' Betty said, repeating what she had heard from the local children. 'Come on, let's go upstairs.'

'I thought you girls wanted to get off here,' the bus conductor shouted up the stairs, as the bus drew to a halt outside a church hall.

Giggling and apologising, the girls clattered down the stairs. Still overcome with fits of laughter, they waved goodbye to the obliging bus conductor before boldly marching up to the door of the church hall. The strains of the latest hit, 'Run rabbit, run rabbit, run, run, run,' could be heard, hammered out by a pianist and the three bandsmen accompanying him.

'Is this really what I've let you drag me out to?'

'Never mind the music, just take a look at those Canadians over there. Come and get us,' Betty whispered out of the corner of her mouth. 'We're ready, willing and able.'

'May I?' Sarah looked up into the smiling dark grey eyes of a Canadian.

Six feet tall and handsome in his perfectly fitting khaki, Tony Bojek had been eyed longingly by the civilian girls in the hall. Decked out in their tight-waisted dresses and high heeled court shoes, they had come to the dance in the hopes of capturing a love-hungry soldier. Oblivious to their glares, Sarah stood up, shyly accepting the invitation.

'I'll do my best not to tread on your toes,' he promised with a twinkle lighting up his eyes and crinkling the corners of his mouth.

'It's ages since I went dancing so it's more likely to be me making the mistakes,' she confessed, half wishing that she had not accepted and yet curiously attracted to this gentle giant. It had been so long since she had been in close physical contact with a man, that she was terrified in case he could sense the wild beating of her heart, as he held her close in a slow foxtrot.

Before the end of the dance they had introduced themselves.

'Sarah, I like that, seems to match your gorgeous hair somehow.'

Shooting a line, Sarah thought, wishing that she had not blushed at the compliment. As the music ended, he muttered something which was drowned by the polite clapping of the dancers, turned on his heels and returned to his group of buddies standing by the bar, leaving Sarah vaguely disappointed at this rejection.

'Never mind, there's plenty of decent fellers here,' Betty beamed, her face flushed with excitement after several dances with a hefty young soldier who seemed in no hurry to let her out of his sight.

Annoyed at her naivety, Sarah bit her lip. How on earth did she think she could compete with these younger civilian local girls? Most of them appeared to be no more than eighteen, a good five years younger than herself. How could she flirt idly with the men here? She was older, a widow, a woman who had gone through the agony of losing a child, not an excitable teenager looking for a bit of romance. Mentally chiding herself for her stupidity at making a fool of herself, she signalled to Betty that she was leaving.

'You can't go now,' Betty urged, still clinging to the arm of her new boyfriend.

'Don't worry, I'll get the bus, see you back at the billet.'

'I'll see her home,' her soldier promised, grinning in triumph at the prospect of having this buxom Betty to himself with no wallflower friend to cramp his style.

It was pitch black outside the hall and Sarah was not sure where the bus stop was exactly.

'Hey there! Sarah!'

'Tony?' Sarah peered at him in the darkness.

'I went to get you a drink and when I turned round you'd gone.' He paused, suddenly gripping Sarah's tiny hands in his. 'I thought I'd lost you.'

'I,' Sarah began, not sure if she ought to admit to

having had the same fear.

'Look, I don't want to go back in there. How about us going somewhere quiet for a drink? We're never going to get properly acquainted with all that noise in the dance hall.'

'Suits me, I was beginning to realise that Betty's idea of a good time and mine don't exactly agree.'

Later that night it was difficult to explain to Betty what had made the evening so magical. Betty's sole interest lay in enquiring how far the relationship had progressed. She was curiously reticent about herself and Bert, admitting only that she had had a marvellous night and was going to see him again. Sarah kept to herself her suspicions that Betty had had too much to drink and might have let things get out of hand.

Tony had told her that he was twenty-six and had lived in Toronto all his life, although his family were Polish immigrants, his mother still speaking Polish at home to his father. 'Once we got the news that Hitler had invaded Poland, I guess I had no choice. I just had to come and fight for what I know has to be right.' Sarah had felt a sudden chill at his words. Fighting meant that there would inevitably be casualties. Many of the young men laughing and flirting at the dance would be killed if Hitler invaded France. It was no use the officers in Sarum House insisting that Hitler would go no further; her gut feeling told her that there would be carnage as in the First World War.

'And what about you? What made you join the ATS?'

This had been a tricky moment for Sarah. She had avoided his direct gaze. 'I was married and my husband died in an accident soon after.' She cut off Tony's murmured condolences. 'The marriage was a mistake. I was going to leave him anyway.'

What she had said was true; burdening him with the story of Rosie's death would have only aroused more pity, which she could not have coped with.

'Yes, I am going to see Tony again, so stop quizzing.' Sarah's eyes flashed icy emerald chips.

'Glad to hear it. The only trouble is going to be getting out of here as often as we want to, especially now Sergeant Pascoe's decided to move in with us.'

'Well, she is the sergeant and entitled to keep an eye on us.'

'More likely she fancies a bit of how's-your-father with that nice Lieutenant Barwell.'

'Betty!' Sarah's upturned mouth and barely concealed giggle at the remark encouraged Betty further.

'We'll have to have a plan of action, letting one another in the kitchen window, that's if old Pascoe is going to be in charge of locking up.'

If meeting Tony meant that a few regulations had to be breached, so be it. 'Right, let's take a look at the window in the pantry.'

'I'd never get my arse through that,' Betty protested.

'No, but I could, then I could open the door for you. We'll just have to make sure we don't put any breakables right under the window.'

Sarah tried to conceal her impatience at the prospect of seeing Tony again. There was something special about their burgeoning relationship that she wanted to protect from Betty's rough teasing. It was not as if she could foresee a long term romance developing. Along with so many others in her situation, it had not taken her long to realise that in times of war, happiness had to be grasped, seized upon for the moment, lest it be snatched away. No one dared dwell on what the future might bring for thousands of the young men who cheerfully filled the pubs and dance halls in the city with their loud laughter and outrageous flirting. Would it be so wrong to give them what they craved most of all, warm human contact with a woman?

'Has he asked you yet? You know what I mean.'

Sarah did not reply that he had not needed to ask. So long denied love, Tony's gentle love-making had escalated into a mutual passion. First of all, Sarah had been afraid that she would be unable to respond, but now the spectre of Fred savaging her after the death of his mother had finally faded. In that artificial atmosphere of living only for the moment, neither she nor Tony had discussed what the future held for them. In fact, whenever Tony had touched on what had been his life back in Canada, he had never placed Sarah in that context. For her own part, Sarah had not even remotely considered the possibility of leaving England and her family at some time in the distant future.

'Do you think you'll go back to Canada with him after the war, you know, get married and all that?'

Sarah shrugged, turning away from Betty to hide the tears misting over her suddenly bright eyes. 'Who knows what tomorrow will bring?' She went into the pantry desperately trying to remember what it was she needed in there.

Betty's arm crept round her shoulder. 'Sorry I spoke, love, it's just, I don't know, it's just such a funny old world at the minute and that's for sure.'

Her suggestion that the two of them should creep out after dinner met with a half-hearted acquiescence from

Sarah. Tony had sent her a note to say that he would not be able to get out of camp for some time, leaving her surmising that perhaps he was afraid that the warmth of their ever deepening relationship was not what he had had in mind. In her blacker moments, Sarah wondered if he had a girl back in Toronto, or even a wife. The latter thought filled her with shame at the image of herself and Tony committing an act of what she saw as betrayal. His note had gone on to say that he would never forget his lovely white Yorkshire rose and the wonderful times they had had together. There was no mention of a future meeting.

'It's not that I was really in love with Tony, oh, I don't know, it's just that I thought we had something special.' Hunched over the kitchen table, she read and re-read the note.

Betty pushed a cup of tea in front of Sarah. 'Here, get this down you. It's the war, everything's topsy turvy and we've just got to make the most of every minute we've got.'

'You think that's what Tony was doing?'

Betty smiled, a gentle, half-teasing look in her round brown eyes. 'And weren't you making use of him?'

Sarah sighed, recognising the truth in Betty's probing. 'Yes, I suppose I was in a way. I'd begun to think that I could never let a man near me.' She looked up, seeing the puzzled expression on Betty's face. 'It's a long story. I promise I'll tell you one day soon. Now, tell me, what's happened to Bert?'

Betty explained that he too was confined to barracks and that if they went for a quick drink, it would be just the two of them.

'OK. You're on, just a quick drink to drown our

sorrows and then it's back here and bed. I'm absolutely drained.'

The quick drink turned into several in the pub where a pianist was thumping out the latest popular numbers, encouraging everyone to join in. With the bar filled with both army personnel and civilians, the air was blue with the haze from dozens of cigarettes.

'How the hell can anyone sing in here?' Betty said, coughing and covering her mouth with her hand. 'You can hardly see across the room, let alone sing.'

'Well, I bloody feel like singing tonight,' Sarah announced, grabbing hold of a surprised Betty's arm and pulling her over to the piano. She nudged the pianist, a stout middle-aged man whose proficiency as a musician did not seem to suffer from his immoderate consumption of innumerable pints of beer. 'Come on, do you know that one? "Wish me luck as you wave me goodbye". My friend and I will start you off.'

'Good God! Who do you think you are, Gracie Fields?' was Betty's shocked reaction to Sarah's bravado. 'I can't sing!'

'You'd better,' Sarah whispered, 'or I won't let you in next time you're late back, so sing up.'

Sarah's sweet soprano backed up by Betty's powerful contralto first silenced the drinkers, then encouraged them to join in.

The loud applause when they reached the final line, 'Till we meet once again you and I, wish me luck as you wave me goodbye,' astonished them both. Offers of drinks and requests for more songs were met with polite refusals, Sarah beginning to wish that she had not succumbed to a sudden whim.

'For God's sake, Sarah, let's get out of here.' Betty's

usual ebullience had deserted her too on finding herself the centre of so much attention.

The piano was positioned on a raised dais in a corner of the bar. In her embarrassment at having made an exhibition of herself, Sarah kept her eyes firmly glued to the floor as she stepped down, barely muttering her thanks to the soldier who had offered a hand to assist her. In spite of his help, she tripped, and was forced to catch hold of his arm and look up.

The choking haze, the heat and the sensation of having had too much to drink clouded her vision. Desperately, she turned round to seek Betty's help, as the room began to turn somersaults and all she could hear were muffled unintelligible voices.

'Let me help you get her out of here,' she heard.

She stood with her eyes closed, leaning against the wall outside in the cool night air. 'Oh, my God, whatever possessed me? I'm so sorry Betty. You can let go of me now, I'm fine, honest I am.' Getting no response, she opened her eyes.

'Betty's gone.'

For what must have been a full minute, Sarah stared at the man in uniform. No, she mustn't make a fool of herself again. Dreaming about the one man she had loved for so many years had made her imagine that one day they would meet again. It was the drink and the lack of oxygen in the pub that had made her brain produce an image of what she so longed for.

'Harry? Is it really you, Harry?' Sarah felt her strength oozing away once more. 'Oh, Harry,' she whispered, as he held her close. It was him, after all this time it really was her darling Harry.

'Don't say anything,' he begged. 'Just hold on tight and

for God's sake, don't let go.' There was a tremor in his voice, a hint that but for a superhuman effort he would break down and cry with Sarah. Finally, he said. 'Come on, sweetheart, let's go somewhere quiet. We need to talk.'

For what seemed like hours, but was only a few minutes, they walked in silence, until Sarah realised that they had reached the cathedral. This majestic edifice, built with sincere religious fervour to the greater glory of God by craftsmen long since gone to their eternal rest, this was the place where she could talk to Harry about Rosie.

They entered the huge doors, Sarah signalling Harry to follow her to sit in the vast silence.

'Why here?' Harry asked.

Her eyes firmly fixed on the altar, Sarah began at the beginning of her life in Blackpool, her pregnancy and failure to find Harry. At the mention of her forced marriage to Fred, Harry buried his head in his hands.

By now her own hands were white and frozen. The chill of the night penetrated every bone in her body, but the worst part of her story still had to be told. Somehow the beauty of the surroundings gave her the strength to tell of Fred's increasing madness, Rosie's death in the fire followed by Fred's death in a drunken stupor on Blackpool beach.

Harry's blue eyes, reddened with weeping, held hers in a look of ineffable sorrow. 'And all that without me. Oh my God! I didn't know. I did come looking for you, but the woman at the café said you had a baby boy as well. I thought you must be happy without me. I just had to let you get on with your life.'

After Sarah's explanation, they sat for a few moments each trying to come to terms with the tragedy of their long separation.

'We'll just say a little prayer for our Rosie before we go,' Sarah said, bowing her head.

On the walk back to Sarum House, Harry told her of his life after leaving Colethorpe. A job in a biscuit factory was followed by a backbreaking stint in the foundry of a car factory. After settling his mother in a comfortable rented house he had moved around from one set of lodgings to another.

'I wanted to forget you, put out of my mind the image of another man making love to you, but you were always there, your lovely sweet face always there in my dreams.'

'Well, it's no longer a dream.' Sarah smiled up at him in the darkness. At the back of her mind there still lay the unspoken dread that Harry was married and that they would have to part once again. 'I expect we can keep in touch,' she added, afraid of what he might say next.

'What do you mean by that? I want to marry you!' His voice startled an air raid warden out on his rounds, who turned to see where this disturbance was coming from.

'You mean, you didn't . . . I thought you and Dolly Redmile were . . .'

'What? Of all the daft ideas! Dolly came south to marry some travelling salesman she'd met in the Co-op. Mam put her up for a while to give her a hand. She wasn't a bad lass, you know.'

Sarah's memory of what she had suffered because of Dolly's attempt to save her own skin angered her. Half crying, half shouting, she turned on him. 'How can you say that, Harry Wilby? If it hadn't been for her, I could have stayed at home instead of being sent away. You've no idea what I had to put up with in that boarding house. Don't you dare mention her name again! She ruined my life!' She wrenched herself free from Harry's arm, half running, half stumbling as she tried to escape, hurling herself ahead of him.

'Hey! Come back here,' he called, racing after her. 'Christ! I'd forgotten what a fiery little bugger you are. Here we are, we've been trying to find one another for years and we're rowing like an old married couple already.'

Sarah's anger subsided just as swiftly as it had flared up. Blissfully happy, she snuggled up against the rough khaki of his battledress. The last few yards to Sarum House were spent in making plans for their next meeting.

'Will you mind not having the full white wedding with the reception at the Co-op hall?' Harry asked, his eyes twinkling.

Her upturned face and ready lips were all the answer he got.

Chapter 24

The newspaper headlines were no longer full of optimistic predictions that the war would soon be won. No one was singing, 'We're going to hang out our washing on the Siegfried Line,' the song which had reflected the earlier mood of the nation.

'It seems that no sooner do we get to know one lot of our fellers and how they like their eggs done, than they're off and we have to start all over again.'

Sarah stirred the porridge, still a favourite with many of the young men, hardly old enough to have left school. Even if she despised their public school accents, her heart was filled with admiration for their courage and determination to defend their country.

'A letter for you,' Betty called. 'France I reckon.'

'Here, stir this.' Sarah thrust the spoon into Betty's hands, grabbed the envelope and tore it open. Shaking and white with fright, she clung to the table. 'It's Harry. I don't understand. He's only written a few words, just to say that he'll be home soon, but his writing is terrible.'

Betty lifted the huge pot off the flame, wiped her hands on her apron, and took the letter out of Sarah's trembling hands.

'Now listen to me. He says what he means. How the hell has he got time to write love letters when there's guns blasting all around him and his mates?'

Sarah's heart was touched by Betty's gruff practical admonition, reminding her that Betty too was worried about her Bert.

'I mean, I've not heard from Bert. For all I know, the bugger's gone and found himself some French bit of fluff.'

'I don't think that he'd be satisfied with a bit of fluff, not after he's had you?' Sarah giggled, wiping her eyes with the end of her apron.

'Here, come on, we'd better get this porridge lobbed up before old Pascoe comes down.' Betty began dishing out huge platefuls of the steaming, glutinous cereal so beloved of the men.

The days went by with the girls anxiously scanning the newspapers first thing each morning, switching on the wireless to catch every news bulletin, trying to decipher what was really meant by, 'The French and British armies are showing Hitler that they are a force to be reckoned with.'

Sarah pored over the maps in the papers which charted the advance of Hitler's armies. Her heart weary with pain, she traced the lines on the maps, wondering where her Harry was, whether he was injured, captured perhaps, or worse. Fate had dealt her so many blows that each day was an ordeal spent waiting for the axe to fall and strike her again.

She tried desperately hard to listen in on the conversation round the officers' dinner table, but lately they had taken to giving one another warning glances whenever Sarah entered the dining room.

Finally, she could stand this cat and mouse atmosphere no longer. Waiting for a suitable moment, she bore in a tray with the men's favourite pudding, jam rolypoly. Setting it down on the sideboard, she banged a spoon on the metal tray. The noise had the desired effect on the men who, one by one, turned to find out the reason for the clatter. One or two reacted with hostility to being called to order by a girl who was on a par with their own servants at home. Others raised their eyebrows curious to learn the reason for this aggressive attempt to gain their attention.

Sarah's courage began to desert her, but she was driven by an overwhelming urge to find out what she felt sure some of them knew. 'Right, gentlemen, I apologise for interrupting, but I think you may have some information that I need.'

Twelve pairs of eyes stared at the lovely young woman with the flaming red curls and blazing emerald eyes.

'Before you get one spoonful of pudding, I want to know what has happened to Harry Wilby's outfit.' She raised a silencing hand. 'No, don't tell me you have no idea, because I've seen the way you all shut up when I come in, and I've not had a single word from him in two weeks.' Hands on hips, aware that her reckless demands could well bring about demotion and a spell in confinement, Sarah glared at each one in turn. 'Well? What is it to be?'

Major Calworthy exchanged a muttered few words with the lieutenant on his right, finally standing up and walking over to Sarah, placing an arm round her shoulder. 'Just come along into the kitchen for a moment my dear,' he suggested quietly. 'The lieutenant will serve the pudding.'

He led her to a chair, beckoning Betty to put the kettle on. 'It's true you've had no word. I'm not going to beat

The White Rose Weeps

about the bush, you can read the papers for yourself. Things are bad over there and, well, we haven't any idea what has happened to a lot of our men. We know where your man's outfit was a couple of days ago, but since then the Germans have made huge advances.'

Sarah nodded. 'I understand.'

'No, I don't think you do, my dear. There are several possibilities. He may have been taken prisoner, in which case you will hear soon enough. However, I have to warn you that fighting has been fierce.'

Sarah's red-rimmed eyes opened wide in horror. 'You don't mean?'

'This is war, and we must be prepared to lose a lot of brave men.' He cupped his hand and placed it under her chin. 'And we're going to need a lot of brave women at home to keep our spirits up.'

Sarah's bleak smile did little to convince him that he had done and said the right thing, but she had asked and he had given as near an honest answer as he could. With the withdrawal of the British Expeditionary Force from France and the accepted view that France would fall, lines of communication were unreliable. He pitied Sarah; she might be small, but she was a plucky little thing, and that pluck might soon be needed.

'I've got to hand it to you Sarah, you certainly have got the knack of getting round these officers.' Betty was staring round-eyed at the departing figure of Major Calworthy. 'I really thought you were done for when you slammed that bloody tin tray.'

Sarah couldn't help giving a sheepish grin. 'I've always been like that. If I want something badly enough, I just have to go for it.' She poured out a cup of tea mainly to give herself something to do, to take her mind of the full implications of what Major Calworthy had said. Harry was in the thick of things, that was for sure. Tears spilled down her cheeks at the thought that he might, even now, be dead. Well, she'd faced adversity before and got on with her life, and that was exactly what she had to do now.

'Shall I clear the tables being as you've probably upset one or two of our well-bred young men, who aren't used to the hired help turning bolshie?'

Sarah thrust her chin forward. 'Not likely. I'm going back in there and heaven help any one of them who tries to treat me as if I'm dirt.'

Betty's disapproving look showed that she was not too happy with Sarah in this belligerent mood. She had enjoyed the posting so far and did not want it to end because of complaints by the officers.

Her fears were allayed when, with a triumphant smile, Sarah re-entered the kitchen. 'All of them absolutely charming, wishing me well and hoping that Harry was safe for my sake. See, it's always worth standing up for yourself.'

Betty did not agree, but thought it prudent not to say so to Sarah in this state of optimism mingled with defiance.

By the end of May the evacuation from Dunkirk was well under way. Every boat in every harbour, marina or dock had been manned and was making the hazardous Channel crossing, ordinary mariners risking their lives, strafed by the deadly fire of the Luftwaffe.

The one fear which haunted those left behind was that the dreaded telegram would arrive announcing. 'We regret to inform you . . .' followed by the news of death, being captured or, 'missing believed killed.' Brought up in an orphanage, Bert had no near relatives and had registered Betty as his next of kin with the War Office before he left to fight in France.

It was a sunny May morning when Sarah saw the telegram boy prop up his bicycle against the brick gateposts at the front of the house, take out a yellow envelope and walk towards the front door. She took a deep breath steeling herself for what was to come. So this was how it happened, the final news, the end of happiness. She opened the door.

'Telegram for Private Betty Lunsher,' he announced perkily.

A feeling of guilt that a wave of relief had swept over her on hearing Betty's name, was swiftly replaced by one of fear for what Betty might learn.

'Would you like me to open it for you?' she asked, first making sure that Betty was sitting down.

'No.' Betty's small voice quavered. 'Give it here.'

The next moment Betty leapt out of the chair, gave a whoop of delight, hugging Sarah and crying, huge tears running down her cheeks. 'It's from Bert. He's safe, been picked up.' Still crying, she collapsed into a chair. 'He sent it from Dover.'

'Well, what the hell are you crying about, you great idiot? He's safe.'

'Well, you're crying too, so why shouldn't I?'

'What the heck's all this row about?' Sergeant Pascoe's plain features scowled at the girls.

Sober now, Sarah thrust the telegram at her superior. 'Sorry, Ma'am, we're just about to start lunch.'

The hard look gradually softened. She handed the telegram to Betty. 'Good. Glad that some of our boys are safe.'

Only some, but what about my Harry? Sarah's heart screamed silently. When would she get some news? His mother would still be named as next of kin and would be the one to be contacted by the War Office. There had been so many things to talk over with Harry before he was posted to France that matters such as his mother's address had not arisen.

Towards the end of June, she had begun to accept that if Harry had been safely back home in England, or even if he had been taken prisoner, he would have written to her. The only place which offered her any solace was the cathedral where she and Harry had sat the night they met. Whatever Father Kelly might have taught them at school about the divisions between Catholic and Protestants, to Sarah this mighty cathedral was a place of God, bringing her peace and comfort when she felt that she was about to fall apart.

The writing on a letter which arrived on the morning of June 27th, looked familiar. Lizzie, of course! It had been ages since she had heard from her sister. Lizzie had carried on with her nursing career in spite of having been deceived by a doctor at the hospital into thinking that he would marry her, when all the time he was engaged to a woman of similar education and background to himself. Lizzie had written only briefly since that unhappy episode in her life. There had been just a couple of postcards from exotic ports of call during her brief stint as a nurse on a cruise liner. In the last one she had written of her dissatisfaction at having to care for a few overfed wealthy travellers on the liners and said she was leaving to resume hospital work. Sarah was intrigued to get a letter from her. It bore the postmark of a town in Surrey.

The White Rose Weeps

> Dear Sarah,
> I bet this is a surprise. Did you think I'd forgotten how to write? Ha, ha! Good news for you. Guess who's in my hospital – Harry Wilby, and asking for you! He was badly wounded in the Dunkirk do, their barge got hit and he copped a bullet.
> I didn't recognise him when he first came in with his hair shaved off. He didn't know me either, which is hardly surprising as his eyes were covered with a bandage. He's on the mend now, but can't write as both arms are still in plaster. You're right, he's lucky to be alive. Anyway, he's expecting a visit the minute you get this letter.
> I'm fine and I've met this really wonderful man, Guy. Tell you all about him when I see you.
> Your loving sister, Lizzie.

Clutching the letter to her, Sarah walked out of the door, turned into the Wilton road and then into the centre of the city, heading towards the cathedral. She spent a few minutes in prayer before returning to Sarum House.

An excited phone call to Flo and Sid to tell them the good news met with a demand to be told the date of the wedding so that they could get Glendale smartened up to receive the bride and groom. Sarah laughed. 'One step at a time. Harry's been badly injured so we'll have to wait until he can at least walk down the aisle.'

Her request for time off to visit Harry was met with a gruff, 'Make sure you're back before lights out, Connolly,' from Sergeant Pascoe, followed by, 'Glad you've got good news.'

The trains were packed out with the military, all the seats taken and the corridors crammed full with men and kitbags taking every available inch of room. It was getting on for three o'clock when she finally reached the gates of the hospital. She paused for a moment taking in the scene; there were men, some on crutches, being helped by nurses, others with their eyes covered in bandages or shades being led like babies round the grounds. How would Harry be? Would he be a helpless cripple for the rest of his life? She felt her courage fade, leaving her apprehensive at what she might find.

The ward at the Military Hospital was full of men swathed in bandages or lying stiffly with legs and arms in plaster. A lump came into her throat as she passed one young lad, who couldn't have been more than nineteen, with the tell-tale pyjama leg pinned up. Lizzie hadn't really given her the full details of Harry's injuries, her letter being in her usual jokey style. Cold fingers squeezed her heart until she heard her breath coming in gasps. Oh, no, please don't let Harry be crippled.

'Sarah?' A man with bandages round his head was lying in the bed at the very end of the ward. What was visible of his face was turned towards the door, as if he were willing the footsteps he could hear to be Sarah's. Sarah could just see spikes of his corn-coloured hair escaping from the white swathes.

'Harry!' She ran the length of the ward until with a sob of relief she was kneeling by the bed, cradling his head in her arms. 'Oh, Harry, I thought I'd lost you all over again.'

'Steady on, love, I told you that you'd never lose me again. Didn't I keep my word?'

'Yes,' Sarah whispered, 'but you look so . . . you're so badly hurt, my darling.'

Harry held her hand tightly. 'Now, you're not to worry. They thought I'd got some shrapnel in my left eye, so I have to keep both covered to be on the safe side, but the good news is that these bandages come off tomorrow, so I'll be able to see my precious darling again.'

'And your arms?'

'Both on the mend.' He leant over towards her. 'I'm counting the days until I can hold you really tightly again.' He grinned. 'You've no idea what you're doing to me, so close and me lying here in bed and can't have you beside me.'

Sarah blushed, a rosy pink which spread over her cheeks making her look seventeen again. 'Just wait till we get married,' she said with mock severity.

Lizzie was waiting outside the ward having watched the two lovers. 'So you've finally got your Harry Wilby.' She hugged her younger sister. 'Don't cry, he's going to be fine.'

'And what about you?' Sarah held Lizzie's hands tightly in hers. 'Who is this man Guy you wrote to me about? Is he a doctor?'

The amber glints in Lizzie's brown eyes sparkled. 'No, he's in some kind of a business, makes oodles of money. I may never have to work again.'

'So which one of us is going to be married first?'

'You and your Harry of course, and make sure you give me plenty of warning so that I can get the time off. Don't you know there's a war on?'

Typical Lizzie, Sarah thought, smiling to herself on the train journey back to Salisbury.

It was another four weeks before a much leaner and fitter Harry was finally allowed out of hospital. The angry scar above his left eye had faded, leaving a white weal, which the doctors said would always be a reminder of how near he had come to being blinded. One broken arm had caused problems, having had to be re-set.

The kindly young doctor had said, 'I'm sorry, but it rather looks as if you'll never be able to hold a rifle again. Active service is out of the question, I'm afraid. You'll never know just how lucky you've been after all that happened to you.'

'I had my guardian angel looking after me,' Harry told him.

Sarah's only fear was that he would be posted abroad again, once his injuries had healed. With Italy in the war and Rommel set to win the war in North Africa, Sarah had nightmares of Harry lying dead out in the cruel, hot desert with vultures circling overhead.

'No fear of that, I told you, it'll be a desk job for me from now on.'

The wedding was arranged for Sarah's next leave, her parents taking over the organisation of the church service. There was to be no big reception, just a few friends and family at her parents' home.

'Well, it is August and the weather's lovely, so we can put the children out in the garden. That swing you put up on the lawn will be ideal. Flo and Sid's two can play with our Bernard and Iris's two.' Joanna Mulvey beamed proudly at her husband. 'I never thought we'd be doing a wedding reception in our own house. We've been so lucky with our Sarah.'

Jim shook his head. 'I just hope she's got the right man for her.'

'Oh she has, Jim, she has, you take my word for it.'

He screwed up his eyes thoughtfully. 'You women, you always know things we men seem to miss.'

'That's the way God made us, Jim, so it must be right.' Joanna did not say that she had had misgivings about Sarah and Harry so many years ago. Now it was different. They were both older, had both suffered at being kept apart and yet they had still remained in love, a love which Joanna was sure would make a solid foundation for their marriage.

Sarah could not have wished for a better day. Surrounded by her friends, Flo and Sid, her dear sister-in-law Iris and her brother Bernard, she felt that all she had ever hoped and prayed for was now coming true.

Betty had her own wedding plans to arrange and was unable to come, but had promised that she and Bert would spend their brief honeymoon at Glendale. Their parting had been tinged with sorrow, but with both of them promising to keep in touch after the war.

'You will spend your honeymoon at Glendale?' Sarah had begged. 'It'll be my wedding present to you for being such a super mate,' she had offered, hugging her tightly.

Betty was as surprised as Sarah when Major Calthorpe handed Sarah a wedding present. 'Some silver candlesticks from home, can't see us having much use for them again, but perhaps they might help you and your Harry to remember us all after the war – in happier times. Good luck my dear.' He kissed her briefly on the cheek. That was the last time Sarah was to see him.

As Sarah and Harry stood at the altar exchanging their

vows, Sarah smiled up at the man she had loved for ten long years, ever since she had been fourteen years old. For Harry's part, he could hardly take his eyes off his lovely young bride, a vision in a cream silk suit and matching hat.

Lizzie had agreed to be a matron-of-honour so long as their little sister Maureen could be a bridesmaid. At ten, Maureen was a carbon copy of Sarah at that age and with all her promise of beauty. Shy, yet pleased to be asked, she had taken her role very seriously, instructing Sarah on exactly the right moment when she was to throw her bouquet. She nodded gravely at Sarah's whispered confidence, agreeing not to mention it again.

As they emerged from the church, Sarah was thrilled to see so many familiar faces. Charlie was there too, his face as spotty as ever, with his young wife by his side holding a baby.

'I don't see Dolly Redmile,' Sarah teased. 'It would have made my day if you'd invited her.'

'How do you know I didn't?' he parried.

'I expect she just couldn't bear to see me carry off the man she always wanted.'

Harry sighed. 'It's too late now for me to change my mind, but is this what our married life is going to be like, with you always getting the last word?'

Sarah giggled. 'I wouldn't be at all surprised.'

The day went by in a flurry of laughter, good wishes, and glorious sunshine to crown it all.

Flo could hardly stop hugging and kissing her old friend. 'I always said things would come right for you.'

'No you didn't you great liar,' Sarah teased, 'you wanted me to marry Fergus and forget Harry.'

Flo boxed her gently round the ears. 'Stop twisting my words, you little bugger.'

The White Rose Weeps

It had been planned that Sid would drive Sarah's old car to Colethorpe for Harry and Sarah to use on their honeymoon.

'How are you going to get back to Blackpool?' Sarah had asked, when this idea was first mooted.

'We're taking the boys on the train for a treat,' he had laughed.

All the goodbyes said, Harry put their cases on the back seat of the car. Carefully watched by Bernard and Sid, he was unable to remove the tin cans tied to the bumper for good luck.

'We'll take them off when we get out of Colethorpe,' he told Sarah, who was so happy that she said she didn't care if the whole world knew she was married to the man she loved.

'You don't mind me driving, do you?' Sarah asked Harry as she drove the car, clattering its way down the High Street. 'I mean your arm isn't a hundred percent yet.'

'Give it time. And in any case I haven't got a licence.'

'I could always teach you,' she offered.

'Not bloody likely! I'll get Sid to do that.'

She drove until they were well away from Colethorpe, out on the open moorland with not a house in sight.

'Come here, Mrs Wilby,' Harry whispered hoarsely. He held her in a long kiss. 'That's just a promise of what I have in mind for later.'

They spent the night in a quiet inn in a tiny village on the moors. They both laughed at the sight of the huge feather double bed which had a hollow in the middle of the mattress.

'Couldn't be better,' Harry murmured.

The landlady, a comfortable Yorkshire woman, had

guessed they were honeymooners.

'I'll bring your supper up on a tray right now. Just you leave it outside the door when you've finished with it. I won't disturb you, my dears, I promise.' An understanding smile and she was gone.

Waking up with Harry beside her, Sarah thought that she would burst with happiness. Their first night together had been one of passionate lovemaking interspersed with gentler moments of shared reminiscences. Harry looked so peaceful and contented that she was beginning to doubt the wisdom of what she had in mind. No, it had to be done; she would tell him later.

Leaving the next morning after a traditional English breakfast which the landlady of the inn told Harry he needed to keep his strength up, Harry enquired what the next plans were. 'You've been very secretive about where we're supposed to be spending the rest of our honeymoon.'

'Well, Flo's prepared the honeymoon suite at Glendale for us. No, don't worry, we'll be totally cut off from the other guests,' she assured him, seeing his shocked expression. 'And we're not expected to get up early in the morning to cook breakfast for everyone. We'll be totally and blissfully alone.'

'Remember that first time I came to see you in Blackpool and the time I came to take you out on your birthday?'

'You gave me a silver pendant.' Sarah smiled shyly. 'I've still got it. I used to hold it, praying that you'd find me again.'

Harry leant over to kiss her cheek. 'I have, and I'm never going to let you out of my sight, not ever again.'

It was midday when Sarah once again found herself

steering the car along the familiar roads. She hadn't had an opportunity to check with Flo whether it had been possible to get what she wanted in time for the wedding. So many times, the excuse given was, 'there's a war on, unless you've forgotten.'

Harry was puzzled when she drew up outside the gates of the Catholic cemetery.

'Come on, my love.' Gripping his hand tightly, she led the way along the path under the yew trees overhanging the older graves until they reached an area where the newer marble headstones in neat rows told them that they were in a more recent addition to the cemetery. Sarah stopped by a tiny mound.

'This is it,' she said quietly, 'our Rosie's grave.'

'Our little Rosie.' Harry struggled for a moment, finally kneeling down and giving way to huge heart-rending sobs. 'I held our little darling just once, just the once. I should have been there for her all the time.'

Holding him and soothing him gently, she drew him to his feet. 'You weren't to know, love, please don't blame yourself.'

They stood together in silence for a while.

'Thank you, Flo,' Sarah said softly. The lovely white marble headstone was exactly what she had always wanted for Rosie. The words,

Rosie
Beloved daughter
of
Harry and Sarah Wilby

were now engraved for all the world to see.

'Our precious white rose,' Sarah said, laying her

wedding bouquet of white roses on the little girl's grave.

Hand in hand, Harry and Sarah walked out of the cemetery to the car.

'A new life beginning for us Sarah? Tell me I'm not wanting the impossible.'

Sarah stood on her tiptoes to kiss him. No further answer was needed.